Amara's Prayer

Steven E. Wedel

MoonHowler
Press

ISBN: 0692610634
ISBN-13: 978-0692610633

Cover artwork by Kirk Alberts

DEDICATION

I would very humbly like to dedicate *Amara's Prayer* to my thesis committee at the University of Oklahoma. Professors J. Madison Davis, Robert Con Davis-Undiano, and Laura Gibbs. Any merit this story has is thanks to your steady and patient guidance.

ALSO BY STEVEN E. WEDEL

Darkscapes

Little Graveyard on the Prairie

Seven Days in Benevolence

After Obsession (with Carrie Jones)

Unholy Womb and Other Halloween Tales

God of Discord and Other Weird Tales

The Zombie Whisperer and Other Weird Tales

The Prometheus Syndrome

Inheritance

THE WEREWOLF SAGA

Call to the Hunt

Murdered by Human Wolves

Shara

Ulrik

Nadia's Children

AS EDITOR

Tails from the Pack

ACKNOWLEDGMENTS

This novel was originally published in 2013 by Bad Moon Books. That edition included a Foreword that is not present in this edition. Otherwise, the text of this edition is identical to the first edition.

The author would like to thank artist Kirk Alberts for kindly allowing MoonHowler Press to reuse the incredible art created for the first edition.

Prologue

Tina Ford sat cross-legged on the hard ground, holding a copy of a picture book version of *Little Red Riding Hood*. Around her sat seven brown-skinned Brazilian children between the ages of four and twelve, all dressed in new American T-shirts and pants or dresses. The night was growing dark, but a battery-powered Coleman lantern provided enough light for her to keep reading. On three sides of the clearing the massive trees of the rainforest reached toward the stars that were beginning to appear in the blanket of sky; birds, monkeys and other animals called from the trees, greeting the twilight as either a time to rest or a time to hunt. On the open side of the clearing a little river slid slowly toward a bigger river that would eventually empty into the mighty Amazon.

Tina suppressed a smile as she peeked over the top of a page and saw fourteen widened eyes watching her. She'd be going home soon, back to Oklahoma, back to her mother, back to school and back to friends who knew her past. She would miss the innocent children who'd learned enough English to enjoy their story sessions.

"My, Grandma, what big ears you have," Tina read in her normal voice. She pulled in her chin and affected a deep, gruff voice for the big bad wolf. "All the better to hear you with, my dear." She turned the pages toward the children so they could see Little Red Riding Hood looking at the wolf's ears poking out of a grandmotherly nightcap as he lay in the grandmother's bed. Tina pulled the book back and turned the page, then stopped. She blinked a couple of times, then raised her head. The rainforest had suddenly become as silent as a graveyard. All around the little village other people were noticing it, too. Tina saw adult natives frozen in their tasks, looking around fearfully while her missionary friends from Oklahoma watched the natives with a puzzled expression on their faces. The children shifted restlessly. Tina

3

smiled at them, but in her mind she thought back to the stillness before a tornado. "What is it?" she asked her audience. "Are the birds and animals listening to the story?"

The children didn't return her smile, but only looked around with frightened expressions, taking in the reaction of their elders.

An old man ran out of a hut to Tina's left. Isawa's eyes were wide with fright, made to look even bigger by the garish red and yellow face paint he wore. The shaman stopped just outside his hut and screamed in his native language, "The goddess is angry! She brings her wrath!" He then seized a hunting spear leaning against the hut, planted the butt against the ground and drove his chest onto the stone tip. The spearhead pushed through his back, dripping fluid that appeared to be black in the gloaming. The shaman remained standing for a moment, then seemed to topple sideways in slow motion.

The village remained silent for another heartbeat. Tina's pulse pounded with anticipation and dread. A woman screamed somewhere behind her, then the chickens that wandered the clearing erupted into a cacophony of shrill clucks as they raced for the deep darkness of the dense forest. Several chickens ran toward Tina and the children, their wings flapping frantically. "Go! Go home," Tina shouted, dropping the book and jumping to her feet. She helped two children up as the others scattered. Bihimi, the youngest girl, hesitated. Tina reached to pick up the child as the nearest chicken exploded. Burning pieces of melted meat and singed feathers showered Tina's body. Bihimi screamed in fear and pain as globs of meat scorched her bare arms and legs. Another chicken ran past and burst into flames behind Tina, covering her back with more blazing meat.

She ignored the pain and picked up the girl.

Tina heard someone screaming the word "goats" and she looked to see the village's small herd falling to the ground. The females' udders swelled, making the animals bleat in agony before the fleshy sacks burst, spewing steaming milk several yards from them. The goats' hair was curling and smoking and Tina was sure

4

she saw the flesh beneath popping wetly as though the blood was boiling.

"Get to the chapel! To the church!"

Tina's eyes were burning and watering, but she saw Paul Kirkland, the chubby youth leader of her Oklahoma City church, waving people toward the little chapel the missionaries had built at the edge of the clearing furthest from the river. Clutching Bihimi to her chest, Tina ran for the building.

All around her, people were screaming and running. Most were running toward the chapel, as she was. But others were shouting the name of their pagan goddess, begging Coadidop for mercy as they fled toward the tree line.

Huts exploded, throwing shards of pottery and clumps of hardened mud and wood across the village. Splinters slammed into Tina's back and sides. She gasped at the sudden stinging pain, then her foot slipped in the hot, messy remains of a dead chicken and her feet flew from under her. She crashed to her back, Bihimi slamming against her chest and knocking the wind out of her.

Tina gasped for air. Bihimi scrambled off her, then stood looking down at her for a moment. "Go," Tina wheezed. The girl ran, her long black hair dripping smoldering chicken goo. A village man jumped over Tina and kept running, never looking down at her. Slowly, she rolled over and got to her hands and knees.

"What is it, God?" Tina asked. "What's happening?"

The village was nearly deserted now. The screaming had become shouted prayers coming from the chapel. Tina looked across the center of the village clearing toward the church, now swallowed in the shadows of the forest.

The air between her and the church was shimmering, reminding Tina for a moment of heat rising from a summer highway; the figure of Paul standing in the church's open doorway was a swimming blur. But this was different than rising heat flickering over asphalt. The shimmering seemed more solid than air, as if something was taking form in the center of the village. Something tall and thick and angry.

Tina pushed herself to her feet and started toward the church, then stopped. Her hair and clothes rippled, sucked toward the flickering air in the center of the village. The temperature rose suddenly to an unbearable heat and something took form in front of Tina.

A figure she could not see, but that she felt like a blast from a furnace coalesced from the air between her and the sanctuary of the church. Up and up the thing rose, pulling Tina's eyes with it until she was looking almost straight above herself. A translucent outline towered above her, gigantic, genderless, crowned with the crescent moon and robed in the starry night sky. A ball of color appeared in the center of the figure's outline and expanded quickly to fill the form with a chaotic mix of colors that swirled and churned like boiling paint.

Tina fell to her knees, her face still upturned, looking into the burning eyes of a towering terror she couldn't have imagined. The thing's head moved, surveying the village, stopping only a moment on Tina before moving toward the chapel.

What big eyes you have.

It was Tina's final thought. A voice roared through her head, bursting her eardrums into fountains of blood. "You abandoned me in life, but you will serve me in death."

Tina's world erupted in red flame and she felt herself flying backward on the edge of a fireball, bursting through shattering huts until she finally hit something solid and stopped, her spine and pelvis cracking loudly. The fireball washed over her and passed beyond her knowing. The burning red of her vision became blackness as her bubbling eyeballs dripped from their sockets, mingling with the flesh melting from her skeleton.

Then the pain ended for her.

1

The smell of burning hung in the air, thick and rank, though the fire had been dead for days. The rainforest was unnaturally quiet. The only sound to be heard was the low sputter of the small gasoline engine that propelled my flat-bottomed, gray boat closer to the heart of the sickening smell.

I am Milton Agnew. That July day in the year 2000, on that particular trip into the Amazon, I was the minister of the Prairie Valley Community Church located in the affluent Prairie Valley housing subdivision in northwest Oklahoma City. I was forty-five years old, married, with two teenage children, getting a little soft around the middle, and more or less happy with my lot in life.

Sitting in the back of the boat that hot and sticky day, I guided it along the winding path of a small river with names that varied depending on who you asked—a waterway that emptied into the Purus River. From the Purus, the water flowed into the Solimnoes, which later became the great Amazon. This river, which I'll call the Gualones, is not deep enough for the bigger boats. A logging company had towed my little American-made johnboat up the Amazon and the Purus to the mouth of the Gualones. From there, I struck out on my own.

I remember how the sun glinted and winked on the white gold of my wedding ring as I adjusted the outboard motor to maneuver the flat-bottomed boat. I remember the splash of fish and the sight of huge snakes—boa constrictors and anaconda—wrapped around even thicker tree branches and the always-frightening vision of crocodiles sunning themselves on the riverbank or gliding through the water like torpedoes filled with teeth.

I dreaded what I knew I would find, but I had to go into the forest and see it for myself.

The aerial photographs were vague, showing only a large area of burned, smoking land with indistinguishable features where huts should have been. The little chapel I'd helped to build couldn't be seen at all in the photos; the area where it stood was hidden in thick smoke. The Brazilian authorities attributed the fire to a lightning strike. The airplane pilot's report said he had seen no living things—no people—in the area.

I wanted to believe that my people—my friends and the jungle natives we had come to lead to salvation—had been able to flee the fire. I wanted to believe they had gotten away. But I knew they would have come back before the pilot flew over to take the pictures that were now in a file folder in one of my packs. If the natives and the missionaries were alive, they would have come back to the village. I was sure of that.

Of course, there was so much I didn't know that day.

The sunlight was starting to fade from the evening sky as I puttered deeper into the jungle. The grass along the riverbank changed from lush green to charred black. The trunks of trees also were blackened, and then, as I moved closer to the village, the trees lay on the ground like the scattered bones of prehistoric skeletons. Only the thick buttress roots were still upright, their jagged ends pointing toward Heaven like broken teeth. Then the trees gave way completely to the clearing beside the river where the village had stood.

Most of the village was gone. Not a single building had been untouched by the fire. Very few structures remained standing at all. The clearing looked as though it had been blasted by an atomic bomb—a bomb dropped in its very center. There was no crater, however, only a circle of green grass in the middle of a huge, blasted area, like the iris of a hideous eye.

Nothing moved. I killed the engine of my boat and glided toward the bank of the river. Silence. I will remember that silence forever. It was as quiet as the country graveyard outside the little Oklahoma town where I grew up. The rainforest should have been full of the sounds of monkeys, birds and other wildlife. I had been to this mission twice before, staying for two months the first time, and I remembered well the cacophony of jungle noises that was a constant soundtrack to those visits. I felt terribly small and alone under the quiet canopy of the ancient forest.

The boat bumped solid earth and I reached out to tie my rope to a burned tree trunk beside the riverbank. My hand touched something that was not wood and I drew back in horror. The strangely shaped log had the remains of human features; it was a body. A man—probably one of the villagers. The burned flesh was hard and flaked away in crusty layers when I touched it. I tied my boat to a twisted root that snaked in and out of the black soil of the riverbank and climbed onto the land. I would not allow myself to look back at the body. Not yet, anyway. The body was proof of what I already knew in my heart.

There were others, though. I saw only a few at first. They appeared to have been thrown by the blast; some were slammed against the burned remains of huts or tangled with the blackened bodies of domestic animals. There were not many, however. There were actually far too few. Slowly, I let my feet drag me toward the ebony skeleton of the church.

Dozens of charred corpses lay on the packed dirt of the floor. They were piled on top of each other or huddled alone against walls. Mothers were crouched over the bodies of babies. Missionaries were indistinguishable from the natives they had come here to save. All were burned, black and ugly. Tears stung my eyes and I turned away.

The elders of this village said it had been here for generations. I wasn't sure, but as far as I could tell, this village was a splinter of the Guarani tribe who had left their friends and relatives and migrated here for some forgotten reason. They had lived as peaceful people beside the Gualones, hunting the game of the rainforest and harvesting a few simple crops from a small field they had cleared to the north. They had been heathens, yes, but not bad people. It had not been hard to turn them away from the worship of their pagan goddess and onto the path of Christ. They had been willing followers, eager for the message of love and forgiveness.

I had read about them almost five years before in an article about a California man who was arrested for hiring the villagers to trap parrots that he then smuggled into the United States to sell. I investigated the village and learned of the inhabitants' paganism. I visited for the first time in 1998. I talked to the village elders about the Holy Trinity. They had been interested— no, fascinated by the concept of a three-part God. They gave me leave to build a mission in their village and, with the blessing of the Brazilian government, I worked for a year to raise the money from my congregation. In early 2000 I returned with the first group of missionaries and we built the chapel. I delivered the first sermon from the pulpit.

I looked back through the skeletal frame of the church to where the pulpit had once stood. There was only a charred, cracked stump of wood where it had been. The thick jatoba wood cross that had stood behind the pulpit was completely gone. The benches were burned splinters, not a single one intact enough to sit on.

A breeze blew off the river and stirred the soot and ashes, sending specks into my eyes. I closed them and rubbed them as new tears rose. When I opened my eyes, a figure stood at the edge of the tree line behind the frame of the church.

She was a creature beyond description. Tall. Her flesh smooth as a rose petal, her limbs like willow branches. Her lips were full and red as a child's might be after a morning in the cherry orchard. Ah, but her eyes were as green as the leaves of the rainforest when seen from above. The color of her hair was red, but a red like can only be seen in the paintings of the great masters. It was not red, not orange, but somewhere between. Her hair was a fire on her head that melted onto her soft shoulders and dripped toward the pink circles of her nipples. Her nakedness did not bother her and her attitude revealed that she did not understand that nudity might bother anyone else, either. Had I been asked to guess, I would have put her age at twenty-five, no more.

I was afraid to call out to her. My voice, had I been able to make it work, might frighten her. I sensed she was like a woodland creature as she stood gazing at me—a deer who would flee if I moved too suddenly or made a loud noise. I couldn't walk through the burned church for fear of stepping on the charred bodies of the worshipers. Slowly, I moved around the rectangular skeleton of the building, never taking my eyes off the woman.

For her part, she never took her eyes off me. She gave no indication of flight as I drew closer, but moved nearer to the trunk of a large tree, putting a delicate hand on the bark near her face, which was now half hidden from me. The one eye I could see remained steadily upon me.

I stopped about five feet in front of her. Still, I didn't know what to say. Her white skin and flaming hair told of European heritage, yet she was not from my Oklahoma church. Where had she come from? Why was she here? Why was she alone in a burned South American village deep in the Brazilian rainforest? Did she speak English?

"Hello, ma'am," I said, the voice that usually rang sonorously from a carpeted pulpit was now shy, hesitant, and overpowered by the silence of the forest. It was as though I'd been transported back to my junior high school drama class and shoved onto the stage for the first time.

Her expression remained impassive. She studied my face, my mouth especially, as if trying to learn how it had moved to form those syllables.

"My name is Milton Agnew," I said. "I'm from the United States."

"Milton Agnew," she repeated. Her voice was smooth and pure, like cool milk. I thought it was tinged with an accent that could only come from the Mediterranean region. Unreasonably, I wanted her to say my name again.

"Yes. That's my name."

"Milton Agnew." Her face remained expressionless, but her voice was even smoother, richer than before.

"What is your name?" I asked.

"Amara."

"That's a Greek name," I said. "It's beautiful."

11

"Yes. Beautiful." For the first time, she smiled. Her face, so pale against the darkening forest, gleamed as her rosy lips turned up at the ends.

"Where did you come from? How did you get here?" A thousand possibilities filled my mind, none more likely than any other. The smile slid from her face and she studied me intently again for several moments before answering.

"My mother died when I was young," she said, her voice now toneless, as if reciting. "My father did not have use for a girl child. He sold me to a sailor. The sailor sold me to another man, a man who lives in a city in the jungle. I ran away."

"You've been living alone in the jungle? For how long?"

"I do not know," she said. "A long time. I saw you when you came to talk to the village elders and I saw you again when you built that." She pointed over my shoulder to the burned church. "You saw me?" I could hardly believe it. "Did you live with the villagers?"

"For a while. But they did not want me. I have been alone in the forest for a long time. I come back here to steal food. And to listen."

"You were a slave?" The whole of her story was slow to sink into my mind. "Your father sold you into slavery? From Greece?"

"Yes. From Greece."

"How old were you?"

"I was young. I do not know."

"How old are you now?"

"I do not know." She turned suddenly and started to walk away.

"Wait," I cried.

She turned her head to look back at me, her red hair like a dancing fire in the gloom. She smiled again and beckoned me to follow her. I did. I couldn't help myself. Her legs were long and firm, her steps sure as she moved deeper into the darkness of the jungle. Her hips shifted deliciously as she walked and my mind was flooded with the most impure thoughts. She turned to look back at me often, smiling as if she knew what I could not help but think.

I tried to pull my eyes from Amara's nakedness. I thought of my wife and children at home in Oklahoma. It was wicked and sinful that I should be looking at this poor lost child as I did. I knew it, and yet I looked anyway and wondered what it would be like to touch the soft curve of her buttocks.

I know now that I have been her slave from that moment to this. Looking back, it is easy enough to see how she manipulated me from the very beginning. But, at that time, I was still very ignorant of many things.

Amara stopped suddenly and turned around to face me. My eyes lingered a moment too long on her full breasts before finding her smiling eyes.

"Am I beautiful to you?" There was no seduction in the question. She simply asked as if it were of no more consequence than asking the time.

"Y-yes," I answered. "You are a very beautiful young woman."

"Who is this?" She pointed to something beside her that at first I had assumed was another tree stump. It was not. It was a statue of the villagers' pagan goddess. The totem stood about nine feet tall, with arms crossed over its breast and legs close together. The figure wore a carved skirt that had once been brightly painted but now was faded and pocked from neglect. "The people in the village used to come here often."

"Yes," I said. "This is a statue of their old goddess, Coadidop. I thought it had been pulled down and burned."

Letters from the mission had told how some of the villagers protested destroying the old goddess' image. Finally, the elders had convinced the missionaries to wait, to let the false goddess stand alone in the forest for a time. Surely the new God would not mind letting those who did not believe in him have their idol. He was a forgiving God, was he not? Still, I had thought after a time the totem would have been destroyed.

"Why did they stop coming here?" Amara asked. "Because my

friends and I told them about the real God,"

I answered. "There is only one God. This is just a statue made of wood."

"The real God?"

"Yes. The real God."

"Your friends are dead," she said. "They all died in the fire. They could not get out of that wooden building. Most of the people of the village died, too."

"You saw the fire?"

"Yes." She paused for a moment and seemed to study me again. "I could not help them. It was too hot and everything was burning. Perhaps Coadidop was angry."

"Nonsense. You said most of the villagers died. What about the others?"

"Some ran away," she said. "Not all of them were in your building. They will not come back. They say the land is cursed. They say Coadidop is angry."

"Superstitious nonsense," I said. "They were the unbelievers."

"Perhaps. There were people calling for mercy from Coadidop as they burned in your church. It was the people who never went inside that building who are still alive."

Her statement shocked me. Despite the fullness of her body, I had been thinking of her as a child. Yet her reasoning, and the tone in which she delivered her statement, told me her intellect was as mature as her figure.

"Yes," I said. "Alive and frightened. Come with me. Let's go back to the village. I have a tent in my boat. Tomorrow I want to look at the village by daylight."

"It will look the same. They are all dead."

"I know." I held out my hand to her and she put her own soft fingers into my keeping. I led her back the way we had come, keeping her beside me so that she would not walk ahead and draw my eyes onto her nakedness again.

2

I lay motionless in my sleeping bag, listening to the sounds of the Amazon night. Sometime after meeting Amara, the jungle sounds had returned, slowly, I think, as if they had to warm up to full volume. Bugs buzzed and chirred. I heard the cicadas plainly and thought how much they sounded like the locusts we hear in the Oklahoma summers. Multi-colored tropical birds, unlike anything living on the plains of the States, called and whooshed through the air; small animals screamed as the birds of prey caught them in sharp talons. Bats squeaked and tree frogs sang. Sometimes, from a distance, a small primate would screech.

About four feet to my right, Amara lay quietly in a red sleeping bag. Her breathing was deep and regular, but I knew she was not yet asleep. I wondered what she was thinking, what she was feeling. Fear? No. I didn't think so. This despite the fact she shared a tent with a man she did not know. I could not name an emotion to fit what I believed the strange woman felt. It was as if she was detached from what was happening around her.

She had allowed me to lead her back to the river and had dressed in the simple, second-hand dress I gave her. We ate beans and Spam I heated over a small open fire outside the blasted area that had been the village. She did not speak much, but she watched me constantly—not nervously, but as if I was a strange animal and she a zoologist trying to make a record of my behavior.

Amara had sat beside the campfire and watched as I pitched the army surplus tent and unrolled two sleeping bags. She accepted her bedding without comment, crawling in and fumbling with the zipper for a moment before I helped her. Then she lay still and silent as I knelt in prayer before putting myself to bed. I wanted to speak, to talk to her and learn more about why she was alone in the Amazon rainforest, but I could not think of the right questions to ask, so I said nothing.

And then I slid into sleep like an uprooted tree slipping away in a mudslide.

I dreamed of my wife. I was in bed with Karen. We were making love. I'm sad to say it was a familiar scene—I was on top of her, pushing with my hips, feeling her around me, not really lubricated enough, her limbs as motionless as the chalk arms and legs drawn around the victim in a crime scene. Her hair smelled of strawberry shampoo and the tiny streaks of gray looked like wisps of sacred silver in the walnut waves surrounding her face. I raised a hand and slid my fingers into her soft hair. She opened her eyes, as if I'd awakened her, then closed them again, not in pleasure, but as if she was thinking of something else, a grocery list perhaps, and I'd distracted her.

As my climax neared, Karen's face changed without ever moving. First, something like a pimple rose on her right cheek. Then another, then one on the left side and one on her chin. Several more sprang up on her chin. The red dots swelled and spread and blended together. Scab-like centers appeared in the sores and quickly ruptured, spilling noxious white nectar that leaked down her motionless face. When the first maggot wriggled from her rotting cheek, I looked away, looked at the bed and saw that Karen's right arm was bleached bone resting in a writhing nest of maggots.

I scrambled off her, my own seed suddenly spurting from my lap to splatter against the curve of her naked pelvic bone. There was a flapping sound; a wind rose around me and I was suddenly staring into the blazing eyes of a giant bird with burning red plumage. The predator closed its great talons on Karen's rib cage and dragged her off the bed. As the bird flapped away into the night, I jumped after it.

And woke up, my hands outstretched, the taste of sweat on my tongue and the sting of salt in my eyes. A scream battered my teeth.

"It was only a night bird." The voice was soft but distinct, matter-of-fact but interested. I looked around the darkness and found Amara also sitting up in her sleeping bag, looking at me, the light of the moon and stars outside the mosquito-net opening of the tent reflected in her eyes and pale skin.

"What?" My own voice was thick. Speaking was like pushing a rock up my throat. "What did you say?"

"A night bird," she answered. "It was close. I think it caught a monkey. The monkey screamed. I think it woke you."

"A monkey?" I looked at her, trying to understand what she was telling me and seeing nothing but my wife's skeleton, a few scraps of skin clinging to the bones as the red bird carried it away from me.

"You were dreaming and the jungle woke you up," Amara said. "It is ancient. Its roots can get into your dreams."

She lay back down and closed her eyes. I don't know if she went back to sleep, or if she had ever been asleep. She did not stir and did not speak. I stared at her for a long while as the sweat dried on my face and left a musky odor in my clothes. I lay down, but could not rest and was soon sitting by the zippered door of the tent, staring through the feathery netting at the dark jungle.

Behind the tent, the river gurgled and whispered. In front, the jungle grew quiet again for a while and then slowly filled with new sounds as the sky turned gray and pink and finally a soft blue. A flock of brilliant red-breasted parrots erupted from the trees to my left, swooped over the burned clearing and vanished into the trees at my right. I slept again, my chin resting against my chest until I slowly toppled over and lay on my side.

When I awoke, Amara was squatting beside me, her long red hair swaying only inches from my face. She had taken off her clothes again. I closed my eyes, but I had already seen the thin, wispy hairs on her legs and the soft patch of fiery satin in her crotch.

"You're naked again," I said.

"I had to...what do you call it? Piss?"

"Close enough. Did you have to take everything off?"

"You don't like looking at me?"

I almost laughed. "You're a beautiful woman. I'm married. I have a wife. I'm not supposed to look at other women." I opened my eyes and concentrated on her face. Her large green eyes gazed back at me. A tiny wrinkle creased the flesh between her eyes.

"Why do people get married?" she asked. "For love."

"I used to believe in love. The men I knew had wives. I do not think they loved them. Does love die?"

I opened my mouth to answer in the negative, but stopped. The dream image of my own wife lying motionless under me, passionless in our most intimate act, slammed into me. "I guess it can," I said.

"Then you find another person? A concubine?"

"No," I told her. "Not in America. Not in the United States."

"In the United States love does not die?"

"Well, I didn't say that. I—Love—" I stopped and shook my head. "I have to relieve myself."

"Relieve yourself?"

"Yes. Urinate." I heaved my aching body to its feet. The hours sleeping on the ground had not been kind to me. Amara rose from the floor, her supple body making me think suddenly of the slippery, undulating pillar of oil in a lava lamp. I unzipped the tent, wondering that she had rezipped it after relieving herself, and walked toward a clump of blackened bushes to the right of our camp. I had opened the fly of my khakis before I realized Amara was with me.

"Could I have some privacy?" I asked. "Privacy?"

"Don't watch me. It isn't polite." The wrinkle formed between her eyes again, but then she turned and walked away.

I pulled my penis out and the urine burst from me in a long yellow arc. I hadn't realized just how badly I needed to go. The morning sun was already bright and hot. I closed my eyes and enjoyed the feeling of relief that came from purging my bladder.

When I opened my eyes, Amara was standing in front of me, just to the left of where my urine was bubbling and foaming on the burned ground. Her head was tilted to the right, the wrinkle still in her forehead as she stared at the stream flowing from me.

"What are you doing?" I stopped the arc and hurriedly tucked myself back into my pants.

"You are not finished," she said. "When it is done, it will... trickle and then drip. You have to shake it."

"I asked you not to watch," I said. All the stress of the last few days boiled in my gut—the burned mission, having to leave home unexpectedly, the cost of coming here to find everything destroyed, my friends and the natives dead or gone...except for this strange creature who had invaded on my private act. "I asked you not to watch," I said again.

"You are angry with me."

"I—I...I guess I am. I don't like to be watched when I do that. I don't let anyone watch that. It's—"

"I am sorry," she said. "Do you forgive me?"

Something about her voice caught me off guard. She sounded so earnest suddenly, as if her very life depended on my answer. I wondered if the man who once owned her had beaten her for disobeying.

"Of course I forgive you," I said. "Just, please, don't do that again. It's a private thing with me. I'd rather not be watched."

"You forgive me?"

"Yes."

"Say it. Please. Say you forgive me."

I looked into her eyes and was again struck by the seriousness of her request, her plea.

"I forgive you," I said.

Amara continued to stare at me for a moment, as if judging whether or not I meant it, then she smiled and was once again the innocent, elf-like girl I had found the day before.

"I'm hungry," I said. "All I brought was canned stuff and field rations. Army food. How about some canned sausages and hard biscuits for breakfast?"

"Yes. Breakfast." She turned around and started back for the tent. I had to force my eyes from her smooth buttocks. But the red hair swaying against her bare shoulders was no less seductive.

"I wish you'd put your clothes back on," I said as I followed her. "It's not good for my soul to see you naked like this."

"Your soul?"

"Yes. Soul. The spirit—ghost. The part of us that goes to Heaven when we die," I said.

"Heaven. Your friends talked about that before they died. Do you think they are in Heaven now?" She paused at the tent flap and looked back at me, the smile playing again at her moist red lips.

"Yes. Yes I do," I said. "I'm sure of it."

"And why does it hurt your soul to see me without those clothes?"

"Well…"

"You think of lying with me." It wasn't a question, just a simple statement. "You cannot get into your Heaven if you think about that?"

"I shouldn't think of it." I felt the blood rushing into my face as I said it. "It's immoral. I'm married. Even if I didn't have a wife, I shouldn't think such things. Thinking them is as bad as doing them. Please. Put the clothes on. I'll wait out here."

"If it will make your soul feel better, I will do it," she said, smiling again before she slipped into the tent. The flap came down and hid her from sight. I looked up at a sky so blue it almost hurt to focus on it. It would be a hot day. Amara's voice came from inside the tent. "I would lay with you, if that is what you want."

The statement shocked me so much I jumped. I didn't know what to do at first, then I moved quickly from the tent, hoping she would think I had been too far away to hear her. I heard her laugh inside the canvas shelter. I pressed my lips together and continued to walk away until I came to the charred remains of a hut. A blackened, child-size skeleton was sprawled among the ashes and debris. The blood ran out of my face; thoughts of Amara's beautiful body receded and I remembered why I was in Brazil.

After a meager breakfast, I took up my shovel and began to

dig. The manual labor was taxing, as I was not used to such physical exertion. Joining a fitness center had always been something I wanted to do, but the real motivation to actually do it had never been there. I worked at the grave, but my mind surely did as much as my body. Thoughts of Amara would not leave my head as I sweated under the Brazilian sun.

She was a strange creature. Amara sat near the edge of the hole, the bits of burned bodies piled beside her like so much rubble. She had gathered the corpses herself, showing no signs of squeamishness as she tugged them out of the burned huts and from under loads of debris. She dragged the bodies near the grave I continued to dig, ignoring the bits of charred flesh that flaked away, ignoring the smell and the buzzing of huge flies disturbed from their feasting by her activity.

Strange creature, *I thought again.*

Why did I keep referring to her as a creature, as if she were a brightly plumaged bird or unusual lizard I had found in the jungle? She is a woman, I told myself. A strange woman with a bizarre past, yes, but a woman.

"Will you toss me that bottle again?" I asked, jamming the shovel into the soft earth and motioning toward the water.

"It is nearly empty," she said as she pitched it toward me. "I brought more. Several bottles," I said as I unscrewed the plastic cap and poured the tepid liquid into my parched mouth. "I know of a fresh spring where the water bubbles from the earth and is very cold," she said.

"You do?" I studied her as I screwed the lid back onto the bottle and tossed it on the ground outside the hole. I took the straw cowboy hat off my head and wiped at my forehead with a bright red bandanna. I replaced the stained hat, shoved the bandanna back into a pocket of my pants and wrapped my hands around the shovel handle. "The villagers never went to a spring for water. They drank from the river."

"They were afraid." The sun made her hair look like a fountain of bronze. She had dressed in a pair of khaki shorts and a thin cotton shirt that hugged her solid breasts. I wondered for a moment that her skin was so pale, not pink from the sun.

"Afraid of what?" I asked.

"The goddess. The water is hers."

"I see. And you're not afraid to drink it?"

"Why should I be?"

"Exactly." I nodded my agreement. "Tell you what. Why don't you take that bottle and fill it up from your spring for me while I keep digging?" I waved away a cloud of buzzing insects. "Those flies are really getting to me."

"Flies have to eat, like everything else. Why do you put these people in the ground?"

"I don't want the flies to eat my friends," I answered. "Besides, it's the Christian thing to do, to bury the dead."

"So the worms can eat them?"

I only looked at her. I didn't think I could explain coffins and the way people were buried in the States. Besides, she'd ask why I wasn't building coffins for these burned pieces of bodies. "Are the worms better than the flies? Is that why you give your dead to them instead of the flies?"

"I guess," I said, exasperated. "I don't know. I just know that buzzing noise is going to make me insane. It'll stop if I get the bodies buried. Will you get the water?"

She laughed, her head thrown back to show her long, milky throat. Then, like a wisp of smoke, she rose from a sitting position and glided away into the jungle.

The strangest creature, *I thought again as I returned to my digging.*

Amara's water was as good as she'd promised. I drained the bottle as soon as she returned and drank another half-bottle before I had the grave dug deep and wide enough to hold all the bodies of missionaries and villagers.

"Shall I begin putting them in?" Amara asked as I crawled out of the hole.

"If you want. Give me a minute to rest and I'll help you."

Amara bent down and wrapped her fingers around a black rib

cage. She jerked the trunk out of the pile, leaving an arm that pulled away from the torso. She dumped the body into the pit and grabbed the arm, tossing it after the rest.

"Wait!" I shouted, reaching to stop her as she took hold of the blistered and blackened arm of one of the bodies. She turned a surprised face to me. "Don't just throw them in," I said. "Be gentle."

"Why?" she asked. "They are dead."

"You should respect the dead."

"Why?"

"You just should." My voice was harsher than I meant it to be. The heat and exhaustion were getting to me. And the flies. Several of the insects swarmed around my head; some had crawled from the dead woman's face onto Amara's wrist. I waved them away.

"They can not feel it. They are dead. Do you think their spirits will come for you if you are not gentle with the bodies?"

"Why risk it?" I said and released her. "Please? Don't just throw them in. Try to space them out a little and drop them in carefully. Okay?"

She nodded, the fold reappearing in her brow as she worked to understand me. I smiled at her, then, drawing a deep breath, I lifted the body of a child from the pile and lowered it as far into the grave as I could reach before letting it roll from my arms. The sound it made when it hit the soft dirt at the bottom was not pleasant. I watched Amara mimic my effort. I smiled at her again.

"That's good," I said. "Thank you."

By four in the afternoon, all the bodies were buried. I straightened my aching back and jammed the blade of the shovel into the soft earth of the mass grave. I put a hand over the top of the shovel and bowed my head, resting my forehead on my hand. I thought about the people beneath me, the villagers who had been so eager for our message as well as those who had been reluctant to abandon goddess worship. But mostly I thought of my friends from home. They were middle- and upper-middle-class people, most of them young, with great futures ahead of them. They should be home, driving sport utility vehicles, mini-vans or Corvettes to important jobs or soccer games. Instead, they were here, under several feet of Brazilian earth, waiting for the worms to find them.

How would I tell their families? Sure, each person I'd buried had come willingly to the Amazon, but it had been my idea to build the mission. I'd encouraged them to take sabbaticals at work, to leave their families and their regular lives to come here and spread the word of God. If I had simply remained content to be the pastor of my church instead of a part-time missionary, these people would still be alive.

I felt the tears running down my dirty face as I began praying again, asking God again to accept each of these departed souls into Heaven and to give me the courage to face their families. I asked him to speak words of comfort through me when it came time for me to tell friends and families what had happened to the missionaries.

"Amen," I said, opening my eyes and raising my head. The last of the tears dropped from my eyes and were absorbed by the muck on my face.

The flies remained, buzzing incessantly through the camp, looking for the feast we had robbed them of. I had to wave my arms constantly as I walked to keep the insects from my face. Amara stayed at my side, seemingly unaffected and unmolested by the flies.

"Show me your spring," I said. "Then I'll rustle us up some grub."

"Grub?"

"Food. Cowboy talk...rustle up some grub. Cowboy's—"

"Like in the movies?"

"You've seen movies?"

"Oh yes. Manuel, the man who owned me, loved movies." Amara nodded as she spoke. "John Wayne was a cowboy."

It was my turn to throw my head back and laugh. Amara

laughed too, but when I was able to stop, she looked at me seriously.

"Why do you laugh?"

"Even in the wilds of the Brazilian rainforest, a woman who's lived most of her life as a slave knows about John Wayne," I answered. "I'm sorry. I just found that funny. Please, show me the spring, then we'll eat. Beans and salt pork, just like the Duke would have eaten on a cattle drive."

The spring was about five hundred yards northeast of the burned village. A fountain of clear, cold water gurgled from a crack in the face of a small rock ledge to form a pool around the base of the ledge. The liquid flowed from the pool in a narrow stream for about twenty yards, then returned to its underground course.

Kneeling, I held my cupped hands in the fountain for a moment then washed my face with the chilling water. I returned my hands and drank from them. The water was deliciously cold and clean.

"This is fantastic," I said to Amara. "It's unbelievable the villagers never used it."

"It is the bathing place of the goddess," Amara answered. "They were afraid to come here because they knew that if they saw the goddess naked she would take away their minds."

"Such silly superstitions," I said as I reached for more water. "Is the pool deep?" I swallowed my water and squatted beside the basin.

Amara walked past me and into the water, naked again. I diverted my eyes for a moment, then looked back at the woman. "Do you think that's safe? I mean, there could be snakes or leeches or who knows what in there," I said.

Amara turned to face me in the middle of the pool. The water came just to her breasts and the ripples made by the cascading fountain broke over her stiff pink nipples. She smiled at me and ducked her head under the surface for a moment. When she came up again, her hair was dark and plastered to her scalp. Water ran in rivulets down her happy face.

"It is cold," she said. "It is safe. Come in with me." She stretched out her right hand, elevating her right breast above the surface of the water.

"Oh no, I can't do that." I shook my head but smiled at her offer.

"But you must be hot after digging the hole for those dead people," Amara argued.

"Yes, I am, and I may take a bath here later, but I can't bathe with you. It wouldn't be proper."

"Proper?"

"It wouldn't be right for a man to bathe with a woman he isn't married to. Especially if he's already married to someone else," I explained.

"Your eyes tell me you want to do it, though," Amara said in a level tone. "Who would know if you bathed with me?"

"I would know. God would know," I answered. "I'll go back and start our supper. I guess you can find your way back?"

"Yes," she said. "I know my way through the jungle. The way through the jungle is not as confusing as the mind of a man who serves your God."

I started, surprised by her statement. I looked at her, wanting to ask what she meant, but afraid she would be able to explain it in a way I couldn't help but understand. I wasn't at all sure I wanted to hear that.

"Then I'll see you back in camp," I said, standing up and starting away from the spring. "Don't be too long."

"I have never known a man like you, Milton Agnew," Amara called. "Any other man I have known would have already made love to me many times. I can see that you want that, too, but you deny yourself. I like you very much."

I stopped and turned back to the naked woman standing breast-deep in the water. I studied her for a long moment.

"You're not the confused child I first took you to be, are you, Amara? No, you're no child," I said. "I don't know what to make of you, either. I can't deny what you say you see in me, but I have taken a vow to forsake all other women but the one I married. A vow before God himself. I can't break that vow." I stopped and smiled slowly. "But, I like you, too, and I want to help you, if I can. Don't stay too long, and be careful coming back."

I hurried away, hoping the woman wouldn't say anything more before I was safely out of hearing.

3

I dumped a can of pinto beans into a steel pot and hung it over the small cooking fire. I stirred the beans slowly, not really seeing them, thinking about Amara and what she had said. Had she really offered herself to me? Did she want to make love to me? Is that what she meant? I tried to push the thoughts away. I simply did not understand her. She was the victim of a unique lifestyle and needed guidance. Even if she had offered herself to me, it was because she believed that's what was expected of a slave woman— a female who had been held captive and used for sex by a powerful man.

"If only Karen would make an offer like that," I murmured as I stirred my pot. "If she would let go of some of her own inhibitions, I wouldn't even be thinking like this."

It was wrong of me to blame Amara for my own carnal weakness. She came from a unique environment where nudity and sexuality were looked at differently. The lust I felt was my own weakness and it was up to me to deal with it.

I took a vacuum-sealed package of salted pork from my food supply and studied it for a moment. Pulling out my pocketknife, I cut the meat into chunks, which I dropped into the beans, wishing for fried potatoes and cornbread to go with the meal. The hard biscuits I'd brought would have to be good enough.

I sat still, looking around the burned village. Since my arrival yesterday, I had not seen another human other than Amara. She said everyone had been killed or fled. If, as she said, the villagers believed it was the wrath of their deposed goddess that sent the killing fire, they might never return. Most likely they would blend into other tribes, forgetting all they had learned about Christianity. There was nothing I could do about that.

But what about my people, the missionaries? I guessed they all were dead. I *knew* they were all dead, though their bodies had been indistinguishable from those of the natives. I knew the missionaries would have stayed and tried to help during the fire. They would not have fled in fear over the anger of a false deity, and they would not have foolishly chased the fleeing natives into the hostile rainforest.

"All dead," I muttered. "All dead. Bill and Linda. Jeff, Kevin, Maria, Daniel, even Cindy. All dead." I tossed another handful of twigs onto my small fire. The missionaries were dead. The villagers they had come to save were either dead or scattered in the jungle. It wouldn't do them or me any good to think of them anymore.

But Amara was still here. A white woman living in the rainforest. A woman who did not know God, who had no home, who had been misused. A woman who needed saving. I could not rebuild the mission here to minister to one soul. I would have to find a way to take Amara back to the States. My attempt at spreading the Gospel in Brazil had failed, but I could take the one lost soul left here back with me and save her on my own turf.

If she would go. And if I could find a way to get her on the plane with me.

I heard a footstep behind me and turned to see Amara approaching. She was dressed, and I felt guilty for the sudden wish that she had waited until I asked her to put the clothes on. I knew my face was reddening, so I turned back to the fire and stirred the food some more.

Amara sat quietly beside me and raked her long fingers through her hair, separating the tangles just as any city-bred female might do after a swim.

"Feel better?" I asked.

"Oh yes. I love the water," Amara answered. "You really must go back and bathe later."

"I'll do that, thank you," I said. "I've been thinking while you were bathing. This mission I started here, I guess it's safe to say it no longer exists. I haven't seen anyone but you since I got here, and you tell me I'm not likely to see anyone else, either. I'm beginning to think you're right. I'll be going home soon. Maybe even tomorrow. I really don't—"

"You won't leave me here, will you?" She gripped my arm with both her delicate hands and held me urgently. "I don't want to stay in the jungle anymore. You won't make me stay, will you?"

"Well—I—well, that's what I wanted to ask you about," I said. "I'd like to take you home with me. I mean, I can't just leave you here. My conscience wouldn't let me do that. This is no place for a woman by herself. So…I guess you want to come back with me? To the States? To Oklahoma?"

"Yes. Anywhere but here." She nodded vigorously.

"Okay then, that part's settled," I said. "Now we just need to figure out a way to get you on the plane without a passport."

"I had a passport," she said. "Manuel took me with him often when he traveled. But he still has it."

"Yes, well, that doesn't do us much good."

"You could say I am one of your friends, one of the dead people, and that my passport was burned in the fire," she said. I looked at her closely. I had been thinking the same thing.

"How did you think of that?" I asked.

"I do not know. It just seemed the easiest thing to do. Would it be hard to make others believe I am someone else?"

"I don't know," I said. "I mean, the government knows about the mission. They know about the fire. But you have no identification. There's no one I can call at home to get a birth certificate or Social Security number…not even a family photo. Plus, if we make too big a scene, your Manuel might hear of it and come looking for you. No, I don't know what to do."

"Is there another way?"

"I don't know." I shook my head. "I don't know. I'll have to think about it. I don't like the idea of saying you're one of…one of the deceased. Are you ready to eat?"

We ate our meal quietly. Amara kept her eyes on the flickering fire, perhaps remembering the flames that swept through the village, perhaps remembering her life before she escaped her master. Perhaps thinking of nothing. I stared into the flames too, wondering how to get the woman out of the jungle and into the United States.

"I will wash these." Amara interrupted my thoughts and gently pulled the empty plate out of my hands. "You go to the spring and bathe. You stink from digging."

"Huh? Oh. Yes, I suppose I do." I stood up, my legs, back and arms protesting at the motion. "Wow. I am so sore. I really should exercise more often."

Amara only looked back at me, her head tilted slightly. I smiled at her, then went to the tent for some clean clothes before going back into the jungle.

"You remember the way?" Amara called as I neared the trees. I stopped and turned back.

"Yes, I remember."

"It will be night soon," she said. "The jungle can be dangerous at night."

"I'll be okay. But, thank you," I said and waved. I entered the dimness of the forest, my clean clothes draped over my shoulder. The floor of the rainforest is soft and moist. Ferns reach from the ground with long, caressing fingers. Decades of old leaves and moldering wood make a blanket that muffles footfalls and holds the sharp smells of life and decay close to the earth, ready to release them whenever a lumbering, heavy foot presses on the soft quilt of time. It is always dim in the forest— dim and damp and timeless.

I found the spring again without any problem and quickly stripped out of my sweat-stained clothes and waded into the cold, clear water. I swam across the pool and back, then dove as deeply as I could go in the depths. I let myself float lazily on my back, the cold bite of the water no longer mattering. Monkeys and birds and insects and reptiles filled the rainforest with their unique sounds and before I realized it, I was surrounded by thick, noisy darkness.

Suddenly the water was cold again and there were sounds in the jungle that I could not identify. Leopards? What predators would come to this pool under cover of night? I splashed toward the shore as quickly as I could swim and pulled myself onto the dry land. I crawled out of the water, shivering, and reached for my clothes.

Something stretched from a bush beside the pool and fastened itself onto my shoulder. I shrieked and rolled away, slipping and sliding back into the water. I flailed there for a moment before I realized what had touched me.

Amara stood up from her place behind the bush. Her laughter was the only sound in the jungle now; my shrill screech had temporarily silenced the animal symphony. Amara pointed at me and continued laughing. She sank to her knees beside the pool, laughing until she was almost sobbing.

"Your eyes are like moons," she said at last.

"Why did you do that?" I demanded. "How long were you there?"

"Not long. You were floating on your back like a dead man. Then you came back to the land as if you were frightened when there was nothing to be frightened of, so I thought it would be a good game to scare you," she said.

"A good game," I said. "Turn around, please, so I can get dressed." She did, so I stood up and waded back to the bank and to my clothes. I could feel my heart hammering in my chest and hear my breath coming in short gasps. "I thought your hand was a snake. I thought I was dead."

"I am sorry." Amara's laughter vanished. She sat on the ground with her feet folded under her and her hands in her lap. "I did not mean to frighten you so bad. It was a game. I am sorry."

"It's all right," I said as I bent to gather my clothes. "Just—"

"I will make it up to you," she said, and before I realized what she was doing, she had turned and reached out to cup my testicles and cold-shrunken penis in one of her hands. She placed her other hand on my thigh. She began massaging my penis.

"Stop that!" I jumped away from her. "Just stop. Why do you do that?"

"I wanted to do something to show I am sorry for scaring you and making you scream like a woman," she said, reaching for me again. I backed away.

"Stop that." I quickly pulled on my underwear and shorts, then slowly pulled on a knit shirt. "You don't have to do anything. I forgive you. It's all right. Just stop that."

"You forgive me?"

"Yes. Yes, I forgive you. Get up. Let's go back to camp." I scooped up my dirty clothes and held a hand out to help the woman up. She took my hand and rose gracefully to her feet.

"You are a strange man, Milton Agnew," Amara said as we began to walk.

"Because I screamed like a woman?"

"Because you do not like to have a woman touch your dick."

"Where did you learn words like that? Not from the missionaries."

She laughed again. "No, not from the missionaries. Why do you not like to be touched by women?"

"I do like to be touched by women—a woman," I said. "My wife. I swore to forsake all others. Remember? That means I can't let others touch me and I can't touch them."

"Yes. The vow before your God," she said. "I remember. You liked for me to touch you, but you think it is wrong?"

"Yes. I mean—" I stopped, realizing I had admitted liking her touch. I could still feel the warmth of her fingers around my penis. "Yes, I suppose I did, and yes, it is wrong."

"Why does your God tell you that you cannot share pleasure with all his people?"

"Can we talk about this some other time?" I asked, wishing I could forget about her touch. "I'm tired and I ache from the digging."

Amara laughed again, quietly, and said no more as we went back to camp and got into our sleeping bags within the tent.

I could not banish the feeling of her warm, soft hand holding my genitals. She was so willing to please, her fingers so long and delicate, her legs firm and inviting. What would it be like, I wondered, to give in, to let her seduce me? Would she let me

33

experience lovemaking in a way Karen never would? I had never been with another woman. Karen and I had waited until our wedding night to consummate our love...and even then she had been a reluctant lover.

When I felt sure Amara was asleep, I gave in to my secret sin and let my right hand pull open my shorts and slide under the elastic waistband of my underwear. I masturbated quietly, remembering the red-haired woman's gentle touch, and brought a drop of blood to my lip as I held my cries in check while the hot, sticky seed burst into my cupped palm.

On the other side of the tent, Amara laughed softly, as if she was having a pleasant dream, or as if she knew a secret.

4

I stowed the folded tent under a seat in the small boat and waded back to shore, the thick, warm water of the river running down my bare legs. Amara sat on the grass not far away, chewing a biscuit. The morning sun caught in her hair and blazed like waves of living copper. I looked away, scanned the area that had once been a village, then walked slowly toward the burned skeleton of the church.

So many people died right in here, I thought as I entered the rectangle of charred wood and ash. I tried hard to picture people—dark-skinned natives and my white neighbors—worshipping in the building. I wanted to recall hymns they would have sung, sermons that would have stirred their hearts. But all I could imagine was the horror, pain and agony of being burned alive in the sanctuary. The screams, the terror…Had the villagers turned away from God and called upon their false goddess in those last moments as Amara claimed?

I knelt in the cinders and bowed my head. I begged God again to show mercy on the souls of all those who had died here. Once more, I named every individual I could remember and called upon the Lord to embrace that person in the glorious kingdom of Heaven. Then I asked forgiveness for my own sins—for my lust, for my failure as a protector of those who had died, for thinking ill of my wife.

Finally, my prayer turned toward the future. I asked that my mission work continue in the person of Amara, and that the Lord would show me the way to arrive safely home with my new charge.

"For, surely Heavenly Father, you have placed this woman in my path that I may lead her to salvation. But Lord, I will need your guidance if I am to bring her home. There are obstacles blocking her path to you, obstacles of earthly means as well as spiritual, and we will need your divine intervention to arrive safely at our destination. We must—"

"Are we leaving?"

I raised my head and turned my face so I could see Amara, who had come to stand behind me outside the ruins of the church. Her green eyes flashed like emeralds as she shifted impatiently from one foot to the other.

"Yes. We're going," I answered. "We're going home." I got to my feet and left the church. Amara followed behind me, and I felt her exasperation when I paused at the edge of the mass grave and whispered a final farewell to those we had buried.

At the bank of the river, I untied my boat from the root and pulled it closer to the land so Amara could board without getting wet. Then I climbed in and pushed away with my foot and used an oar to get us into the middle of the sluggish current. I didn't start the engine yet—the rainforest seemed too quiet, too peaceful, to be interrupted by the puttering drone of the engine.

"Did your—Did the man you used to live with ever take you to the States?" I asked.

"Once," Amara answered. "We flew to Houston, and from there to New Orleans. He was selling cocaine."

"Did he use cocaine?"

"Of course. He would not sell anything he did not use."

"Did you? Did he make you use cocaine?" I asked.

Amara laughed. "I had to steal it from him," she said. "Sometimes I would do favors for my bodyguards so they would give me some."

"Favors?"

"Favors like I tried to give you yesterday."

"I see." I adjusted the boat with the oars to keep us in the middle of the current and thought about how to proceed. "I've been thinking, Amara. Most people in the village were killed in the fire. And yet, when I came back, I found you. You've led a…well, a strange life so far. Do you want to know the Lord?"

"I would rather not talk about your God," Amara said. "He

did not care enough to save your people."

"Perhaps he was calling them home—to Heaven," I answered.

"Or maybe the goddess was angry with them for turning against her and she killed those who had worshipped her and those who came to turn them against her," Amara said. She leaned forward on her seat, her eyes suddenly very earnest and her voice firm. The line on her brow was deep as a knife wound. "Maybe they would still be alive if you and your God had left them as they were."

"They would never know the glory of Heaven if that were the case," I said, startled by her passion.

"You do not even believe that," Amara said. Her countenance changed, as if she had suddenly realized how harsh she was being. "Sometimes when you talk, it sounds like you are reciting things you have memorized."

I was taken aback by her statement. No...I was shocked. I would have been less surprised if she had leaned forward and bitten off my nose.

"I make my living preaching the Word of God," I answered. "A lot of people come to me as unbelievers and use the same kind of arguments you're using. I guess I'm so used to giving the stock answer that it sounds memorized. That doesn't make it any less true."

"We should talk about something else," Amara said. "How far is it to where we are going?"

"A long way," I answered. "This river goes into the Purus and the Purus goes into the Solimnoes, which becomes the Amazon River where it joins the Rio Negro at Manaus. I expect we'll find a cargo boat on the Purus that will take us on as passengers. We'll go a lot faster then.

"When we get to Manaus is when we'll have to figure out a way to get you home," I said. "I know some people in Manaus. That's where the airport is—the airport I landed at when I got here."

"You do not yet have a plan?" Amara asked. "Not yet," I said.

"But the Lord will provide."

Amara laughed, but she did so kindly and kicked off the sneakers she had been wearing. She wiggled her bare toes in the rainwater that had collected in the bottom of the boat, then kicked some of the water at me. I smiled and tapped my foot to splash her back. Drops of water glistened on her ankles and she laughed again. "You're getting me wet," she said.

"You speak with less of an accent the more I know you," I said. "How is that? You sound almost like an American. If you keep it up, you'll be sounding like an Okie."

"An Okie?"

"That's a name for someone who comes from Oklahoma," I explained. "It didn't used to be a good name. What about your accent?"

"I learn languages easily, and I already knew English," she said. Then, in Brazilian Portuguese, she asked, "Is this better?"

"No," I answered in Portuguese, then English. "I'm not skilled in languages and would rather stick to good old English since you know it so well. It took me forever to learn enough Portuguese to communicate down here. However, your ability may come in handy when we get to Manaus. Maybe you can help us find someone to take us home to Oklahoma."

"I will do whatever you tell me," she said.

"Well then, you can hand me that gas can and I'll fill up this engine and start her up so we can get home a little bit faster."

Within minutes, the forest was filled with the buzzing sound of the outboard engine and our little johnboat was skipping downstream toward an uncertain future.

5

We left the narrow tributary Gualones and had been on the sluggish Purus for nearly an hour before a larger boat approached us. I killed our little outboard motor, which I'd been using mostly just to hold a steady course as we drifted with the current, and waved to the chugging cargo vessel. A dark-skinned man in the prow waved back and soon I heard the boat's diesel engine shifting down to an idle.

I took up the oars and rowed the johnboat closer to the bigger boat, whose name had been obscured by time and weather. Amara sat very still in the front of our boat, studying the larger vessel. When we were close enough, someone from the cargo ship threw us a rope and I attached it to the prow of the johnboat. A rope ladder was lowered to us and Amara and I climbed onto the deck of the ship.

We were confronted by a motley crew of unwashed, unshaven men of various races and ethnic mixes. As if they were one body with many eyes, they looked me over from head to foot and then fastened their gaze on Amara, smiles splitting their whiskered faces.

Was it fear for her safety that I felt, or was it jealousy? At the time, I would have laughed at anyone who suggested I was concerned about anything other than her physical wellbeing. Whatever my motive, as the men ogled her, I put an arm around her waist and pulled her closer to me.

"Who is the captain here?" I asked in Portuguese.

A thick man separated himself from the leering pack, stepping forward and grinning at me, his eyes flicking between me and Amara. He wore a shirt that I'm sure had once been white but was now a dingy gray from weeks or months of sweat stains. The shirt's red vertical stripes had turned brown. His pants looked as if they could stand on their own. A filthy yachtsman's hat was pushed high on his head; long, straggly black hair hung in mats from beneath the hat.

"I am Antonio Vargas, captain of the *River Lily*," the man said.

I introduced myself as the Reverend Milton Agnew from the United States and made some vague indication that Amara was my traveling companion. No doubt they assumed some lascivious definition of that term.

"We are going to Manaus," I said. "We would like to buy passage on your ship. You could tow our boat behind or bring it on board."

"We will be docking in Manaus for a short while," Vargas said, raising a grease-stained hand to rub his chin. "What will you pay?"

"What is your price?" I asked. I made a mental count of the cash I had on hand—about eight hundred Brazilian *real*, or four hundred U.S. dollars. I hoped we could get passage cheap since the captain had already said he would be docking in Manaus.

"Share your woman with us and I will take you to Manaus," Vargas told me.

I was shocked. Perhaps I shouldn't have been. No, I should not have been so shocked. I knew the kind of men that usually transport cargo on the rivers of Brazil. However, when dealing with them before, I either had been alone or with a larger group. Now that it was only me and Amara, I felt vulnerable and afraid they would simply take what they wanted. I wondered if we could get over the side of the *River Lily* and back into our johnboat before these men caught us. How long would it be before another boat came? Would our luck be any better with another crew?

"No," I said. "That is out of the question."

The captain laughed, showing a full mouth of yellow teeth in his tanned face. "Then you will let her lay with me tonight. Me alone, the captain."

"No, I cannot do that," I said. "She is under my care and I cannot allow anything to happen to her."

"Nothing bad will happen to her," Vargas promised.

"Nothing bad, though she may scream." He grinned and his crew laughed and slapped him on the back.

"No," I repeated. "We will go back to our boat. Thank you for your time." I started to turn away, pulling Amara with me. "One thousand *real*," Vargas said, reaching out to take my arm.

"I am a missionary. I don't have that much money. All I have belongs to my church. You are going to Manaus anyway. Would you take so much money from Christian people who gave their wages to help your countrymen?"

"I would take as much money as I can get from anyone, especially from rich people who have enough to give away," Vargas said. Again, his crew cheered him on.

"I cannot pay that price," I said. I made to pull my arm away.

"Seven hundred," he said, tightening his grip on my arm. "Three hundred," I countered.

"Six."

"I will give you two hundred *real* and let you keep my boat," I answered. "With the motor, it should be worth another six hundred."

Vargas agreed, his grinning face showing that he thought he had scored a good deal.

"But," I added. "If you or any member of your crew touches the woman, the deal is off. We will take the boat and go and you will get no money."

Vargas cast one more appraising glance at Amara, his lips pressed together as if frustrated I'd guessed that he'd planned something for later. I knew if it came to that, there was really no way I could protect her from the crew.

"She will be safe on the *River Lily*," Vargas said finally. "If you don't pay me as we approach the dock of Manaus, I will cut your throat, throw you in the river, and we all will rape the woman before I kill her and throw her in the river with you."

"I am a man of God and you can trust my word," I said, surprised that my voice did not quaver.

Vargas turned away and shouted to his crew to get the ship

moving again. He ordered two burly sailors to pull our johnboat onto the deck. The *River Lily*'s diesel engine roared and we began moving faster than the current of the river.

"Captain," I called as Vargas made to move away. He turned to face me. "Where will we sleep? Will we have cabins?"

"There is only the captain's cabin on this ship," Vargas answered. "The men sleep on hammocks in the hold with our cargo. You will sleep there or on the deck." He walked away from us.

"He is angry with you," Amara said quietly.

"Yes, he is," I said. "But, I think we'll be safe. He wants the money too much."

"He could always kill you and take it," she said.

"Yes, he could. I don't think he will. He knows there are people who know where I am. I'd be missed. He could probably get away with it, anyway, but I don't think he'll risk it."

"Why didn't you agree to his demands? It would have been safer."

"What?" I looked from the men raising our johnboat to Amara's innocent face. "Let him, or his crew—all of them— have their way with you? Never."

"You will not give them what you will not take for yourself?"

"Selling human flesh is wrong. It's immoral and ungodly," I said. "Besides, they would have hurt you."

"You think of me as a child, Milton Agnew. I am no child. They would have rutted on me like animals, but it would not have hurt me."

"Is that what you wanted?" I asked softly. "Did the man who owned you damage you so badly that you think you need that?" She smiled her radiant smile at me. "My needs are simple enough. I do not need what they wanted to give, but I would have agreed to it for you."

"What is it you do need, Amara?"

She was silent for so long I began to think she was not going to answer. Finally, in a soft, distant voice she said, "I think I have found what I need, Milton Agnew. I need what you can give."

"Amara, I can offer you food and shelter and salvation through Christ our Savior, but I cannot offer you physical love. I've told you that."

Her smile turned sad, but it remained. "Is that so?" she asked. She turned away from me and walked to the bow of the ship. I watched her, her small hands gripping the steel cables that made a rail across the bow. Many members of the crew looked after her, too, but none approached her.

When the johnboat was on deck, I removed our supplies and made a pile of them near some coils of rope in the bow of the ship. When I had everything secured, I went to join Amara, but she was no longer standing at the rail.

6

I found Amara in the stern of the ship, facing a man who was crouching near a mooring post on the ship's deck. The ship, I should mention, was about seventy-five feet long and Vargas used it primarily, he said, to transport vegetable oil from the upper Amazon to the Atlantic coast. I know on that voyage there were dozens of fifty-five gallon drums stored in the hold of the *River Lily*. Whether they held vegetable oil, a legitimate and common commodity in Brazil, I do not know.

The man facing Amara was crouching as if trying to put the metal, spool-looking post of the ship between himself and a dangerous jungle animal. His weathered face was drawn tight, his dark eyes large and round. He clung to the post, but his posture said he was ready to spring away and flee at the slightest provocation.

"What's wrong with him?" I asked Amara in English.

She didn't take her eyes from the wiry little man. "I do not know," she said.

I turned to the sailor and spoke in Portuguese, "What is wrong with you? Why are you acting like that?"

"She is a demon," he hissed at me in a sharp whisper, turning his head in my direction but keeping his eyes fixed on Amara. "Throw her off the ship or we will all be damned."

"That's nonsense," I told him. "There's no need to fear her pale skin and red hair. Such things are not uncommon in other parts of the world. She is not a demon."

"She is the demon-spirit of the jungle," the man said. "She wears her flesh like you wear your shirt. She is—"

"Below! Go below." I looked up to find Vargas standing a few feet behind the crouching man.

Without looking away from Amara, the man backed away

44

from the post. When he was even with Vargas, he spat on the deck in Amara's direction, then fled toward the hatch leading below the deck.

"Belo's father was a shaman among the natives," Vargas said. "Belo left his village, or was driven away, several years ago when his wife became unfaithful." Vargas laughed. "From what I can put together, she got lost in the jungle one night. When she came back, she became the village whore. Belo says she was possessed by a demon in the jungle. I think he just finally got suspicious when she didn't come back to their hut that night and he claimed the demon got her.

"No matter. I will see to it he does not bother you again," Vargas said. He cast another lingering look at Amara, then went back to the pilot house of the ship.

"Superstitious natives," I said, walking up to Amara. "Did he scare you?"

"No. Like you say, such people are silly."

"Yes. I have our stuff stowed on deck," I said. "We'll sleep on the deck tonight. I think I can put up some mosquito net to keep the bugs off us. There's no way we're staying down in the dark cargo area with these men."

Amara only nodded her agreement, or acceptance.

"I hope you'll stay close to me. Don't wander off. Vargas may or may not keep his word, I don't know. I don't know how much control he has over his crew. He—"

"Are you going to fight to protect my honor?" she asked. "Would you kill these men for trying to force themselves on me?"

"I...I pray it doesn't come to any kind of confrontation," I said.

"If these men came to take me, would your God stop them?"

"Probably not," I answered. "And you would not fight them."

"I don't have any weapons and I haven't been in a fistfight since junior high, but if I had to fight to protect you, I'd do it," I said.

She chuckled at my promise of defense. "How long will it be

until we get to Manaus?"

"Tomorrow, probably in mid-afternoon," I said. "What then?"

"I'm not sure. When I was there last week, a friend of mine was in the city. He's an archeologist. He's a Texan, too, and a fun-loving heathen, but a good man who knows…things. I hope he's still there and I can find him again."

"An archeologist?"

"Yes. He looks for artifacts—things from old civilizations—and brings them back to sell to museums. Usually he gets everything out of the country without any trouble. But I know there have been times he's had to persuade people to help him. He has the money to do that kind of thing."

"You do not have much money?"

"Not much. What I have was given by the church to help the mission in whatever way I saw fit. Using it to smuggle you out of the country might not be what they had in mind. But… you're all that's left of the mission and this is the way I've decided to help you."

We went back to where I'd put our supplies. I have to admit I was a little surprised that it looked like no one had touched our things. Looking back, maybe I judged the crew of the *River Lily* too harshly. They gave us less trouble than we gave them.

Several of the sailors were fishing from the sides of the boat. As the sun sank behind the trees of the forest, a fire was made in a metal barrel on the deck and the various fish that had been caught during the day were cooked on spits over the flames. Vargas ordered his men to share with me and Amara. I felt obliged to distribute a portion of the food items I'd brought, so I gave each man of the crew one of my hard biscuits and some dried fruit.

My fish was charred on the outside and nearly raw close to the bones. I ate what was warm and gnawed on beef jerky to supplement the meal. Amara ate what was given to her without comment. Scraps were thrown overboard.

With Amara's help, I spread our tent on the deck, held it

46

down with ship parts that were laying around, and rolled the canvas sides up so that we would be protected by the mosquito netting but still able to see anyone approaching the tent. Vargas watched us with great interest and a broad smile, but no offer of help. I moved all our packs into the tent, unrolled the sleeping bags and watched Amara slip into hers. Kneeling, I hurried through my nightly prayer, then got into my sleeping bag, pulling the top over me but not zipping it.

I tried very hard not to sleep. I was afraid I would wake up to find Amara dragged away by the lustful crew, or at the least to find one of the greedy sailors rifling our supplies or picking my pockets. Despite my fears, I did sleep.

I awoke to screaming. Of course, I turned to Amara first. She was a dark shape within her sleeping bag, her back turned to me, her long red hair a glistening fountain in the moonlight. The scream came again, from beneath the deck, and I rushed out of the tent.

Vargas shoved me aside at the hatch leading below the deck. He was stopped from running down the steep stairs by his crew rushing up from the hold.

"What is it? What's going on?" Vargas roared at them as they came on deck, many of them stripped down to their underwear. All of them appeared to be afraid of something.

"Is the ship sinking?" I asked.

"There's something down there," one of the men said. "Yes, something that is not human," another added. "A ghost. An evil spirit."

Vargas cursed at them. "You are all as bad as Belo with your talk of ghosts and vampires. There is nothing down there but cowards and vegeta —"

"Where is Belo?" someone asked.

"He is still there, in his hammock. He did not move."

"Go get him," Vargas ordered. "He started this, I think." None of the men moved to obey their captain. Finally, Vargas grabbed the closest man to him and threw him bodily at the opening in the deck. The man stumbled, cast fearful eyes back at his captain, then slowly moved into the dimness below. I sensed that the men around me were truly afraid. I was sure this was not an elaborate trap to separate me from Amara. And, I was curious. I had heard the stories about missionaries who battled devils in the jungles. I admit the idea of doing such a notable thing was not unappealing.

"I'll go with him," I said, and followed the sailor into the hold.

Battery-powered lamps hung from beams beneath the deck. Stacks of blue metal drums lined the sides of the hold. A line of hammocks was suspended between the center support beams. Most of them were empty. The one holding a man was near the back of the hold. The sailor who had descended ahead of me turned his head back to look at me.

"You are a priest?"

"A minister," I said. "There's nothing to be afraid of down here."

"No? You do not feel the cold? You do not know that it is supposed to be very hot down here?"

It *was* cold. There was no doubt about that. Now that he'd mentioned it, I couldn't help but compare the cool air of the hold to the sticky heat on the deck. It was peculiar, but I was not deterred.

"Yes, it's cooler here than above," I said. "Is that Belo back there?"

"Yes."

"Let's go see what's wrong with him."

As God is my witness, the air of the cargo hold of the *River Lily* got colder as we approached the man in the hammock. By the time we stood beside him, our breath was leaving our bodies in a frosty cloud. The sailor was trembling and I knew it was less from the cold than from fear.

Belo's back was to us. His right hand was across his body and entwined in the mesh of his hammock as if he'd turned away from something and had been clawing at his bed. My companion wouldn't touch him. I reached out to untangle

Belo's fingers. I knew the man was dead as soon as I touched his flesh—he was as cold as a cadaver saved in a science lab. I pulled his fingers from the mesh and rolled his face toward us. The sailor shrieked and ran. My first impulse was to follow, but reason won out and I remained. Belo's face was frozen in what could at first be considered a look of abject horror. His mouth and eyes were open wide, a trickle of saliva sticking to his cheek. I tried to close the mouth but the man's jaw was stiff. The air moved around me, as if stirred by the motion of someone passing by. I looked around, expecting to see Vargas coming up behind me, but there was no one there. I heard a sound and turned back to the corpse. His left hand, which had been closed, was now open, the skin blistered and scorched.

A burning stick of wood rolled from beneath his hammock toward my bare foot.

I jumped out of the way, then thought of the barrels of cooking oil and stamped on the small fire. The flames burned my bare flesh and the force of my effort bruised me. I pulled my foot away and looked down at the thing.

It was easy to tell the bit of wood was some sort of native charm. I recognized some of the symbols carved around the face, symbols that were supposed to ward off evil. The face carved onto the charm was familiar. I bent down to get a better look, then picked the thing up and held it close to one of the lamps.

The face was that of Coadidop—the same face that was on the totem of the villagers who had been the subject of my mission.

I should say something about this Coadidop. Legends vary, some saying she is a beautiful goddess who created the earth from her own milk, created a companion for herself named

Enu and that other companions created by herself and Enu mated to create the first humans. It also is believed Coadidop brings the rain, looks after women in childbirth and protects children in the forest. Other legends say she is a short, hideous creature that feeds on blood. Legends among the villagers I had known said Coadidop was benevolent unless crossed, that she oversaw the welfare of all within the forest, but her payment was blood. It is said she preys primarily on the most beautiful of women and that, after a visit from Coadidop, her victims become nymphomaniacs. Such women are usually stoned to death.

All this was going through my mind as I studied the little idol Belo had dropped from his dead hand. Suddenly, the air swirled around me once more, again as if some figure was passing. The idol was knocked from my hand and burst into flame again—a flame so intense it was nearly white. By the time the wooden object hit the floor of the ship's hold it was nothing but smoking ash that shattered upon contact with the floor.

"What was that?" Vargas shouted from the bottom of the stairs leading to the deck. His voice, booming and echoing in the frigid air of the hold, caused me to jump. My heart began hammering in my chest and my mouth was so dry it took me several tries to answer.

"I don't know what it was," I finally managed. "Belo is dead. It looks like he had a heart attack in his sleep."

"Yes, Fernando said he was dead," Vargas said as he came toward me. The cold was suddenly gone. The hold was filled with close, oppressing heat, just as it should have been all along. "Fernando said Belo's devils got him."

Vargas stopped beside the hammock and looked at the dead man. "It is a fright," he commented. "Who knows what devils he saw in his dreams before he died. Probably just his wife." Vargas laughed softly and pulled Belo's blanket up to cover his dead face.

I bowed my head and whispered a prayer for the deceased, asking that God forgive the man his paganism. My prayer was interrupted by Vargas.

"Save your words, padre," he said. "Belo would not want them. I'll see to it he gets a burial he'd like in Manaus.

"Where is your concubine?" he asked.

"Amara." I hurried away from Vargas, back up the steep wooden stairs into the night air of the deck. It felt good to be out of that cargo hold, to breathe the fresh air, even if it was still warm and filled with the smell of scared, sweaty men huddled around the opening leading below. I pushed through them and went to our tent.

Amara was still asleep. I bent over her, then paused. I could not detect her breathing. One slender arm was exposed. I gently took it in my hand and felt for a pulse. At first I didn't feel anything.

"Amara!" I shook her shoulder with my free hand. She jerked and her eyes slowly opened. The movement of her arm had put her pulse beneath my searching fingers. I sagged with relief. "I'm sorry," I said. "You've slept through quite an adventure."

"Belo is dead," she said. "How—"

"I heard the men talking. I had just gotten back to sleep."

"Oh. Yes, he's dead. It was very strange. I guess it was a heart attack. But…"

"But what?"

"Well, it was very cold below deck. For a while. And it felt…Oh, you'll think I'm being as silly as Belo. It just felt like there was something moving down there…something I couldn't see."

"Milton Agnew, there may be things in this world that you do not understand. You should open your mind and give up some of your inhibitions."

"You believe in ghosts?" I asked.

"I do not disbelieve in anything," she answered. She snuggled deeper into her sleeping bag and closed her eyes.

More bewildered than I'd been since I met her, I returned to my own sleeping bag. This time, I did not sleep. It was many hours before dawn finally brightened the sky.

7

The remainder of our voyage with the crew of the *River Lily* was a quiet one. I suspect word got around that poor Belo had believed the fiery-haired Amara was a devil. At any rate, none of the men spoke another word to us until it was time to leave the cargo ship.

Sometime during the night we flowed with the water of the Purus into the Solimnoes. At Manaus, the Solimnoes joins the Rio Negro, a sight that always makes me think at first that someone has spilled oil into the water. The Rio Negro is black, like dark tea, making a sharp contrast to the brown water of the Solimnoes. But, like the races that have joined to mold today's Brazilian citizen, the black and brown rivers mingle and become one living thing known all over the world as the mighty Amazon River.

The dock at Manaus actually floats on the river to accommodate the annual rise and fall of the river. During the rainy season, between October and April, the Amazon has been known to rise as much as fifty feet at Manaus.

The *River Lily* hardly had bumped against the old tires tied to a slip of the dock before Vargas' crew began pitching my packs and supplies off the ship. Vargas, still smelling of sweat and grease, approached me for the first time since we left the hold the night before.

"I will have my money now," he said.

"We really appreciate your generosity," I said as I counted off the money. "And I want to personally thank you for keeping your crew under control in regards to Amara."

"Belo might have been crazy," Vargas said, glancing over my shoulder to where Amara was waiting for me on the dock. "But maybe he wasn't." He took the money from me and turned away.

Shaking my head, I put the rest of my money back into my

pocket and descended the plank to join Amara on the dock.

"It seems they all think you're a devil now," I joked with her. "Maybe I should have told old Vargas you'd cast a spell on his rusty boat if he didn't cut his price in half."

"Maybe you should have," she laughed. "I could play the part of the evil jungle queen and curse them all."

"Sounds like you might enjoy that a bit too much," I said, picking up a couple of backpacks and the rolled tent. "I hate to ask, but can you carry some of this stuff?"

Amara picked up the remaining items, another backpack and an old army rucksack, and together we left the dock and the river behind.

It didn't take long to find a taxi. We loaded our supplies into the trunk of the ancient car and got into the back seat, which smelled of millions of cigarettes and various other unidentifiable odors. I gave the driver the name of the hotel where William Barlow, my archeologist friend, had been staying.

It was a depressing ride through the *favelas*, the slum areas that surround most of the larger cities in Brazil. The *coboclos*—poor European/Indian people who live in the Amazon basin—spent their lives working for little or no wages, living in shanties made from scrap wood, cardboard, pieces of tin or whatever else they could find to hold off the elements. William usually rented hotel rooms in the neighborhoods separating the *favelas* from the next level of society. He hired the poor mixed-race people to do the manual labor on most of his expeditions because, he said, they would work hard and if the worst happened and they died—and many of them did—their families were as happy to get the cash bonus William offered as they would have been to have the worker come home.

The hotel was a solid, square building made of stone, reminding me of a New York City brownstone. Amara and I dragged our bags up the steps to the main entrance and into the lobby. The desk clerk told me that Mr. Barlow was still lodged there but that he was out for the afternoon. I asked for two rooms.

"We have only one room available," the thin, brown-skinned man said. He had very dark, wavy hair and a thin moustache. His shirt collar was limp from the heat.

"Only one room?" I asked. "But…" I glanced at Amara, who was studying a print of Dante Gabriel Rossetti's *Astarte Syriaca* on the wall near the desk. She seemed not to be paying any attention to the conversation. "Okay. We'll take it," I said. I paid for the room, signed only my name on the register, and helped a bellboy who didn't seem to be more than ten years old carry our things up two flights of stairs and down a long, narrow hallway to our room. Amara followed behind us. I gave the boy a generous tip and closed the door after him. "Are we to sleep together?" Amara asked.

"Of course not," I said. "This was the only room left."

"Perhaps fate is pushing us toward this big bed." She sat on the side of the bed, then lay back, stretching her arms above her head and arching her back. "Perhaps you are meant to plow my vulva here."

"Now you're just being silly," I said. "I'll figure out something later. Maybe I'll sleep in Bill's room and you can have this one all to yourself."

"You'd rather sleep with a man than with me?" Her tone told me she was teasing, but I didn't like the implication, even as a joke.

"Of course not," I said. "But I—" She had trapped me. There was no good answer. She laughed at me, and I suppose I wore an expression that deserved it. "Maybe you are a jungle devil," I said.

"Maybe I am. But, you already have promised me salvation, and I expect you to give it to me."

"It isn't mine to give," I said. "And all you have to do is accept it. It's already there waiting for you."

"Is it?"

"Paid for on the cross."

"Umm. The Crucifixion," she said, closing her eyes and smoothing her shirt over her stomach. "Your dead missionary friends talked about that a lot."

"You seem to have heard an awful lot of what they said for not having actually lived in the village," I said.

"I would sneak up to the side of the little building where they died and listen when they told the village people about the new God. Some of the stories were fun. Some made me cry. "What will we do now?" she asked. "I heard that your friend will not be back this afternoon."

"I'm starving," I said. "I plan to go find a restaurant and eat something other than field rations or half-raw fish. Are you ready to go?"

We left the hotel for the street—a street that is unlike anything you'll see in Oklahoma…or anywhere else I've been in the United States. Brazilians like to touch those they talk to. It's a custom I've never been comfortable with, but one that cannot be avoided while in Brazil. Clerks in stores are likely to cling to your arm as you discuss their wares. Vendors will clasp both your hands in theirs as they take your money. Waiters will put a hand on your shoulder as they lean close to hear your order.

Amara was the only exception I ever saw to that custom. From a safe distance, men would stare at her, some not bothering to hide their leers, but any who approached her soon backed off. Other people, those who seemed more civilized, would look to her face in greeting, then move past her as if she were marked as one who was not to be approached. I do not know how many hands I saw outstretched toward Amara, then moved to another before ever touching my companion's pale flesh.

It seemed as if Amara was being shunned. I couldn't explain the behavior of the people and I hoped Amara wouldn't notice it and ask why no one touched her as they did me. With all she'd been through, and with me taking her away to a new life, she had enough to think about without worrying over her exclusion from a custom I myself often found annoying or even distasteful. She did not seem to notice it, or maybe she thought I had already met the myriad people who handled me as we moved about the city.

After our meal, we returned to the hotel. I was very tired from the excitement of the night before. Amara sat in a chair, fascinated by the television in our room. I stretched out on top of the bed covers and fell asleep within moments.

When I awoke, Amara was snuggled against me, one of her legs over mine and her hand resting on my chest. Her blazing red hair was near my face and I could smell its feminine fragrance; it bore no trace of perspiration or hint of river smell.

"I can feel your heart," she said.

"I'm glad to hear it's still pounding away."

"It is strong." She gently traced circles on the chest of my shirt, tickling me more than I let on.

"I thought you were watching the television."

"You looked so…how would you say it? Inviting?"

"Oh really?"

"Yes. You are very comfortable."

The smell of her hair and the feeling of her soft skin nestled so close to me was intoxicating. I admit that she felt very refreshing and…inviting, as she would have said, as she lay there, her exquisite limbs draped over me. It felt right. It felt good and natural and for a moment I wished I could forget that I was a married man.

"We should get up," I said. "I can't believe you're lying so close to me. I know I have to stink of sweat and the river air."

"You smell like a man," she said, not moving.

"Yes, well, a dirty man who needs a shower. Let me up." She still didn't move, so I gently pushed myself from under her arm and leg and swung my feet off the bed. "I'll just be a few minutes, then you can take one if you want. Or, you can go first."

"Or we could bathe together," she said, smiling at me and laughing at whatever expression I made. "Oh no, you cannot do that," she said in a stern mockery of my own voice.

"I'll go first," I said, gathering my clothes and heading for the bathroom.

Standing under the hot water, I could not help but think of the beautiful woman in the next room and how she had felt snuggled against me. It grieves me to admit that for the second time since meeting her, I gave in to my own carnal cravings and masturbated while thinking of fornicating with my seductive charge. The orgasm I had was so powerful that for a moment I feared I would black out and fall out of the bathtub. When my head cleared, I washed the semen from my hands, washed my hair and got out of the tub. I felt horribly guilty, as I always do after giving in to such desires, but at the same time I was able to convince myself that my bath-time exercise would help to curb the male appetite I felt toward Amara—an appetite she encouraged so playfully.

She was watching the television again when I came out of the bathroom. She turned her smile on me and it was a knowing smile, as if she had been peeking through the keyhole and knew what I had done. But, that was silly since the bathroom door had no keyhole and the shower curtain was opaque, anyway.

"You do smell better," she said.

"As if you can tell from there," I said, balling up my dirty clothes and pushing them into a canvas bag. When I turned back to her, she was directly behind me.

"I can smell you even better here," she said. She took one of my hands and brought it to her face. She sniffed it and I couldn't help but think how only a few minutes ago the fingers she held had been coated in milky white semen spilled over thoughts of her. Then her tongue slid from between her soft red lips and traced lightly over the area where my seed had been.

"Stop that." I jerked my hand away from her. I could feel the blood rushing to my face. I tried to turn away, but there was nowhere to go. "Why do you do such things?" I asked angrily. She laughed at me, her voice again like small ringing bells.

She turned away and started for the bathroom, pulling off her clothes and dropping them as she went. She didn't bother closing the door behind her as she turned on the water and stepped into the tub. She gave me a lingering, teasingly inviting look before she drew the shower curtain.

I could hardly believe it, but I felt my manhood stirring in my pants again as I saw her dark silhouette slowly rubbing soap over her skin. I took my hat and fled the room.

In the hotel lobby, I asked the desk clerk if William Barlow had returned. I was a little angry to learn that Bill had indeed returned and no one had told him I was expecting him or sent word to me that he was back. I thanked the clerk and started for Bill's room, then stopped. I decided it probably wouldn't be wise to leave Amara alone in our room without at least telling her where I was.

When I opened the door to our room, I found Amara lying on the bed, her long white legs spread, her knees pulled up slightly and one of her delicate hands vigorously rubbing her vagina while the other hand gripped and released a breast. Her eyes opened to slits and fixed on me, but her hands never ceased their activities.

She grunted several times, then raised her buttocks from the bed, the muscles of her calves and thighs straining as her face contorted. The frantic activity of her hands ceased. The one between her legs slid deep into the glistening cavity of her vagina and she let out a long, low, deep moan. She stirred the fingers in her juices for a moment as she slowly lowered herself back to the bed. Now her eyes were open completely and still fixed on me.

"What—" My voice was nothing but a croak. I realized I was still standing there with the door opened and quickly slammed it, not bothering to see if there was anyone in the hallway who might have heard or seen Amara. "What are you doing?"

Her fingers were still lazily rubbing circles between her legs as she answered. "I am touching myself. In my thoughts, it was you touching me. I hope you do not mind that I was thinking of you that way. You can think of me when you touch yourself. I will not mind."

It was several long beats of my heart before I could answer her. Had she known about my own masturbation? Was she mocking me? Did she really feel such desire for me?

"Why? Why do you do such things?"

"Because it has been a long time since a man touched me," she said. "I want to be loved."

"The men who…who touched you, weren't you their slave?"

"Yes."

"And you enjoyed that?"

"They were not always mean to me," she said. "That is what you are thinking. That they came to me with fists instead of caressing hands. It was that way sometimes, but not always."

"Please stop that," I said, tearing my eyes from the hand still working between her legs. "If you have to do that, fine, but please do it somewhere private. And for the record, it's just as wrong as if you were actually committing adultery."

"You did not enjoy watching me finish?" Her eyes moved from my face to my groin, where, I am sad to say, it was obvious I had enjoyed her show.

"Amara, please, do not torture me," I said, my voice suddenly tired, begging. "Will you stop these games if I tell you that my wife is a woman who does not put much value on sex and that I do find you incredibly desirable? But still, I cannot, will not give in to any desires I may feel for you. It is wrong. It's wrong."

"Please get dressed."

"I did not mean to make you feel bad," she said, sitting up, then getting to her knees. Her large green eyes were serious and apologetic as she moved to the end of the bed, her long red hair brushing her soft white shoulders. As she came nearer, I could smell her musky sex. "Will you forgive me?"

"Yes, Amara, I forgive you," I said, waving her back and turning my side to her so that I wasn't looking at her.

"Look at me. Please." I looked back, keeping my eyes fixed on hers. "You forgive me?"

"Yes," I repeated. "I forgive you. Please don't do it again, or at least do it where I won't walk in on you."

"You forgive me?"

"I said I do."

"Then it will be like I did not do anything wrong?"

"If you get dressed now. Please." I turned my head away again. "And wash your hands."

When she had her clothes on and had washed, I told her that Bill was in the hotel and that we should go talk to him.

"What if he does not like me?" she asked. "He will."

"He might not. I think a lot of people here do not like me. No one would touch me in the streets. No one wanted me to touch them."

"Don't be silly," I said. "People just have strange customs here. You should know that."

"If your friend does not like me, he might not help us."

"He'll help us," I said. "Now come on."

Together, we went up the two floors to Bill's suite of rooms.

8

William "Bill" Barlow is a slight man, not more than five feet, eight inches tall. His dark hair looks much lighter because of the many flecks of gray that have begun to appear in it. He is always clean-shaven, at least when I have met him, and the graying hair I just mentioned is always immaculately combed, with a part to the left. The casual observer would never guess him to be a cunning, sometimes ruthless hunter of ancient artifacts. He looks like a man who should be ensconced in a corporate office, doing nothing more strenuous than tapping a computer keyboard.

When he opened the door to my knock, he was wearing his usual khaki outfit with the shirt unbuttoned at the throat— his casual look. His weathered, browned face split into a smile when he saw me, the lines around his eyes crinkling and breaking the dust that was still on his skin.

"Milton, it's good to see you again. I expected you'd still be in the jungle," he said as he reached for and pumped my outstretched hand. Then his eyes landed on Amara. "What's going on?"

"Can we come in?" I asked.

"Yes, of course. Come in." He moved aside to let Amara and I slip past him. I noticed that his eyes remained on Amara. His brow was furrowed and he looked troubled. He closed the door behind us.

Bill almost always got a suite of rooms when he was in Manaus. He slept in the smaller room to the back and used the front room as an office to organize his ventures. He often held interviews with natives he planned to use as guides or laborers in the front room of his suite. There was a desk in this main room and I could see stacks of papers and a few photographs on it. Bill's battered straw cowboy hat was sitting on one end of the desktop.

"Do you want to sit down?" he asked, waving at the two hotel chairs in front of the desk. "Do you want a drink? I have a few cans of Diet Coke."

"That would be nice," I said. "Does your friend want one?"

"Amara, do you want one?" I asked.

She turned away from her examination of the room and smiled at me, her large green eyes filled with light. "I am not sure what it is, but if you are having one, I will have one."

"You've never had a Coke? A soda pop?" I asked. She shook her head. "Well, you're in for a treat, then."

We sat down while Bill fished three silver cans from an ice chest. He rattled some melting ice cubes into Styrofoam cups and handed two cups and two cans to us. I helped Amara open the can and pour the foaming soda over the ice. I watched as she sipped it, smiling as the bubbles touched her skin.

"Do you like it?"

"It is very bubbly," she said. "Yes, I like it very much."

"Good," Bill said. "There's a couple more cans in there, so if you finish that and want some more, you can have it."

"Thank you, Bill," I said.

"No problem. Now, tell me about the mission. What brings you back to Manaus so soon? And with your present... companion?"

"The village—and the mission—is destroyed," I said. "Everything was burned. The people are either dead or scattered. We buried the bodies we found. Then...there was nothing else we could do, so we left."

"Yes, but you were alone when you went in," Bill said, his eyes moving from me to Amara and back.

"Amara, would you like to watch the television again?" I asked. I turned to Bill. "Would you mind if she watched in your room?"

"No, I don't mind," he said. "Of course, the TV is a piece of sh—" He broke off before saying the word. "Sorry, Milton. You know my mouth. It's one of those black-market 'Sonee' sets brought in from Paraguay. The damn buttons have been falling out since I got here."

"That's fine," I said. "Come on, Amara, I'll show you where it is. You don't mind, do you? I just need to talk to Bill privately."

"I do not mind that you are going to tell him about me," she said, smiling again. "But I will go in the other room and watch the television again."

I led her into the smaller room and found a dubbed version of a popular American sitcom. As Bill had warned, the channel selector button fell off the set when I took my finger off it. I replaced it.

"You'll be all right?" I asked Amara, who had settled on Bill's bed.

"Yes. Go tell your friend how you found me naked in the jungle and ask him how you can sneak me home with you," she said.

"Are you upset that we're going to talk about you? I just don't feel comfortable talking about all the things we're going to talk about with you sitting beside me. Bill will probably have to suggest some things that it might be best you don't hear."

She laughed at me. "Go on, Milton Agnew. But I am not as naïve as you might think."

Shaking my head, I closed the door and returned to my place across from Bill at his desk.

"She's quite a woman," Bill said.

"Yes. I don't know what to make of her."

"Tell me."

"I found her in the village—what was left of the village, that is. She was stark naked, standing next to a tree, watching me." I told him Amara's story about being sold into slavery, escaping and living near the village and how she'd seen the fire. I left out the parts that concerned her seductive endeavors and my own weaknesses, of course. I also didn't mention the accusations made by Belo, or the sailor's strange death.

"She's no slave," Bill said. "Come on, Milton, you know that. Look at her. Look at how she carries herself. No slave woman is going to hold her head up and meet your eyes like that.

"Besides, a woman like that would probably be marked, branded like a prize cow, so everyone who sees her would know who she belonged to. Or at least that she belonged to someone. She's no slave."

I sat and stared at Bill for several seconds. I remember my eyes blinked a few times, like an owl's, as I digested this information.

"She was used for sex," I said. "Maybe she wasn't marked because it would have marred her...well, obviously, her beauty."

"Maybe," Bill agreed. "I'm not sure I'd buy that. The Brazilian drug runners I know wouldn't care much about a little brand or some carved marking as long as she's able to do what he wants.

"And there's still her demeanor."

"I don't know what to say. Maybe her spirit was never broken."

"And she's been a slave since childhood? Sold by her own father? Do you believe that?"

"It's what she told me," I answered.

"What did you say this drug runner's name is? I can check on him."

"No, don't do that," I said. "It doesn't matter. So what if she wasn't a slave? She was lost in the jungle. She's alone and needs help."

"Your help?"

"She's all that's left of my mission."

"She didn't live in the village. She wasn't part of your mission, Milton."

"She listened outside the chapel sometimes, she said. She... she has a soul, Bill, and it's my duty to bring her to Jesus."

"She could be a fugitive who was hiding in the jungle."

"That's ridiculous. She's like a child."

"What are you going to do with her, Milton?" he asked. "I'm afraid I know the answer, but I want to hear you say it."

"I want to take her home with me."

"Christ, Milton, listen to yourself. She's not a tame parrot you found in the jungle. Even if she was, you can't just put her on a plane and take her home. She doesn't have a passport, I'll bet."

"Well, no," I admitted. "That's why I came to you. I thought you could help."

He blew a great gust of breath between his lips and rolled his eyes up to look at the dirty ceiling of the room. "Milton. Do you know what you're doing?"

"No, Bill, I don't. That's why I'm asking for your help."

"Do you understand what you're asking?"

"I'm not sure."

"That's what I thought." He sipped his Diet Coke. "She doesn't have any identification?"

"None. She was naked when I found her, so she didn't have any pockets for a driver's license or passport or anything." I tried to smile. Bill only grunted at my humor.

"Why didn't she steal some clothes from the villagers?"

"I—I don't know," I said. "She seemed, I don't know... naturally naked. As if she was comfortable that way. Almost like Eve before...well, you know the story."

"Yeah, I know the story. That's what worries me. I'm afraid you're making her out to be some jungle waif that you're going to save, both physically and spiritually, when she might be a murderer looking for a way out of the country."

"That's just crazy," I said. "I think I'm a fair judge of character, Bill. That woman's no murderer."

"Fine. Fine," he said. "I'm not going to change your mind arguing that way. You want to take her home, to Oklahoma City, I guess. Then what?"

"Then...I'll see that she learns to fit into our culture and that she has the chance to accept the Lord."

"Where will she live?"

"I don't know. I'm sure someone in the church will take her in."

"You know there's no legal way to get her out of Brazil and

into the U.S. when she has no ID."

"I suspected that."

"You knew it, Milton."

"Okay. Fine. Should the laws of man stand in the way of God's work?"

"You're the preacher, you tell me."

"Laws don't usually stand in the way of your own work, Bill."

He sighed. "That's true," he said. "The things I take out of here, though, are relics. Pieces of rock, wood and clay. Not human beings."

"I know. Still, I thought you might know how...how to get her out."

"I can make some suggestions," he said. "Just because I don't smuggle immigrants doesn't mean I don't know people who have done it. Some of them are even still alive and not in prison." He gave me a pointed look.

"I understand there is risk involved."

"Do you? Suppose you pull it off and get her home. What will your church think of you, shall we say, *bending* the law?"

"I think they'll understand it's necessary."

"Okay. I'll let you worry about that." He rubbed at his eyes, then looked at the dirt on his fingers. "I need a shower. I've been out all day looking for strong backs to help me carry some old idols out of the jungle."

"There's an old idol not far from the village," I said. "I thought it had been destroyed. Amara showed it to me. Coadidop, they called her. That was the name of the pagan goddess."

"Coadidop?"

"Yes, that was her name. There is an idol, like an Indian totem pole, not far from the village"

"That myth is ancient," Bill said. "They worshipped Coadidop? I'd like to take a look at that idol. I might have to do that."

"Yes, they worshipped that goddess," I said. "But Amara says most of the villagers were attending services in the chapel by the time the fire broke out."

"And you don't know what caused the fire?"

"No. I couldn't figure it out. But, I'm no expert investigator. My guess would be lightning, which is what the government says caused it. There was a central place where it looked like there had been an explosion and I think the fire moved out from there."

"That's the likely explanation," Bill agreed. He sighed again, sipped his soda, and put it gently down on his desk. I took a drink of my own. "Well, how are we going to get you and her out of here?"

"Fake passport?"

"That would be the obvious way," he agreed. "I have a couple of suggestions regarding that, and one other idea."

"I'll listen to anything."

"Umm-hmm. It's easy enough to get a fake passport in Brazil," Bill said. "Depending on where you go, the quality isn't too bad. It'd probably cost you between five hundred and one thousand dollars. That's just for the passport. If you want corroborating documents—and I would highly advise it—that'd cost you even more. You can get those here in Manaus and fly out from here, probably in a couple of days.

"The drawback to that plan is that Brazilian customs can be tough. You get a fake passport that doesn't look right, and you'll get busted. Of course, *your* passport is fine, so you could put the rap on her for having the fake, if push came to shove."

"I couldn't do that."

"Of course not." Bill snorted and rubbed his face. "The other problem is that the Brazilian cops have been raiding passport makers pretty hard lately. If you got caught having one made, it wouldn't go well with you."

"What are the chances of that?"

"I have no idea. I don't have any connections that way—nobody to tell me when a passport raid's coming. Remember, I don't have a need for that." He smiled. "You could pay off the cops, they're corrupt as hell, but that'd take a lot of money."

"No thanks. Okay. So, what are the other plans?"

"You could go down to Paraguay, get a fake passport there and fly out from Asuncion to Miami."

"I didn't know there was an international airline in Paraguay."

"It's a crappy one. They mostly fly old DC-8s or 707s, planes no respectable airline would even put in a museum."

"Okay, besides the plane falling apart, what are the risks that way?"

Bill snorted. "Well, it's Paraguay. Stuff's cheaper, but it's like my 'Sonee' TV, man. The quality isn't there. You could get out of Paraguay easy enough, but getting past customs in Miami could be a real bitch. Excuse me, a real problem. If the airport TSA agents are really busy, with Amara's white skin, you might be able to slide right through. If not…if they have time to take a good look at her passport from Paraguay…you could find yourself in trouble again. Back before 9/11 this kind of thing would have been easier to do.

"And then, like I said, you'd be leaving from Paraguay. You mess up down there, go down the wrong street at the wrong time, you could be kidnapped slick as shit, excuse me, kidnapped easy enough. They might hold you until you gave them all your money, they might call your church in the U.S. and demand more money. They'd almost definitely have some fun with your friend. But, they'd probably let you go. Eventually. It's not likely they'd kill you."

"Who are 'they'?"

"Whoever gets you first. The police, a street gang, an organized crime outfit, whoever. There's almost no law down there."

"I see. What was your other plan?"

He took a deep breath and chewed his lip for a moment. "This one's getting a bit closer to home. Tomorrow there'll be a private jet leaving Manuas for Belem. I have a few artifacts on the plane. Those will be loaded onto a ship at Belem and taken to Brownsville, where they'll be stored until I get there to pick them up."

"That would be perfect," I said. "We could just sail right into Texas."

"Not so fast, Milton. Like I said, this one is closer to home. There's a damn good chance you could sail right into Texas, get off the ship and go about your merry way. But if you're caught, they're sure to search the ship. Now, my cargo isn't too bad, although it is leaving Brazil without the consent of the government. But I'm not the only one using the ship for transport of questionable goods, if you know what I mean."

"I think I understand."

"Good."

"What about the Coast Guard? Won't they stop the ship once it's in U.S. waters?"

"It's unlikely. The ship has a legitimate registration, the captain has a clean record and a good deal of the cargo is going to be Brazil nuts—perfectly legal, and a major export of Brazil.

"With you and your friend in there being white, I don't think you'd be harassed by the Coast Guard if the ship was stopped. The captain and crew are very good at hiding any cargo that might be questioned, should the ship be stopped.

"I think this is your safest route, though the slowest."

"Okay, but how do we get home if you don't want us getting off in Brownsville?"

"You'll get off in Matamoros, Mexico, which is just across the Rio Grande from Brownsville," Bill said. "There's two bridges across the river. I can have someone leave a car for you in Matamoros. You drive the car over the bridge, through the checkpoint, and into Brownsville. Leave the car wherever you're told, and go about your business."

"How hard will that be?"

"Should be a piece of cake. You're an American; she can pass for one. Just say you were visiting friends in Matamoros and you're on your way back home."

"Will they check identification?"

"I doubt it. They might check the trunk of the car to be sure there's no wetbacks hiding in it, but that's it. You've got your ID. She can say she left hers at home."

"It sounds good," I said. "I think it'll work."

"How long do you think all this will take?"

"I suspect you'll be in Matamoros within a couple of weeks, providing the ship leaves on time, and she usually does."

"I can't thank you enough, Bill."

"I still think you'd be better off getting rid of that woman and just going home, Milton. You're taking a lot of risk, and I don't mean just the smuggling. You could lose your job over this. It could be the end of your career as a preacher."

"I'm doing the work of God," I said. "I'll be all right."

He shook his head. "Okay. Fine. You're staying here in the hotel?"

"Yes."

"I'll make arrangements to have you on the plane to Belem tomorrow. It leaves Manaus at 10 a.m. I'll drive you to the airport."

"Thank you, Bill."

"You know I'll feel like crap if all this blows up in your face."

"It won't," I said. "I can feel that the Lord is guiding me. He brought Amara to me and us to you and you will get us home."

"I wish I had your confidence."

"You could. All you have to do is accept—"

"Yes, yes, I know the drill. I need a shower. Take your little maiden and get some rest. Let me take a shower."

"She's no maiden."

"Oh?" Bill's eyebrows went up. "She was a slave. Remember?"

"Right. Sure she was."

I got up and started for the door to the room where Amara was waiting, then hesitated. "Bill, I don't suppose you'd let me sleep in this room tonight, would you?"

"Why?"

"Well, when we checked in, they only had the one room available, and it only has one bed in it."

He laughed, a deep, hearty laugh for such a small man. "Don't trust yourself, eh Milton? I can't say I blame you. She's quite a woman. I'd have her checked over, though, before you go doing anything with her."

"Bill, that's not even an option. You know I'm married."

"I also know you're a long way from home, in the company of a beautiful woman who says she was used for a sex slave and has no qualms about being naked. You're only human, Milton, no matter how hard you try to be a saint."

"You're a heathen, Bill. An absolute heathen."

"I'm sorry, Milton. I'm sure you haven't even thought of committing an immoral act with her. Of course you can sleep here, though to be honest, I'd rather you sent her down here. You know, before you teach her that women shouldn't run around naked."

"An absolute heathen."

"And proud of it."

"And a Texan, to boot," I said.

From there we exchanged a few football barbs concerning the universities of Oklahoma and Texas, then I took Amara and we went back to our room. I made sure she had all she needed for the night, then returned to Bill's suite and fell asleep in his extra bed while he sat at his desk mapping a new journey into the jungle.

9

Bill ended up buying all my supplies, saying he would use the tent, sleeping bags, cooking utensils and such on his expedition. I knew he was being gracious, but I was grateful for the offer since finding a shop to buy the items, and haggling over the prices, would have taken more time than I really had to spare. Plus, Bill gave me a better price than I likely would have gotten anywhere else.

"You're sure you won't change your mind about this?" he asked me again.

"No, Bill, I can't," I answered. I'd left Amara in our room with a new hairbrush, comb and handheld mirror. She was delighted with the gifts I'd bought at a nearby store early in the morning, cheap though they were. She had been sitting on the bed, combing her glossy red hair, the mirror held before her, when I left the room. "What would she do if I left her?"

"Scam somebody else, probably," Bill said.

"Come on, Bill, you know she's no scam artist. Who would she have been scamming out there in the deep jungle?"

"I still think you're biting off more than you can chew," he said. "But, if you're determined to do it, and it seems that you are, so be it. Here." He held out a piece of paper with several lines of his sharp handwriting.

The paper was a list of instructions and contacts that he said would guide me from the time he left me at the airport until I dropped off his friend's car in Texas.

"Ron will park the car in Matamoros about five days from now," Bill said. "The keys will be with the garage owner, Old Man Sanchez. You can trust him, but tip him. Now, when you dock in Matamoros, get your ass off that boat *el pronto*. You understand? Don't be obvious. Don't run down the gangplank. Be casual but quick. Get off and get away from the port. Mexican authorities are pretty lax compared to ours, but eventually they'll get around to checking the ship, and you don't want to be around for that because if you're there, they might decide to check your paperwork, too. Got it?"

"I understand."

"Good. Get away from the port, get a cab and go to Sanchez's garage. Do you have a plan to get from Brownsville to Oklahoma City?"

"I thought we'd fly," I said. "That shouldn't be a problem once we're back in the States, should it?"

"Probably not. I'm not sure you can go from Brownsville/South Padre Island International Airport to Oklahoma City, but it'll at least get you to Houston or Dallas and you can get home from there."

"That's good enough."

"If your friend is ready, let's catch a taxi to the airport."

I went to get Amara from our room. As I approached the door, I heard her speaking to someone.

"I'm going with him," she said. There was no response. Amara spoke again. "I have changed. I'm different now. This man will help me. He is the key. If he—" She stopped suddenly, as if warned that I was eavesdropping.

I coughed into my hand, rapped at the door once and entered the room.

Amara was still sitting on the bed. The hairbrush and comb were laying beside her, but she continued to hold the mirror before her face, looking at herself as if she'd never before seen her own reflection.

"Do you like those?" I asked, glancing to the brush and comb, then back at the mirror. They were all made from red plastic, the cheap kind of travel set you can buy in any corner drug store in America. I looked from them to the old black rotary phone on the table beside the bed.

"I love them," Amara said. "It had been so long since I was

73

able to comb my hair. I had almost forgotten what it felt like to have it combed. And the mirror…it is much clearer even than the pool of the goddess in the forest. Thank you." She suddenly jumped off the bed and threw an arm around my neck, still holding the mirror, and planted a kiss on my cheek. This kiss, however, was not that of the seductress, but the kind a pleased daughter would give her father.

"Are you ready?" I asked. "Bill's getting a taxi and he's going with us to the airport."

"In a minute."

She grabbed another gift from me, a black canvas purse, from the nightstand and carefully put her brush, comb and mirror into the purse, zipping it closed. I hefted the only other item we had to take with us, a large army surplus duffle bag that held fresh clothes for Amara and me and the food I'd taken into the jungle and carried out, mostly dried meats and fruits with a few bags of nuts.

"Does the phone work okay?" I asked.

"What?"

"The phone. Does it work?" I tipped my head toward the telephone. Her gaze followed my lead, but her expression never changed.

"I do not know," she said.

"Oh. I'm sorry. I thought I heard you talking to someone before I came in."

"No, I was alone," she said.

"Well, yes, I can see that. I thought maybe you'd called someone."

She looked again to the telephone. "There was no one."

"Okay. You ready to go?" I wanted to go to the phone and pick it up just to see if the receiver would be warm from her hand. Probably useless, I thought, considering the heat of the room.

We left the room and returned to the lobby. While I paid the bill, Amara wandered back to stand before the Rossetti print of *Astarte Syriaca*.

The smiling little man at the desk hadn't added any extra

charges to our tab.

"I think my friend may have just made a phone call from our room," I said quietly. "I should pay you for that."

He agreed and went into a small room behind the desk for a moment. He came back a moment later.

"No, sir," he said. "No calls were made from your room."

"Are you sure? It would have been just a few minutes ago."

"Yes, sir, I am quite sure."

"Oh. Okay. Thank you."

Puzzled, I joined Amara before the Rossetti print to wait for Bill. The print was actually a poster that had been matted and framed. The woman, Astarte, held some resemblance to

Amara, with her long red hair and fair skin. In the painting, two angels bearing torches stood behind Astarte.

"Who is that?" Amara asked.

"Astarte. From the Old Testament," I said. "She was worshipped as a goddess of love and fertility by the ancient Jews, but eventually they turned away from the worship. She had a counterpart in most other ancient religions. She was Inanna to the Sumerians, Ishtar to the Babylonians and Aphrodite to the Greeks, so that would make her Venus to the Romans. I don't remember the rest."

"Why did the Jews stop worshipping her?"

"She wasn't a real goddess. She was just a figure depicted in art, given the personality men wanted her to have. Men and women used to think a god or goddess controlled everything... the wind, water, earth, sea and heavens. You've never heard of Homer's *Iliad*?"

"Is that a book, like your Bible?"

"Well, it's a book," I said. "It's about a war between Greece and Troy and how the mythical gods got involved. A lot of what we know about the ancient Greeks comes from that book."

"For a man who says he believes in only one God, you know a lot about other gods and goddesses," Amara said, glancing from the picture to me and back again.

"I took some mythology classes in college. I like reading the ancient poems, even if the religion isn't right."

"Are you two ready to go?"

Bill's voice startled me, as I hadn't heard him come up behind us. I gave him a sheepish grin and said we were ready. I picked up the duffle bag I'd stood beside me and walked with Bill toward the door. Amara followed, but kept her eyes fixed on the Rossetti print until it was hidden from her view.

The air outside the hotel was even hotter and stickier than it had been earlier when I'd gone out to buy Amara's gifts. I immediately felt my shirt grow moist and stick to my back. Beads of sweat jumped out on my forehead and stung my eyes. Bill hailed a taxi for us. I put my bag in the trunk and joined Bill and Amara in the back seat of the ancient car just as a mist of rain began to fall.

The car had no air conditioning and the window beside me would not roll down. The other three side windows were down. As we moved through the crowded streets, the wind blowing into the car carried the ripe smell of our sweaty driver to the back seat, but not out the open back window.

We were quiet for the most part. Amara sat between me and Bill, her bare legs pressed together at the knees, her eyes fixed straight ahead of us. Bill kept his face near his open window and I envied him the fresh air whipping past his lucky nose.

We made it to the airport and Bill paid our fare. He gave the driver a large tip and told him in Portuguese, "Buy some soap and take a bath, friend." To which the driver responded with some profane suggestions that are not unique to Brazil. I got my bag out of the trunk and barely stepped away before the driver sped off.

"That man smelled bad," Amara said. Bill and I laughed. "Yes, honey, he smelled bad, all right," Bill agreed. "Let's get you two on the plane."

He led us through the airport and onto the tarmac where we met the pilot standing beside his small jet. The pilot greeted Bill with a handshake and a smile. Bill introduced us quickly and bade the pilot take good care of us.

"This is it, Milton," he said, herding me and Amara away from the pilot and nearer the steps leading into the jet. "Are you absolutely sure about this?"

"You know I am."

He nodded his head. "All right. You have the instructions?"

"Yes." I patted my buttoned shirt pocket.

"Okay. Well then, good luck to you," he said, taking my hand in his small one and shaking it slightly. He turned to Amara and took her hand. "It was nice meeting you. I hope you like the States."

"I am sure I will," Amara answered. "Thank you for helping us."

"Think nothing of it," Bill said. "Milton, I'll be talking to you again. Take care."

"You too, Bill. Thank you."

He walked away, casting a final wave to the casually dressed jet pilot. I helped Amara up the steps and into the crowded airplane. We had adjacent seats near the back. Knowing it would be a treat for her, I let Amara have the seat near the window.

A few minutes later, the airplane moved onto the runway. As I always do when I fly, I bowed my head and whispered a short but fervent prayer, asking for protection as the jet's powerful engines revved, making me think of a cat tensing to spring on a trapped mouse. The plane lunged forward, charged down the runway like a raging bull and lifted gracefully into the air. It was a pleasant flight. The clouds broke apart beneath us and the sprawling majesty of the Brazilian rainforest was laid out like a carpet. The Amazon River and its tributaries were like the glistening veins in a fresh maple leaf. It was beautiful and peaceful. Amara was delighted by it all, staring out the small window all the while we were in the air, occasionally grabbing me by the arm and pointing out a flock of birds below us or some other variation in the scenery.

I was happy on that short flight from Manaus to Belem. They say ignorance is bliss. Had I known what the rest of our journey would be like, I might never have left the jungle. Funny, but even now, when all is over, I still must remind myself that all is as God wills. I was thankful then for the uneventful flight and I still am, although the path I've traveled between then and now has not been an easy one.

But, I get ahead of my story.

10

We took a taxi from the airport to the sprawling dock of Belem. I remember moving through the streets of the city, seeing the dark-skinned, brightly clothed Brazilian people going about their daily routines. They seemed a happy bunch of people and I hope they still are.

The driver took us as close as he could to our dock. I hefted our bag out of the trunk of his car and he chugged away. The smell of the ocean was strong. Gulls soared and called overhead. Anchor chains rattled, men shouted, horns blasted the early afternoon air. For a while, I entertained the idea of thinking of myself as a Jack London or Robert Louis Stevenson adventure character. I can laugh about it now, but I was soon to find out the Atlantic Ocean is no place for an Oklahoma preacher who sometimes gets queasy on roller coasters.

We found the ship, a dark, hulking, black thing with an unromantic name that translates to be something like *Sea Plow*. An on-deck crane was lifting pallets of burlap bags from the dock to the ship as we went up the gangplank. A sweaty young man with a lazy eye accosted us and demanded to know our business, which I told him.

"Follow me," he said, his good eye fixed on Amara. I thought then that I probably should have suggested she wear long pants for our journey, but it was too late. Her shapely white legs seemed to gleam with a demand that every man on deck should look at them as we followed our guide. We were taken to another man who was yelling orders as the pallets were lowered into the bowels of the ship.

"Captain, these are the people the archeologist sent," our guide said. Then he turned around and walked away, but he kept his head turned to watch us. No, I kid myself. He was watching

Amara.

The captain glanced at us, then did a double-take. "Good God," he exclaimed, gaping at Amara. He laid a long, low curse on poor Bill, using words I'd never heard in Portuguese before. "She cannot be on deck," he said, finally looking at me.

"What?"

Without answering, the captain grabbed me and Amara each by an arm and hustled us toward a door in the side of the ship's pilothouse. He pushed us through the doorway, into a dark, dank place, and closed the door behind us. A moment later I heard a click and the place filled with yellow light.

"Down those stairs," the captain barked.

There was a very narrow set of metal stairs leading into the lower levels of the ship. The yellow light from the bulb above our heads could not illuminate the bottom of the stairwell. The captain gave us a push and I started down the steps, the strap of the duffle bag pushed up on my right shoulder as my right hand slid along the handrail. I kept hold of Amara's free hand with my left. When the captain's bulk started down the stairs behind us, the yellow light was blocked out, making the passage very dark and dangerous feeling.

I came to a landing and the captain ordered me to go on.

I found a corner and started down more stairs. This seemed to go on for a very long time, but that could simply be attributed to the fact it was so dark and I was having trouble finding my way. The ship was rocking gently and I could hear creaks and groans as it moved.

Thinking back on it, there's no way we could have gone down more than a couple of levels in that tub of a ship. The vessel simply wasn't that big. Not being familiar with the sea, I can't say really what kind of ship it was, how big, how much displacement and whatnot. It was much bigger than the *River Lily*, but much smaller than the luxury liners I've seen. It was bigger than a fishing ship or yacht, too. Even had I known how to measure these things, I simply didn't have the chance to do it.

The captain, whose name, by the way, was Delmar Ferdinand de Santo, finally stopped us. He groped around somewhere and came up with a flashlight, which he used to guide us around more pallets of burlap bags and several wooden crates of various sizes. We soon came to a rusted metal door that I guessed to be very near the front of the ship. Captain de Santo selected a key from his ring and unlocked the door. It squealed when he pushed it open.

"This is where you will stay," he said.

"What?" I asked again. The area he had revealed was no bigger than a jail cell and was not so well equipped. "This is outrageous. Bill Barlow said you would treat us right. He said—"

"Bill Barlow did not tell me what he was sending here," de Santo interrupted. "This woman, she is dangerous. If they see her, my men will not work until they have had her. She must be hidden. I can tell them she is diseased, but that may not stop them. Many of them, too, are diseased. You will stay here or you will not sail on my ship. Or the woman can satisfy my men as they desire it. I will not have mutiny over a woman."

"I don't understand this. Surely your men can control themselves. They're not animals."

"In time, men at sea will do most anything to touch a woman," the captain said. "They know you are sneaking out of Brazil. The people who do that, the women, are willing to give themselves in exchange for safe passage. Is she willing?"

"Of course not," I said. "That's the most barbaric thing I've ever heard of."

"Then you will stay in here." He motioned again to the little cell.

"There's no bed, no toilet, not even a sink or window in there," I said.

"If you want comforts, one of your American cruise ships is docked nearby. Perhaps you would like to buy passage on her."

"Fine," I said. "Are we both supposed to stay in this one little room?"

"You would leave her alone?"

"No."

"I will bring you what you need or have my mate do it. He is the only man I would trust with such a duty. This woman you have brought on my ship, she will cause problems. Many problems." He waved again at the room. "I must return to deck now. Lock the door. It is for your safety I tell you to do this."

Reluctantly, I motioned Amara into the room and followed her inside. The door closed and I could dimly hear de Santo moving away from us. I bowed my head and asked God why things were going wrong. There was no answer, so I threw the latch on the deadbolt and turned my attention to Amara.

She was sitting in a corner, her naked knees pulled up and her delicate chin resting on them. Her large green eyes were fixed on me.

"I'm so sorry," I said. "It isn't supposed to be like this."

"It does not matter," she said. "It will be a short voyage and then we will be back on the land."

Her words were comforting and I couldn't help but smile at her. Maybe God had answered me, after all.

Sometime later, maybe a couple of hours, I felt movement. I had fallen asleep sitting in another corner of our little chamber. When I woke up, the metal wall was thrumming with the vibration of the ship's engine. But it was somebody banging on the door of the room that had awakened me.

I jumped to my feet and was ready to open the door when I remembered de Santo's warning.

"Who is it?" I called, my hand on the lock.

"Captain de Santo." The voice sounded authentic, so I opened the door. The heavy, sweaty captain stood on the other side, his shirt plastered to his body. He held a couple of blankets under one arm and a metal bucket with a lid in his hand. He had a gallon bottle of water in his other hand. "I have brought you these," he said, passing the items to me.

"What's the bucket for?"

"For you to shit in," he answered. "Someone will come to

empty it each day."

"But—"

"I must go. Keep your door locked." With that, he turned around and left us.

I remember being outraged and thinking evil things about my friend Bill Barlow. However, I believe Bill had no idea how Amara and I would be treated on that voyage.

That voyage…from the time de Santo brought the blankets and bucket until the day of the tragedy was mostly a nauseating blur. I had never been to sea. I assume we were actually a good way from the port, on the open sea, before the ship began to roll. But, I really don't know. I just know that the rolling began suddenly and that at first I likened it to a hog leisurely rolling and squirming in a fresh wet mud bath. But pretty soon I was hunkered over de Santo's metal bucket heaving and vomiting until there was nothing left inside me and then heaving some more.

I remember sweating, vomiting, sleeping, vomiting, praying and vomiting some more. I remember Amara cradling my head in her lap. She seemed to be totally unaffected by the violent motion of the ship. I remember de Santo and another man, his first mate, I guess, laughing at me when they came daily to give us food that I couldn't eat and a fresh bucket to hold my vomit.

The only good thing I can report about our time on the *Sea Plow* is that none of the crew harassed us. Perhaps the captain said something to control them, but I like to think that it was because the men really were not the beasts de Santo made them out to be. Whatever the reason, I was grateful to God that they left us in peace.

My sickness went on for a long time. I'll never know how long it really was. There did finally come a day when I woke up, felt that the ship was still wallowing in the ocean and did not immediately feel the need to vomit. When I opened my eyes, I was looking into Amara's face. My head was in her lap. Her own head was down, her chin on her chest, and she appeared to be sleeping, although her eyes were open a little bit.

I sat up carefully so I wouldn't wake her. I felt terribly weak and my stomach growled like an angry lion. I found the latest portion of food we'd been given—a few pieces of hard bread and two bruised apples. I dug in my duffle bag, found some beef jerky, and made a meal of what I had. It was a meal I ate very slowly, expecting with every mouthful to feel the need to lunge for the metal bucket. But, I was able to keep it down.

I checked my watch and saw that it was just after three o'clock. I didn't know if it was a.m. or p.m. I looked at Amara, thinking there was something wrong with the way she was sleeping. She was too quiet...

And that's when an explosion rocked the ship.

I got to my feet, still feeling shaky and weak, and opened the door of our little room. From far away I could hear the sound of men yelling. Within moments I caught the smell of smoke.

"What happened?" Amara had come to stand behind me. "I think there's been an accident. We should get on deck and see how bad it is," I answered.

Amara went back and picked up the little purse I'd given her. I thought at the time it was a silly gesture, but I picked up my duffle bag, too. I suppose, the truth be told, I was more worried about leaving it behind for fear the sailors would go through the few things I had in the bag while we were out of the room.

Feeling our way carefully, we made it back to the metal staircase and started up. By this time, the smell of smoke was very strong. It only got worse as we moved closer to the deck. The ship was still rolling as bad as it ever had. I clung to the handrail as we pulled our way upward. The meager meal I'd eaten bubbled in my stomach, but I was determined to keep it down.

We emerged from the stairwell into an inky black night. Men were running everywhere on the deck, shouting and waving. I think I noticed that the front of the ship was tilted up at about the same time I first saw the glow of the fire at the back end of the ship— the stern, I think it's called.

"Milton." Amara's hand took me by the arm. I turned to face

her. "We should go." She tilted her head slightly to one side, toward a wooden lifeboat not far from the stairwell opening.

"We should help," I said.

"I think it is too late. Do you not feel how the ship is sinking?"

"Yes," I admitted. "Yes, I feel it."

She pulled me toward the lifeboat. Before God, it was my intention to try to get the boat ready to launch and wait for the sailors to get in before we lowered it into the water. However, that was not Amara's intention. Her skill with the knots holding the little vessel amazed me. When she told me to get into the boat, I assumed she knew what she was doing. No, I assumed she had the same intentions as me. She knew exactly what she was doing.

She swung the lifeboat over the side of the ship, which was now very noticeably sinking. In the glow of the fire, I could see that there was a massive hole in the ship's side. Water was pouring into the hole. The fire now seemed to be coming from the deck. Steam rose from the ship's wound and I guessed the seawater had doused the source of the initial fire.

I saw all this as I sat in the lifeboat, clutching at the sides because the boat was swinging in its pulleys over the side of the ship, suspended over the dark, rolling ocean. At the moment, I gave no thought to the fact that I would soon be riding those waves in that tiny little wooden boat.

The crew had decided to abandon ship. I could see them preparing another lifeboat between ours and the fire. Some of the men were coming toward us.

Amara jumped into the boat, flung her purse at me, and began lowering us. Again, she amazed me. How could her thin arms have the strength for such a task? Why was she doing it? "Amara, wait," I said. "This boat will hold several more people. We can't take it for ourselves."

She didn't even acknowledge me. The sailors reached the railing on the ship above us. They shouted in Portuguese for Amara to let them raise the boat back up. She ignored them.

"Amara, we can't leave them," I said. I started to get up, daring the rocking of the boat to try to stop her. I knew she was afraid. I was afraid, too.

She let go of the rope while we were still about five feet above the water. The boat smacked onto the surface and I fell flat, knocking the wind out of myself as my gut slammed into one of the boat's wooden benches. Amara fell, too, but in a moment she was up, holding a wooden oar. She used the oar to push the boat away from the side of the ship. We were caught in a swell and suddenly shot around the front of the ship—the prow—and away.

"Amara, what are you doing?" I gasped. I drew myself into a sitting position, my hands over my abdomen as I sucked greedily for oxygen. "Can't leave them."

"There are many lifeboats," she said. "They will live."

I looked back. We were on the other side of the ship now and I could see two more boats being lowered into the water. That made three boats, not counting the one we were in. The crew of the cargo ship couldn't have been made up of too many men. Were there enough lifeboats for everyone aboard the *Sea Plow*? I just didn't know.

"We have to get away from the ship before it goes under," Amara said. "It will suck us down with it."

I'd heard of this, or read it somewhere. I picked up a set of oars and together we rowed away from the ship. I watched the *Sea Plow* go down. It was quite a sight. Nothing as spectacular as images of the *Titanic* rising from the water, but impressive nonetheless. The rear of the ship was submerged when another explosion blew the top off the area very near where I guessed the stairwell leading to our little room had been. Shrapnel rained down on the ocean, but we were out of range of the debris by that time. The deck was aglow for another moment, and then the wallowing, black, rusty tub of a ship simply went under, reminding me of a dog slipping beneath a blanket.

There was a stiff wind blowing over the sea. At times I thought I could hear the calls of men coming in fragments over the water.

"Shouldn't we try to find the other boats and stay with them?" I asked.

"Do you think we can find them?"

"I think we should try."

We tried, but we lacked the skill necessary to maneuver the little boat against the persistent waves of the Atlantic. We both tried using the rudder, or tiller…the steering device of the boat. Neither of us could hold the handle steady against the waves, and even if we'd succeeded, the other of us couldn't use the oars to give the boat momentum in the direction we wanted to go.

And, I must admit, once the adrenaline boost began to wane, I became sick again. The bread and beef jerky were expelled over the side of the little boat and a moment later the sea swelled up and slapped me in the face as I clung to the boat's side.

I sank to the bottom of the boat. Amara sat beside me. The waves were high, or seemed so to me, but the boat rode them and it was a rare occasion for a wave to break over the side and drench us.

We rode for a long time. I slept, rocked by the sickening waves. When I opened my eyes again, Amara was still sitting nearby. The sun had risen and the waves had calmed considerably. In fact, the surface of the sea wasn't rocking the boat much harder than a strong Oklahoma wind would do on the surface of Canton Lake, a body of water in the western part of the state where my father used to take me fishing. I looked at my watch and saw that it was just after nine.

I slowly got to my knees, felt okay, and slipped onto one of the benches. I looked around us. Of course, there was nothing to see but rippling blue ocean. For a moment, it was a beautiful, majestic sight. Then the reality of our situation sank in.

"So, here we are," I said. "Here we are," Amara echoed. "We should start rowing."

"Where?"

"Well, the sun rises in the east. The ship was heading north,

so if we go west we should reach the coast of Mexico. Eventually."
I looked to the west and saw nothing but water stretching to the
horizon. I sighed. "I would have thought they'd stay within sight of
land. I guess that shows what I know."

"Do you think we can do it?"

"I don't know, Amara. I don't have any idea. This is more
desolate than the Oklahoma prairie. This is worse than Kansas." I
tried to laugh but couldn't.

"Are you hungry?" I asked. "I still have some food in my bag.
I think there's at least one bottle of water, too."

"We should save it until we need it," she said. I knew she was
right, but the rumbling in my stomach wanted to argue. "You
should eat some, though," she said. "You have been very sick."

"I hate to eat any of the little bit of food we have if I'm just
going to throw it up," I said.

"The sea is calm now. Eat now. You will be okay."

It made sense. I dug into the duffle bag and pulled out the
plastic bag of beef jerky. There were still several strips of meat in
the bag. I also still had a bag of my hard biscuits and two bottles of
water. One biscuit was starting to show a green spot of mold. I
took that biscuit from the bag, tore off the tiny green patch, asked
for a blessing on the food and ate the rest of the biscuit with a half-
strip of jerky and a swallow of water.

"Did you sleep at all while I did?" I asked. "No. I was not
tired."

"You should sleep now," I said. "I'll stay awake. I feel fine.
Maybe Captain de Santo was smart enough to send a distress call
and somebody will come looking for survivors."

"I do not think so," she said. "I do not think the captain
called for help."

"Why not?"

"He was taking cocaine to Mexico."

"How do you know that?"

"His friend who brought us food told me. He said he would
be a rich man when the ship docked. He wanted me to leave you

and be his wife."

"He—" I was speechless. Amara nodded.

"He called you a lot of names because you were sick."

"Oh. Well." I didn't know what to say. "You didn't want to go and be rich?"

"No."

I nodded. "You should wear something with sleeves," I said. "And pants. You're going to get sunburned."

"Sunburned?"

"Yes. Sunburned. Your skin will turn red, like my neck is doing. And the top of my head." I raised my hand to my scalp and wished I'd grabbed my old straw cowboy hat as we fled the ship.

"I will not burn," she said.

"Red-haired people always burn easily," I argued.

"I am not burned." She held out her arms and stretched her legs toward me. She was right. Her flesh was still very white. And, I noted, there was no trace of hair growth on her legs.

"Hmm. How about that," I said. "Okay. Well, good. You're not burning. I wish I wasn't." I laughed, but couldn't take my eyes off her legs, thinking they should be fiery red and covered in short hairs. "You should get some rest now."

She lay down and closed her eyes but I don't think she slept. I sat in the boat and watched the ocean...the unchanging, uncaring ocean. I prayed, too. I prayed quietly and I prayed out loud. Of course I prayed for deliverance from the sea. I prayed that our food and fresh water would last until we were rescued. The day wore on. Evening came, and with the coming of darkness the sea became restless again, tossing us about, sending spray into the boat to keep us wet. Another day dawned and the waves quieted. Our clothes and skin dried but were coated in a crust of salt. We drank very little, ate less. We had drunk nearly three quarters of the contents of one water bottle by the coming of the next night.

We rowed some during the day, but we likely lost any ground we gained when the waves came up again. Rowing was despairing work and we didn't bother with it much. We simply drifted. We didn't talk much. I tried to get Amara to tell me more of her past, but she was reluctant and I didn't want to push her into talking about such a bad part of her life.

Days blended into one another, broken by the nights, but they soon lost any meaning as far as time. Looking back, I want to say we drifted like that for six days, but it could have been more or less by a day or even two.

I know I had a pretty scraggly beard by the time we spotted a boat to the right of us. From the distance, it was impossible to make out what kind of boat it was, but I guessed it to be quite a bit smaller than the sunken *Sea Plow*. The sea was relatively calm and I'd finally grown accustomed to the motion of our little lifeboat. I stood up, pulled off my sweat-stained shirt and began waving it and yelling.

It was a natural but foolish thing to do. We were much too far away for anyone to have seen or heard me. Fortunately, Amara had not grown lax in her new grooming habits while we were drifting. She was combing her hair when I saw the other boat. As I stood waving my shirt, the sun glinted in her mirror and hit me full in the face.

Surely it was a sign from God. I snatched the mirror from her hand and wiggled it until the sun flashed on it again. I aimed it toward the other boat and wiggled again until I was able to get another flash. I tried flashing the S.O.S. code. Who knows if I got it right? It didn't matter. Within a few minutes, praise God, that boat, which had been a profile to us, turned in our direction.

I stood in our lifeboat for about half an hour, flashing Amara's cheap mirror in the sun. Eventually I sat down, but I kept signaling with the mirror until the ship was close enough for me to see its crew gathered in the prow to get a look at us. The ship, which now even I could guess was a fishing boat, flew a Mexican flag.

I handed the mirror back to Amara, who seemed much calmer than me. On impulse, I grabbed her in a bear hug, then released her to catch a rope that was thrown to us. I tied our boat as a rope ladder was lowered. Amara went up the ladder first and I followed.

As it would happen, none of the sailors spoke English. I knew very little Spanish. Amara, however, knew a fair amount of Spanish. There seemed to be no end to the surprises she had waiting for me. She later told me that Manuel, her former owner, had employed several people who spoke Spanish and she had learned from them.

I was not able to follow all of the conversation between Amara and the captain of the fishing boat. I picked up words here and there, but the gist of the conversation was lost on me. The words I did understand left me puzzled. Amara mentioned my wife, a ship, and said "no" several times in answer to something the captain kept saying. She also mentioned money; I understood her to say "*mucho pesos*," which, of course, means "a lot of money."

Later, she told me she'd explained to the captain that we were both Americans. She said we had been sailing in my yacht when the engine exploded and the yacht sank. The captain said he would radio the shore and let the authorities know we had been rescued. Amara told the captain that I was married, but that she was not my wife. She said I was a wealthy man and that I would reward him if he didn't report the sinking of the yacht or our rescue because my wife would be angry.

She told me this in the captain's private room on the boat. That room was smaller than most bathrooms—it contained a narrow bed that ran the entire length of the chamber. We had the door closed, but I was still worried someone would hear. That was the only thing that kept my voice in check.

"You told him that?" I demanded. "You told him you're my—my *mistress*? How could you do that?"

"He would have used his radio to call the authorities," she said. "They would have asked questions about me."

"Oh Amara. I can't believe you did that. They'll think I'm an adulterer. That I run around with women other than my wife. They'll—"

"I'm sorry," she said. She lowered her head and repeated it.

"I'm sorry, Milton. I was scared somebody would take me away from you and send me back to Brazil. Back to Manuel. He would be very angry with me. He probably would kill me." Her humbleness, her tone, her attitude were enough to remind me that I was working for a higher purpose. So what if a group of sailors on a Mexican fishing boat thought this redhaired woman was my mistress? Who would they tell? They likely thought our predicament was funny.

"It's all right," I said. "Actually, you probably did the right thing. Stupid me probably would have told them the truth and the American Coast Guard would be coming to meet us now. That'd put an end to getting you home with me. You did right. I'm sorry I got mad."

"You forgive me?"

"Yes, I forgive you." I took her chin and lifted her head so she was looking at me. "I'm sorry." She smiled.

"How much did you say I would pay them to keep quiet?"

"I said only a lot. You can pay them some now and promise them more when we get to shore. Maybe we can get away before you have to pay them again."

I had to laugh. "So, you've lied to them, and now you'd cheat our rescuers, too?" Her face started to crumple and I immediately apologized again. "Come on," I said. "Let's go back out and ask the captain where we're headed."

The boat was on its way home. Fishing had been excellent. The captain said we'd be docked in Tampico by nightfall. His price for silence and for taking us to shore equaled about five hundred dollars, which was most of what I had with me. I paid him half right then and gladly gave him the rest when the fishing boat was safely moored to a Mexican dock.

I led Amara ashore. I was never so glad to be back on dry land. It was funny, but all that time in the rocking boat made it seem strange to be walking on a surface that was not moving beneath me. I laughed as we walked away from the dock, barely remembering Bill Barlow's advice that we get away from docks as quickly as possible. We got a few amused looks as we walked, due no doubt to the odd sight of a laughing white man being accompanied by Amara, who was still, after so long at sea, a stunning vision of womanhood.

I don't remember much about Tampico. It seemed like a nice city, but after our ordeal on the Atlantic Ocean, any city on dry land would have been a paradise. We hailed a taxi and I instructed Amara to tell the driver we wanted to go to a bus station. Once we reached the station—a very shabby little place with a few wooden benches—we booked passage north to Matamoros. We used the two-hour wait to clean ourselves up a bit in the bus station restrooms and ate at a nearby restaurant; authentic Mexican tacos are nothing like what we get at an American fast food place.

As darkness claimed the city, we boarded a dirty, smoking bus and began rolling north.

11

What is there to say about the bus ride north to Matamoros? It was hot, the bus was dirty and had to stop once for a blown tire and again for some minor engine trouble. We didn't talk much. Amara sat near the window and spent a great deal of time watching the Mexican countryside inch by. I watched the other people.

There were a lot of them. The bus was pretty full when we left Tampico. Very few people got out as we stopped in small towns along the way. Several more boarded, though. Soon, the bus was packed with hot, sweating humans. Many of them were carrying suitcases or rolled clothing. There was a lot of conversation among the other passengers and I heard southwestern states mentioned, including Oklahoma.

They were immigrants, I guessed. Like Amara, they were going to the border and hoping to find a way to cross into the United States, the land of opportunity. They were poor people, mostly. Clothing showed patches and was dusty. Hair, especially on the men, was unkempt and oily. Their faces showed wear but their dark eyes were lit with hope.

How ironic, I thought, that a nation founded by immigrants would try to bar these people from entering.

A wide-hipped woman with several children opened her blouse for a crying infant. She was standing with her husband near me and Amara. Except for the baby, her children sat in the aisle. The baby couldn't keep fastened to the woman's nipple because of the jostling of the bus. I pulled myself out of my seat and got her attention. I made motions that she should sit. *"Gracias,"* she said, nodding and giving me a thankful smile. She sat, the baby latched onto its mother and was happy.

Amara, however, gave me a desperate look, as if I'd left her in a trap. I tried to reassure her with a smile and a small wave with my free hand; I had to hold onto the back of a seat to keep my feet as the bus bumped along. Amara gave the mother sitting next to her a look—an annoyed look, I think—and turned her attention back to the window.

When the baby finished, it fell asleep. The mother tried to give my seat back to me but I was able to convince her to stay. Amara didn't look away from the window as the conversation in English, Spanish, and hand gestures went on beside her.

We rode into Matamoros that way. When the bus finally stopped and the engine died, people gathered their belongings, rose and pushed toward the door. I felt something in my hand and looked down to find that Amara had taken my hand in hers and was holding tightly. I met her eyes and smiled again as we pushed with the crowd to get out of the stifling, stinking air of the bus.

"I'm sorry about giving up my seat," I said to Amara when we were off the bus and away from our fellow passengers. "She was having trouble nursing. I wasn't leaving you."

"She was disgusting," Amara said.

I was shocked by her bluntness. "What do you mean? Why?"

"I just didn't like her. All those children. Why does a woman have so many? Look what it did to her body."

"She's likely Catholic," I said. "They don't use birth control. Do you know what that is?"

"Of course. Manuel didn't want me getting pregnant. She should keep her ugly breasts covered."

"Amara, you surprise me," I said. "Don't forget that you were naked when I found you. And you'd probably be naked right now if I didn't make you keep your clothes on."

"I do not look like that." She pointed toward the mother, who was standing with her family near the door of the bus station. The mother thought Amara was waving and waved back. I waved and pulled Amara away.

"No, you don't look like that. But you don't know that she doesn't have a medical problem that affects her weight and appearance," I said. "Now please, be nice. You have to accept people as they are, physically, and help them to be beautiful spiritually."

"I'm sorry, Milton. I have made you angry."

"No, I'm not mad. I'm surprised. I didn't expect you to be…to be so rude."

"I'm sorry."

"It's okay."

"You forgive me?"

"Yes, I forgive you."

"You are a nice man, Milton Agnew."

I sighed. "Thanks. Now, do you think you could use your amazing Spanish skills to get directions to this parking garage?" I held Bill's note up and Amara read the name.

We finally had to go into the dark, foul-smelling bus stop and ask a tired-looking clerk before we found someone who could tell us where the parking garage was. As it turned out, it was only a few blocks from the bus station, so we walked the short distance.

"Once upon a time I thought it was good for a mother to have so many children," Amara said as we walked.

"Once upon a time, huh? What changed your mind?"

"The earth cannot feed so many people. Isn't that why so many are poor?"

"That may be one reason, I guess. There are others. Bad government, ignorance, lots of things."

"A woman who cannot make her children happy with enough food should not have so many," Amara said. I couldn't argue, really, so we walked on quietly.

The car Bill had arranged for us was a late model Buick Skylark, light blue in color, and blessed with the most wonderful air conditioning I've ever felt. We sat in the dark, covered garage for a few minutes with the cold air blasting into our faces. I bowed my head and thanked the Lord for our success so far, asked him to help us across the border…and then asked that he also help those we'd traveled with on the bus.

"Thy will be done in all things. Amen," I said. I dropped the transmission into gear and we left the garage—but not before I gave about half of my remaining cash as a tip to Senor Sanchez, Bill's friend and the owner of the garage.

The sun was sinking to our left as we approached the bridge that stretched to Texas, to home. I laughed at myself for thinking of Texas as home. Bill Barlow would have roared with mirth. I didn't care right then. The sky was turning orange. The wait to go through the checkpoint was short. I felt my pulse increase steadily as we approached the uniformed guard. "Howdy," he said as we pulled even with his guardhouse.

"How you folks doin'?"

"Oh, we're fine," I said. "Just going home."

"Did ya have fun?"

"Yes. We were on a mission trip. We delivered Bibles to some of the villages south of Matamoros."

"That's fine. Anything you need to declare? Fruit, alcohol? Oh, sorry about that. I suppose there wouldn't be any booze."

"That's okay," I said, forcing a smile. "We're not bringing anything back."

"You won't mind if I ask you to pop the trunk, will ya? Sorry, but we've had some trouble with Mexicans coming back over in missionary car trunks from time to time."

"No problem," I said. I pulled the latch to open the trunk. "And if I could just see some ID when I get back," the young man said.

"Sure." Despite the air conditioning, I was suddenly sweating. I watched in the mirror as the guard meandered to the back of the car and peeked into the trunk. He slammed it closed and moseyed back to my window. I handed him my driver's license. "This is an Oklahoma license," he said. "Your car has Texas plates."

"The car belongs to a friend at our sister church in Brownsville," I said. "We flew down from Oklahoma City."

"I see. What about you, miss? Do you have some ID?" He bent over and craned his neck to look at Amara. I saw his blue eyes widen a bit as he took her in.

"No, she didn't bring her purse," I said. The man's eyes flicked to Amara's feet and I saw her purse resting against her ankle. "I mean, her pocketbook. Wallet. Whatever women call the thing they keep their license and money in." I tried to smile. A drop of sweat dripped into my eye and stung like fire.

"I'm sorry," Amara said. She picked up her purse and opened it, holding it where the guard could see inside. There was nothing but the brush, comb and blessed mirror. "We can go home, can't we?"

"Of course ya can, ma'am," he said, touching the brim of his straw cowboy hat and giving a quick nod. "You obviously ain't Mex. You folks go ahead and have a nice evening."

"You too," I said as I hit the switch to raise the window with one hand and dropped the car back into gear with the other.

Amara threw her head back and laughed. "Your God does not mind if you tell a lie every once in a while, does he?"

"He would rather I didn't," I said curtly. "But you are so good at it."

"It's not a skill I'm proud of. And one I try not to use." Her laughter was infectious and, really, it was pretty funny how the right words had come to me. Perhaps God had provided them. I hoped so, but frankly, once we were over that bridge and back in the good ol' U.S. of A., I figured even if the lie wasn't Heaven sent, it was worth it to be so close to home.

We left the car where Bill had instructed and got a taxi to take us to the airport. From there, I decided to do something I probably should have done back in Manaus. I went to a pay phone, pulled out my long-distance phone card and called David Ross, the church bookkeeper and one of our elders.

David is older than me by about fifteen years. He's a small, manicured black man with extremely soft hands, a retired accountant whose wife always did the lawn work. He has snow-white hair and a disciplined beard. He's a fine man, but I always thought he stuck to the book at times when maybe his heart should have guided him. I wasn't looking forward to talking with him. He answered on the third ring. "David, it's Milton," I said.

"Milton? Where are you?"

I told him where we were, told him the aerial photos had been right, the mission was destroyed.

"Everyone was dead, David. Dead or gone," I said. "It looked like most of them were in the church and died there. I couldn't tell one from another. We—" I choked on a sudden sob as I remembered the black, crispy bodies. "We buried them."

"We?" David asked. "You went alone. Did someone survive?"

"Sort of," I said. "There was a woman there. A white woman. She's an escaped slave who lived in the jungle outside the village. She used to listen to the sermons from outside the chapel."

"Why wouldn't she go inside?"

"I guess she was afraid somebody would send her back to the drug lord she escaped from," I said. "She helped me bury everybody. David...I brought her back with me."

"I'm sorry, Milton. What did you say?"

"I brought her back with me. I couldn't leave her. She's... she's in need of salvation, David. She needs us."

"How in the world did you get her into Texas?"

"You don't even want to know."

"I think a lot of people will want to know."

"I'll tell you when I get home," I said. "It's been quite an ordeal. Shipwrecks and everything. I just wanted to let you know that I'm out of cash. I'm going to have to use the church credit card to get us plane tickets home."

"You bought a roundtrip ticket when you left," David said.

"I had to sell it. I needed the cash."

"Milton, I have to tell you, the elders were not happy that you left so suddenly, practically without giving us any notice that you were going. And without asking for authorization for the expense. That's not an inexpensive jaunt you're on."

"David, our people were down there," I said. "Nonetheless, you know the rules concerning expenses.

That mission was your idea and we went along with it despite a lot of misgivings. You have to check with us before you buy plane tickets and run off to South America."

"David, I'm checking with you now. Can we come home? Can I come home and tell the families of our dead missionaries that they'll never see their loved ones again? Can I come home and tell them I buried their sons and daughters and friends and neighbors the best I could? Can I have the money to do that, David? If not, say so and I'll use my own money."

"Calm down, Milton. Yes, use the credit card. Come home. No one is angry with you. We just wish you'd play by the rules."

"Fine. I'll play by the rules. I'll see you soon, David." I hung up the phone.

"I'm causing problems?" Amara asked.

"No," I said. "It isn't you. Not really. It's money. I don't know what the problem is. Our church has one of the richest congregations in the state, yet that man holds the purse strings as if they were the only things holding him to the earth."

"We can go home? To your home in Oklahoma?"

"Yes, we can go home," I said. "Come on. Let's get some tickets."

We were booked onto a small propeller plane to fly to Houston. From there we were put on a commuter jet, much like the one we rode from Manaus to Belem, and flown to Dallas, where we waited three hours for a flight to Oklahoma City. I slept a little in the waiting area of our terminal in Dallas, something I hadn't been able to do on the dirty Mexican bus. I woke up remembering that I hadn't called home yet. I still had about half an hour before we could board the plane, so I found a bank of pay phones and called my house. It was close to 11 p.m., but my daughter picked up on the second ring. "Hi, Lori. Are you doing okay?" I asked.

"Hi, Daddy. I'm fine. I thought you might be Dan."

"Isn't it too late for your boyfriends to be calling the house?"

"I only have one."

"It's past 10:30, Lori. But I'm not calling to check up one you. Is your mom around?"

"Just a sec. She's in bed." Lori put the phone down and pretty soon I heard two voices approaching the receiver.

"Where is he?" Karen asked.

"I don't know," Lori answered. "He just griped me out because I said Dan might be calling."

"Hello?" Karen said into the phone.

"Hi, honey, I'm sorry to wake you up," I said. "I wasn't asleep yet. Where are you?"

"I'm in Dallas. Listen, I'll be home in a couple of hours. I need somebody to pick me up at the airport."

"So late? Why are you coming home so late? How was the mission? Was everyone okay?"

"No, Karen, they were dead. Everyone. It was…it was really bad. There was one person left, a woman who was an escaped slave. I brought her back with me. Can you or Lori pick us up? We'll be in at 12:48."

"You brought a native woman home?"

"She's Greek," I said. "She's all that was left there. I couldn't leave her alone in the jungle."

"Of course not. Greek? Yes, somebody will be there to meet you. Everyone was really dead?"

"Yes."

I heard her sigh. "Okay."

"I better go. I love you."

"I know," she said.

"I'll see you pretty soon."

"Okay. Bye." She hung up.

"She didn't say she loves you back," Amara said.

I started, surprised that I hadn't noticed her coming to stand so close behind me. I tried to smile at her. "No, she didn't. She'll meet us at the airport and take us home."

Once we boarded the plane, my excitement about getting close to home picked up. After such a long adventure, we were finally really getting close to our goal.

"Tell me about your wife," Amara said. "She's not going to like me."

"Oh, she'll like you," I said. "We've been married for almost twenty-five years. We met in junior high and started dating in high school. She's a year younger than me. We got married about a month after she graduated from high school and she worked while I was in college."

"Tell me about her. What does she like?"

"She's into ceramics," I said as I reached for my wallet. "She's been going to classes and making ceramics for a couple of years now. She sells most of what she makes in a shop a friend of hers has downtown. This is her." I opened my wallet and showed Amara a photo of Karen.

The photo was several years old and didn't show the tiny streaks of gray that had crept into my wife's long brown hair.

Her face was composed, looking to the left of the picture. She was wearing a white shirt, open at the throat to show the goldanddiamond heart pendant I'd given her for our fifteenth wedding anniversary.

"Why isn't she smiling?" Amara asked.

"Well, I don't know. I guess she wanted it to be a serious picture."

"Is she happy?"

"I think so. Here's Lori and Eric, my kids," I said, flipping the plastic sleeves in my wallet.

The photo of Lori was two years old, taken during her short-hair days. She was smiling, but keeping her lips together so her braces wouldn't show. The braces were gone now and her hair was longer.

Eric's picture was from last year—a copy of the picture taken for the school baseball team. He was grinning happily, his red hat shading a wedge of his face. His brown eyes had a twinkle in them, some orneriness he hadn't yet outgrown.

"They're good kids," I said. "Lori is a senior in high school this year. She'll be eighteen in October. Eric will be in tenth grade. He hopes to get a baseball scholarship for college. He's pretty good."

"I saw American baseball on the television once," Amara said. "They look happier than your wife. Your children. Will they like me?"

"I'm sure they will," I said. I put my wallet back in my pocket. "Don't worry. Everyone will like you. It's going to be fine."

"If they don't, are you going to send me back?"

"Of course not. There's no way I'm going through all this again just to drop you off back in the jungle somewhere." I smiled at her, and, after a moment, she grinned back. "Thank you."

"Everything will be fine," I said.

The plane landed and we found Lori waiting for us in the Will Rogers World Airport terminal. She was wearing khaki shorts and a red T-shirt with her hair pulled into a thick ponytail that bounced behind her as she hurried toward us. I opened my arms and accepted her.

"Hi, Daddy," she said, hugging me back. "You're not mad that Dan was going to call, are you? He was supposed to get a raise at work and was going to call me when he got home to tell me if he did."

"No, baby, I'm not mad. Even if I was, I'm too glad to be home to care anymore. It's so good to see you again."

"You haven't been gone *that* long," she said, releasing me and stepping back.

"No, it hasn't been a long time, but it's sure seemed like it. Your mom told you about it?"

"Yes. Everyone's dead. I can't believe Tina and everyone is...is really dead. She was just a year older than me. We used to sneak little dolls to church and play in the pew."

"I know."

"You knew?"

"Of course. I can see pretty much everything from the pulpit." I looked behind me and found Amara hanging back. I took her by the arm and gently pulled her forward.

"Lori, this is Amara. She was living near the village. She's had a hard life, but agreed to come home with me. She can use our help."

"Hi," Lori said, holding out a hand. Slowly, Amara reached out and took Lori's small hand in her own. "I'm glad you… well, you know…weren't part of the tragedy."

"Thank you," Amara said. "You are very pretty."

Lori blushed deeply. "Thanks. You guys ready to go?"

"You wouldn't believe how ready," I said, picking up the duffle bag I'd dropped as Lori approached. "You ready?" I asked Amara.

"I think so," she said.

"Everything will be fine, Amara," I said again. "Let's go home."

I believed that as we followed Lori's bouncing ponytail out of the airport. We'd survived the jungle, the Amazon River, plane rides, a shipwreck, a Mexican bus ride and the Texas border guard. I thought the ordeal was over.

The real trials—the challenges that would test everything I'd ever known or believed in—were just about to begin.

12

Lori chattered all the way home. I sat in the front seat of the two-year-old Cadillac with her while Amara rode in the back; Lori was still saving her money for a down payment on her own car. As Lori talked, I kept glancing to the backseat to see how Amara was doing; for the most part, she sat perfectly still and looked out the side window as we traveled north from the airport, up Meridian Avenue to the Northwest Expressway, then west, toward Prairie Valley.

"I mean, like there's nothing wrong with being a cheerleader, but that doesn't mean you have to sleep with the quarterback, right?"

"Huh? I'm sorry, Lori. Who are you talking about?" I asked. "Dana. You know, from work?"

"Oh. Yes, the cheerleader. What's she done now?" Lori worked as a carhop at a drive-in restaurant close to the high school. She'd been there for about a year and considered it part of her job to minister to her co-workers, many of whom had no college aspirations or goals beyond their next paycheck, which, Lori said, was used mostly to pay for parties.

"Well, she just made the team, which is good because she is pretty, but that isn't enough. She wants to go to bed with Monty Hanson, the new quarterback. She says she only tried out for cheerleader to get to Monty."

"And what did you tell her?"

"Well, I dropped the God-bomb on her," Lori said. "I gave her chapter and verse about fornication. I don't think it did any good, though."

"No? Well, sometimes it takes people a long time to see the error of their ways," I said, glancing again at Amara and wondering what she was thinking, if she was paying any attention to the conversation between me and Lori.

As if realizing I was looking at her, Amara turned from the window and smiled at me. "There are so many lights," she said. "Are we close to your home?"

"We're almost there," Lori said before I could answer. "I can't wait to hear all about you, Amara. How did you ever live in the jungle? What did you eat? What did you wear? You don't look anything like I expected. I thought you'd be all thin and bony and scratched up with dirty hair and everything. You look like a supermodel, though."

"Supermodel?" Amara asked, her eyebrows rising as she looked at me.

"They're beautiful women who try to sell you things, like expensive clothes and perfume," I said.

"You are very pretty, too," Amara said.

"Oh, I'm not," Lori answered. "I mean, I'm not a hag, but I'm no Sarah Michelle Gellar, either."

"I do not know who that is," Amara said.

"An actress," I answered. "Never mind that. Lori's always too hard on herself. We're almost home."

We had left the lights of restaurants, retail stores and apartments buildings behind and were on the outskirts of the Oklahoma City limits. Lori turned the car off the Expressway and we passed through the entrance of Prairie Valley, a housing subdivision that had nearly grown into being its own tiny suburb. Still mostly made up of large, very expensive houses, there was an area at the western end of the subdivision that had been given over to commercial property, with a small strip mall that included some retail clothing stores, a couple of eateries and a drug store. The subdivision has its own golf course with a small lake, an elementary school and three churches, counting mine. The people who live there mostly are bankers, doctors, lawyers or retirees.

Lori drove through the winding streets to our home, where she pulled the car into the driveway and killed the engine. The house actually belongs to the church; my salary included the cost of the rent. It's a four-bedroom brick house, two stories high, with two bathrooms and a two-car garage. There's a small in-ground swimming pool in the backyard; the yard is surrounded by a six-foot privacy fence. The porch light was on over the front door.

"This is it," I said to Amara.

"You live here?" she asked, her eyes moving from edge to edge and top to bottom of the house. "It is like a castle. All of these buildings are like castles."

"It's not bad," Lori said as she threw open her door and got out of the car. "Wait'll you see the pool. Can you swim? You'll love it."

"She is like you and not like you," Amara said as Lori passed by her window to open the trunk of the car. "She does not like sex, but she talks much more."

"She's a good girl," I said, smiling. "Let's go inside."

I carried my rucksack and guided Amara toward the front door by gently keeping a hand on her back as we followed Lori. My daughter had opened the screen door and was looking for her house key in the illumination of the porch light when Karen opened the heavy wooden door. Karen stood between the glow of the light on the porch and the light of lamps inside the house. She pulled her terrycloth bathrobe closed at her throat and cinched the belt more firmly around her trim waist as she looked at us. I noticed her eyes traveling down my arm to where my hand was pressed to Amara's back. Karen's eyes flashed back to my face. I gently pushed Amara forward.

"Karen, this is Amara," I said. "Amara, this is my wife, Karen."

"It is nice to meet you," Amara said. "I feel like I know you already."

"Do you?"

"Yes. Milton talks about you all the time."

"Let's go on inside," I said, pushing Amara into the house. As I came even with Karen, I took my hand away from Amara and leaned in to kiss my wife. "It's nice to be home," I said.

"You weren't gone as long as I expected," Karen said, closing and locking the front door.

Lori led us into the living room, where my son, Eric, sat in my recliner eating a bowl of ice cream and watching television. His blond hair was wet, as if he'd only recently showered. I saw his blue eyes widen as Amara stepped into the room. He slowly stood up and put his bowl on an end table, his gaze never leaving Amara, but moving up and down her as if he'd never seen a woman before.

"Amara, this is my son, Eric," I said, motioning to him. "Eric, Amara. Did your mom tell you about her?"

"Mom said you were bringing home some jungle woman," Eric answered. "She didn't say she'd look like this."

"Eric, mind your manners," I said. "Isn't it way past your bedtime?"

"I'm gonna finish my ice cream," he said. He picked up the bowl and started to sit down again.

"Why don't you finish it in the kitchen?" I asked.

"But I'm watching this." He motioned at the television with his bowl. A repeat of "Seinfeld" was playing.

"You've seen it. Now go on," I said.

His eyes darkened and he looked to Karen as if expecting her to protest before he left the room. I heard him pull a chair away from the table in the kitchen and the clink of the bowl hitting the table.

"That boy is going to get himself in trouble with that attitude," I said.

"He's just being a boy," Karen said. "I don't—"

"Amara, are you going to stay with us?" Lori interrupted. "I don't know," Amara answered. "I don't know what Milton is going to do with me."

"Of course you're staying here," I said. "We'll put you in the guest room. I'm sure you're tired. Lori, will you show Amara the bathroom and the guest room and help her get settled in?" Chattering about various things in the house, Lori led Amara out of the living room and up the stairs. I fell into my recliner, put my head back and sighed deeply, my eyes closing involuntarily.

"She is not staying here," Karen said.

"What?" I opened my eyes and found Karen standing over my chair, her arms crossed over her chest.

"That woman. She is not staying in my house."

"Why not?"

"Why did you have to have your arm around her outside? You two seem to be awfully close."

"Oh Karen, don't. Don't say that. You know nothing's happened between us."

"How would I know? Besides, she'll be a bad influence on Eric. There's no telling what some jungle nymph like that might try to do to him."

"There could be a problem there," I agreed. "I saw the way he looked at her. Like a lion eyeing dinner."

"He did no such thing. He was probably just shocked you would bring that kind of woman into our house."

"Karen, I'm too tired to argue with you. I don't mean for Amara to live here forever. We'll see if somebody in the church will take her in. She needs a roommate, some other woman her own age, to show her how to live in America. She won't be here long. Won't you be nice to her while she's here?"

"I'm always nice. Do you want something to eat?"

"I would love a real meal," I said. "But even more than that I just want a hot shower and to be in my own bed." I pushed myself out of the chair and took my wife in my arms. I hugged her close to me, her own arms pinned between us. "Are you going to be all right with this?"

"Aren't I always all right with your schemes?"

"You tolerate them." I kissed the top of her head. It looked like there were more strands of gray in her dark hair than there'd been when I left.

"I'm going on to bed," she said. "There's no sense in the kids waking up to go to school in just a few hours. They might as well stay home," she added, slipping away from me and moving toward the back of the house where our bedroom and bathroom were. I followed her, stopping at the laundry room beside the kitchen to drop off my rucksack. Eric had finished his ice cream and gone upstairs. I shut off the lights and went to the bathroom, stripped out of my sweat-stained clothes and spent at least thirty minutes washing under the hot water.

When I came out of the bathroom I saw the light was back on in the kitchen. I went up the hall and found Lori and Amara sitting at the table eating pickles and slices of cheese.

"We were hungry," Lori said. "For pickles and cheese?"

"We were lazy, too. I didn't want to actually fix anything," Lori said. "Want one?" She extended a bitten pickle toward me. "No thanks. Amara, are you doing all right? Anything I can get you before I go to bed?"

"No, Milton. Thank you," Amara said. She was wearing a long cotton nightshirt that belonged to Lori. Her wet hair was brushed away from her face and her skin seemed to glow in the kitchen light.

"I got her covered," Lori said. "Go to bed."

"Yes, dear." I kissed Lori, waved to Amara, and went to my bedroom.

I closed the bedroom door and got into bed, turning off the lamp on the table on my side of the bed. Karen's back was to me but I could tell from her breathing she wasn't asleep. I snuggled close to her, putting my hand on her hip.

"You're not going to touch me and think of her," Karen said.

"What? I would never do that."

"It's too late. Besides, I heard her and Lori come down the stairs."

"They're having a midnight snack."

"It's after midnight."

I slid my hand from her hip to rub Karen's buttock and thigh. She was wearing a knee-length satin nightgown I'd bought her a couple of months earlier. Her body felt firm and warm and smelled of lavender soap and I wanted her very much.

"I said no," she said. "Go to sleep."

I pulled my hand off her and rolled away, knowing from long experience it would do no good to press the issue. I lay in the darkness thinking of contrasts. Not so many days ago and I'd been in a South American hotel room telling a beautiful woman I would not have sex with her. Now I was home and my wife was telling me she would not have sex with me.

And that beautiful woman who was so willing was so close. I could hear the low tinkle of conversation between Amara and Lori in the kitchen. Not enough to make out the words. I heard them go back up the stairs and I heard the door close to the bedroom directly over my own...the bedroom where Amara would be sleeping alone in my guest bed.

I closed my eyes and prayed for strength.

13

The next morning I awoke late. When I dressed and left the bedroom I found Amara sitting alone on the sofa watching a talk show on the television. She looked up as I entered the room and smiled at me, her face bathed in sunlight from the sliding glass doors that opened onto our patio. Her eyes looked incredibly green and her red hair was a living fire around her glowing face.

"How are you this morning?" I asked, noting that she was wearing a pink blouse and pair of white shorts that belonged to Karen.

"These people are not afraid to talk about sex," she said, pointing to the television. I looked to the screen in time to see that somebody was being introduced to the audience as the lover of his sister's boyfriend. I turned off the set.

"Some people have no shame in their sins," I said. "You shouldn't pollute your mind with that filth. Where is everybody? Karen said the kids could skip school, so I expected to find them in front of the TV."

"Gone."

"Where did they go?"

"You did not make love to your wife last night."

"What? How would you know that?"

"I would know."

"Listen, Amara, we don't talk about that kind of thing here. Okay? What happens between me and Karen is our own business and we don't talk about it."

"But nothing happened. You wanted to make love to her. I saw it in your eyes last night."

"Amara, we won't talk about it. Where did everyone go?"

"Lori went to be with someone named Dan. Is he her lover?"

"Dan is Lori's boyfriend," I said, sitting down in the recliner and thinking I was in for a longer conversation than I'd intended. "They've been together for a long time. They're not lovers, though. I should have known he'd skip school if she did. What about Karen and Eric?"

"Your wife said she had a meeting to go to this morning. She didn't want to go. She didn't want to leave me here alone with you. I could tell."

"Umm. The neighborhood committee. I forgot today was Thursday. She'll be back after lunch."

"Your son went to hit baseballs. He told me he is a great athlete in his school. He was the last to leave the house. He showed me the muscles in his arms."

"He did?" I shook my head and wondered how much of a problem Eric would be with Amara. His sixteen-year-old hormones were already raging. Amara's lack of modesty could present a real problem.

"Amara, I want to talk to you about Eric."

"When he looks at me it is like when you look at me, but he doesn't feel guilty for it."

"He's young. He's going through that time in his life when all he can think about is girls," I said, ignoring her remark. "I'm asking you to not encourage him. Don't tease him. Don't give him any more reason to think impure thoughts of you. It'll be hard enough for him as it is."

"Why is that?"

"Why? Well…well, because you're a beautiful woman. He's noticed that."

"You think I am beautiful?"

"Oh, we've had this conversation before," I said, laughing. "Have you eaten anything yet?"

"Lori cooked eggs and bacon for me. She is very pretty. She has only one lover? Dan?"

"She is pretty," I said. "Thank you. She only has one boyfriend, yes. No lovers."

"She is a virgin?"

113

"She tells me she is and I believe her."

"Like a temple priestess," Amara said. "Or a sacrifice."

"I'm going to get something to eat. And I won't be eating Spam, let me tell you." I went to the kitchen and opened the refrigerator, taking out two eggs and the package of bacon. I nearly bumped into Amara as I stepped back. "Sorry. I didn't know you followed me."

"What will we do today, Milton Agnew?" she asked. "We have no burned bodies to bury, no boats to ride and no guards to lie to. What will we do?"

"I'll need to call a meeting of the church elders to discuss the mission," I said. "And, I guess I'll have to go visit the families of the missionaries who died."

"Will you tell your elders about me?"

"Yes. We'll talk about you."

"What will they do with me? Will they send me back?"

"No, they won't send you back." I cracked the eggs and let the yolks fall into a skillet, putting the shells on the counter while I peeled off four strips of bacon to add to the frying pan. Amara picked up the pieces of one egg and gently pushed them back together.

"An egg," she said.

"Yes. Do you want another one?"

"Regeneration. The egg was precious to the goddess. It was a symbol of birth. New life."

"Yes, that's true. A lot of old pagan cultures believed that," I said.

"You do not?"

"Only at Easter."

"Easter?"

"When Christ rose from the grave," I said. "Kids celebrate it by hiding colored eggs."

"Then the egg is sacred to you?"

"No. It's just an egg."

"Then why is it used to celebrate the rebirth of your god?"

"It's a holdover from pagan times," I said. "The church couldn't stamp out all the pagan beliefs, so it adopted them and gave them new meanings."

"Oh." She slowly closed her hand, crushing the broken egg, her eyes watching her own hand become a fist.

"There's a trashcan behind you," I said. I pretended to pay no mind as she slowly turned around, went to the garbage can and scraped the pieces of eggshell from her palm. She rinsed her hand at the sink and came to stand beside me again just as I was taking my breakfast from the stove. We sat together at the kitchen table.

"Did Lori say when she was coming home?" I asked between bites.

"After lunch."

"What about Eric?"

"He did not say."

"I thought maybe this afternoon you might want to go shopping with Lori and Karen. You can buy yourself some new clothes so you don't have to wear Karen's."

"If you want."

Her answers were too short, her voice distracted. "Amara, are you all right?"

"Why would your god steal the egg from the goddess?
Doesn't he have his own symbols?"

I know I stared at her for a long moment, a fork loaded with egg held halfway between my plate and my face. "Why are you upset about that?"

"I am not upset."

"Okay. Well, God didn't steal the symbol. God doesn't even like symbols. The early church just adopted the egg because they couldn't make the people stop believing in their old ways."

"Is that because their old ways were true?"

"No. People are just stubborn creatures. We don't like to change. Those people had worshiped the egg, or the goddess the egg represented, for centuries. They didn't want to believe their goddess was false, so they refused to give up the egg. So the church just said 'Fine, have your eggs, but from now on it will be a symbol of the true Christ.'"

"So it was your church and not your god that stole the egg?"

"Well, not *my* church exactly. The old Christian church. The Catholic Church. But let's save the Protestant Reformation for another time, okay?"

"Are you going to leave me alone here today?"

"I hadn't planned to. I guess I could make some calls from here and have the elders meet me early this afternoon. We could divide up the duty of notifying relatives. No, I should do that myself. The whole mission idea was my responsibility. You'll go shopping with Karen and Lori this afternoon, won't you? You're okay with that?"

"I think Lori likes me, but your wife does not."

"You'll be fine. She just needs to get to know you."

I finished my breakfast quickly and studied Amara for a moment before speaking again. "Okay, I'm going to go into my den and make some calls. Do you want to watch TV again? Something besides those talk shows? I'm concerned about you getting bored."

"If you want me to."

I sat Amara in front of the television and tuned in a cable program about vacation destinations in America, then went into my study, closing the door. I called David Ross first. The call wasn't as bad as I'd anticipated. At first, he was more interested in how much I'd spent on plane tickets than on the fact I was actually home, but then he agreed the elders should get together immediately. We decided he would call six other members and I would call the final five and we would meet at the church at one o'clock.

"Milton, what is the status of the woman you smuggled into the country?"

"Amara is here and she's safe and well," I answered. "She saw the fire in the village?"

"That's what she told me."

"I think she should come with you and tell the council what she saw."

"No, David, I don't think so," I argued. "I don't think she's ready to be grilled by twelve church elders. Besides, I told her she was going shopping this afternoon with Karen and Lori. She doesn't have any clothes of her own."

"How is Karen taking this?"

"Karen's fine."

"I'm sure she is." I couldn't tell if he was agreeing or being sarcastic. David's humor, on the rare occasions he uses it, always is dry.

"I'll see you at one."

"Milton. We will want to talk to her. It won't be grilling her, but we do want to know what she saw. Not only did we lose a great deal financially in that fire, but the cost in lives demands an account."

"I understand, David. And I agree. But you may be surprised to hear what she has to say."

"What do you mean?"

"I wouldn't want to spoil the surprise. You've never met anyone like Amara. Let's leave it at that for the moment."

"Good-bye, Milton."

After calling the other council members, I spent some time making sure I had the addresses and phone numbers of relatives for all the people who had died in the mission. Then I spent a while praying to God for the wisdom to comfort those relatives. After that, I went back to the living room and watched television with Amara. At noon I was ready to make us peanut butter sandwiches for lunch when Lori and Dan came in carrying sacks of sandwiches from Arby's.

I should say something about Lori's boyfriend, Dan Ward. He was a nice kid while they were together. Maybe he still is.

He was tall, with black hair and brown eyes and very good manners, always calling me Mr. Agnew or Reverend Agnew. He treated Lori with respect, ran with the school track team and attended church regularly. I wasn't crazy about the idea of Lori having only one boyfriend for so long at her young age, but I have to admit I really liked Dan and wouldn't have been overly disappointed if he'd become my son-in-law.

Dan was better able than Eric to hide his emotions upon seeing Amara. His eyes widened a bit and I saw his throat move sharply as he caught his breath, but he recovered quickly and shook her hand.

"See that," Lori said to Amara. "See what you do to guys? He thinks you're so hot he's speechless."

"Lori…" Dan protested, but his blushing face gave him away.

"I'm not hot," Amara said. "I am very comfortable."

"She means pretty," I explained.

"Oh. You think I'm pretty?" Amara asked Dan.

"Yes, Dan, tell us," Lori mocked. "Do you think she's pretty."

"Lori, don't tease him," I said. I had to hide a grin behind my hand.

"Well, ma'am, I think you're quite attractive," Dan said. "You could be a movie star, that's for sure."

"Thank you," Amara said. Then, to everyone's surprise, she leaned forward and kissed Dan on the cheek.

"Okay, that's enough of that," Lori said, pulling Dan away by the arm, but smiling at Amara. "This one's taken. You'll have to find your own."

We sat down to a lunch of roast beef sandwiches. A few minutes later, Eric came in, looked at us, then grabbed a sandwich and some French fries before going up to his bedroom. Karen came home just as we were throwing away the wrappers. I explained my plans for the afternoon to Karen and Lori.

"Shopping?" Lori asked. "With your credit card? I'm in."

"I suspected as much," I said.

"Lori can take her shopping," Karen said. "I have to write the neighborhood newsletter this month and I have a migraine already."

"Are you going to be okay?" I asked. "I'll be fine," Karen

answered. "Lori, do you mind?"

"No, Daddy, I don't mind taking Amara shopping," Lori said. She turned to Dan and asked if he wanted to come.

"I'm sorry, but I can't. I have to be at work by three," he said.

"It's just you and me and Daddy's credit card," Lori said, squeezing Amara's arm.

"Yes, and a three-hundred-dollar limit," I added. "Now, I have to go so I can get to the church before David Ross. I don't want to have to listen to him tell me how important it is to be punctual."

14

"Damn you, Milton Agnew! You bastard! You bastard! I hope you die!"

Selena Ford's words still ring in my mind. She was the mother of Tina Ford, one of Lori's best friends and the youngest of the missionaries to die in South America. Pictures of Tina were placed throughout the living room of the Ford home...Tina as a baby, Tina as a small girl in braids, Tina in her YWCA softball uniform and Tina in the blue gown she'd worn to the junior prom only a few months before. A sweet girl, she and Lori had met in school and Lori convinced her to come to my church even though she lived a fair distance from Prairie Valley.

Tina had joined the church despite protest from her mother, a divorced woman whose ex-husband was an alcoholic, herself the daughter of an abusive father, a hypocrite of a man who took his family to church every Sunday but never hesitated to use his fists in anger.

"I'm sorry, Selena. I truly am." My response sounded flat, empty and pathetic, nearly drowned out by the woman's crying. "We'll work with the authorities to exhume the bodies, identify Tina and bring her home for a proper burial. We already—"

"Go to hell," she sobbed.

"Mrs. Ford, Reverend Agnew wants to help you. We all want to help you." Henry Hopkins, one of the church elders, had accompanied me on my visits to relatives of the deceased. He was a retired psychologist, a tall man with a golden tan, thick white hair and a very deep, soothing voice.

We'd saved the visit to the Ford house for last, knowing it would be the hardest. Most of the relatives already had resigned themselves to the expected news I brought. There were tears at each stop. So many tears. But in every other case the relatives were members of my own congregation and they found some sense of solace in prayer. Selena Ford was another matter.

"Please, Selena, believe me," I begged. "I never would have sent Tina there if I'd suspected anything like this would happen. She wanted to go. We prayed about it and we felt good about her going. God—"

"God? God!" she shrieked. Selena rose from her chair, her cheeks wet with tears, her mascara like smears of paint on a face that had become red with fury. She advanced toward me a step, her fists clenched at her sides. "I know all about you and your God. 'Give me your money,' you preachers say, then you tell men they can hit their little girls. You give all the power to men and then you send my baby to the jungle to die. You killed her. You *killed* her!"

"Mrs. Ford..." Henry stood up and reached for the woman, but she turned on him and shoved him away. Henry tripped over an ottoman and crashed to the floor.

I tried to stand up, but something slammed into my forehead. Stupidly, I looked down and saw a heavy decorative bottle made of thick glass. It bounced as it hit the carpeted floor, just as it had bounced off my head. As I stared at it, a drop of blood fell past my eyes and spattered on the glass. I raised my hand to my forehead and felt a large, warm, wet lump growing there. Slowly, I looked up in time to see Selena Ford grabbing a china plate decorated with painted kittens from its wall mounting. She flung it at me. I couldn't back away because of the chair behind me. I raised an arm to block the missile. The plate hit my elbow and shattered. I felt a piece of it dig into my right cheek.

Selena was reaching for a brass candlestick holder when Henry tackled her. He did it as gently as he could, twisting so that his body hit the floor with the woman on top of him. He held on as she fought him, clawing at his arms and kicking at his shins, all the while screaming and cursing both of us, the church, God, her ex-husband and her father.

"Milton! Call 911," Henry shouted to be heard over the distraught mother. "Tell them to send an ambulance so she can be sedated."

I know I did what I was told to do, but I can't remember what I actually told the emergency operator. I was still holding the phone when the sirens approached and stopped in front of the house.

"Let them in," Henry yelled. I did, the cordless phone still in my hand.

Selena Ford was given an injection of something that calmed her down. Two men and a woman put her on a gurney and loaded her into the back of the ambulance. One of the men came to me. He took the phone out of my hand and gave it to Henry, who hung it up. Then the paramedic bandaged my wounds and asked repeatedly if I was going to be okay. I guess I convinced him I was fine. The ambulance left.

"Milton? Are you sure you're all right?" Henry asked. "Pray with me, Henry. Please," I said, looking him in the eye and reaching for his arms. He took me by the wrists, his tanned, usually happy face lined with concern.

"Of course, Milton," he said.

We dropped to our knees and I prayed as hard as I've ever prayed, asking God to help that poor woman. The words I used escape me now, but I know I was crying before it was over and Henry was supporting me so I wouldn't topple over. I felt horrible for Selena, but looking back now I can say I also wept because of the guilt I felt over the death of her daughter and the others. Deep inside somewhere, I wondered if it really was my fault those people were dead.

After a time, and with Henry's help, I pulled myself together. Tears had soaked through the new bandage on my cheek and the salt was stinging the wound. I gently pressed the gauze patch and smiled sheepishly at Henry.

"Thank you," I said. "I feel so sorry for her. Do you think she'll be okay?"

"In time, yes, probably," Henry said, his face earnest. "She hasn't had an easy life, herself. This will be hard for her. How are you holding up?"

"Oh, I'm fine," I said. "Very sad that so many of our friends died, but they were doing the Lord's work. Still, it's very sad."

"Yes. Yes, it is."

We decided to find and check Selena's purse for her house key. Once we'd done that, Henry agreed to take it into his keeping and get it to the attending physician at the hospital where Selena had been taken. We locked up her house and got into my car.

"How is Karen doing, Milton?" Henry asked.

"She's fine. Why?"

"During our meeting this afternoon you said something about her not being happy about this woman you brought home."

"Oh. Well, she's not, really," I said, suddenly uncomfortable and very aware of Henry's former profession. "But she'll come to like Amara, I think. And, it's only for a while."

"Do you have any likely candidates in mind who could take her in? Amara, that is?"

I drove several blocks in silence. "No," I admitted. "I guess I don't. I thought I would mention it this Sunday and see if anyone steps up."

"Can I be honest with you about something, Milton?"

"Of course."

"When you spoke of Amara this afternoon, you had a tone in your voice that seemed to be something more than compassion," Henry said.

"Oh? What do you mean?"

"Milton, did you have relations with Amara?"

"Of course not," I said. Maybe I said it too quickly, too shrill. Even I didn't believe it, and I knew I hadn't done anything wrong. "Really, Henry, nothing happened between us. She's…she's like a child in a lot of ways. But then…"

"Yes?"

"She is from a completely different culture," I said. "She thinks of things differently than we do. Maybe it's childish, but then she'll ask these deep, innocent questions and it's just…I don't know. She's an enigma."

"What was she wearing when you found her in the jungle?"

"Huh?" We were turning into the church parking lot. The shadow of the steeple was long and thin, pointing at the entrance to the lot, pointing at me, as if accusing.

"I asked, what was Amara wearing the first time you saw her?"

"I...I don't remember," I said. Yes, I lied. A blatant, noway-to-justify-it lie. To a man I considered a friend but who also influenced my employment, my career. "It was some rags, some old stuff like the villagers wore."

I parked the car and turned to face Henry. He was watching me, his gray eyes steady, his face darkened by the shadows of the setting sun. I offered a smile.

"She wasn't wearing anything spectacular," I said.

"No, I guess not," Henry agreed. "Milton, I hope you'll take my advice, as a friend, as a psychologist and as a member of the elders, and get that woman out of your house before there's trouble. You know what kind of trouble I mean. If not between her and you, then between her and your son."

"Oh Henry, you haven't even met her," I argued. "You'll like her. Just wait and see."

"It isn't a question of whether or not I will like her, Milton," he said. "I am concerned about the attachment you already have to her."

"That's nonsense. She's a waif. A...a lost soul found in the burned remnants of a mission I—we—worked so hard to create. She's a nice girl. A pagan needing direction. Nothing more."

"I hope so, Milton. I really do. Now, I should get home. I don't need to remind you how David and the rest of the council felt about your sudden trip to South America. About the whole mission experiment. I suggest you lay low for a while. Just do your job. Tell people what you found in the mission, then let it go. Don't mention it again for a long time. Do you understand?

Nobody will want to hear about it again."

"Yes, Henry, I understand."

"Good evening," Henry said. He got out of my Cadillac and I watched him get into his own blue Lexus. I backed out and drove away, heading for home, Henry's warning heavy on my mind.

15

David Ross was waiting for me at home. He and Karen were sitting in the living room, drinking iced tea and talking softly when I came in. Amara and my kids weren't in the room. David stood up as I entered. Karen gave me a strange look, then focused her gaze on her glass of tea.

"David, I didn't expect to see you again today," I said.

"I wanted to talk to you about a few more issues," David said in his crisp voice. I remember how his glasses reflected the lamps in the living room as he said that. David is shorter than I am, about five-feet, nine-inches, with short, curly hair that had turned whitish gray. He is very proper. Perfect manners and perfect teeth.

"What can I do for you?" I asked. "How did it go this afternoon?"

"What happened to your face?" he asked, flicking his eyes to my bandage.

"Tina's mother did not take the news well. She went into hysterics. We had to call an ambulance for her."

"I see. Could we speak alone?" he asked. "Somewhere private?"

"Of course. Karen, please excuse us. We'll go to my study."

I led David into my book-lined study. He sat in a leather wingchair beside my reading table; I took the chair behind my desk and watched as he moved a coaster on the table and put his glass on it. "What's wrong, David?"

"I'm very disturbed, Milton," he said. "My task of telling families about loved ones lost and buried in a strange country was quite taxing on my conscience. It was unpleasant. It will not happen again."

"Of course not."

"There will be no more missions sponsored by the church."

"David, I wouldn't dream of asking," I said.

"Good."

We looked at each other for a long moment. His face was firm, his eyes set, but I could see something beneath his iron will. Despite his adherence to rules and his curt way of speaking, David is a compassionate man. Talking to the families of the deceased must have been very hard for him.

"What of this woman you brought back?"

"Amara? What about her?"

"Where is she?"

"Well, I can't really say. I just walked in the door. I take it she wasn't here when you got here?"

"I haven't seen her."

"She's probably out with Lori," I said. "They hit it off very well. I sent them out to buy clothes for Amara earlier. They're probably still shopping."

"You've committed a serious offense by smuggling that woman into the country, Milton."

"I thought we'd covered this in the meeting this afternoon," I said, controlling my voice and hoping my annoyance didn't show.

"I want to be absolutely sure we understand one another. I do not approve of what you have done."

"You wouldn't have done the same?"

"I wouldn't have hopped on a jet and gone to South America on the church's money without proper approval in the first place."

"Granted," I agreed. "But, suppose you had gone through all the channels. You got down there and everything was gone. Burned. Destroyed. The only thing there was one single woman who obviously had no business being alone in the jungle. A slave woman escaped from a drug-dealing owner. What would you have done, David? Tell me."

"I would have obeyed the laws of Caesar as well as the law of Christ," David said. "I would have helped her out of the jungle and turned her over to the proper authorities."

"Oh David, there are no proper authorities down there," I

argued. "She would have been sent back to her owner. She can't do that. She's…she's like a flower. Plant her in filth and she'll die. We can nurture her and make something of her."

"I will look forward to meeting your jungle flower, Milton. You say she saw the fire?"

"Yes. That's what I told all the elders this afternoon. Remember?"

"Did she try to help anybody?"

"I don't know."

"Could it be she started the fire?"

"No. It looked like a huge blast hit the center of the village. Like a lightning strike. I don't think any human started that fire."

"What will your sermon be about this Sunday, Milton?"

"I haven't had time to put a lot of thought into it," I said. "Henry has advised me to talk about the mission this one time, then never speak of it again. That's what I'll do. Talk about what happened, the souls we saved, the sacrifices made in the name of Christ, then introduce Amara as the continuance of our mission work."

"I agree with Henry. This is an issue best dropped soon. This isn't the first time you've mentioned Amara being the new mission. You think that's wise?"

"Yes," I said. "She is a unique creature. She's so…I don't know…wild. Pagan, maybe. But she's like a sponge. Very eager to hear about Christ. And the questions she asks…"

"Having this woman in your house is going to create trouble. I don't mind telling you, Milton, that I think very highly of your wife. Karen reminds me very much of my own Felicia, God rest her soul. She is a good woman. You are challenging her by bringing this woman into your home. Your voice tells me you are infatuated with this jungle woman."

"Oh David, come on. That's nonsense. I think of her as a child. A waif to be educated and brought to the Lord. Nothing more. She is no threat to Karen."

"If you say so." He lifted his glass and sipped his tea. "I must go. I admit I came here mostly in hopes of meeting this waif of yours. For the time being, Milton, we will not notify the authorities that she is in this country. But, I give you fair warning, it is an issue the elders will have to consider. We will have to meet with her and hear her story so that we can decide what is best done."

I hesitated a long moment before answering so that my voice would remain calm. Suddenly, David seemed to be nothing more than a smug figure of authority lording his power over me. I wanted to snap at him, to say something ugly. It was a moral victory that I did not. "Very well," I said.

I showed David out, then returned to my study, closing the door behind me. I sat at my desk, my head held in my hands. Never had I considered that rescuing Amara from the jungle would cause so much trouble with fellow Christians. Not just Christians, but the elders of my own church. I fervently prayed that God would open their eyes to the fact I had done the right thing, that I was doing His will.

My prayers were interrupted by a knock. "Who is it?" I asked.

"Me," Lori answered. "Can we come in?"

Lori and Amara entered my study. "What do you think?" Lori asked, extending her open hands toward Amara. "Doesn't she look great?"

Oh, she did. Amara was wearing a short, lightweight skirt, brown with large pink and white flowers on it and a loose-fitting, sleeveless pink shirt with a deep neckline adorned with ruffles. On her feet she wore brown shoes with two-inch heels. She had just the slightest bit of makeup on, just enough to tinge her cheeks and highlight her eyebrows.

"You must smell me, too," she said, stepping forward and throwing her arms around my shoulders. "Thank you, Milton. I love the clothes."

"You're welcome, Amara," I said, reluctantly but firmly separating myself from her. "And that's a very nice perfume you're wearing."

"I told you he'd like it," Lori said. "It's Obsession."

"Do you like my clothes?" Amara asked.

"Yes. But, aren't they kind of…well…skimpy?" I asked, looking more at Lori. "Autumn is coming on and that skirt isn't going to do much to keep your legs warm."

"I told you he'd say that," Lori said to Amara. "Don't worry, Daddy, we got some pants and some longer skirts. She'll stay warm. But this was the cutest outfit."

"The cutest, huh?"

"Oh Daddy, you know what I'm talking about." Lori turned to Amara again. "He'd never let me wear this. But you're a grown woman and he can't stop you." She winked.

"All right, Lori," I said.

"You would not let Lori wear clothes that show how beautiful she is?" Amara asked.

"I don't really control her clothes," I said.

"Daddy, that's not true," Lori said, smiling. "Remember my favorite green dress? The one that looked like velvet?"

"Lori, you were six years old and you outgrew that dress," I said. "Every time you bent over in that dress you showed off your Tweety Bird panties."

"Yeah, but ever since then, you've told me no skirts shorter than two inches above my knees."

"Well, that's what a father's supposed to do," I said.

Lori laughed, then came up and pecked me on the cheek. "Good night, Daddy, you old fuddy-duddy."

"'Night, Lori. Good night, Amara."

"Good night, Milton. Sleep well," Amara said, her eyes meeting mine and holding me for a moment.

I turned off the light and followed them out of the study. They went upstairs and I went to the living room, where Karen was sitting on the sofa, watching a news show. I sat on the sofa with her and watched the television for a moment as it showed footage from the latest conflict in the Middle East.

"Everything okay with David?" Karen asked.

"I think so," I answered. "He wasn't quite finished griping

about me going to South America. Or about how I got Amara out of the jungle. He's threatening to turn her over to the government."

"Would that be so bad?"

"It would be like I've betrayed her if I let that happen," I said. "They would probably deport her back to Brazil and she'd end up back with the man she escaped from."

"She could apply for asylum."

"She isn't politically persecuted. I doubt she'd get it."

"Milton, I don't like her staying in our house."

"Why? What's wrong?"

"I don't like the way she looks at you, for one thing. Or Eric. She'll be trouble."

"The way she looks at me? What do you mean?"

"Don't pretend you haven't noticed," Karen said, facing me now. "Maybe it's only a school-girl-type infatuation since you rescued her. I don't know. But I don't like the way she looks at you."

"Karen, it's sweet that you're jealous, but there's nothing to be jealous about."

"Promise me you'll find somewhere else for her to live. Soon."

"Of course, Karen. That was always the plan. I'm going to talk about her Sunday. Hopefully somebody will come forward then and volunteer to take her in."

"Uh-huh. I'm going on up to bed."

"I'll be right up."

"Leave the screen door unlocked. Eric isn't home yet."

"He's not? It's a school night."

"I know."

"Where is he?"

"With his friends?"

"Where are they?"

"I don't know, exactly. Maybe they had band practice," she said as she walked away.

"Karen, I wish you'd keep better track of where he is. He's at an age where he needs guidance."

Karen paused and looked back at me. "You know we wouldn't be having this conversation if it was Lori out late. You let her get away with murder. You're a lot harder on Eric."

"I am not," I argued. "He's not as responsible as Lori. If Lori was out, we'd know where she was."

"We'd know where she told us she was going."

"I'll wait up for Eric. Good night, Karen," I said, suddenly angrier than I should have been. I looked away from Karen, fixing my eyes on the television.

About a half-hour later I heard the door open behind me and Eric came in. He closed and locked the doors behind him and started for the stairs.

"Where have you been?" I asked.

"Out," he answered, starting up the stairs. "Come back here. I'm talking to you," I said.

He came back and stood beside the sofa in his baggy, ragged jeans that Karen had bought for him in that condition. He was wearing a red and black T-shirt with a leering skull on the chest.

"You smell like cigarettes," I said. "What have you been doing?"

"Not smoking."

"Eric, what have you been doing?"

"Come on, Dad, I was just hanging with the guys. Darren and Joe smoke. It's Darren's car. I couldn't tell him, 'Hey man, put out the cigarette so my dad won't think I've been smoking.' They'd kick me out of the car. It's bad enough..."

"What's bad enough?"

"Come on, Dad. I get a lot of crap because I'm a preacher's kid."

"That's a bad thing? It doesn't bother Lori."

"Yeah, well, I'm not Miss Goody-two-shoes."

"Watch it, Eric. You're in enough trouble. You're late."

"Oh man, I can't believe you're busting me like this."

"You knew I would."

"You wouldn't do it to Lori."

"That is enough," I warned. "You're staying home tomorrow evening and all weekend."

"Dad, that's bullshi—"

"What did you say?"

"Nothing."

"Get up to your room."

"I gotta shower."

"Do it, then you go to bed. You better not give your mother any trouble getting up in the morning."

He muttered something as he turned and stomped up the stairs. I thought about calling him back, but let him go. I was too mad to deal with him and afraid I'd do something I'd regret if I kept at him. I flicked off the television and went to bed.

The first dream came almost immediately. I was back in my study, working at my desk though the room was very dim. I heard the door close and looked up to see Amara standing before me, her new pink blouse unbuttoned and open just enough to show her cleavage and her naval.

"I'm working on a sermon about you," I said.

"I have a better idea." She opened her blouse and shrugged her shoulders so that it slid down her arms and fell to the floor behind her. "Worship at the altar of my breasts and make your offering in the collection plate of my loins." She leaned over the desk, put a hand behind my head and pulled me closer until my face was enveloped in her new perfume and pressed against a soft breast, the nipple pushing at my lips. I opened my mouth and accepted it, sucking greedily, my hands rising to grip her arms, her shoulders and finally cradling her breasts as I kissed them hungrily.

Then I got up and went around my desk. She stayed where she was, leaning forward over the desk, her new flowered skirt riding up the back of her thighs. I pushed the skirt higher, until it was bunched around her waist, then bent forward and kissed her firm, smooth bottom. I opened my pants and took her from behind, thrusting deeply and smoothly into her. I watched her back arch, her long red hair moving on her pale flesh as I pushed into her.

I heard a scream and looked over my shoulder to find Karen had entered the study. She was looking at us, a horrified expression on her face. Amara was laughing. I couldn't stop my hips from thrusting. I stayed fastened to Amara, my eyes fixed on my wife.

I awoke a moment before ejaculating into my underwear. "What's that?" Karen asked, sitting up suddenly in the bed. "Huh?" It was incredibly cold in the room. I pulled the covers to my chin and raised my knees to hide the erection still throbbing in my lap.

"It woke you up, too," Karen said. "Somebody was in here."

"What? There was nobody here."

"There was. Go check." She grabbed at the covers and huddled under them. "Go check."

Carefully hiding the way my pajama bottoms protruded in front of me, I sat up and swung my feet off the bed. The air was frigid. My penis began to shrink, though, so it wasn't such a bad thing, except that the semen in my underwear had cooled and felt disgusting. I stood up and hurried out of the bedroom.

The downstairs level of the house was empty. I checked the doors and found they were still locked. I hesitated at the stairway, then hurried to the laundry room. There was no clean underwear available, so I took the pair I'd worn the day before from the clothes hamper and quickly changed. Then I went upstairs.

Lori's door was first and it was open a crack. I looked inside. Lori was on her bed, her covers thrown off, her arms and legs splayed out, the long T-shirt she wore to sleep pushed up too high on her legs. Her room also felt unusually cold. I pushed the door open and slipped inside, moving as quietly as I could to her bed. I gathered her covers and spread them over her, which disturbed her. Her eyes fluttered and opened.

"What's wrong?" she asked sleepily. "You looked cold," I said.

"Umm." She raised a hand and scratched at her shoulder. In

the pale light coming through the curtains over her window I saw that there was a small, dark stain on her shirt where she was scratching.

"What's that?" I asked, leaning close and pulling the collar of her shirt to the side. There was a small welt on her shoulder, slightly swollen, with a bit of dried blood in the center.

"Mosquito bite," she said.

"You should put something on it."

"Morning." She fell asleep again.

I left her room and went to Eric's. His door was closed. No light leaked from beneath the door and it was quiet within. I opened the door cautiously, well aware of his demand for privacy and the argument we'd had just hours before. His room was not cold; the temperature within was the same as that in the hallway. Eric was asleep in his bed beneath a poster of Marilyn Manson I'd asked him to take down numerous times. I closed his door and turned away, toward Amara's room.

It wouldn't be proper to go into her room the way I had the rooms of my children. I couldn't knock, for fear I would wake her if she was asleep. But, with both kids asleep, I had to assume it had been Amara moving about that had awakened Karen. Unless I'd cried out when…

I very carefully opened the door and looked into the room. Amara was lying belly-down on the bed, naked, facing me, her eyes closed. Her curtains were open and her room filled with soft moonlight, making her milky flesh seem to glow. My eyes moved slowly from her dainty feet, up her long legs to the buttocks I remembered kissing in my dream, then along her back to the mass of burning red hair and finally to her eyes. She was looking at me.

"I'm—I'm sorry," I said quickly and closed the door. I turned around and hurried away, down the stairs and back to my own bed.

"What was it?" Karen asked.

"Nothing. I don't know," I answered, my heart hammering in my chest. "Maybe it was Lori. Some kind of bug bit her. It bled a little. She'll need to clean it in the morning."

"A bug? Is she all right?"

"Yes. It's just a bug bite. She was uncovered. You probably heard her flopping around or something."

"Why was it so cold in here?"

"Huh? Oh. I don't know. It's not anymore."

"Hmm-umm," she said, putting her head back on her pillow. A few minutes later she was sleeping deeply again.

It seemed a long time before I slept again. But when I did, Belo was waiting for me.

16

The son of a shaman was waving his arms and shouting at me, but I couldn't hear his words over the sound of a rushing wind that rippled the leather loincloth around his waist and buffeted me where I stood. Belo's black hair whipped around his head; he cupped his hands around his mouth and shouted, but I couldn't hear him. I tried to move forward, closer to him, but I could make no progress against the wind.

We seemed to be standing on nothing, surrounded by nothing but blackness and I wondered for a moment how I was seeing Belo if there was no light in this place. Then I caught a fragment of what he was saying. It sounded like, "A star."

I looked up and, to my surprise, saw a single star in the darkness. It was hurtling toward us. No…it was coming at me, growing bigger and brighter as it neared, throwing heat in front of it and lighting the empty space around me as it came closer. I turned to run. I ran as hard as I could, but no matter how fast I moved I could feel the heat increasing behind me, could see the glow of the pursuing star growing brighter.

I dared a glance over my shoulder and could see nothing but the ball of fire burning behind me.

"Milton!"

I fell from the emptiness and crashed onto a hard surface. My eyes popped open and I found myself looking up into Karen's face, her expression something between concern and suppressed mirth. She was leaning over the edge of the bed I had just fallen from.

"Are you okay?" she asked. "What happened?"

"I guess you were chasing rabbits in your sleep," she said. "You were kicking, or running, or something. I tried to wake you up and you fell off the bed. You're okay?"

"Yeah. Yes, I think so."

"What were you dreaming about?"

"I think I was about to be crushed by a falling star," I said, slowly pushing myself up from the floor. I got back under the covers, lying on my side so I could face my wife. "It was a very scary, vivid dream."

"You're telling me." Now she did laugh, just a little, and I didn't mind that she was laughing at me. Over the last few years, laughter from Karen was something I hadn't heard often. "You kept kicking me in the back, so I rolled over to see what was going on and it looked like you were running a race."

"I'm glad you threw me off the bed before I lost that race."

"I just nudged you and you jumped off the bed," she said.

"It was pretty funny."

"Well, I'm glad I was able to entertain you," I said.

"Can I get some sleep now? Between people walking around the house and you running races in bed, I haven't had any sleep tonight. You know I have to meet with the Thanksgiving Day committee in the morning. I don't want bags under my eyes."

"I'll try to keep it to a quick lope if anything else chases me."

"Good." She rolled away from me into her usual sleeping position and was soon breathing deeply again.

I slept only fitfully after that and was glad to finally see the glow of the morning sun behind the drawn curtains of the bedroom. I got out of bed and went to the kitchen to cook breakfast. Lori was the first one to join me. She came into the kitchen still dressed in her nightshirt and plopped into a chair, rubbing her eyes with one hand and her shoulder with the other.

"Did you put anything on that bite yet?" I asked, putting a plate of scrambled eggs, bacon and toast in front of her.

"No. I forgot."

"Are you feeling okay?"

"Just tired. I had weird dreams."

"Were the ducks from the park after you again?" I asked, referring to a childhood dream she'd had about the breadcrumb-eating ducks that lived in a small park.

"No. They were about Dan, mostly. Weird. And I could have sworn you and Amara were in my room last night."

"Oh? Well, you know, I was in your room. That's how I knew about the bite on your shoulder."

"Oh yeah. You were in my room," she said, some of the grogginess lifting from her eyes. "Was Amara?"

"Not that I saw. We can ask her. What about Dan? He wasn't in there after curfew, was he?"

"Oh Daddy, of course not," she said, smiling, but just a little.

Eric and Karen came into the kitchen at about the same time and I gave each of them a plate of food. Karen was wearing a tan business suit and Eric was dressed in some black concert T-shirt and jeans. Lori finished and started back upstairs for her morning ritual of dressing and applying makeup.

"Will you check on Amara?" I asked. "Tell her breakfast is ready."

"What do you have planned for today?" Karen asked me. "I have to write Sunday's sermon. It won't be an easy one."

"What are you going to do with your friend upstairs?"

"I'm not sure. Hopefully she can find something to do to entertain herself."

"I could take her to school with me," Eric said, a fleck of egg flying from his mouth as he spoke.

"See what I mean?" Karen quipped. "She's a bad influence."

"Eat your breakfast, Eric," I said.

We ate in silence for a few moments, then I saw Amara coming down the stairs. She was dressed in a black skirt that fell to mid-calf but was split up both sides to mid-thigh and a yellow satin blouse. She was barefoot and her hair was loose around her face. I cleared my throat to discreetly remind Eric not to stare, but it didn't work.

"Eric? Are you finished?"

"Yeah, Dad, I'm done," he said. He left the table, but never took his eyes off Amara as he went back upstairs.

"Good morning," I said as Amara approached. "I put a plate

on the counter for you. Just help yourself to what's on the stove."

"You cook a lot, Milton," she said.

"Well, Karen has plans for this morning, so I made the breakfast so she wouldn't have to mess with it."

"Is it customary for the man to cook the food?" Amara asked.

"Oh, well, we believe in equality," I said, laughing. "Karen actually is an excellent cook. I think she's making dinner tonight. Aren't you, Karen?"

"Yes. I'm making a roast."

"I will help you, if you like," Amara offered.

"You can cook?" Karen and I asked at the same time.

"Of course I can cook. Cannot every woman prepare food?"

"Nope. Not all of them," I said. "I'm sure Karen would be glad to have the help. Wouldn't you?"

"Yes. I planned on stopping at the farmer's market on my way home to get some fresh green beans," Karen said. "Have you ever snapped beans?"

"Oh yes, I have snapped beans," Amara said.

"What else can you do that Milton hasn't told me about?" Karen asked.

Before Amara could answer, Lori interrupted by calling to me from the stairs. "Dad? Can you come here for a minute?"

I excused myself and went to my daughter. "What is it?"

"I need you to look at something on Dan's car," Lori said, starting for the front door.

"You know I'm no mechanic," I teased, following her out of the house. "Wait. Dan's not here yet." Her boyfriend usually drove her to school.

Lori stopped and turned to me, her face drawn in concern. "What's the matter?" I asked.

"I'm a little worried about Amara."

"What do you mean?"

"Well, when I went up to tell her breakfast was ready, she was talking to somebody in her room. There's no phone in there. After she went downstairs, I went in and looked around, you know, to see if she had a tape recorder or a cell phone or something I didn't know about."

"What was she saying?"

"I couldn't hear her very well," Lori said. "She had her door closed. It seemed like she was arguing with somebody, saying something like 'It will work' over and over."

"Did she say a name?" I couldn't help but remember the same thing happening with me in Manaus.

"I don't know. There was a word she used in a way that sounded like a name. It was…I don't know. It started with an 'az' sound."

"Hmm. Well, I wouldn't worry about it too much," I said.

"Dad, what if she's, you know, mental or something?"

"Did she seem that way when you were together yesterday?"

"Well, no. But that was only one day."

"I'll keep an eye on her," I promised. "That's all I can really do."

"Yeah. Okay. Dad?"

"What?"

"What did she do before she got lost in the jungle?"

"She was a slave."

"Yeah, but, what kind of slave? Sex?"

"Yes, I think so. Why?"

"She was giving me makeup advice yesterday. And telling me how to remove hair from my legs and armpits. But she was telling me all these weird ways, what kinds of berries to mix and that bee's wax is better than tallow to take off the hair. Didn't she have real makeup and a razor?"

"I really don't know. I didn't ask her that kind of detail about her previous life."

"Well, I don't want to be all snitchy," Lori said. "I mean, she seems nice and all. But that talking to herself was kind of spooky."

"If you hear her doing it again, come and get me, okay?"

"Okay, Dad."

"Did you do something about that bug bite you were

scratching last night?"

"Yeah. I put some antibiotic ointment on it. I gotta go."

"Okay. Study hard."

"I will, Daddy." She leaned forward and gave me a peck on the cheek, then got in her car. It was the last kiss I got from my little girl for a very long time. I went back in the house as she backed out of the driveway.

I had barely stepped through the front door before Karen almost ran into me on her way out. She glared at me, her eyes blazing.

"I will speak to you when I get home," she said, keeping her voice low but filled with anger. "But I want that whore out of my house."

"What's wrong? What happened?" I asked.

She didn't answer, but stormed out of the house. I went after her, but she wouldn't turn to face me. She got into her Ford Explorer, slammed and locked the door, refusing to acknowledge that I was knocking at the window. She started the truck and drove away, leaving me standing in the driveway.

The sound of heavy metal music filled the air. I looked up the street to see a black Trans Am filled with teenage boys approaching. The car stopped at the curb and a moment later Eric raced past me. He got into the car and the music faded as they left.

"What is going on?" I wondered aloud. Once again, I went into the house. "Amara! Where are you?"

"In the kitchen," she answered. I found her washing the breakfast dishes at the sink.

"What's going on around here? What was Karen so upset about?"

"I think I might have caused that," she said. "I tried to give her help about making love."

"You did what? What did you say? You told her…"

"It is important for a woman to like making love and you said she does not. I wanted to help."

"Amara…" I pulled a chair away from the table and fell into

it. "You told her I said she didn't like sex?"

"She became angry and asked how I would know such a thing. I told her I had offered myself to you and you refused me because you are loyal to your wife, even though she doesn't like sex. I thought she would be proud of you."

"Oh Amara. Oh no. No."

"I have done a bad thing."

"Not intentionally. I know you meant well, but…"

"I am sorry, Milton."

"You were trying to help. I know that. You just have to understand that we don't talk about sex so openly here. I've told you that."

"I am sorry."

"It'll be all right. Somehow." I wasn't at all sure just how it would be all right. I had no idea on earth how I would fix this problem.

"Do you forgive me?"

"What? Yes. Yes, I forgive you."

"You mean that?"

"Yes."

"I should go away so I do not cause you more trouble with your wife. She does not like me."

"You don't have anywhere to go."

"I could get by. I am very good at finding my own way in the world."

"No. You're not leaving. I'll just have to explain to Karen that you are from a very different culture where sex was looked at differently."

"She wants me to leave."

"Yes." I sighed. "And we do need to find you another place to live. A roommate with an apartment, or something. I have to admit, Amara, I'm not sure what to do with you. I didn't think this thing through enough. I was so focused on getting you out of the jungle and my only thought after that was bringing you to Christ. I didn't think about, or just wouldn't admit to myself, all the other realities that go along with what we did. I mean, how are you going to get a job? Earn a living? Get a driver's license? Or anything?"

"What do you mean?"

"You need paperwork for all that stuff. Birth certificate. Social Security number. I don't know. I'll just have to check into it. I know illegal aliens come to the U.S. all the time and are granted citizenship. We'll find a way."

"I have caused you much grief, Milton Agnew. And I think I will cause you much more."

I couldn't help but smile at her as she stood there with her hands in the dishwater, the morning sun coming through the window over the sink and lighting one side of her face and hair as she looked over her shoulder at me.

"If you are the greatest tribulation I ever face in my life, I'll count myself a lucky man," I said. "Now, I have a sermon to write for this Sunday. I'll be in my study if you need me. Help yourself to the TV or books or the radio or whatever you need to have something to do."

"Thank you, Milton."

"You're welcome, Amara." I pushed myself from the chair and headed for the study.

It took a long time for me to begin work. I couldn't shake the thought of Karen's anger over Amara's words. I knew I was in for a storm of fury when my wife returned. Unfortunately, I felt myself taking Amara's side in the matter. Amara had been trying to help, in her own way. And Amara was right in saying that Karen should be happy that I had resisted the temptation. I could only hope Amara hadn't told Karen just how often I'd had to resist. Although that should be even better, I reasoned. I had withstood a barrage of temptation that would have conquered many other men. I had done no wrong, other than some impure thoughts and masturbation, and Karen could hardly hold that against me. Especially if she didn't know.

Because I had been thinking about this sermon almost from the moment I'd heard about the disaster in Brazil, I was prepared and able to put the words together once I was fully able to devote my thoughts to the work. It would be less a sermon than a eulogy for those who were lost. I began writing down memories I had of all our church members who had died, as well as notes about some of the villagers who had turned to Christ while I was with them.

I compared our lost loved ones to the early Christian martyrs who died preaching the love of Jesus to the world.

"True, these people from Prairie Valley Community Church were not killed for their belief," I wrote, "But they died in the service of the Lord, just the same. They are the martyrs of our family. Their sacrifice must inspire us to go forth into the world around us and preach that same message they were delivering when the fire trapped them inside that little church deep in the jungle."

Suddenly the words were flowing from my pen as if inspired from a divine source. My hand moved almost as quickly as my thoughts, moving from those lost to the one new lamb found among the ruins of the mission. I would introduce Amara to the congregation, tell them a little of her past and how I found her alone and vulnerable and without Christ in the jungle.

"And in her our mission work in Brazil will carry on," I wrote. "She is confused. She has been sold by her own father to be a living toy for a man who lives outside the law, outside justice, outside salvation. Who among us will take up this mission? Who will take this woman into their home and help guide her to the glory of Christ? Who will save this poor woman?"

What if no one wants her?

My pen stopped. That was a ridiculous thought. Of course somebody would take her in. My congregation was made up of good people who would eagerly do the right thing.

What if she becomes the lover of someone else?

So what? I would wish that she found a man who would be her husband. A man who would make her happy.

What if Bob Schrum takes her in? He and his wife are having problems. He said as much. Perhaps his will might not be strong enough to resist temptation.

No. I couldn't allow that. There would have to be a screening process.

Why not just keep her here?

That might be the safest thing, but...

I heard the front door open and close. Then Karen's voice called, "Milton?"

17

Time had slipped away from me as I worked. I didn't realize it was after 1 p.m. My stomach growled as I got up and opened the door of my study. Karen was standing at the foot of the stairs. "I'm in here," I said. "Will you come in?"

She came in and closed the door behind her. Her jaw was set, her eyes still blazing as she faced me. "You better tell me exactly what happened in that jungle. And I mean you better tell me everything. Then you better get that woman out of my house."

"Nothing happened, Karen. Amara already told you that."

"You told her I'm frigid."

"I said no such thing." I couldn't hold her gaze any longer. I turned away and went back to the chair on the other side of my desk. She sat in a wingback chair near a bookcase.

"Exactly what *did* you tell her?"

"I don't really remember."

"Don't you lie to me, Milton Agnew. You better remember what you said."

"All right, Karen. All right. I told her you don't like sex. I told her you don't like making love to your husband and I told her that made it even harder to resist her and I told her that's what I had to do. I had to resist her, even though my wife doesn't care at all for my needs as a husband. I told her I wouldn't take her because I made a vow before God that I would forsake all others when I married you. And that's what I've done, Karen. That...is...what...I...have...done."

"Don't you get mad at me," she said. "Don't you put this on me. If you don't like the way I am, you shouldn't have married me."

"The way you are? The way you are? This isn't how you were when I married you. Remember? You laughed more then. You teased me and made promises about all the love we would make as soon as we were married. Do you even remember that, Karen? And do you remember how you resisted on our wedding night and how, when I was finally reduced to tears and begging, you just lay there and cried while I took you? Do you remember the last time you allowed me to do that? How it was just an interruption in your discussion about some function you're planning? You just lay there like, like—"

The words wouldn't come. Her set jaw was quivering, her eyes glassy with tears. She was no longer the angry woman who had come into my study. She was my wife and I had hurt her deeply. She lowered her head and dug through her purse for a tissue. The light caught the strands of gray in her dark hair as it fell from her shoulders to hide her face. She blew her nose and wiped her eyes.

"Oh Karen." I hurried back around the desk and knelt in front of her, taking her hands in mine. "Forgive me, Karen. That was cruel of me. I never should have said those things to you. And I never should have said anything to Amara about our physical relationship. It was wrong. I just wasn't thinking."

"I'm sure you were thinking, just not about me," Karen said, more tears running down her face.

"That's not true, Karen. It was thoughts of you that kept me from accepting her offer. I couldn't hurt you like that."

"Maybe you'd be better off with her. Maybe she'd do everything you want that I won't do."

"Don't be silly, Karen. I married you because I love you. It's wrong of me to push myself on you."

"No, I have a wifely duty," she said, trying to make air quotes with the fingers I held in my hands.

"I think Eric and Lori are proof you've done your duty," I said. "What more could a husband ask for?"

"You ask for more."

"And I shouldn't. I'm sorry."

"What if she makes the same kind of offer to Eric? At his age, with the pressure he's getting from his friends, do you think he'll turn her down? I'm not blind, Milton. She is a desirable woman."

"I've talked to her about the proper meaning of sex, and about Eric specifically," I said. "I can't guarantee she won't try something, though she hasn't given any indication she's leaning toward it. But, in the end, we'll have to trust that we brought Eric up in a manner that will help him to make the right decision if he's tested."

"And if he makes the wrong decision? What if she has AIDS or something? How would we know? We don't know anything about her."

"I should take her to a doctor, I guess. She should get some immunizations, just to be safe."

"And she should be put on the pill."

"What for?"

"So she doesn't get pregnant. Why did she offer herself to you?"

"I don't know. My animal magnetism?"

"Don't be facetious, Milton. Why? And when?"

"She thought it was expected of her, I guess. It's the way she was raised."

"When did she do it?"

"I guess it was the day after I found her. After we buried everybody. She told me about a spring and a pool and I went there for a bath after she did. But she came back while I was in the water."

Karen pulled her hands away from mine and her eyes narrowed. "She told me it was in a hotel room in Manaus, after you caught her touching herself on the bed."

I couldn't answer. Although I hadn't said anything that wasn't true, I felt as if I'd been caught in a lie. Apparently, my face showed as much.

"How many times did she try to get you to sleep with her?"

"I don't know. And it doesn't matter. What matters is that I didn't do it."

"Was it more than those two times?"

"I don't know."

"You don't know, or you're not telling me?"

"What harm would there be in telling you? Maybe it was a hundred times. Maybe a thousand. The point is, I didn't do it. Not even once."

"You wanted to. And I want her out of this house." Karen pushed me away and stood up. "And don't you *ever* tell anyone another word about our private life."

"Karen…"

The door slammed and she was gone.

I sat on the floor and put my head in my hands. I remained there for a long time, until finally some glimmer of a plan formed in my mind. I went back to my desk and picked up the phone, dialing Henry Hopkins' number from memory.

It took some persuasion, but I was able to talk Henry into taking his wife and Amara to dinner and a movie that evening. I explained that Henry had been right, that Amara's presence was causing some problems and I really needed an evening with Karen.

"Just handle her carefully, okay? She has a completely different set of values than we do," I said.

"We'll be fine, Milton. What time should I pick her up?"

"Would six be okay?"

"That's fi e."

"I owe you, Henry. I really do."

"Think nothing of it. I'll see you this evening."

We hung up. Convincing Amara to go was a harder sell.

She protested, saying she didn't know "those people" and would be uncomfortable around them, that she wouldn't know how to talk to them, that they wouldn't like her, and finally that I had turned on her and was trying to get rid of her, suggesting that Henry was going to take her to the airport and send her back to Brazil. At long last, I convinced her that it would be good for her to go and meet new people. I assured her that Henry and his wife, Pat, would like her just fine and that nobody was sending her back to Brazil.

"I really need this evening with Karen," I said. "We've had a disagreement and I need to do something special to make it up to her. Please, Amara. For me?"

Reluctantly, she agreed. I helped her pick out some conservative clothes from the array she and Lori had bought the day before. I didn't want her to go to join Henry wearing a mini skirt and halter top, which she might have done.

"One more thing," I said. "Will you kind of lay low until Henry gets here? Karen is very upset and it would be better if you two were separated for a while. Hopefully, after this evening, everything will settle down."

Amara agreed and I left her in her room while I went to find Karen. She was lying on our bed, reading a novel. She looked up when I came in, then doggedly fixed her gaze on the pages she held in front of her face.

"Karen, I'd like to take you out to dinner this evening, then we can come home and talk. Just the two of us."

"What about *her*?"

"I've asked Henry and Pat Hopkins to take Amara out for the evening. Lori has a date with Dan and Eric has plans with his friends."

"I thought you grounded Eric."

"I ungrounded him for this."

"Why did you really turn her down?"

"I told you that. I'm married to you. Happily married."

"If you had slept with her and left her there, or just turned her over to the authorities there, I'd probably never have known it."

"What's your point?"

She sighed and lowered the book so I could see her face. "Maybe I shouldn't be mad at you. I believe you didn't do anything. It probably would have been funny to see your reaction when she came on to you. Maybe I'm really mad at myself for not being more like her."

"Oh, that's crazy talk. Come on, say you'll go to dinner with me. We can talk about this later, if you still want to."

"All right. I'll go. Where are you taking me?"

"McDonald's. I think we could both use a Happy Meal."

"I want lobster."

"You always did have expensive tastes. Lobster you shall have."

The rest of the afternoon and early evening went as planned. I returned to my study and typed the notes I'd made for Sunday's sermon. I heard Lori and Eric come home from school; Lori popped in for a moment to tell me she was leaving. Then I took a quick shower and dressed in slacks and a sport coat for dinner. At six I met Henry and Pat, a tall blonde with a solid handshake, and introduced them to Amara.

Like most people who first saw her, both Henry and Pat seemed taken aback by Amara's physical appearance. But, they recovered quickly and gracefully. Amara acted very demure and shy and it was obvious she was hesitant about leaving my side, but eventually Pat simply took her by an arm and led her away, chatting about restaurants as they went out the door.

"I see now why you need an evening with your wife, Milton," Henry said. "You need to move her out of here soon. No wife should have a woman like that in her house."

"I plan to, Henry. Thank you so much for doing this."

"It's no problem. It may turn out to be an interesting experience, if she starts talking."

"Yes. Well, you may get more than you bargained for if that happens. Don't let that act fool you. She has a habit of making you think she's a child, then hitting you with some very difficult questions."

Henry laughed. "I'll take that into consideration. Good luck to you." We shook hands and he left.

A few minutes later and Eric ran down the stairs and out the front door, wearing jeans that looked ten sizes too big for him and a shirt he'd turned inside out. I heard more hard rock music approaching the house, pause, then move away. Karen finally decided she was satisfied with her clothes and makeup and came out of our bedroom. She looked very attractive in a dark green skirt and matching jacket. She'd curled her hair and all traces of the crying and anger from earlier in the day were gone from her face.

"You look stunning, Mrs. Agnew," I said. "Simply stunning."

"I do, don't I?" she agreed, smiling.

Surprisingly, the subject of Amara occupied very little of our dinner conversation. Instead, we talked about the kids and about the families who had suffered losses in the mission tragedy. We talked about Christmas gifts and what we should get the children and whether or not we spoiled them. Overall, it was a very nice dinner and I felt very close to my wife as we left the restaurant, my arm around her waist and her shoulder pressed against me.

"What would you like to do now," I asked. "A movie? We could go over to Lake Hefner and walk along the shore? Just drive around? Whatever you want."

"Let's just rent a movie and go home. It'll be nice to have an evening in the house by ourselves."

"I'll remember that in a few years when both the kids are away in college," I teased.

We went to the Blockbuster store in the Prairie Valley shopping center and rented the latest Harrison Ford movie. I don't remember the name of it. We never got to watch it.

Dan's car was parked in the driveway when we got home. Parked beside it was the familiar black Trans Am with three of Eric's friends sitting inside while electric guitars screamed from the stereo. Eric wasn't in the car. Karen and I both looked at each other with a "There goes that idea" expression.

"Maybe they just forgot something," I suggested. "I think Lori and Dan had planned to go to a movie and then do that midnight bowling thing. It looks like Eric won't be staying long, anyway."

"Maybe."

We got out of the car and went into the house. Nobody was in the living room. Karen said she was going to make some coffee and went to the kitchen. I went upstairs and was surprised to find Eric with his ear pressed to Lori's closed bedroom door. He had a huge grin on his face, which faltered only a little when he saw me at the head of the stairs.

"What's going on? What are you doing?"

"Your baby girl just got her cherry popped," Eric said. "What?" Oh God, I remember the way it seemed, everything—all the blood, every organ, every bone—inside my body seemed to suddenly become heavy and pull toward my feet. I felt as though I'd been punched in the gut by a champion heavyweight boxer. I felt sick. I felt old, tired and defeated. "Go away," I told Eric. "Go to your room. Leave. Why are you here?"

"Don't worry about me. I'm outta here," Eric said. He slipped past me, went down the stairs and out the front door.

Like a condemned man approaching the gas chamber, I moved down the hall to Lori's bedroom door. I raised my hand to knock."

"That's it? That's all? You can't be finished." It was Lori's voice, surprised and angry.

"I'm sorry," Dan answered.

I knocked on the door. It sounded feeble, weak, empty. I tried again, forcing my hand to strike the wood harder, but couldn't muster anything resembling authority. "Lori?" I called.

"Oh my God, it's your dad," Dan said, panic in his voice. "Don't open that door," Lori yelled, but it was too late. Dan opened the door, his Polo shirt untucked from his slacks, his hair messed up, his face pale and scared as he looked at me.

"I am so sorry, Reverend Agnew. I swear, I didn't mean to. I didn't want to. I tried to stop her. Shit." He turned and ran. I watched him fly down the stairs and again I heard the front door of my home close.

Slowly, as if my neck had become stone, I turned my head back and looked into my daughter's room. Stuffed animals lay on the floor, along with the shorts and shirt Lori had been wearing when she told me good-bye earlier. A bra and pair of white panties with small blue flowers also lay discarded on the floor.

"Milton? What's going on up there? Was that Dan who just

ran out?"

"Yes, Karen. It was Dan."

"What's going on?"

My eyes moved onto the bed, where Lori sat up against the pillows, a blanket pulled to her chin to cover her nakedness.

"Oh Lori. Oh baby. Why?"

18

I remember Lori sitting on her bed, the covers clutched under her chin, a guilty look in her eyes as she yelled, "Daddy, go away! Get out!" And I did. Slowly, as if in a dream, I backed away from the door, backed to the edge of the staircase, and stood there dumbly for what seemed a long time. Then, I saw the tips of Lori's fingers on the door as she slammed it closed.

"What is going on up here?"

My head swiveled and I realized Karen had climbed the stairs and was standing beside me. She looked from me to Lori's closed door.

"They were in bed. Together." The voice coming from my mouth didn't sound like my own.

"Lori and Dan?" I nodded.

Karen took a deep breath and released a long sigh. "I hope she at least used protection. I'll go talk to her. Go on downstairs. I think it's safe to say our evening out is over."

Not knowing what else to do or say, I did as I was told. I went to the living room and sat in a chair, staring stupidly in front of me, wondering what my women were talking about upstairs. Had Karen really said she hoped Lori used protection?

Was that really her first thought in the matter? Our daughter was defiled and Karen was thinking of condoms. I reached over and picked up the phone from an end table. I punched in the phone number for the Ward house. Dan's mother answered on the second ring.

"Hello, Ann, this is Milton Agnew. Is Garry home this evening?"

"Sure, Milton. Hold on," she said, her voice happy, unsuspecting.

"Milton? How are you?" Garry Ward asked.

"Well, Garry, I've been better. Karen and I came home early from an evening out and found Dan and Lori in bed together. Karen's upstairs talking to Lori now. Dan ran out of here as soon as I found him."

"What's that? They were in bed? Having sex?"

"Well, I assume so. They didn't have their clothes on."

"Milton, they are seniors in high school. They've been dating for a long time. Surely you suspected they were doing this." I couldn't believe what I was hearing. Was this man actually defending what his son had done to my daughter? I felt my face flushing. My hand gripped the receiver so tightly my knuckles popped.

"Garry, Dan is no longer welcome here. Lori is not eighteen years old yet. If I find your boy anywhere around her again I will have him arrested for statutory rape." I hung up the phone.

"You know that's only going to make it worse." Karen had walked up behind me. I started a little at her unexpected voice but didn't turn to face her. "Tell her she can't see him and she'll just make sure she does."

"She will not see him again."

"Milton, I'm as upset as you are," Karen said, coming around the chair and sitting on the couch across from me. "I'd hoped she would wait until she was married, but a lot of girls just don't do that anymore."

"You don't seem as upset as I am," I said. "Garry Ward sure wasn't upset. He said he thinks they've been…going at it…for a long time."

"That's not true," Karen said. "I can promise you that. Tonight was Lori's first."

"She told you that?"

"Yes, but she didn't need to. The evidence is on her sheets."

"Why? Why did she let him do it?"

"Milton, it wasn't Dan's idea," Karen said. "What? What are you talking about?"

Karen sighed deeply and looked away from me for a moment,

then faced me again. "Lori told me it was her idea. She said she'd felt funny all day. How'd she put it? She said she felt all hot inside. When she was with Dan this evening she just had the overwhelming urge to have sex. He tried to talk her out of it, reminded her how they'd agreed to wait. But, she was done waiting."

I stared at my wife for a very long moment. I had no idea how to respond to what I'd just heard. My little girl had practically raped her boyfriend. I couldn't believe it.

"I don't know if this is good or bad, but Lori didn't seem to think much of it. Of her first time," Karen said. "She asked me if that's all it was."

"How did you answer that?"

Karen looked away from me, a sudden flash of guilt filling her face. "I told her it was different for different people."

"I'm going to go talk to her," I said.

"No. Don't do that. Wait," Karen urged. "You're too upset. You're both too upset. It can wait until morning, after you've both slept on it."

"I'm not sure I want to sleep on it."

"There's nothing to be done about it, Milton. Going up there and yelling at her about how she did the wrong thing won't make her a virgin again."

"Fine." I pushed myself up from the chair, went to the bedroom for my pajamas, then went to the bathroom. I stood under the shower until the water ran cold, wishing the water could wash away what I'd seen, what I now knew about my little girl. I left the steamy bathroom with pink, wrinkled skin and the image of Lori hiding her nakedness under her bed covers still at the front of my mind.

"Amara's back," Karen said. She was still on the couch, watching the evening news. "That should make you happy."

"Where is she?"

"Upstairs. I asked her to stay in her room tonight. We're having a family crisis."

"All right. I'm going to bed." I went to bed, but only lay on my back in the dark room, staring up at the ceiling, wondering where I'd gone wrong, what I could have done differently to protect my daughter from the bad decision she'd made that night. In the living room, I could just make out the voices from the television. Eric came home. I heard him and Karen talking, then his feet pounding up the stairs. A few minutes later and Karen was running her bathwater. I was still awake when she drained the water and came to bed, though by that time I was lying on my side pretending to sleep.

But no sleep would come to me. Karen, on the other hand, soon slipped into a deep slumber. That she could fall asleep after the tragic events that had transpired irritated me. I pushed the blankets off myself and carefully got out of the bed and left the room.

I went to my study first, but couldn't even pretend to work. Finally, I just steeled myself and went up the stairs. Lori's bedroom door was open. I looked in and saw that the reading lamp beside her bed was on, but she wasn't in the room. I moved farther down the hallway, heard the tinny sound of heavy metal music coming from the headphones Eric wore after bedtime. I paused, thinking I should tell him the music was too loud, but just wasn't in the mood to fight another battle in the music war.

Voices were coming from Amara's room. I moved closer but paused at the door, which was only open a crack. In the dresser mirror I could see Lori and Amara sitting on the bed, Lori in her two-piece pajamas and Amara in a short gown. Lori was talking as Amara brushed her shining red hair with the brush I'd bought her in Manaus.

"But it wasn't any good," Lori said. "I mean, I thought it was, like, going to be all explosive and powerful and I'd feel wonderful and weak afterward. But it wasn't like that. He barely got it in me before he finished. I didn't get anything but the pain and the mess."

"The first time often is like that," Amara answered.

"Especially for men. They have no control the first several times. But a young man who has gained enough experience to have control of his orgasm is a treasure. Maybe you should try someone older next time."

"I don't know," Lori said. "What if it still isn't any good? What if it's like Mom said, just something women have to endure?"

"It is a pity your mother doesn't enjoy sex. But that doesn't mean you shouldn't. I have had many lovers, Lori, and I enjoyed each of them. We come closest to being like gods during sex."

"Maybe I'm just no good at it. Maybe that's why that happened to Dan."

"No. He's not good at it. I could teach you to be a skilled lover," Amara said.

I shoved the door open and stepped into the room. Lori jumped from the bed and looked around desperately, as if searching for an escape route. Amara sat calmly, facing me, a small smile on her face.

"I wondered how long it would take you to come in," she said.

"Lori, go to bed. You will stay in your room," I ordered, standing aside so she could scurry past me.

"You would punish her for doing what comes natural?" Amara asked.

"Leave her alone," I said. "I don't know why she did what she did tonight, but I know that you are the last person she needs advice from. You leave my daughter to me."

Amara hung her head as I spoke but nodded when I'd finished. "I'm sorry, Milton," she said. "I meant no harm."

Her voice sounded pitiful, like the whine of a beaten puppy. I suddenly felt deflated; my shoulders sagged and an unexpected sob broke from my chest. I lifted a hand to my face, where tears suddenly had sprung to my eyes. When I wiped them away I found Amara standing before me. She took me by the wrist and led me to the bed, where she pushed me to a sitting position. She sat beside me.

"What have I done wrong?" I asked.

"Your daughter is not a little girl anymore, Milton," she said. "She is a woman."

"I guess she is after tonight."

"Tonight was only her first lover. She is a beautiful woman and will have many lovers. Better lovers."

"No. Don't you see? That's not right. She should wait until she's married. One lover, her husband, for all her life."

"And be as happy as you are? Never knowing if another lover would be better or worse than the only one you've ever had?"

"Stop it. Don't say that. Karen is upset enough with you without you talking like that."

"You did nothing wrong with Lori," Amara said. "I saw the bite on her neck. Maybe it was a lobishomen that caused her to take a lover."

"A what?"

"A lobishomen. It is a demon that lives in the forest. It feeds on the blood of women and makes them crave lovers."

"And you think one of those bit my daughter?"

"Maybe you brought one home from the forest without knowing it."

"Amara, I want you to stay out of this," I said. "If Lori comes back to you, you send her to me or Karen. Do you understand?"

"Yes, Milton. I am sorry."

"That's all right."

She reached over and put a hand on my wrist, holding gently. "You forgive me?"

"Yes. I—"

"What is going on in here?"

I looked up to see Karen standing in the doorway, looking at me in the same way I'd stood in the same place looking at

Lori only moments ago. I was very aware of sitting on Amara's bed, her hand on my wrist. Though I knew the moment was innocent, I felt my stomach clench and my heart sink.

"Milton was chastising me for giving Lori bad advice," Amara said. "I still do not understand all the ways of your society."

"Uh-huh. Milton, are you staying up here or are you coming back to bed with your wife?"

"Don't do this, Karen," I said. "You know nothing is happening here."

"I know you left our bed and I found you sitting on another woman's bed."

"I'll be sleeping in my study tonight," I said, getting off Amara's bed and sliding past Karen. She pulled Amara's door closed and followed me down the hall.

"It wouldn't surprise me at all if that red-headed harlot isn't behind what Lori did tonight," Karen said.

I rounded on her in the hallway, in front of Lori's closed door. "We've raised our daughter for almost eighteen years, Karen. Do you think Amara can come in here and in just a few days undo everything we've done? That's crazy. It's our fault. Ours." I left her standing there, went to my study and locked the door.

I tried to sleep propped in the chairs but couldn't get comfortable, couldn't shake the images of Lori in her bed, Dan running past me, Lori and Amara sitting on Amara's bed as Amara promised to teach her how to be a better lover. Finally, crying like a baby, I slid out of my chair and knelt—huddled, really—in front of my desk. It seemed I prayed for hours, usually without words, just pouring my heart and tears out to God, begging for guidance, telling him over and over that I knew

Lori was a good girl and that I knew it was my own failing that had caused her to fall from grace that night.

And finally, curled like a baby on the floor, I slept.

19

The status quo deteriorated quickly from that point. There are many signposts on the road of life. The night my little girl gave up her virginity turned out to be a truly ominous signpost on both her road and mine. Unfortunately, though, there were no flashing lights, no workmen in orange vests, not even a printed warning about the hard road that lay ahead. I thought things couldn't get any worse. I was so wrong. But, I get ahead of myself.

Lori was sullen and quiet when she came down for breakfast. She sat at the kitchen table and put one spoonful of Honeycomb after another into her mouth, her eyes fixed on her bowl, her hair mussed, her hands steady. I tried sitting at the table with her, but couldn't bear the silence and the thought that today she was not the little girl I'd sat with yesterday. I took my toast and grapefruit and coffee to my study.

Amara had not come down. Eric was under strict orders from Karen to be silent and go about his own business. Surprisingly, he did that. Karen tried to make idle conversation about the fog lingering into the morning, but gave up and was eating in silence when I left the table.

I mostly played with my food, digging the pulp of the grapefruit out and squeezing the juice from it between my spoon and the plate. I heard the kids leave for school. I heard the clink of dishes as Karen cleaned up in the kitchen. She was still mad at me; that much had been obvious by her attempt at conversation. She hadn't directed it to me, hadn't tried to engage me to help her make things seem normal. She hadn't even looked at me. I was sipping my coffee when she opened the study door without knocking and came in, closing the door behind her.

"Your harlot isn't up yet."

A sharp reply rose to my tongue, but I bit it off there, tried to think of a civil response to her comment, couldn't, and sat quietly sipping coffee I couldn't taste.

"I want her out."

"I think I've mentioned that's the plan," I said.

"You say that, but I know how you are. You'll let her stay here, like a dog nobody will take, until she ruins us all. Maybe you haven't slept with her. I have to believe you haven't, Milton. But I know what she wants. She'll tear this family apart. You know as well as I do that it was her influence that drove Lori to do what she did."

"I don't know that. Lori is a teenager. They have…urges." It sounded weak and ugly when I said it. "She could have been fighting it for a long time and, I don't know, maybe it just overwhelmed her."

"You really think she would have done it if she hadn't been spending so much time with your harlot?"

"Please. Stop calling her that. Even if she were a harlot, she isn't mine. And no, I don't think she's responsible for Lori's actions. Only Lori controls what Lori does. Isn't that what I preach every Sunday? That we are responsible for our own actions?"

"We can be influenced," she snapped back.

"Why have you changed your mind about all this?" I asked. "First, all you cared about was if Lori had used a condom. Now all you want to do is blame Amara."

"I have to meet with the Christmas dinner committee this morning," Karen said. "I don't mind telling you that I don't like leaving you alone in the house with that woman."

"Take her with you."

"I will not." The color drained from Karen's face. "Do you think I would take her to meet those ladies? My friends? And have her tell her story about trying to seduce you in the jungle?"

"Fine, Karen. Fine. Will you feel better if I promise not to go to bed with Amara while you're out today?" I regretted the sarcasm, but I thought I felt as low as I could ever possibly feel and I just wanted the conversation to end, even if it meant she stomped away and slammed some doors.

"I'll feel better when I know that whore is out of my house." Karen turned and calmly but quickly left the study. She left the door open and I saw Amara standing in the living room, facing us, her red hair tousled, wearing nothing but a long T-shirt nightie. Even from behind, I felt the angry glare Karen threw at her as she went past Amara and up the stairs. I lowered my head into my hands and exhaled deeply. When I looked up, Amara was in the doorway.

"Your wife is very angry with me," she said. "Yes, I guess she is."

"Are you sorry you brought me here?"

"No."

"She blames me for Lori's decision to make love to her man."

"Yes."

"Do you?"

"No." I shook my head vaguely. "Lori is old enough to make her own decisions."

"It hurt you that she chose as she did."

"Yes."

"If all women remained little girls, there would be no new people in the world."

"I suppose that's one way to look at it."

"What shall we do today, Milton?"

"Work. I still have work to do. This sermon on Sunday will be very important. You…I don't know what you should do." I looked around my study, at the books, the knick-knacks, the computer, the open Bible on my desk. "You could read. Or play on the computer. After you get dressed. Have you ever used a computer?"

"No."

"Here, let me show you. You can use the computer in here and I'll take my laptop and work on it." She came around to my side of the desk. I showed her how to boot up the computer, gave her a quick tutorial on the games that had come pre-installed with the operating system and showed her how to connect to the

Internet. I pulled up the main page of my favorite search engine and saved it as my home page.

"Now, anything you want to find, you type in this box," I explained. I typed "history of Greece" into the search field. "Then hit the 'Search' button and..." I paused as the computer screen changed. "There you go. Hundreds of pages with history information on your homeland."

"Oh Milton, that is amazing," she said, her eyes wide. "Yes, it is. You can find out almost anything you want on the Internet. History, recipes, you can see museum collections, go shopping. It's almost endless what you can do."

Amara clicked on one of the Greek history links. A page loaded with images of Greek deities. "Look, Milton, it's Aphrodite, goddess of love."

"You know about Aphrodite?"

"Oh yes. I remember her. I can really use this?"

"Yes. Have fun with it. When you're done, just click here," I said, showing her how to disconnect the modem. "I think I'll go out on the back patio to work since it's a beautiful morning. Just come get me if you need anything."

I gathered up my laptop computer and my handwritten notes and left her alone in my study. The late-August morning was warm and I knew it would be another hot day. Summers in Oklahoma often linger well into late September or early October, with a few weeks of autumn before the first cold fronts come roaring in on north winds in late November or early December. I sat in a patio chair at the umbrella-covered table on our deck and turned on the laptop. Morning sun gleamed like diamonds on the ripples in the swimming pool. Birds called, sparrows and robins mostly, though I heard a blue jay somewhere to the east. I loaded my sermon into the laptop's word processor from a flash drive and read over what I'd written so far. It sounded wrong...timid, not worthy of those who had died.

Soon, I was focused completely on my work. Hours went by unnoticed. The sun climbed, peaked over my head and slid a little toward the west before the heat got to me and I suddenly realized how thirsty I was. My skin was shiny with perspiration. I looked at the clock on the screen and realized it was 1:30. I had been working for nearly five hours without interruption.

The sermon was nearly finished, a bit long, but all things considered, I figured a long sermon was necessary this time.

I wondered that nobody had disturbed me. Karen either hadn't come home yet or wasn't speaking to me. Amara...I saved my work and went to see what she was up to. I found her where I'd left her, at the computer in my study. She had eBay on the computer screen.

"What are you doing?" I asked. "Shopping."

"For what?"

"Everything. It's amazing what you can find at this place, this eBay. Everybody in the world can offer money for things others are selling. Whoever offers the most money wins the item."

"Uh-huh. I know. I've been there and bought some things at auction."

"Oh I know. I used your account. I hoped you would not mind."

"You what?" I asked. "Used my account? How did you do that?"

"The computer had your username. I just had to put in your password."

"And how did you know that?"

"It was not hard to figure out. You just combined the names of your children into one word."

"But, how would you know to do that?"

"I just tried to think like you would."

A feeling of dread stole over me. "What did you do after you figured out the password?"

"I bought things," she said, her large green eyes fixed on me as if I was a curious bird she was studying.

"I didn't know you had any money," I said, forcing a smile. "There was an account already set up to pay for things."

"Yes. That's my credit card. Everything I—or you—buy while logged in to my account is charged to my credit card. I have to pay for that."

"I should not have bought things?"

"You should have asked first. You really shouldn't use other people's accounts. Even when you are smart enough to figure out the passwords. Now, what did you bid on? Let me see."

I pulled up the screen to show recent bids from my account. I could only stare in silence for a long moment, unable to say anything. The list was long and impressive. She had bid on artwork, books, jewelry and antiquities. It was easy to pick out the theme of goddesses in what she was bidding on—oilon-canvas prints of Venus, Phoenician coins bearing the image of Astarte, necklaces dedicated to a moon goddess of various names. The total amount for all the bids currently placed came to almost $7,000.

"Amara," I said slowly. "This is very bad. This is a lot of money."

"It is?"

"Yes. It is. How did you plan to pay for all this?"

"I did not think of that," she said. "I guess I thought you would. You have been so nice to me, buying me clothes and everything."

"You needed clothes, and they didn't cost this much. I'm not even sure my credit card has that much available."

"I am sorry."

"Well, maybe somebody will outbid you on most of the stuff so we won't have to pay it."

"I am sorry, Milton," she repeated.

"Hmm. Well, don't worry about it. We'll figure something out when we have to."

"I am really sorry."

I pulled my eyes from the computer screen to look at her anxious face. Her large green eyes were filled with remorse and sheened with tears. "It's all right, Amara. Just don't do it again. Okay?"

"I won't. You forgive me?"

"Of course. You didn't understand what you were doing," I said. "Let's shut this down for now." I logged off the Internet and turned off the computer. "Are you hungry? Want some lunch?"

"Yes. That would be nice."

I made ham sandwiches for us and we sat at the table to eat. "I noticed there was a theme to the stuff you were buying," I said. She gave an innocent smile. "Seems everything had something to do with a pagan goddess."

"I guess it did," she said. "Why is that?"

"Some of it was very old. But some of it, like the books and jewelry, is new. Belief in goddesses hasn't gone away, has it?"

"No, it hasn't. Never will." I bit into my sandwich and chewed for a moment. "Most modern people who worship a goddess are, shall we say, on the fringes of society. Radical feminists, lesbians, some bohemian artists."

"People your god doesn't like?"

"I wouldn't say that. Just people who don't follow his Word. He loves them anyway."

"And will take them up to the Heaven you talk about?"

"Not unless they accept Christ as their savior and repent for what they believe now."

"Savior from what?"

"From sin," I said. "God sent his son, Christ, to die on the cross so we could all be forgiven for original sin."

"Original sin," she said, her voice expressing recognition. "Yes. Adam and Eve. The forbidden fruit. Defying God. You know the story?"

"Yes, I know it," she said. "The serpent tricked Adam into putting on its skin, then Adam made Eve do it."

"What? I've never heard it that way," I said, my sandwich halfway between my plate and open mouth.

"The serpent explained to Adam that he was naked because he had no flesh," she explained as if I were a child. "He was... a ghost, a spirit. Naked. The serpent told him that. Then the snake shed his skin and Adam put it on. It fit tightly over his spirit. Then he asked for another skin and made Eve put it on. She hated it, but Adam made her wear it. He was fascinated by the way she looked in her new flesh. But God wasn't. He was mad and kicked them out of Paradise."

"Where in the world did you hear that?" I asked.

"I don't know. Maybe my father told me before he abandoned me."

"You certainly didn't get that from the Bible."

"No. I read your Bible. The beginning, anyway. The one you left in my bedroom. It seemed...silly. Would your god really make Adam and Eve leave Paradise because they ate a fruit?"

"But the fruit allowed them to see that they were naked," I said. "But that isn't the important part. They had everything—everything—but God commanded they should not eat the fruit and they disobeyed."

"See, you said yourself they were naked."

"They didn't have clothes. They had flesh."

"After the snake gave it to them. Then the Grigori tried to help Eve by showing her herbs to heal the flesh she was stuck in and how to make potions to make the flesh look more beautiful. So God banished the Grigori from Heaven."

"Amara, you amaze me," I said. "That's a very creative interpretation of Genesis. I'm glad to see you've been thinking about what you read in the Bible. But, you see...Wait. The Grigori isn't named in the Bible. How did you know about them?"

For a moment, the very briefest of instances, her face froze in a mask of fear, as if she'd been caught in a lie. Then she recovered and smiled shyly. "I read some of your other books, too," she said. "I was bored the night before last and went into your study after you'd gone to bed. I found the name in one of those books. I don't remember which one."

"I see," I said, thinking her explanation sounded hollow. "Well, the important, and very good thing is that you've been reading about God and Christ and it has inspired you to think. But, you should accept the Bible as it is and not add your own interpretations to it."

"It is just as it was originally written? There have never been changes to the text?" she asked.

"Umm. Well, no. There have been changes as clarifications were made or more reliable documents were found."

"Maybe I just clarified the serpent story," she said. "I feel almost like I was there."

"I'm glad your reading felt so vivid, but I don't think that's how it was." I reached over and took her empty plate, put it on top of mine and put the small knife I'd used to cut our sandwiches into halves on top of that. I picked those up with one hand and the Miracle Whip jar with the other, then stood. As

I rose, the plates tipped forward and the knife slid off. "Watch out!" I called, but it was too late.

The point of the knife struck Amara's left pinky finger, stuck in the wood surface of the table for a fraction of a second before falling over. I looked at her finger as she drew the hand toward herself. I expected to see the opened flesh spilling blood. Instead, it seemed that the flesh had opened to reveal a riot of swirling color encased in skin. Like a rainbow in a tornado, I remember thinking. I stood, dumbfounded, staring at her hand, now held protectively to her chest and covered by the other hand.

"I should go wash off the blood," she said, getting up quickly and hurrying toward the bathroom.

"The blood," I said. I shook my head and looked back at the table. A swath of sunlight reached from one corner of the table to the other, the wooden-handled knife laying in the middle of it. "It must have been the sunlight reflecting on the blood," I said to myself. I looked at the knife; there was no blood on the blade, but I knew that wasn't so unusual considering how the wound was inflicted. "Sunlight on blood," I said again.

I picked up the knife and took the dishes to the dishwasher and the Miracle Whip to the refrigerator.

20

About a half-hour later, the phone rang. It was Dave Koehn, the principal at the high school. "Mr. Agnew," he began, "I'm going to need you to come to my office. Immediately, if you can." His voice was firm, icy. I lowered my head and rubbed my eyes with my free hand.

"What's Eric done?" I asked.

"It isn't Eric. I'm afraid it's Lori."

"What? What's wrong? Is she okay?"

"Please come, Mr. Agnew. I'll see you soon?"

"Yes. Yes, I'll be right there."

It was a relatively short drive to the high school. I parked in a visitor spot near the front door just as a bell rang. Hundreds of kids came pouring from the buildings, flowing around me as I moved against the tide toward the entrance, my mind racing with possibilities. I knew Lori couldn't be hurt. Principal Koehn would have told me that, he would have said he was sending her to a hospital. Was she in trouble? Lori never got in trouble at school. But then, that was before last night...

I entered the school. The hallways were already nearly deserted. My adult footsteps sounded incredibly loud on the tiled floors as I walked toward the office. A middle-aged secretary greeted me from a desk in the principal's office. I told her my name and a pained, embarrassed expression passed quickly over her face. She picked up a phone and punched three numbers. "Mr. Koehn, Mr. Agnew is here." She hung up and looked back to me. "Right through that door and to your left."

I passed from the main office into a hallway with three closed doors and two benches. Lori sat on one of the benches. She met my gaze for only a moment before looking away. "What is going on?" I asked.

Before Lori could speak, one of the doors opened. A boy came out, followed by an angry woman. The boy looked at Lori and grinned. "See ya later," he said. "Shut up and get your ass home right now," his mother said, casting a glare at Lori and one at me as she shoved the boy ahead of her. They went into the office I'd just left. I looked away and found the principal standing in the doorway of the office the boy and his mother had left.

"Mr. Agnew," he said, reaching out with his right hand. I shook it. "Please come in." He looked at Lori. "I'll call for you in a moment."

"Whatever," she said.

"Lori! Show some respect to the principal," I said. She just looked at the bench without responding.

"Mr. Agnew, please. Come in," Principal Koehn said. I followed him into his office and he closed the door behind us. "Please sit down." He motioned to a pair of leather wingback chairs before his desk as he went around to his own chair. I sat, afraid of what was coming.

"What's happened?" I asked.

"I'm very worried, Mr. Agnew. Lori has always been such a good student. A model student. Not just in grades, but in conduct." He paused and picked up a red pencil. He held it before his face, rolling it between his palms. His brown eyes, framed by gold-rimmed glasses, were fixed on the pencil. "How are things at home?"

"Well, okay," I said. "I mean, well, there was the mission accident. Lori lost some friends in that, but she seemed to be doing okay. At home, anyway."

"No unusual behavior?"

"No…" I paused, a mental image of my daughter in her bed, her blankets clutched over her nudity as her first lover raced past me to escape the house. "Well, yes. She, umm, she… I'm not sure how to say it. She lost her virginity yesterday." My voice caught as I said it and I knew I was blushing.

"Hmmm. Interesting," the principal responded, nodding, his

eyes fixed on the pencil that was held still before his nose. Slowly, he lowered it and met my eyes. "Lori skipped her sixth hour class today, Mr. Agnew. One of the local policemen we have patrolling the campus found her and the young man you saw leaving my office having sex in his car in one of the parking lots. He drives a station wagon. They appeared quite comfortable, the officer said."

"Oh God. Oh God." I dropped my head into my hands. It took all the strength I could summon to keep from breaking down and sobbing. Without looking up I asked, "Who was he? She's been with Dan for so long…"

"I'll leave it to Lori to explain her relationship with the young man. As I'm sure you can imagine, students are not permitted to, well, to engage in sexual intercourse on school grounds," the principal said. "If you're ready, I'm going to bring her in here with us." I nodded and he got up and went to the door of his office, opened it and leaned out. "Lori, come in here." She came in and he closed the door, motioning her to the empty chair beside me as he went back to his own.

"I've told your father about what happened," Principal Koehn continued. "I—"

"Lori, how could you?" I blurted. "Why? Why are you doing this?"

She didn't answer, only looked at her hands in her lap. "Lori, would you like to answer your father?"

"I don't know," she said. "I just…I couldn't help it. I just *wanted* it. We didn't get caught this morning when we did it during homeroom."

"What?" Principal Koehn and I said together.

"Yeah. We skipped homeroom and went to his car and did it the first time."

"Lori," I moaned. "Lori. You know about fornication and—"

"Oh come on, Dad. Don't drop the God-bomb on me. I mean, it's just sex. It's natural. And Mom is wrong, it can be incredible."

"Lori Lynn Agnew! You watch your mouth," I said.

She huffed and threw herself into a slouching position, acting like a spoiled child. Acting like her brother often did. I was shocked and had never in my life felt so disappointed.

"As I was saying," the principal interjected. "As I was saying, sexual intercourse on school grounds is a punishable offense. So, I am forced to take action. I'm suspending Lori for three days. She will not be able to make up missed work during that time, so any grades collected in her class will be recorded as zeroes during her suspension. You both understand?"

"Yes," I said, nodding. Lori made no answer. "Lori. Answer the principal. Now."

"Fine. I understand. Big deal," she said.

"You'll think it's a big deal when I get you home, young lady."

"Yeah, whatever. Mom'll just blame it on Amara."

"Amara?" the principal asked.

I sighed. "She's a woman I brought home from Brazil. The only survivor of the burned mission."

"Could she be the negative influence on Lori?" he asked. "She's not a negative influence," Lori said.

"I didn't think so," I said. "Maybe I was wrong."

"Well, that's up to you to decide," Principal Koehn said. "Today is Friday. Lori's suspension will begin on Monday. She can come back to school on Thursday."

"Okay. I understand," I said. "I'll try to send her back like she was last week."

"I hope so, Mr. Agnew. Thank you for coming in." He stood and shook my hand again.

"Lori, let's go," I said. I herded her out of the office, across the deserted campus and into my car. We drove home in silence. I didn't know what to say to her. I wasn't sure I even knew her.

21

What to say? I look back and marvel at how life can seem so normal one moment, then suddenly a man's world can be turned upside down. This is how tornado victims or relatives of murder victims must feel, I remember thinking.

I grounded Lori to the house. I forbade her to drive, to have phone calls. I lectured her, pleaded with her and cried and prayed over her. She only acted fidgety and disinterested. Her only explanation was that she felt an overwhelming urge for sex and did it with the first boy who was agreeable.

Karen blamed Amara. And Amara's presence was my fault, so Karen blamed me, too. She grew very cold toward me, speaking only when necessary and then using as few words as possible. She flinched at any attempt to make physical contact, as if my touch scalded her.

Both Eric and Amara stayed out of the way. For the first time in several years, it seemed something regarding the family had penetrated Eric's shell of heavy metal music and bad attitude. His eyes were wider and seemed filled with surprise every time he looked at anyone in the house, as if he was seeing them for the first time. Amara stayed mostly in her room. Sometimes I heard her talking in there, as if she was not alone, but whenever I knocked and looked in on her she was always sitting on the bed, often reading a Bible.

That is how Friday evening and Saturday went. Sunday was worse. Lori would not get up and dress for church. She claimed she was sick. Ordinarily, I would never have questioned her. Her devotion to the church had always been strong; if she had an excuse to miss service, I knew I could believe her. Now, however, I knew she was lying.

"You need church now more than ever, young lady," I told

her, standing in her doorway and adjusting my necktie. "You don't have a fever and you're not showing any other signs of illness. Get out of that bed and get ready to go."

I stepped away from the door and a moment later I heard her gagging, then vomiting. I hurried back to her doorway to find a stream of vomit down the side of her mattress, dripping onto the carpet. The smell was overpowering.

"Happy now?" she asked.

I was furious. I fully suspected she'd stuck a finger down her throat and made herself throw up. But what proof did I have? I had a teenage girl who, until a few days ago, was the most trustworthy person I'd ever known. She said she was sick. There was vomit on her bed and floor.

"All right, Lori," I said. "You can stay home. Fine. But clean that up."

"Whatever."

I started to respond, to scold her for her bad attitude. Instead, I walked away. I checked in on Eric and found that he was dressed and ready to go and playing a video game while he waited. I went next to Amara's room and knocked on the door. She called for me to come in.

"Amara, you're not ready to go?" I asked when I found her sitting on the bed in a bathrobe.

"I am scared, Milton," she said. "What if they do not like me? What if they drive me away with stones?"

"That's nonsense, Amara. That would never happen."

"Then they are full of sin?"

"What?"

"Is everyone in your church sinful? Only he who is without sin can stone the whore. Is Lori worried about her safety, too?"

"I don't under—" Realization hit me like a slap. "Lori is not a whore. And neither are you. There is nothing to be afraid of. Please get dressed." I started to walk away, but she called me back.

"Milton, what if your God does not want me in his church?"

"Amara, I don't have time for this. All are welcome in God's

177

church. Please. Get dressed. Be ready to go."

I found Karen downstairs, wearing a navy blue dress with a white collar. She looked prim and somehow severe. She diverted her eyes when I tried to hold her gaze.

"Lori is sick," I said. "She vomited. I told her she could stay home. Eric is ready and Amara is getting there."

No answer. I picked up my Bible and the notes for my sermon and sat down, holding the items in my lap. Soon, Amara came down the stairs wearing a demure dress covered in tiny flowers. She wore white shoes and her red hair was swept back from her face and held with a white ribbon. "You look very nice," I said, rising from the chair. I called up the stairs for Eric and he came bounding down the steps.

"Let's go." I ushered them out the door and into the car. The ride to the church was tense and quiet and I was glad when we arrived. I saw by the cars in the parking lot that a few of the elders and the associate pastor were already in the church.

The church is a massive structure of blond brick. The main part of the building is round with a roof like an inverted funnel running up to a gleaming white steeple. Two wings reach away from the body of the building to accommodate Sunday school classrooms. It is typical of modern Protestant churches, which I've always thought lack in character when compared to most Catholic cathedrals or mosques and synagogues.

At the front door, Amara froze in her tracks, staring at the interior of the vestibule as I held the door open. Karen and Eric walked past, not noticing Amara's hesitation. "I cannot enter," she said without looking at me.

"Amara, it's all right. Please come—" I reached for her arm, but when my fingers touched her flesh, she jumped, let out a shriek and began running.

Dumbfounded, I could only stare at her as she raced across the parking lot, crossed the street without checking traffic and vanished into the neighborhood.

"I'm not at all surprised." I looked away from where Amara

had disappeared to find Karen looking at the same spot. She turned her head and stared at me for a moment, as if to be sure I understood she'd been right all along, then went back inside. "Milton, what was that about?" David Ross had replaced

Karen at my side.

"I—I...I really don't know," I said. "She was worried earlier that nobody would like her, that she'd be stoned, actually. But she seemed fine driving over and walking up here. But then... when I opened the door she said she couldn't come in. When I reached for her, she ran. She ran like a frightened rabbit."

"This won't help your effort to find someone to take her into their home," David said, then he, too, left me. Not knowing what else to do, I followed him into the building.

It seemed more than a little surreal to stand at the door and greet my congregation as they arrived. I shook hands. I smiled and listened to tales of ailments, listened to men and women express their regret over the happenings in Brazil. Finally it was time to begin. I went through my office and took the stage from the back door, as usual. I welcomed everyone again, then let Brenda Carlisle, the associate pastor, lead the morning hymns and opening prayer. At last, I stepped to the podium to deliver the sermon I'd worked on for the past few days.

"As the apostle Paul wrote to the Romans, chapter six, verses seven and eight, 'For he who has died has been freed from sin. Now if we died with Christ, we believe that we shall also live with Him'," I began. For a half-hour I spoke about the mission, naming each lost member of my flock and offering some memory. I named many of the villagers and recounted stories of their coming to Christ.

"They are all gone now," I said. "Gone from us, but living forever in the glory of Heaven. I would like now to read from Hebrews, chapter eleven, verse thirteen, 'These all died in faith, not having received the promises, but having seen them afar off were assured of them, embraced them and confessed that they were strangers and pilgrims on the earth.' Our friends, those you knew personally and those who never left the jungle of Brazil, no longer are strangers and pilgrims on this earth. They have gone on to the home that awaits us all. Let's bow our heads and give thanks to God that we knew these people." I led them in a short prayer, then stood uncertainly for a moment, looking at the hundreds of faces peering back at me from the rows of wooden, padded pews. I saw tears in some eyes. Small children played with toys, their parents uncomfortably aware yet thinking it was better to leave them alone so they were quiet.

"It was my intent to introduce someone to you at this point," I said. "All the villagers were killed or fled from the fire, as I said. But there was one person among the ruins when I arrived in the jungle. One woman, alone, naked and without God. It struck me as very unusual to find her there, for she is a white woman and speaks English very well. She told me a horror story of how her own father sold her into slavery from her home in Greece when she was a child. Sold her to a Brazilian drug lord. This woman, Amara, escaped her captor and fled into the jungle, where she would listen to the services outside our mission church, taking food from the villagers but living alone in the dark depths of the jungle.

"I stand before you today and confess that I broke international law. I brought this woman home with me. Yes, I broke international law, but I was following God's law, following the words of Christ our Savior. The village is gone. The church is gone. But our mission work continues in the form of this one waif, this childlike woman who does not know Jesus.

"For the past few days she has lived in my home with my family. However, that is not the best environment for her. She needs to be with people her own age, or with someone without children, someone who can devote more time to nurturing her in the Word of God and the ways of our society. And so I call upon you today to look into your hearts and consider opening your home to Amara. Be the next generation of missionaries from our church."

I paused, looking at my flock as they looked back at me. I

could see the question in their eyes: *Where is she, this woman you ask us to foster?* I closed my eyes; images of Amara fleeing, of Lori covering herself in her bed, of defying me in school, of

Eric with his unholy music and Karen's hard, cold eyes rushed through my mind. *Lord, what have I done wrong?* I opened my eyes, called the ushers forward for the offering and sat down while the plates were passed and the choir sang. After another hymn and a closing prayer, I sent the flock home. Though I went to the main door of the church and shook dozens of hands, no one asked about Amara.

With all the laymen gone and only a few elders and ushers left, I retired to my office. Karen and Eric were waiting for me. "No one offered to take her, did they?" Karen accused.

I dropped myself into my desk chair and put my face in my cupped hands. "No. No one even asked about it," I answered.

"One way or another, you are getting that…that Jezebel out of my house."

"Yes, Karen."

"Can we go now?" Eric asked. "I'm hungry."

"Yes. Let's go." I stood up and ushered them out of the office and through a back door. We drove home in silence.

The house was quiet as we entered. I found Amara sitting in the living room. She looked up at me sheepishly, then lowered her face.

"Lori is gone," she said. "She packed her things and left in a taxi."

22

I raced up the stairs and burst into Lori's room. Clothes were scattered across the unmade bed and the floor. Dresser drawers hung open like broken jaws, clothes spilling out like lolling tongues. A framed family portrait that had stood on the dresser lay on the floor on the other side of the room, the glass broken into long, jagged shards. A single piece of notebook paper was taped to the mirror. I pulled it down with a trembling hand.

I have left home for good. Maybe someday, when I think you can accept me for who I am, I will come back to visit. For now, I have changed from the little girl I was just a week ago. I am a woman and have gone out into the world to live as a woman. I have friends outside Daddy's church, friends who will help me as I am without trying to change me back into what I was. Don't try to find me. I will be 18 before you could find me and then you couldn't stop me, anyway.

"Oh Lori. Oh baby. My baby girl." I staggered to her bed and sat down. Karen had entered the room and now snatched the note from my hand. Eric stood in the doorway of the bedroom.

"See!" Karen shrieked, brandishing the letter in my face. "See what your little slut has done now? Just last week, she says. What is different this week? That red-haired whore was not in our house last week, that's what. You find my daughter!" She fled the room, nearly knocking Eric over before he could get out of the way.

"Dad?"

"Yes, Eric?"

"I'm sorry."

I took a deep, shaky breath and looked at Eric. He was blurry through my tears. "It's not your fault, son. I don't…I don't know what's come over Lori. But thank you."

"Can I see the note?"

I picked it up from the floor where it had fallen when Karen threw it at me and held it out toward Eric. He read it quickly. "I'm going to go call some people," he said. "Maybe somebody knows who her friends are."

I nodded and he turned to go. "Eric," I called. He came back. I stood up and folded my arms around him. It had been years since he'd allowed me to hug him like this. I savored it as much as I could in my sorrow. "Thank you," I said, releasing him. "Thank you."

"No problem, Dad." He hurried out of the room.

I fumbled my cell phone from my pocket and turned it on. My finger was still trembling as I dialed 911. My voice broke several times as I explained that my daughter had run away from home. The operator promised to have a police officer at my house soon.

Within twenty minutes there were two police officers in our living room. Amara had gone to her bedroom sometime earlier, no doubt as soon as Karen had gone downstairs. The officers, a tall black man built like a linebacker and a short but stout blonde woman, asked numerous questions. Karen and I answered them all. I wasn't able to look at the police as I explained Lori's sudden change in behavior over the past few days.

"It was that woman he brought home," Karen spat. "What woman?" the female officer asked.

"A survivor of a mission fire in Brazil," I explained, realizing that I was likely setting myself up for serious trouble discussing Amara, a woman I'd smuggled into the country.

"Can we talk to her?" the male officer asked.

I nodded and turned to Eric, who was seated near the kitchen. "Will you go get Amara?" He ran up the stairs and a few minutes later came down ahead of Amara. I could see the fear in Amara's wide eyes. Both police officers sucked in their breath at the sight of her in her tight shirt and jeans, her hair unbound and falling over her shoulders. Amara came to sit in the only unoccupied chair in the room.

"This is Amara," I said. "She is staying with us temporarily."

"Tell us about your relationship with Lori," the female cop prompted.

"Lori is a very nice girl," Amara said.

"Were you two good friends?" the male asked.

"I think so, although I only knew her for a few days. We went shopping together."

"Did you encourage her to run away from home?"

"No. She was waiting for her taxi when I came back to Milton's house this morning." Amara turned to me. "I am sorry I ran from the church. I couldn't go inside. I just couldn't."

"That's fine," I said. "It's not important now."

"Please say you forgive me. Say it now," she pleaded. "Fine, Amara, fine. I forgive you. Please, tell us about Lori.

She was already packed?"

"You forgive me?"

"Answer us, whore!" Karen screamed, rising from her place on the sofa, her arms raised as if she was ready to attack Amara. "Mrs. Agnew, please sit down," the male officer commanded, his deep voice suddenly hard with authority. Karen sat slowly, her eyes burning as she looked at Amara.

"Amara, I forgive you," I said. "We'll talk about your fear later. Okay? Now please, tell us about Lori."

"She was sitting there," she said, pointing to where the female police officer sat. "She had two suitcases by her feet. She jumped up when I came in and I saw that she was scared. Then she laughed and sat back down. 'It's only you,' she said. 'Why aren't you at church?'" Amara paused. "She said she was leaving, that she couldn't stay here anymore. She said you don't understand her anymore."

"Is that all?" I asked. "Her taxi came then."

"You didn't ask where she was going?"

"She said she was going to stay with some friends who would understand her."

"*Some* friends?" the female officer asked. She looked to me. "Who does she know who lives together as a group, or at least two people living together who might harbor her without telling you?"

"I—I don't know," I said. "I thought I knew all her friends. There's no one like that. No one who would help her hide from us."

"There's obviously someone."

"I don't know."

"All right, Mr. Agnew, Mrs. Agnew," the black man said.

"We'll take this picture and circulate it among the local offices and the other districts around the metro. I'd say there's a good chance she's still in the Oklahoma City area.

"However, her birthday is less than two weeks away and she'll be eighteen then. She's no longer a minor at that point. I know this is hard for you to hear, but when she's an adult, she's no longer a runaway. I'm sorry to say it, but with this note, and at her current age, we won't dedicate a lot of time and manpower to this investigation. We don't have reason to believe she's in any danger at this point."

"What? You're not going to look for her?" I asked.

"We'll check around. We'll contact her employer, talk to teachers and some classmates, but if you're thinking of sweeping the city, no, I'm afraid not."

"But she's my little girl," I begged.

"Mr. Agnew, maybe it was that attitude that made her leave," the female cop offered.

I could only stare for a long moment, disbelieving. Finally I took a deep breath. "Please leave my house. Do what you can. I'll look for my daughter."

"Mr. Agnew, please understand, we'll do everything that is reasonable in this case," the man said, casting a harsh glance at his partner.

"Thank you," I said, making sure it was obvious I was addressing him and not the woman.

"Let's go," the man said, rising from his chair. His female partner also rose. "We'll be in touch. Please call me at the number on the card if you have any additional information," he said. I glanced at the white business card on the coffee table and nodded, then followed them to the front door and closed it after them.

"Should I have stopped her?" Amara asked.

Karen was on her like a cat, her arms flailing as her hands, open and balled into fists, pummeled Amara as the redhead cowered in her chair. Karen was screaming and cursing as she pounded Amara's back and head. I jumped forward and pulled Karen away. She continued to flail her arms and began kicking at me. I couldn't hold her, but couldn't release her to attack Amara again. I turned toward the couch just as a foot connected with my groin. I released Karen and doubled over with such force that I threw her forward. She hit the couch, bounced off, hit the coffee table, knocking it over so that it fell on top of her as she hit the floor.

"Dad, you threw Mom," Eric yelled, rushing past me as I sank to the floor, both hands cupping my genitals, the pain stealing my breath and making my eyes water. Eric's eyes were accusing as he pushed the coffee table aside and asked his mother if she was all right. He helped her up and together they went into the kitchen.

"Are you hurt badly?" Amara asked.

I turned my head to look at her. She was sitting up again, her hair sticking out wildly where Karen had been pulling at it. I shook my head and managed to croak, "I'll be okay. You?"

"I am not hurt."

I nodded and groaned.

23

We heard nothing from Lori. We called the police station relentlessly, begging for information, for more intense searches, for some shred of hope. There was nothing. People from church called. They brought food and put flyers in store windows, on telephone poles and windshields of parked cars. Nothing. It was as though the city had swallowed my little girl.

Karen was brutal. She would not speak to me in a civil manner, even when relaying the latest lack of news from the police. She was emphatic that Lori's fall and disappearance were Amara's fault. Her simmering glare and sharp words drove me from our bed so that I slept on the sofa; I considered going to Lori's bed, but simply could not do it.

Eric, who it had seemed for the briefest of moments I might be able to reconnect with, took his mother's side, as he generally did. He still believed I had thrown Karen to the floor when she kicked me in the testicles. Maybe I had. Eric was sullen and uncommunicative to me. I eavesdropped every afternoon as he recounted conversations about Lori he'd had with people at school. Nobody knew where she was.

Amara kept to herself, hiding in her bedroom. She would not come down to eat because of Karen's open hostility. I took food to her and gathered her dishes. She would peer from her door, then scurry to the bathroom when she needed to. I felt sorry for her, but at the same time was reluctant to show too much compassion for her for fear of giving Karen more reason to be angry.

Not one member of my congregation asked about taking Amara into their homes. As people would come with casseroles or baskets of fried chicken, I would ask if they had considered my request. "We simply can't do it," they would say. No, they didn't know of anyone who might be able to take her in. They were sorry.

They knew it must be very hard on us.

They had no idea how hard it was.

Several days passed this way. I was unable to work; I simply couldn't concentrate, couldn't pull my thoughts together to form a sermon. I called Brenda Carlisle and asked her to take the duties of pastor that Sunday. I spent the weekend sitting by the phone, avoiding Karen's glance, wondering where Lori was right then, what was she doing. Did she have food? She had never returned to work and no one from the restaurant admitted to having any clue where she might be. That was the only news we received from the police. I felt sure somebody from her job wasn't being honest. Where else would she have met anyone who would help her hide from her parents?

I called one of the local television news stations and told them about Lori's absence. They sent a reporter and cameraman out; the reporter, Kristi Simpson, was a perky young woman with short brown hair and a too-bright smile. Her sadness was feigned and when I showed her Lori's note she quit pretending. "Mr. Agnew, I'm not sure we'll run this story," Kristi said. "In a few days your daughter will be eighteen and not a missing person, based on this note."

"But she's not eighteen now. Not today," I argued. "She's a missing child today. I just want her to come home." I broke down and buried my face in my hands, crying, my tears being soaked up by the single sheet of notebook paper Lori had left us. I felt Karen rise abruptly from the sofa.

"Please excuse my husband," she said curtly. Her footsteps moved away, leaving me alone with the news crew. I pulled my hands from my face and wiped my eyes.

"I'm sorry," I said. "It's been a very hard week."

"I understand," Kristi said. "Listen, I'll try to get this on the air. You said I could use this photo?" She waved a print of Lori's senior picture at me. I nodded. "Okay. We need to get going. Good luck to you, Mr. Agnew. I hope she comes home."

"Thank you," I mumbled. I didn't bother getting up to show

them out.

That night, the TV news station showed Lori's photo, her note and a few seconds of me crying. I turned it off.

Two more days crawled by. It was the eve of Lori's birthday. I lay on the sofa in the dark house, staring at the ceiling and thinking back eighteen years to when Karen and I were young and she was pregnant. It had been a restless night. She was having contractions, but the hospital had sent us home, saying it wasn't time yet. We couldn't sleep. We'd walked around the small house where we lived then, gone outside and walked around the block in the dark, and finally returned to our living room and sat down to watch a videotape of "Casablanca." About thirty minutes into the movie, Karen's water broke. We rushed to the hospital, crying and laughing, checked in and were shown to a delivery room. Two hours later I held a red-cheeked, beautiful baby girl in trembling hands; photos showed my eyes were round as an owl's as I gazed at Lori for the first time.

I didn't realize I was crying again until my breath caught in my throat, making my body hitch under the thin blanket. I wiped at my eyes. I wasn't the only one weeping. I listened, thinking Karen must be having the same thoughts alone in our bed. But the sobbing came from upstairs. I threw off the blanket and went quietly up the stairs. Amara's door was slightly ajar and the crying was coming from within. I opened the door and stepped inside.

Amara was sitting on her bed, dressed in a white cotton nightgown that came to mid-thigh. Her head was bowed, her hair hanging around her and hiding her face. Her shoulders shook slightly with her sobs.

"Are you okay?" I asked.

She lifted her head and fixed me with green eyes that seemed all the more intense behind her tears. Her lips trembled. She shook her head and dropped her gaze again. I stepped into the room and pushed the door to where it was almost but not completely closed, then went and knelt before her.

"What's wrong?"

"I've made your daughter leave and am ruining your marriage," she said.

"No, Amara. No. None of this is your fault. I don't know what happened to Lori. Somebody was giving her bad advice, but it must have been going on for a long time. Long before you got here. Even if you'd meant to...to corrupt her, you didn't have time to do it. As to Karen...that one is harder, but it's not your fault."

"Oh Milton, you're always too kind to me," she said. Without warning, she pushed herself off the bed and embraced me where I knelt. Her arms around my neck were soft but securely locked. Her hair covered my face, filling my nose with her fragrance as her head pressed against my lips. Without thought, I kissed the side of her head.

She lifted her face and gazed into my eyes for a moment. In that moment we both knew that I was lost. Our lips met, pressed together, needing one another, opened and my tongue found hers. My arms unlocked and my hands roamed over the thin cotton of her gown. She stood, pulling me up with her, then lowered herself onto the bed, compelling me to follow with deep kisses and eager hands.

I pushed the gown up, my hands finally sliding over the perfect white skin of her back, around her sides until they cupped her firm young breasts. She broke our kiss and pulled the gown over her head, dropping it to the floor behind me as my hands held desperately to her breasts. I dipped my head and kissed first one beautiful erect pink nipple and then the other. Her hand slid down my arm, over my stomach and onto my painfully hardened penis. She squeezed it, causing me to moan. With both hands she began tugging my pajama bottoms down. I let go of her and tore away the pants, pushing them into a ball under the covers, my underwear tangled up with them. She slid her panties off and tossed them aside.

I lifted the blanket and looked at her nakedness. She was exquisite, smooth and pale, young and firm. The triangle of her red pubic hair pointed to what I needed most. I slid my hand down her belly and through the small patch of hair. Her legs opened to receive my needy fingers. She arched her neck and moaned slightly as my middle finger entered her. With the hand closest to me she groped for my own sex organ, found it and squeezed it hard, pulled it quickly in a few short strokes, then pulled me toward her.

I slipped over one leg and positioned myself over her groin.

The blanket fell away, revealing our nakedness. She was open, wet and ready for me. Her hand continued to pull at my penis, directing it toward her gleaming vulva.

And without warning I ejaculated, shooting stream after stream of sticky semen over her body from breasts to pubic hair. She released me and relaxed, a playful smile on her face. "Oh Milton, you wanted me too much," she said. With one hand she began to caress herself, rubbing my semen over her body as if it were a moisturizing lotion, while with the other she reached between her legs and masturbated ferociously. I could only crouch between her legs and watch. Just as she was near her climax, her body tensed and arching from the bed, I heard the bedroom door fly open behind me.

My heart and soul came loose, melted and sank into my bowels in that moment. I couldn't turn around, couldn't face Karen. I didn't have to. She left the room, yelling for Eric. I heard her in his room, demanding that he get dressed, pack what he needed for school and get in the car.

"Your father is in bed with his whore!" she screamed as she passed Amara's door, heading for the stairs.

Amara said nothing and did not move as I scrambled off the bed and clawed under the blankets for my pants and underwear. I dressed and hurried out of the room, almost running down Eric in the hallway. He looked from me into Amara's room, saw her lying naked on the bed, saw the guilt in my eyes. "I hate you, Dad. I hate you. How could you do that to

Mom?"

"Eric—"

"Fuck off." He slapped away the hand I held toward him,

hitched his backpack up and walked away, a duffle bag held in one hand.

I passed him on the stairs, racing toward our bedroom where I heard Karen slamming drawers. A wooden jewelry box flew at my head as soon as I stepped into the room. I ducked and it crashed to the floor behind me. Bottles of fingernail polish, vials of makeup, framed pictures and other bric-à-brac followed. I couldn't avoid it all. But finally she ran out of projectiles. I jumped onto the bed, ran across it and jumped off to catch her in my arms. She fought, slapping at me, screaming, but I held her tightly.

Until Eric's fist slammed into my left kidney. The unexpected blow caused me to release my hold on Karen. I turned my head toward my son in time to see his fist coming at me again. The second blow was to my stomach. I doubled over and caught the next one on the temple. I fell sideways, against a dresser, then to my knees on the floor. I looked up at Eric and saw that he was ready to hit me again, aiming for my nose.

"Stop it!" Karen shouted. "Stop. Get in the car, Eric. We're going somewhere else for tonight. I'll decide what we'll do next later. Come on."

Without another look at me, she left the room, dragging a suitcase behind her. I watched her leave the room, then turned back to Eric.

"This is for all the years of being a fucking hypocrite," he said just before his fist smashed into my mouth. Blood flew from my busted lips as I rocked back on my knees. "Let's see you fuck her now," he added, kicking me in the crotch. I fell to the floor, my hands in my lap as blood poured from my mouth. The pain was incredible. The white pain turned black as my eyes rolled into my head.

When I opened my eyes again I was lying on my bed and Amara was holding a Ziploc bag filled with ice on my genitals.

24

The next two days were similar to those days Amara and I spent in the jungle of Brazil. It was just the two of us, living together in unfamiliar territory. With Karen, Eric and Lori gone, Amara abandoned her room to become my constant companion. We talked a good deal about very little, mostly whatever happened to be on the television at the moment. Often, I wept piteously and she comforted me with soothing words.

During those two days I had no word from my family. And then, mid-morning of the third day, the telephone rang. It was Karen. She didn't bother with a greeting.

"I'm divorcing you," she said. Her voice wasn't completely clear; I knew she was on a speaker phone. "We can do this the easy way, or you can make it hard. I have a lawyer. We've drawn up papers for you to sign. I get half of everything. If you sign them, it's over. If you don't, we go to court and everyone finds out what you've done."

"Karen? Divorce? But—"

"Mr. Agnew," a male voice interrupted. "My name is Robert Parker. Karen has hired me to represent her in divorce proceedings, if it comes to that. Based on the information she's provided me, I feel certain the most lenient of courts would grant Karen what we have asked for in the papers she's mentioned. Probably, she could get more."

"But Karen, a divorce? Can't we talk about it?"

"No."

"But Karen, after so many years—"

"She's still there, isn't she?" Karen asked. I couldn't answer at first.

"Isn't she?"

"Yes."

"Sign the papers, Milton," Karen said.

I was sitting at the kitchen table, staring through the window in the back door, watching a sparrow on the porch railing as I held the cordless phone. I couldn't find my voice. The sparrow flew away. "I'll sign," I said at last.

"Very good, Mr. Agnew," Robert Parker said. "Can you come by my office and sign the papers today?"

"Yes."

"How soon?"

"Now. Will you be there, Karen?"

"It isn't necessary for her to be here," the lawyer said. "I'll have her sign now."

"Fine."

"Shall I count on seeing you, say, an hour from now?" Parker asked.

"Yes."

"Good. I'll see you then. Good-bye."

"Bye, Karen," I said.

There was a silence, as if the lawyer was looking at her for a response. I could imagine her shaking her head. Then the line went dead.

I considered leaving Amara at home when I left, but thoughts of her possibly logging onto the computer and spending more money forced me to rethink that. I knew it wouldn't look very respectable to show up to sign divorce papers with the woman accused of being my lover at my side, but it seemed my best option. Together, following the directions we had been given, we drove southeast on the Northwest Expressway, turned south on Classen Boulevard and went to the lawyer's office, an old Victorian-style home converted to a law office.

A perky young receptionist with knowing eyes ushered us right into a conference room and told us to sit at the long, polished wooden table to wait for Mr. Parker. I sat in a very comfortable chair made of chrome and thick gray cushions. Amara sat beside me on my left, reaching over to hold my hand under the table. After a moment, a petite man in his late thirties entered the room with a hand extended toward me. His other hand held a brown folder. I rose slightly and shook his hand.

"I'm Robert Parker," he said, taking a seat at the head of the table. "Thank you for coming. Shall we get right to this?" I nodded. The lawyer pulled a sheaf of papers from his folder and spread them out before us.

"Basically, since you don't own the house, this doesn't have to be very complicated at all," Parker said. "You will sign over ownership of the 1999 Ford Explorer Karen drove away in, although you will continue to make the payments and cover the insurance premium. You will divide your IRA in half, depositing half the current amount into an account I will set up for Karen."

"And Eric?"

"Custody of your son will be given to your wife. Soon to be ex-wife."

"Why? Why is she doing this?"

"Mr. Agnew, it is my understanding that Karen caught you in an act of adultery and that there was a physical dispute between you, her and your son immediately afterward."

I couldn't answer. I couldn't face him. I stared at the papers as new tears came to my eyes. "What about visitation?" I asked. "Will I get to see Eric?"

"Karen is against it, but I have advised her that a court very likely would give you monthly visitation rights because there is no previous history of violence from you."

"Violence? Did she tell you how she was throwing things at me? I was only trying to stop her. I ran across the bed to grab her and we fell. And then...and then Eric...beat me. I never raised a hand. Not against either of them."

"We assumed you would sign the paperwork today and not let this matter degenerate into a costly and embarrassing court battle. You *are* a minister, right?" The man smiled a shark's smile. "Do I take it that you would prefer to bring this matter to court?"

I thought about it. A court case would be humiliating, both personally and professionally. And what could I win? I knew that the accusation would be just as damaging as confirmation. And, what could I hope to win? Getting Karen to come back? She'd left and filed for divorce after being gone for only two days, during which she'd made no effort to contact me, no effort to try to fix what was wrong or even hear my explanation. Nothing but a phone call to announce she was divorcing me.

"No," I whispered.

"Then sign here," Parker said, pushing a pen into my limp hand and pointing at a line on a sheet of paper. "We also have decided on an equitable amount of alimony and child support you will pay monthly. Sign here. And here." I signed my name many times.

"I feel that Karen is being very fair, considering that she holds all the cards in this case," Parker said.

"Not even talking to me is fair? Not giving me a chance to explain? That's fair?"

"I see you brought your concubine with you today," Parker said. "At least, I assume this is the same woman Karen found you in bed with. Unless you have others she doesn't know about."

I was as angry then as I ever remember being before that moment. I know my face flushed deeply and I remember gritting my teeth. I held back most of what I wanted to say, but not all. "Shut your mouth," I said.

The shark smile never faltered. "Karen has hired a moving crew to take her things out of the house tomorrow. You'll be required to leave the house while she's there."

"Required? I doubt that."

"Oh Mr. Agnew, I think you'll do as I ask. You will be somewhere else. The police will be standing by. I assure you that if you harass Karen tomorrow you will be arrested and we'll go to court to settle this divorce. She may even decide to file charges for the earlier attack."

Amara's hand gripped my left bicep. I bit my tongue and didn't respond to the lawyer's statement. "Where is she going?" I asked.

"Karen has made arrangements to rent a house in Woodward, near her sister. The Woodward police will be notified of your history and likely will be present when you arrive in town for your monthly visitations with Eric."

"Woodward."

"Mr. Agnew, do not entertain hopes of harassing Karen in her new home. She is very angry with you and has told me repeatedly that there will be no reconciliation. Leave her alone. Stay here with your jungle queen." His eyes flicked to Amara.

"You're gay."

"What?" Finally, I had said something that caught him off guard.

"No straight man looks at Amara that way. With scorn," I said. "Only a gay man could look at her without desire." It was a petty thing to say, a cheap shot, but it was the only offensive I could muster.

"My sexual orientation is of no concern here," Parker said. Amara's laughter was sudden, loud and ringing. Parker glared at her as he crammed his papers back into his folder. I turned so I could see Amara behind me. Her head was thrown back and she was laughing heartily. Our eyes met and she winked at me. "Milton, I am very proud of you," she said between bursts of laughter.

"Enjoy yourselves," Parker said to me, rising from his seat. "Just remember who it is who just lost half of everything he owns. I trust you can find your way out." He left us in the conference room, Amara still laughing and me grinning more than I should have considering I really had just agreed to give up half of everything and still make the sizable payments on the SUV Karen had taken. We got up and left the office, the receptionist looking at us very queerly as we walked past her desk.

The drive home was mostly quiet, though we did trade some off-color comments about Karen's lawyer. We stopped off at a Sonic drive-in and bought two huge Diet Cokes, sucking on the red straws as we continued the drive to Prairie Valley.

There was a sheriff's car parked in front of my house when we got home. I pulled into the driveway, opening the garage door with the remote, but turned off the car's engine when I saw a uniformed man getting out of the patrol car. I threw open my door and hurried to greet him, leaving my drink in the cup holder.

"Did you find my daughter?"

"Are you Milton Agnew?" the man asked. He was an Oklahoma County deputy sheriff. His uniform was mercilessly pressed. His gold badge gleamed in the early afternoon sunlight. He wore a hat with a round brim, large mirrored sunglasses, a groomed brown mustache and no expression at all on his face.

"Yes. Yes, I'm Milton Agnew. Did you find Lori? Did you find my daughter?"

"Mr. Agnew, this is a restraining order," the policeman said, pushing a folded piece of paper at me. "You are hereby ordered to remain no nearer than one hundred feet from Karen Agnew and her son Eric Agnew. Do you understand?"

"What?"

"The restraining order is specifically to ensure that you will not be present between the hours of eight a.m. and five p.m. tomorrow when a crew hired by and overseen by Karen arrives to gather her belongings from this house," the deputy said. "But it remains in effect for six months."

"A restraining order?"

"Mr. Agnew, do you understand about the restraining order?" the deputy asked. "If you need me to read it and explain it to you, I will do so."

I looked at him for a moment, noting that he had a large brown mole on his right cheek. He hadn't bothered to remove his sunglasses and I could see two reflected images of my own confused face in the lenses, Amara standing behind my left shoulder, looking on with an interested expression.

"I understand what a restraining order is," I said. "But why? Why would she do this?"

"It's my understanding there was a physical altercation between yourself and your wife and son," the deputy responded mechanically. "Personally, I'd like to whip the shit out of you myself. I don't like men who hit their wives and kids."

"I never, *never* hit them. Never."

"Milton, is this more bad news?" Amara asked, placing a comforting hand on my shoulder.

"The other woman," the deputy said, his face still devoid of expression. "I figured as much."

"I understand the restraining order," I said. "Is that all you want?"

"Watch your tone, Mr. Agnew," the man said, reaching up and slowly removing his sunglasses. His blue eyes danced with dark light. "I may interpret it as a threat to a police officer. I am done with you and will be on my way. You violate that order, though, and I'll come visit you again." He gave Amara a lingering look, his eyes finally showing some emotion—lust, tinged with something violent—then he put his sunglasses on and turned away. I watched him walk back to his car and get in. The engine started and he drove away.

I looked around the neighborhood, but didn't see the flick of curtains falling into place, couldn't tell how many of my neighbors had just witnessed what had happened. Amara's grip on my arm tightened.

"Come, Milton. We should go inside," she said. I let her lead me into the house through the garage door. I sat at the kitchen table, staring at the restraining order, unable to focus on the text.

And then Amara was leaning over my shoulder, her hair covering our faces like a veil of fire as she kissed my cheek and ear. "You no longer are a married man, Milton Agnew," she said.

"A judge has to sign those papers, I think," I answered dully. "A technicality since I agreed to everything." My mind was telling me to make her stop, that it was still wrong, but my body was responding to Amara's kisses and to her roving hands.

"She is divorcing you for adultery and we did not even really have intercourse," she whispered.

"No. We didn't." I felt my blood beginning to pump faster.

"She told the police and her gay lawyer that you beat her and your son."

"She did." My heart hammered in my chest. "Will you come to my bed?"

"No." I stood up, very aware of my penis jutting forward in my pants. "I'm taking you to my bed."

She smiled as I took her arm and pulled her after me. In the bedroom, I tore away my clothes, throwing them as they came off. She had only removed her jeans by the time I was naked. I grabbed the front of her shirt with both hands and ripped it open; buttons flew off, bouncing off my chest like bullets off Superman's pectorals. I grasped one of Amara's breasts firmly and kissed her hard on the mouth. She responded with her hot tongue and her hands pulling me tighter. I pushed her onto the bed and entered her, thrusting angrily, taking her in the violent, uninhibited way I'd always wanted to experience but had never been allowed. I grunted as I rutted on her, finally growling and slobbering like a rabid animal as my climax neared.

"Damn you, Karen!" I screamed as I emptied myself into Amara. My body was tensed, my back arched and my knuckles white where I held Amara's arms pinned to the bed. Her face flushed red as she experienced her own orgasm. Spent, I sagged forward, my face buried in her hair as it fanned across the pillow.

25

We spent most of the rest of the day in bed and slept together there that night. The next morning we arose early and showered together, making love again under the hot spray of water. We dressed and left the house at a quarter before eight. As we were leaving the Prairie Valley subdivision I saw Karen entering, a large moving van following her. I know she saw me but showed no acknowledgement, so I didn't either.

"Are you hungry?" I asked Amara. "Very."

We drove to the nearest International House of Pancakes and ordered huge breakfasts, eating slowly and talking about the headlines of The Oklahoman newspaper.

"Milton," Amara said. "I am sorry."

"For what?"

"For what has happened to you. It is my fault."

"No, it's not. If Karen hadn't been so…so inhibited, let's say, I never would have thought to go to bed with another woman."

"If I had not been there, you would not have had another woman available."

"True," I agreed around a mouthful of hash browns. I swallowed and took a drink of orange juice. "I won't kid you, Amara. I can't say I'm happy about what happened. I mean, Karen is—was my wife. For a long time. But now…it's so strange. She threw it all away. Yes, I made a mistake by getting into your bed. Never mind how that actually turned out. That was wrong. But she isn't even willing to discuss it. She won't even consider forgiving me. It feels almost like she wanted some excuse to get out."

"She will not forgive you," Amara said quietly. I wasn't sure if it was a question or if she was simply repeating what I had said.

"In all her years as a Christian she hasn't learned to forgive," I said.

"That is the most important element of your faith, isn't it?"

"Absolutely. Christ went to the cross so that we can be forgiven. He forgave the Jews and Romans who sent him there. And Karen won't even hear my apology."

"Would you change it now?" she asked. "I think you enjoy making love to me. If Karen would hear your plea and accept your apology—if she gave her forgiveness—would you bring her back into your bed?"

"Yes, Amara, I would." I expected her to pout, to look away, to show some sign of anger or jealousy, but she only gazed back at me, smiling faintly. "Don't get me wrong," I said, compelled to explain myself despite her lack of complaint. "You are fantastic. You are—" I suddenly stopped and looked around, then lowered my voice. "You are everything I—any man—could ever want from a lover. But I took a vow to remain with Karen until death do us part."

"But you are not dead."

"Then we should stop," I said, smiling at her.

"I do not believe you want to stop, Milton Agnew."

"It all feels very strange to me," I said. "I was very angry. I'm still sad. Sad over losing Lori, of not even knowing where she is or what she's doing. Sad that I've lost my wife and my son. Sad that my son, my only son, turned on me the way he did. And yet, I feel renewed, like a weight has been lifted from me that I never really knew I was carrying. And I feel guilty that I feel that way." I shook my head.

We turned our attention to our food for a while, until my cell phone rang. It was Henry Hopkins, the church elder who had accompanied me to the homes of the lost missionaries.

"Milton, we need you to meet us at the church today," Henry said. "We have some serious matters to discuss with you."

"What's up?" I asked. "Is it about exhuming the bodies?"

"No, Milton, it's not. It's about…it's about your adultery." My heart beat several times before I remembered to breathe.

"How did you hear about that?"

"Karen's divorce attorney phoned David late yesterday. When can you be here, Milton?"

"Henry, what is this about? Really, what is it about? Please tell me how bad it is."

"Milton, I'm sorry. I truly am. When can you be here?"

"Half an hour."

"Make it an hour so I can get the rest of the council gathered," Henry said. "Okay?"

"All right, Henry. An hour." I put the phone back into my pocket and took a shaky breath.

"More bad news," Amara stated.

"Yes. I suspect I now have one hour left as pastor of Prairie Valley Community Church."

The council of elders was waiting for me in the sanctuary of the church. Their faces were grim; some would not meet my gaze nor return my greeting. Henry came forward and shook my hand. "Milton, I want you to know I'm sorry about this."

"I understand, Henry. Thank you," I said. "I'm glad Amara didn't come with you."

"She's in the car. She wouldn't come inside."

David Ross stood up and took charge of the gathering before Henry could say anything else. "Milton, will you come up here and sit on the edge of the stage here?" David called, pointing to a place on the stage in front of the first pew where the rest of the elders were settling in. I did as he asked, taking a seat and looking at the council, twelve men and women over the age of forty. Henry took a seat among them; David remained standing between me and them and a little to my left.

"We all know why we're here," David said.

"I'm not completely sure I do," I said. David cast an exasperated look at me.

"Very well, Milton," he said. "We are here to excuse you from your position as minister of this church. Unless you can convince us why we should not." He paused. "Can you?"

"Just so it's in the open, upon what grounds are you seeking

Steven E. Wedel

to fire me?"

"Adultery," David replied. "We cannot have a minister who is engaging in adultery. Not to mention the accusations of violence brought against you by your wife and son."

"Karen's lawyer spun you his full story, I see. For what it's worth, I never actually had sexual relations with Amara—or anyone else—prior to Karen filing for divorce. And I have never hit any member of my family."

Lisa Turner, a woman in her mid-fifties, a secretary at one of the local community colleges, spoke up timidly. "Milton, we were told that Karen caught you in bed with this young woman. The one you brought home from Brazil. Is that true?"

"That is true," I confessed.

"Have you adopted President Clinton's definition of sex?" asked Adam Brahm. "If you're in bed with a woman, and from what we were told there were no clothes involved, that is sex by most standards."

"You may define it how you choose," I said. "I acted inappropriately with Amara. I do not deny that. I've been under a huge amount of stress, with Lori running away from home and Karen blaming Amara for that and, just for Karen's jealousy in the beginning. She was accusing me when there was no crime. She was cold and distant. This is no excuse, I know. What I did was wrong. It seems there is no Christian forgiveness here."

"Have you repeated the offense?" David asked.

"I have signed the papers Karen sent and the divorce she wants will be finalized as soon as a judge signs them."

"That is no answer to what I asked," David said.

How to say it? It was no easy task. I knew that any selection of words I used now would damn me in their eyes. I looked for a way of admitting it without it sounding so cheap and tawdry. "Amara has become my companion," I said.

"Milton, please, just answer the question," Henry said. "This is painful enough. Are you having sex with her?"

"Yes, Henry," I said. "Yes I am."

204

"Milton, how could you?" Lisa asked. "Karen is such a lovely woman. So kind and giving and always standing by your side."

"I'm sorry, Lisa," I said. "I won't speak ill of my soon-to-be ex-wife. That won't help anybody. However, I will say that I was hurt by her immediate actions. She never gave me a chance to explain, to apologize or anything. She left the house and the next message I had from her was delivered by her attorney and a deputy."

"The restraining order," David said. "I see that your lip is slightly swollen. I understand Eric did that during your altercation with him."

"Altercation? I was trying to hold on to Karen to keep her from throwing things at me when Eric attacked me."

"So you admit you physically fought with your son?" Adam asked.

"No, I do not. I say that he beat me. That I never raised a hand against him." The image of Eric standing over me, his eyes full of hate as his fist drove toward my face nearly brought tears to my eyes. I looked to the floor and forced the memory away. Somebody addressed me but I couldn't respond at first.

"Milton?" David called again. I looked up at him. His face was stern, but maybe there was sorrow in his eyes. "There also is the matter of your reckless spending of church money. Alone, that would not be such an issue. Certainly you and I already have discussed it and I felt like we'd reached an agreement. However, it seems that in the past week you have used the Visa card issued to you by the church to access pornographic Internet sites."

"What?" I stared at David, thinking he had to be lying, making the charges against me worse than they were. "But I've never done that. Never."

David reached into the inside pocket of his blazer and pulled out a folded piece of paper. He handed it to me and I unfolded it. It was an activity statement printed from the Web site of the bank that issued my church credit card. There was a short but expensive list of pornographic Internet sites listed in the expense record.

"I didn't do this," I said.

"The statement shows the last four digits of the card issued to you and your name is on the statement," David said.

"Eric?" I wondered aloud. Could he have taken the card from my wallet and used it from the computer in his room?

"Your son did this?" Henry asked.

"I don't know," I said. "Last week I would have defended him. I would have thought he'd never do such a thing. But now…I just don't know."

"I have contacted the administrators of three of these sites," David said. "The username associated with this card number is 'astarte.' Are you familiar with that name?"

"Of course," I said. "It's a variation of the name of the consort of Baal."

"Yes, we know that," David said. "Do you use that name?"

"No."

"Is it likely Eric would have used a feminine name to log on to these sites?"

"I don't know."

"Milton, could it have been Amara?" Henry asked.

"No, she—" I stopped, thinking of the eBay bids. I had forgotten about those and wondered suddenly what had become of the items she'd purchased. "She could have," I said.

"Milton, I really don't see that we have any choice in this matter," David said. "The adultery alone is enough grounds for us to dismiss you. The accusations of violence and the spending, both going off to the Amazon without approval and these porn sites, though maybe circumstantial, just make the case against you more compelling."

"I understand," I said, my voice cracking.

"Let's vote and get this over with," David said. "All those in favor of terminating the contract of Milton Agnew and awarding the severance package we spoke of, say aye." He paused and then all twelve members, even Henry, responded in the affirmative. "Those opposed?" Silence.

"I'm sorry, Milton," Henry offered. I nodded without looking at him.

"We've agreed to give you one month's salary as a severance package," David said. "You also have that month—thirty days from today—to vacate the house. Please, Milton, don't make us take action to evict you."

"No, David. I wouldn't do that," I said.

"I think we're adjourned then," David said. Ten of the members on the pew stood and hurried away from me. Henry stepped before me and put a hand on my shoulder. I didn't want it there, but resisted the urge to knock it away.

"I'm sorry, Milton," he said again. "If you…well, if you want to come see me sometime, I'd be glad to talk with you."

"As my therapist?" I asked, finally looking up at him. "No thank you, Henry. I think your vote showed how you would treat me."

"Milton, I had to vote in the best interest of the church," he said. "It wasn't personal."

"I suppose not, since it wasn't your career being voted on." Henry pulled his hand from my shoulder and walked away without speaking again. To my surprise, David took a seat beside me.

"He was telling the truth, Milton. We all voted in the interest of the church."

"Uh-huh."

"Milton, I'm going to tell you something I've never told another person," David said. I looked over at him and his deep brown eyes caught mine and held me glued to him. "Five years after we were married I found out my own Felicia had been having an affair with another man. It had been going on for about eighteen months when she finally told me about it." He paused; I couldn't speak. That Felicia Ross had been unfaithful to her husband was something I found very hard to accept.

"I forgave her for it," David said. "It wasn't easy. It was my fault, really. A young black man trying to earn a living as an accountant in the 1960s, I guess I spent too much time on my career and supporting the civil rights movement and not enough time with my new wife. I forgave her for it and it was a wake-up call for our marriage. We became much closer after that."

"Why are you telling me this, David? Karen won't even talk to me."

"This isn't about you and Karen. I understand it's too late for that, Milton. Karen is gone. You've made that choice. I'm telling you this because I want you to understand that, even though I forgave my Felicia for her adultery, I would have voted against her today just as I did you. A minister has to be a role model. Does that mean he or she is perfect? No, of course not. Only Christ Jesus is perfect. We could forgive you for what you did. But the fact you are continuing to engage in sexual activity with this young woman you brought home shows a lack of remorse.

"And, as elitist as this may sound, this church is not interested in a reformed minister," David continued. "We do not want a minister who will stand in the pulpit and tell us of his past sins. That just isn't the style of this congregation. Do you understand?"

"Yes, David. I understand. I'm still fired and have a month to get out of the house I don't own." I made to stand up, but David grabbed my hand. The gesture was terribly out of character for him. I looked down into his lined face and saw real compassion.

"As a friend, Milton, I forgive you and will help you if I can. As an elder of this church, I have to enforce the church's rules, but as a Christian I am available to you if you need help."

"Thank you, David," I said, my voice tense. I extracted my hand and walked away.

I left the church, unsure if I would bother to return for my personal things left in the office. Mostly they were photos of a family I no longer had. The parking lot was empty except for my Cadillac, David's Lincoln Town Car and the little compact car owned by the church secretary, Linda Addison. Amara was watching me as I walked toward my car.

"It did not go well," she said as I slid in behind the steering wheel. "The faces of those who left earlier showed they were not happy."

"It didn't go well for me," I said. "As to them being unhappy, I can't be so sure about that."

"You are not the priest anymore?"

"Minister, not priest. And no, I'm not." I started the car and dropped the gearshift into drive, but did not release the brake. I turned to Amara. "What happened with that stuff you ordered on the computer?"

"Some of it has arrived," she said. "I put it in my room in your house. You were angry that I bought it, so I did not show it to you."

"Did you—" I was going to ask about the pornography, but decided I didn't want the answer yet. The folded credit card statement was crumpled in my pants pocket. "Did I what?"

"Never mind," I said, beginning to back out of the parking slot. "We have to find a new place to live. And I have to find a job."

26

Since I couldn't go home, we ate a quick lunch and went house-hunting. It was a very surreal experience to be looking for a place to live with a woman who wasn't Karen. I kept asking myself, *Can this be real? Is anything from the past few weeks really happening?* It was happening. My daughter was lost somewhere, my son had beaten me and my wife had left me. How can a life fall apart so quickly?

Oh, but the downward spiral was still in the early stages.

Money was a problem already. My salary with the church had by no means been extraordinary. Living in the house owned by the church had been a large chunk of what I earned. My bank account was healthy enough—certainly not bloated, but not anemic—but I wasn't sure how long I would have to live on that money before finding another job. I vowed not to touch the money remaining to me in my individual retirement account.

Obviously, I was not going to go out and buy a house for me and Amara. We looked at homes for rent. I was torn, on one hand wanting to get as far away from Prairie Valley as I could, but on the other wanting to stay close just in case Lori should come back. That was ridiculous, though, as living in the subdivision was out of the question considering the scandal I'd caused with Amara. And I knew the houses were out of my price range now that I'd have to pay for my home.

I went to a home finder and paid a fee I felt was too high to look through stacks of notebooks at available houses without sufficient descriptions. I made a long list of addresses and phone numbers, then took Amara and we drove around the Oklahoma City metro area looking at the houses on our list. Precious few of them were worth calling about, but we eventually made arrangements to look inside a two bedroom house in a neighborhood that seemed to be well kept. The rental was being handled by a national realty company; the name of the agent was, I think, Virginia Dillon, a small but energetic woman in her mid-sixties, I'm sure.

"Will it just be you and your daughter living here?" she asked as she opened the door of the house for us.

"Amara isn't my daughter," I said, then realized I should have just let her believe her misconception. But, with Lori missing, I reacted without thinking. Virginia gave me a disapproving look and didn't respond. "Yes, it'll just be the two of us."

"What do you do for a living, Mr. Agnew?" she asked. "I'm a…I'm a minister."

"Oh really? At what church?"

"I'm sort of looking for a new flock," I said, looking around the small living room but suddenly feeling so embarrassed that I couldn't take in any details of what I was seeing.

"Does that mean you are unemployed?"

"Yes, ma'am, I guess it does," I said.

"You have some other source of income we can verify?" she asked.

"Well, no. I don't. Other than a month's severance from my last job."

"You know you'll have to have a source of income before we can rent to you."

I looked at her for a long moment, the reality of my situation sinking in a little deeper. I nodded. "Amara," I called. She had wandered off toward the back of the house. She appeared in a doorway. "Come on. We'll have to keep looking."

"I'm sure you understand," Virginia said. "We have to know you'll be able to pay the rent."

"Yes, ma'am, I do understand," I said. "I completely understand and I'm very sorry we've taken up your time this afternoon." I ushered Amara out of the house and back into the car. We drove away as Virginia was locking the front door of the house.

"Did it cost too much?" Amara asked.

"In a way, I guess it did. This is going to be a problem. Any respectable landlord is going to expect me to have a job so I can pay the rent. I don't have a job. I've never been fired. I've never been unemployed. Even as a teenager I never lost a job and never quit one until I had another one lined up. I'm not sure what to do."

"Can you not get another job?"

"I don't know. I really don't know. I...we...Our relationship will seem scandalous and that's going to make it difficult. Ministers are not supposed to commit adultery, lose their wives and jobs and run around with women half their age."

"This is my fault," she said quietly.

"No, Amara. It's mine. I was weak. I was supposed to be the leader, the mentor guiding you on the path to God. I strayed from that path."

"I lured you from that path. Milton, I am sorry."

"What's done is done."

"I am sorry."

"Don't worry about it, Amara," I said, driving aimlessly.

There was still almost an hour before I could return home. "Please say you forgive me," Amara said. I looked over at her and saw that she was once again staring at me very intently, as if her life depended on my answer.

"You always seem so desperate when you ask me to forgive you for something," I said. "Why is that?"

"I need you to forgive me."

"You act like you'll be cast into the fires of Hell if I don't forgive you."

"Perhaps I will."

"Nonsense. I'm just a man. My forgiveness doesn't mean that much."

"You are made in the image of your God. That is what your book says."

"The Bible. Yes, man is made in the image of God."

"If you cannot forgive me, why would your God forgive me?"

I chuckled and reached over to squeeze her leg. It was a familiar gesture that somehow felt right. "I guess I see what you mean," I said.

"Then you do forgive me for ruining your life?"

"Amara, you haven't ruined my life. True, my life isn't what it was just a short time ago. But I don't blame you for it."

"Milton, please forgive me."

I looked at her again, this time feeling confused over her insistence. "Okay, Amara. It isn't your fault, but I understand you feel guilt about recent events. I forgive you for any part you think you had in what's happened. Feel better?"

"You really forgive me? You are not just saying you do?"

"Of course I do, Amara. I really, really, really forgive you."

"Thank you, Milton."

"Are you ready to go home?"

"Yes, I think so. Will your wife be gone?"

"By the time we get there, yes, I think she will. I can't believe she won't be there when I get home. That she'll never be there again. She's gone."

"I am sorry."

"No, let's not go there again," I said.

The moving truck and Karen's car were gone when we arrived a few minutes before five. I parked in the garage and we went into the house. It felt vacant, cold and somehow unfriendly. Looking around, I quickly learned why it felt empty—it nearly *was* empty. Karen had taken almost everything, from the dishes to the living room furniture. As I walked through the house I found that the only room completely untouched was my study. In our bedroom, the bed, dresser, chest of drawers and night tables were gone. The mattress Amara and I had slept on the night before rested on the box springs on the floor. My clothes and personal items were thrown in piles around the room.

Eric's room was completely empty; the closet door stood open as if to advertise the vacancy. Lori's room, which we'd left virtually intact after she left, also was stripped to the bare walls. I wondered why Karen would bother to take Lori's things all the way to Woodward with her.

Amara's room was missing all the furniture except the mattress and foundation we'd been on when Karen caught us. Amara's clothes also were strewn around the room. The purse I'd bought her in Manaus lay on the floor, the cheap hairbrush and mirror spilling onto the carpet.

"She took the things I bought from the computer," Amara said.

"What?" I turned to face her. She pointed to an empty corner of the room.

"They were there. I stacked them against the wall to show to you when you were ready to see."

"What were they?"

"Paintings. Coins. The most beautiful jewelry, made for a goddess, or at least her priestess. Some books. Oh, a lot of things."

"Yeah," I said, sighing and making a note to check my credit card balance, close my eBay account and make sure the cards were safely hidden from Amara. "Karen really cleaned us out."

The sudden sickening thought that she may have emptied our bank accounts crossed my mind for the first time. I hurried downstairs and called the automated system. She had. There was an available balance of eight dollars in the checking account and seventeen dollars in the savings account. Very slowly, I hung up the phone, realizing that my life was continuing to get worse with each passing hour.

27

I dreamed of Belo again that night. The jungle shaman's son was standing in the pulpit of the Prairie Valley Community Church, standing in the place where I'd delivered countless sermons, while I sat in a front pew. He spoke to me in the language of the natives, but I understood him better than I'd ever understood the primary language of my friends in the mission. "Evil," he said, repeating it over and over again. "She is destroying you. You will die by her hand."

"Why are you saying that?" I asked. "She is harmless."

"Evil," he said again, pointing to his left. I followed his finger and saw a wavering mirage of sand. The sand seemed to move, or rather, it seemed I was flying above it. Ahead I could see greenery and a wide, snaking river. I soared over the river and followed its course. I wondered where I was. Not over the Amazon, at least no part I'd seen or ever heard about. A large tree grew near the river and carved in the trunk of the tree was a throne. A man stood before the throne and a woman sat on the seat.

I raced closer to the couple, my speed seeming to increase as I drew nearer. Just as I realized the woman on the throne was Amara, I slammed into the back of the man and entered his flesh so that I became him. The force of the blow knocked him to his knees. He remained there with me inside him, then he bowed before Amara.

"First Daughter of the Moon, Lady of the Evening! I sing your praises," the man called in my voice. "Mighty, majestic, radiant, and ever youthful. To you, Inanna, I sing!"

The woman stared down at me, her green eyes cold and calculating. But then it seemed she looked deeper, beneath the flesh and saw me within the man. She smiled and the world brightened. She made to speak, but before any sound issued from her mouth I heard Belo calling me again.

"Hide your head in the grass. Your demons are coming for you," he said. I turned to find him and felt myself torn from the flesh of the man beside the river.

I was in darkness, spinning faster and faster until I felt sick. I closed my eyes but the darkness remained the same. Suddenly my motion stopped. "Hide your head in the grass. Your demons are coming for you," Belo's voice said again.

I opened my eyes and found myself on the mattress on the floor of my bedroom. Belo's words ran a loop in my head. "Hide your head in the grass. Your demons are coming for you." I looked beside me and studied Amara's sleeping form.

"Inanna?" I whispered. I had no idea why I would dream about the Sumerian goddess. *Probably because of Amara's obsession with goddess worship.* I laid back on my pillow and put a forearm over my face, still feeling a little queasy over the dream-vortex in which I'd been spinning. The room was quiet. Very quiet. Too quiet. I took my arm from my face and looked at Amara again. She was not breathing.

I jumped to a sitting position and clutched her shoulders. I shook her gently, but when she did not respond I shook her harder. Her flesh was cold under my hands. "Amara!" I screamed. I put my hand on her neck, feeling for a pulse. I couldn't find one. I moved my fingers, panic filling my mind. Still no pulse. I patted her cheeks and called her name again. Nothing. I slapped her hard, but she still did not respond. My blow did not turn her cheek red.

"Oh God, why?" I asked. "I've lost everything. Am I to lose her, too?"

Amara's eyelids fluttered and opened. She looked up at me and smiled drowsily. "What are you doing, Milton?" she asked.

I stared at her, disbelieving. "Thank you," I whispered. "For what?"

"I thought you were dead. You weren't breathing and I couldn't find a pulse. I…well, I hit you and you didn't move."

"You hit me?"

"I was trying to wake you up?"

"You cannot wake the dead by hitting them."

"I know that. I was just hoping you were in a deep sleep."

"I was," she said. "I was dreaming about you." She reached forward and put her hand over mine. "I took you to see my father."

"Your father? In Greece?"

"No, it was not in Greece, but it was my father. I can never forget being in his presence."

"Why did you take me there?"

"So you could ask him to let me come home."

"What did he say?"

"You woke me up too soon."

"Oh." I laughed. "I had a dream about you, too. It wasn't so good, though. Do you remember Belo, from the *River Lily*?" Amara's lips pressed together and the line of consternation formed on her brow. "Yes, I do remember him. He did not like me."

"He still doesn't."

"But he is dead."

"Yes, I know. But I keep dreaming about him. Tonight he kept telling me you are evil, that you would kill me. He showed me something. It was you, sitting on a throne carved in a tree. And I— I possessed a man standing in front of you and I— he—knelt down and said something. I don't really remember what. You knew it was me inside him and were about to say something, but Belo pulled me back. Belo kept saying something just before I woke up."

"What did he say?"

"I can't remember. You scared me so bad that I forgot. Something...something about demons and grass. Demons hiding in the grass? I don't know."

Amara stared at me for a very long time with an emotion that seemed to be anger trying to take control of her face.

"Are you all right?" I asked.

"You should not dream about dead men," she said. "Dead is

dead. The dead have no cause to speak to the living."

"It was just a dream, Amara. Just a strange dream." I laid down and pulled the blankets over me.

"Yes, Milton. A dream," she agreed, turning toward me, her hand lighting on my chest, then sliding under the covers and down my stomach to slide into my pajama pants. "But this is real."

28

Finding a job was no easy task. There simply were not many openings for ministers in central Oklahoma at that time, particularly ministers not affiliated with any denomination. Prairie Valley Community Church is non-denominational, another reason the job had initially appealed to me. I was free to bring in various aspects that would not have been accepted in some churches.

Over the course of the next two weeks I found one job to apply for. It was as minister for a Pentecostal church in Moore, a suburb to the south of Oklahoma City. I left Amara at home and made the drive, finding the little brick church nestled in a residential neighborhood. The gravel parking lot was small and I knew it couldn't accommodate more than three dozen vehicles. I left my car and went through the double doors into a foyer with three doors. One of the doors was open and I could see a man at a desk in the small room. He looked up at me, then rose from the desk and came to greet me.

"Milton Agnew?" he asked, extending a hand. "I'm Richard Tate."

He was just what I'd expected. Richard Tate was a young man, in his early thirties, tall, with bright eyes, a narrow face and pulsating enthusiasm. He wore a green golf shirt and tan slacks; a gold wedding ring glinted on his left hand.

"It's nice to meet you," I said. "Thank you for agreeing to meet with me."

"I'm glad to do it," he said. "Come into my office and let's talk a bit." He led me into the little room and offered me a seat in a wooden chair. Pictures of a woman about his age and a young boy adorned one wall. A bookshelf was on the opposite wall. His desk was littered with loose paper. "Tell me about yourself," he prompted.

I hesitated, not knowing where to begin. Finally, I decided to be honest. "Well, I've just experienced some problems in my life. I guess maybe God decided I wasn't where I needed to be and shook things up so I would move. A Brazilian mission my former church founded burned, killing everyone in it a month or so ago. My daughter left home just before her eighteenth birthday. Then…well, my wife left me because…" I stopped and had to drop my eyes from his steady face. "I committed a sin against her," I said.

"I see," Richard said. "Adultery?" I nodded. "Yes," I said.

"God forgives all sins through Christ Jesus. All you have to do is repent," Richard said, then grinned. "But what am I telling you? I'm sure you've done that."

Again I hesitated. Had I asked God to forgive me for committing adultery? Had it been adultery that first time? When was the last time I actually prayed? I couldn't remember. I smiled back at Richard Tate and said, "Of course I have."

"And you are the minister of Prairie Valley Community Church, right?"

"Well, no. Not anymore. I quit…I was relieved of my position about two weeks ago."

"Why?"

"The adultery had a big part in it," I said. "I didn't mention it, but I went to Brazil after the fire. There was a survivor, a white woman I'd never met. She needed help, so I brought her home. Smuggled her home. The adultery was with her. My wife also put a restraining order on me, saying I physically abused her and my son. That part isn't true, though." I knew I sounded like a junior high kid trying to transfer blame for some stupid crime.

"The woman you smuggled home," Richard asked in a measured tone. "She is still with you?"

"Yes. When my wife and son left, with my daughter already gone, Amara really was all I had left. And there's still nowhere else for her to go. In my last sermon I tried to find somebody in my congregation to take her and be her mentor, to teach her to live in our society and help her find salvation, but there was no response."

"I see." He looked down at his desk, shuffled some papers and looked back at me. "I'm sorry, Milton, but I'm just not sure you are the right candidate for this job. We're a small church, and forgiving, but I just feel sure you are, well, bringing more baggage than we're ready to take on here."

"I understand," I said. My voice betrayed my despair and that only made me feel worse. "Thank you for your time." I stood up and he extended his hand over the desk. I shook it.

"Good luck to you, Milton. God will provide if you just let him."

"Yes. I'm sure he will," I said.

My spirits sank lower and lower as I drove home. There was a stack of unpaid bills waiting for me in my study. I knew I had to face them. I'd opened a new checking account and deposited my severance check into that account so Karen couldn't withdraw it, should she have a mind to do so. But it wasn't enough to pay the two car payments, insurance premiums on the cars and my life policy, the credit card bill that had gone over the limit because of Amara's online spending, the money I had to pay Karen for alimony and child support, buy groceries, gasoline, utilities and eventually rent and deposit on a new place to live.

There would be no way around it. I would have to take money from my IRA, an account that hadn't been huge before Karen took half of it. There would be tax penalties, of course. How much should I take out? No job. No prospects. Huge bills. It was a depressing thought.

Amara greeted me at the door with an embrace and tantalizing kiss. "Did you get the job?" she asked.

"No. I didn't."

"Because of me."

"Because of me," I corrected. "You have to have a job?"

"Only to buy food and pay the bills," I said, slipping out of her arms.

"You have a lot of debt?"

"Yes. Yes, I do. Too much debt." I went to the kitchen and made a peanut butter sandwich. Amara hopped up and sat on the counter beside me. She was wearing a light dress that came to mid-thigh despite the first autumn chill on the outside air. It was late September then. I couldn't help but smile at the sight of her shapely white leg. I tickled the bottom of a bare foot and trailed my fingers lightly up her calf, over the knee and up her thigh to the hem of her dress. She was smiling back at me.

"Will you plow my vulva again?" she asked.

"That is the most bizarre invitation to sex I have ever heard. Where did you ever pick up such an expression?"

"It is very old."

"That may be. But you are not. Where did you hear it?"

"I do not remember. Shall we go to the bed, or would you have me here?"

I sighed. "Not now. I have to do something about the stack of bills on my desk. I'll have to empty my retirement account, I suppose."

"What is that?"

"Money I put away now to live on when I'm too old to work."

"That is very wise," she said.

"Thanks. It would seem wiser if I had more of it." I stuffed the last of my sandwich into my mouth, patted her leg and went toward the study. She pushed herself off the countertop and followed me. I sat at my desk with the phone in my hand, the toll-free number of my IRA administrator dialed except for the last digit. Reluctantly, I pressed the final button and gave instructions to have the total amount deposited into my new checking account. I hung up and looked at Amara.

"So much for the security net," I said. "You are worried."

"Yeah. I'm worried. That was a tiny church I applied at today. Not getting that job...well, I have to wonder if anyone will hire me if they wouldn't."

"Do you have to work as a priest?"

"Minister," I corrected. "No, I don't have to. It's just that I've trained for a long time for this. It's all I know. I really don't know what else I could do."

I did expand my job search over the next week, applying for a position on an assembly line at a local computer manufacturer, manager of a fast food restaurant, counselor at a children's shelter and various other jobs. Then, one evening as Amara and I sat watching the tiny television in my study—the only set Karen had left in the house—the phone rang. It was Jim Hall, the president of a community college, asking if I would be interested in an adjunct position teaching a humanities class on Western civilization.

"Yes," I answered too quickly.

"It's only one course, three evenings a week," Jim said. Your resume and cover letter says you were looking for a faculty position teaching philosophy or religion. This isn't really what you were looking for, but the instructor we had left for medical reasons. Do you feel comfortable teaching humanities? The course will require you discuss various religions, architecture, literature and customs."

"Yes, I remember my own undergrad course," I said. "I'm sure I can do that with no problem."

"I can't offer you a very high salary because it is only one course, but since we need to fill the position quickly I can give you a modest signing bonus." He gave me some numbers.

"That sounds fine," I said.

"Can we count on you to stay in this position for the duration of the semester? You won't quit when you find full-time work?"

"No, sir. I'll honor my commitment."

"Thank you. We should meet in person, and with the dean, before I officially hire you. When can you come in?"

I made an appointment for early the next morning. Amara was watching me intently, smiling over my obvious excitement.

I hung up the phone and told her about it.

"I am so happy for you, Milton," she said, leaning in and kissing me, a simple gesture Karen never would have offered.

"It isn't much money. Certainly not enough to pay the bills, but having a job, any job, should help us find a place to live."

It did. My meeting with the school president and dean of the college's liberal arts school went well and I got the job that morning. That afternoon we found a small, furnished one-bedroom apartment on the south side of Oklahoma City. The next day we began moving the possessions that remained to us into the apartment. I had to hire a moving service to bring my desk, bookshelves and other furniture that wouldn't fit in my car and were too heavy for Amara and me to lift.

The apartment was crammed with stuff to the point it was difficult to move around. We arranged the furniture, bookshelves and boxed items we didn't have room to unpack as best we could. Finally, we collapsed on the plain sofa that was one piece of the furniture that came with the apartment. Above us, somebody walked across the floor of their third-floor dwelling. Country music drifted up from the apartment below us.

"I should shower and get to class," I said. "First day on the new job and all."

"You will do well."

"Thank you."

"I will shower with you," she offered.

"I'd rather you called and ordered us a pizza. I don't have a lot of time."

"You would rather have food than me?"

"I would rather have food with you," I said, putting an arm around her and pushing my nose into her hair. Despite all our labor she still smelled amazingly fresh. "Just this once, okay? I'll plow your vulva, as you like to say, tonight."

"A woman has needs. Are there laws in your country to tell you when you must make love to your wife?"

"No," I said, laughing. "That's silly."

"It was not always silly."

"Well, whatever you say. I'm going to shower. Make it Pizza Hut, okay? The phone book is by the phone in the kitchen."

The pizza arrived as I was getting dressed. We sat at the small round table of the apartment and ate while watching the evening news. A bus bomb had killed several people in Israel earlier in the day.

"The Hebrew people are still hated by their neighbors," Amara said as she bit into her slice of pizza.

"Yes," I said. "I'm surprised you'd know about that. No TV in the jungle."

"It is an ancient conflict."

The news was replaced by a commercial. I checked my watch and realized it was a few minutes later than I'd thought. I kissed Amara good-bye and rushed out the door.

I spent that evening catching up with the class, learning names and how far they'd gotten in the textbook. The class was a mix of young students looking to cram all the hours they could into one semester and adults who were slowly earning their degree at night. For the most part, they seemed like a nice group and I looked forward to working with them. After class, as I was putting in my required office time, a few students came by to welcome me. I was very pleased and thought I would really enjoy teaching.

The job lasted just over a week. During that week, I turned over the keys to the Prairie Valley house to David Ross. He asked if I was doing well, had found work and a place to live. I answered curtly that I was doing fine, that I was teaching and thoroughly enjoying it.

"And Amara?" he asked, looking around at the emptiness of the house where I'd lived for so many years.

"Amara is fine, too. Thanks for asking."

"You were a fine minister for us, Milton," David said, meeting my eyes again. "I'm sorry it ended this way."

"So am I."

"There seems to be nothing else to say."

"No," I agreed. "Except..."

"Yes?"

"Lori. I'm just worried that someday she'll come back here looking for me." I offered him a slip of paper with my new address and telephone number. "If she ever comes back, will you make sure she gets this."

"Of course, Milton. Of course." He took the paper in one hand and gripped my arm with the other. "It must be incredibly hard for you."

I nodded, shook his hand and left the big house in the affluent subdivision for the final time. There was a lump in my throat as I drove away, watching the house in my rearview mirror. I drove back to the small, crowded apartment, to Amara and my new life.

I'd continued monitoring the classified advertisements in the newspaper, but to no avail. Mostly I spent my days studying the material I would teach to my class. I knew Amara was becoming bored, but we didn't have the money for me to entertain her, so we spent our time in the apartment, me reading while she watched television or played games on the computer, or we made love. She was insatiable to the point that, for the first time in my life, I wished for a break from sex.

One evening she asked to go with me to class, promising to stay in my office while I was teaching. I didn't see how it could hurt, so I agreed. We left early, as I had to make copies of some information I'd pulled from the Internet to supplement material from the textbook. I dropped off my papers at the copy department and led Amara to my classroom.

"This is it," I said, gesturing at the rows of desks. "Not much to see without the students."

"It is very nice," she said.

"Yeah, well, come on and I'll show you my office." The office was pretty small, with white walls and no window. A computer covered most of the desk. I shared the office with two other adjunct faculty members, so I'd done nothing to personalize the space. There was a chair for the instructor behind the desk, an old swivel office chair, and two scuffed wooden chairs for visiting students in front.

"You'll be okay in here for an hour?" I asked. "I will be fine."

"All right. Keep the door closed and stay inside, okay? I'm not sure the administration or security would like the idea of you wandering around."

"I will stay inside," she promised.

"Okay. I gotta go pick up my papers and head back to the classroom. I'll see you in just over an hour." We kissed quickly and I hurried away, closing her in as I left.

Class was uneventful. We discussed the differences between Doric and Ionic columns in ancient architecture and I showed photos I'd taken from the Internet to show how both styles were still in use in modern buildings.

After class, the president of the college met me outside the door. "Milton, how's it going?" he asked. "Enjoying it?"

"I love it, Jim. I should have thought about teaching a long time ago." Students were spilling out around us.

"Let's go to your office. I wanted to talk to you about maybe adding an intersession class after this semester," he said.

"That would be great. I'd be very interested." We began walking toward my office and I remembered Amara. "There's somebody waiting in my office," I said.

"Student?"

"No. She's my...well, I guess she's my girlfriend. She wanted to come tonight, so I left her in my office while I was in class."

"That's fine, if you're comfortable with her being there while we talk about employment and pay," he said.

Jim Hall is a tall man, a good four inches taller than me, mostly bald, with a smile that comes on as if it's controlled by a switch. We walked together the short distance to my office. I pushed open the door. A smell hit me and I thought the room must be on fire. Amara sat in the faculty chair, smoking a huge marijuana cigarette.

"Amara? What are you doing?"

"I was bored," she said.

"Milton, what's going on?" Jim asked, his eyes fixed on me as my own gaze flicked from him to Amara to the joint she held before her face.

"Where did you get that?" I asked.

"Milton, this is totally unacceptable," the president said. "Of course it is," I agreed. "I'm sorry. I don't know what's going on."

"If you do this on your own time, Milton, that's your own business. But you can't bring it to campus."

"But I didn't."

"Milton, your girlfriend is sitting at your desk smoking pot."

"But—"

"I'm sorry, Milton. Please gather your things and leave. I'm relieving you of your duties here. Security will be by in half an hour to make sure you're gone." He turned on his heel and strode away. I looked back to Amara.

"What have you done?" I shouted. "What—Why—Where did you get that?"

"I found it in your desk," she said. "Why did you not bring it home?"

"It's not mine."

She sucked the butt of the joint again, closing her eyes as she did. She released the smoke slowly. "It is good," she said.

"Stop it." I stepped into the office and closed the door. "I've never smoked pot in my life and now I'm losing my job because of…that." I waved at her hand.

"I have caused you more grief," she said, her face crumpling into a mask of sadness. "I apologize."

"Apologize? Do you even understand what you've done? I've lost my job. Again. And now the president of this college thinks I smoke pot. On the job, probably. Amara, this is bad. You know how hard it was for me to find this job and it's barely enough to pay our rent. What are we going to do now?"

"I am sorry, Milton," she said.

"There's nothing to do about it now," I said. "Maybe I can call the president tomorrow and explain that you found it in the desk. I'll offer to take a drug test. Maybe he'll give me a second chance."

She stood up and came around the desk to stand next to me. Her large green eyes were turned up to me, pleading. "Milton, please forgive me."

"Amara…" I took a deep breath and released it slowly. "I do forgive you. I just have to remind myself you're still not familiar with the way we do things here. That stuff is illegal. You're not supposed to own it, sell it or smoke it. Please get rid of that joint."

She dropped it onto the floor and smashed it out under her foot. I picked it up, made sure it wasn't burning anymore, and buried it in the trashcan. I didn't have much to collect, just a few books I'd brought from home and a notepad. I put them under my arm and ushered Amara out of the office.

We drove home in silence.

I called Jim Hall the next day, mid-morning, and explained the situation to him. "Milton," he replied. "I've already talked to the faculty members you shared your office with. Of course they both denied having any illegal substances on campus. We took a drug dog in this morning and the only evidence we found was the butt of the joint you put in the trash. I'm sorry, but my decision stands."

I hung up the phone. I was sitting at a chair in the kitchen area of the apartment. I stared into the living area where I could see the back of Amara's head over the back of the couch. She was watching cartoons on the television.

"Lord, are you testing me as you tested Job?" I whispered. "Scripture says you will not give a man more than he can endure. How much more can I handle?"

Amara turned and smiled a knowing smile at me.

29

Another job search. My education made me overqualified for most of the positions. Others, I lacked the necessary experience. Once, I thought I had a good shot as music director for a large Baptist church, but I made the mistake of being too honest and mentioning that I hadn't worked since a brief stint at the college. When I had to admit why I was let go there, on top of how I lost my job as a minister, the hiring panel smiled weakly and thanked me for my time.

One by one we lost our utilities. My cell phone went first, then cable television. I paid car payments and credit card bills and Karen's monthly support. My checking account was down to under one thousand dollars and I had no prospects for employment. The day the natural gas service was shut off, Amara came to me when I was sitting at the kitchen table, the checkbook and various unpaid bills scattered in front of me. She dropped a bag of crumpled brown leaves on the table.

"What's that? Potpourri?" I asked. "Marijuana."

"More pot? Why? I thought we went over this."

"It is what I found in your office at the school. I knew you would not want to leave it behind and make someone else get in trouble for it."

"Amara…Actually, this time, I would have liked for someone else to have gotten in trouble for it. Go flush it down the toilet. Not all at once, though. And not the bag."

"It would relax you," she said. "I'm not smoking that."

"Because it is against your law?"

"Yes."

"It was against your laws to bring me into your country. You said God's law was more important."

"Nowhere in the Scriptures does it say I should smoke pot."

"Would you not say your God made this plant?"

"He did. He also made the tree of forbidden fruit and told man not to eat from it."

"I told you that story is wrong," Amara said. "There was the serpent and he shed his skin and—"

"Yes, yes, you told me that. But that's just a story you made up."

"I have read your Bible, Milton. It does not say you should not smoke this plant and reap the benefits of using it. All things of the earth were given to men to use." As she spoke, she opened the bag and fished out a packet of white rolling papers from among the leaves. She tore one from the pack and dropped leaves on it, rolling it quickly and expertly. She held it toward me. "Try it," she said.

"No, Amara, I can't."

"Try it for me," she urged. "Just once. If you do not like it I will never ask you to try it again. But I think it will relax you and take away some of your sorrow for a while. You take those white tablets to make headaches go away. Why is this different?"

Why did I do it? Her eyes? Her manner? Her logic? To make her leave me alone about it? I don't know. But finally I did agree. She produced a book of matches and lit the joint, inhaled deeply from it and passed it to me. I'd never held a lit joint or cigarette before. I tried to emulate what I'd seen in the movies, what Amara had done. I put it to my lips and sucked. Immediately I began to cough. Amara giggled as I doubled over in my chair, coughing until my eyes watered. When the coughing fit had passed and I sat up I realized that I did, indeed, feel somewhat more relaxed.

"Suck it slowly," she said. "Just as if you were breathing naturally, then hold your breath for a short time."

I looked at the joint in my fingers dubiously, then put it back to my mouth and breathed through the burning paper and leaves. The smoke came in slowly, tickling, soothing as it flowed down my throat and into my lungs. I held my breath, moved the joint away from my mouth, and exhaled slowly. It was as if all the worries of my overdue utility bills and worry about paying the next month's rent slipped out of me on that tiny stream of fragrant smoke. Honestly, I was scared that it was so easy to breathe away my trouble like that. But, just thinking of how I wouldn't be in my current situation if Karen hadn't emptied our bank accounts and still demanded thousands of dollars from me every month made me angry all over again. *Why had I signed those papers from her gay lawyer?* I took another pull and breathed away those smoky thoughts, too.

We passed the joint back and forth until it was gone. I was soon acting silly. I knew it, knew I was stoned, but I could only laugh about it. Amara laughed, too, but even in my euphoric condition I knew that she had not been affected by the marijuana. We made love on the floor of the living room, then went to bed and made love again, like animals, with me taking her from behind as she crouched on her elbows and knees. I howled like a wolf as I climaxed, then fell on the bed beside her. We laughed until we fell asleep.

Of course, the next day I was called for a job interview as assistant manager of a chain bookstore. I failed the drug test.

I spent the next week in a deep state of depression. That is, when we weren't getting high, which seemed to be every evening and, toward the end of the week, sometime after noon when I'd checked all the classified ads in all the local papers. Soon, the bag of marijuana was empty.

"I guess that's it," I told Amara. "No more escaping reality."

"We can get more," she said.

"No. It's bad enough we've been smoking this that you found. We can't go buying it. We could get in big trouble for that. Besides, I'll never find a job if I don't stop."

Stopping wasn't so easy. With no job prospects, I finally turned to the state for help and was issued a welfare card with which to buy groceries. I filed for unemployment, agreeing to do at least two job searches each week, but the income still wasn't much and I slipped deeper into depression with the arrival of each check because every time I accepted the check it was proof that I was a failure.

"I have a Ph.D.," I muttered once as I sat on our sofa, unshaved, a new unemployment check in my hand.

But that was part of my problem. I was overeducated for many jobs, or my degree didn't apply for others. And I was too old. Companies didn't want to hire a man in his mid-forties, especially for jobs they usually filled with teenagers. Yes, I'd begun applying for any openings at fast food places, as a clerk at department stores, almost anything, some of which would have paid less than my meager unemployment check.

Amara never offered to find work. I didn't think much of it at the time. What could she do? No Social Security number, no birth certificate and she was in the country illegally. I knew she couldn't help gain income, so I never asked her to.

And then one day she left the apartment to walk around the neighborhood. It was morning and I was still poring over the classifieds for the day. Amara was gone for about half an hour, then returned and put a small baggie of pot on my newspapers as she sat down across from me.

"You have been tense again," she said. "I know you said not to buy any, but it helps you relax."

"Amara," I said, picking up the bag and looking at the contents. "You shouldn't have bought this." However, seeing the bag made me crave it strongly.

"But it is here now. You will use it and feel better?" she asked, her emerald eyes glowing over her gift.

"Where did you get the money?"

"From your wallet," she said.

"You took money from my wallet?" She nodded. "Amara, don't do that. Our finances are so tight. Unbelievably tight. Don't ever take money out of my wallet. Every dollar we have matters."

"I am sorry," she said.

"Well, it's all right this time." I opened the bag and sniffed the marijuana. "Just don't do it again."

"You forgive me?"

"Yes. I forgive you. Where did you get it?"

"One day when I went walking I found a man, a young man, who sells it. He lives in this building," she said.

"You shouldn't be around those kinds of people. They'll get you in trouble."

"He was very nice. He said he would worship me as a goddess if I would go to his bed."

"What? He asked you to sleep with him?"

"Sleep is not what he wanted."

"Amara, stay away from those kinds of people. They don't have the kind of morals you need to copy." I realized the absolute irony of what I'd just said. Me, a fallen minister, sitting in an apartment I shared with my adulteress lover, holding a bag of pot. I sighed. "Just be careful out there, okay? There are a lot of people who would hurt you."

"I am always careful," she said, smiling at me. "I have been taking care of myself for a long time."

"Do we still have papers?" I asked. We did. We rolled and smoked and I felt better than I had for many days.

It had been just about two months since Karen left me and I lost my job as minister of Prairie Valley Community Church. It seemed much longer in many ways. The weather had turned colder. The presidential election was a mess, with votes recounted and lawsuits filed as Al Gore and George W. Bush fought for the Oval Office. Thanksgiving Day was approaching. I bought Amara a new coat from a department store; it seemed more necessary than buying a turkey for the holiday. On Thanksgiving Day we ate hamburger patties and instant mashed potatoes. I made out another round of checks for Karen, paid her car payment and insurance premium, and paid half of the utility bills for the apartment, hoping our power wouldn't be cut off. Then Amara and I smoked pot and had sex as the Minnesota Vikings defeated the Dallas Cowboys on the television set.

Later that evening, as Amara took a long hot bath, I puttered around the apartment, the effects of our afternoon joint wearing off. I was hungry and bored, pacing, trying to think of something to do other than eat the last potato chips in the house. From a bookshelf, my Bible caught my eye. I had several bibles, actually. Different versions, some I would mark in to highlight passages, some I would never think to write in. It was a thick, leather-bound New King James version that I preferred and that I'd spent the most time reading for my own enlightenment. I pulled the book from the shelf and held it in my hands for a while, then let it fall open as I held it. My eye lighted on John 14:14. I read it aloud. "If you ask anything in my name, I will do it."

For the first time in many, many weeks I was forced to stop and think about my relationship with God. It wasn't where it had been. Obviously he was testing me. And I was failing that test. With every challenge he threw at me, I retreated further into sin rather than putting my life in his hands and doing what I should do.

"Amara, I'm going out for a short walk," I called, putting the Bible back on the shelf. I didn't wait for her response, but slipped out the door, putting on my coat as I headed for the stairs to the ground level.

It was cold. The wind was blowing from the north and darkness already had fallen over the city. Traffic on the roads was light as people stayed inside to eat leftover turkey and dressing. I walked aimlessly, thinking of how life used to be. Three months ago I was a minister to one of the richest congregations in the state, we had a successful mission established in the Brazilian jungle, my family was happy and I was very content with my life. Perhaps too content. Had I been taking my success for granted? Had I grown distant from God then and not even realized it? I don't remember feeling differently at the time. I had prayed regularly, did charity work, gave blood and offered counseling to those who asked. "What did I do wrong to deserve what has happened to me?"

The cold drove me to shelter. I walked across the dark playground of a school until the building blocked me from the wind. I sat down and stared across the flat playground, watching swings move gently. Across the alley, lights burned in homes where people lived ordinary lives.

"Adultery," I murmured. Yes, I'd done that. But my life already had begun to sour. Lori had lost her moral bearings, then left home before I'd first gone to bed with Amara. True, Karen would still be with me, I'd still have my job and home if I hadn't committed that one sin. But wasn't God supposed to forgive those sins?

I hadn't asked.

For all my adult life I'd been telling people to bring their sins to Jesus, but I had not yet done that with my own greatest sin. I almost laughed at the silliness of it. Wasn't it apparent that the reason for all my problems was that I'd drifted away from God since Lori ran away? I'd been so distracted by losing her that I'd submitted to my own carnal desires and gone to bed with Amara and then I continued to focus on myself rather than God as things spiraled down to where I was then.

I bowed my head and asked God to forgive me for my mistakes as a father, for being a poor husband, for the adultery and for straying from him during my time of trouble. "In the name of Jesus I ask you to forgive me for these things and set me back on the right path. Amen."

At the final word, it was as if a great weight had been lifted from me, even greater than that first time I'd smoked marijuana with Amara. Warm tears rolled down my cold face. A voice in my head reminded me that I had not forgiven Karen and Eric for leaving me, that I still held anger over that.

"I forgive you," I said. But I needed to tell them that. It was Thanksgiving Day, the perfect opportunity to call them. I got to my feet and hurried back to the apartment.

I arrived in the parking lot just in time to see the tow truck pull my Cadillac out of its slot and drive away with it. I gave chase, but didn't have a chance of catching my car. I stood puffing clouds of steam, my hands on my knees as the truck, labeled Big Joe's Repos, pulled out of the apartment building parking lot and carried my car away from me.

"Is this it, God?" I yelled. "You're still testing me, even when I do everything right? You take my car away from me?"

I was two months behind on my own car payment. But I'd made the payment on the sport utility vehicle Karen had taken from our garage when she'd left.

"Bitch," I spat the word, so unfamiliar to my lips, then turned and went up the stairs and into the apartment where Amara was waiting for me.

Steven E. Wedel

30

Two weeks later, during the first week of December, we lost our apartment. We were a month behind on the rent. Out of fear and guilt, I'd made sure I always paid everything I'd agreed to give Karen first and my own bills second. The rent payment was something I'd skipped in an effort to keep the lights burning and the water flowing from the tap. And the phone turned on in the hope of getting a job offer.

I dreamed of Belo again the night before we were kicked out of the apartment. He showed me images of the sea under the light of a bright full moon. I stood on a hill with a valley on one side and the sea stretching away on the other. Beside me was a massive stone statue carved of gray rock. The statue was of a horned woman standing among lionesses, a serpent twined around her.

People came up the hill to worship at the statue. They threw jewels at the feet of the statue, sang praises and offered prayers. Some cut their hair and scattered the shorn locks around the base of the statue, the wind picking up strands of hair and blowing them into the valley. One man came forward, tore away the robes he wore and took a knife to his genitalia. In the dream language he called out to the statue, saying, "For you,

Mother of All. I offer myself as a priest to the Lady of Byblos." Then he cast his bloody testicles at the statue and fell to his knees. Other men, priests of the goddess, rushed forward and carried him away as he lost consciousness.

"Who is she?" I asked Belo, who had appeared again beside me. For answer, he pointed to the sky. The people and the statue were gone. A star was hurtling toward us. I was frightened because the burning asteroid seemed sure to hit us where we stood on the hilltop. I fell to the ground and the rock roared past. I stood in time to see it crash into a lake in the valley.

"She fell from the sky as a star and so they named her," Belo said. I looked at him and the statue was again with us on the hill, looming above him. He pointed to its face and there I saw Amara's features carved into the stone. "She is Astarte."

I remember waking up at that point, mumbling something to Amara, who lay motionless beside me. She did not respond, though, and I dropped back into sleep. There was only blackness and Belo's voice. "She fell from the sky."

On Tuesday of that first week of December, the apartment manager knocked on our door bright and early, dragging me out of sleep. I opened my eyes and said, "Enoch walks with God." Before I could think of why I would say that particular phrase, the knock at the door was repeated with great force. "Enoch walks with God," I said again as I swung my legs out of the bed and pulled on a bathrobe. I knew it had something to do with a dream fragment, but beyond that I had no clue.

I opened the front door to find our landlord, Mr. Rodriguez, as he liked to be called despite being about fifteen years younger than me, standing on the walkway with another huge Hispanic man behind him. The big man had his head shaved, but it showed a few days' worth of growth. He wore sunglasses and a goatee and a tight black T-shirt and jeans. Mr. Rodriguez wore a dress shirt and pressed slacks, his thin black hair combed back from his forehead.

"You have not paid your rent," he said. "You need to get out."

"I'll pay it," I argued. "No. You get out."

"But I'm only a month behind."

"You don't have a job. You get welfare checks and your woman spends it on drugs. Get out by five o'clock or we'll come back and Juan will help you leave. You understand?" Mr. Rodriguez asked, jerking his head back to indicate the big man. The thug grinned, showing a gap where he was missing a tooth. "Five o'clock? Can't we have more time?" I pleaded. "We don't have anywhere else to go."

"Five o'clock," he repeated.

I nodded and closed the door. Amara stood behind me, one of my button-down shirts covering her, though she only held the front closed. "The man you bought the marijuana from?" I asked. "The one who wanted to have sex with you? Was it our landlord? Mr. Rodriguez?"

She nodded. I sighed. "All right."

It took more than half our money to hire a moving crew with a truck who would work on such short notice. I called and rented a storage facility and convinced the movers to put our furniture and boxes in the storage space and deliver the keys to a motel I found with weekly rates. I told Amara to gather what she needed most; we put our clothes, toiletries and various other necessities into white trash bags and I called a taxi to take us to the motel.

While we were waiting for the taxi, the mailman came by and delivered another unemployment check, a couple of bills and a cardboard tube. I put the check and bills into a box of things going to the motel with us and examined the tube. It was from my friend Bill Barlow who'd helped me get Amara out of Brazil; it had originally been sent to my old home in Prairie Valley. I popped the plastic top off the tube and shook out the contents.

First to fall out was a rolled note written on Bill's business letterhead. I shook the tube again and a rolled piece of canvas came out; it had a rubber band around it so it didn't immediately unroll. I picked up the note and read.

Milton,

I'm very glad to know you survived the sinking of the *Sea Plow*. I received word you made it safely across the border and back into the States with your cargo. Unfortunately, mine is at the bottom of the sea. Only a few crew members were lost when the ship went down and most of them were killed in the explosion. The captain has laid many curses on you and your friend for going off alone in one of his lifeboats.

Enclosed you'll find an old print of a painting I thought of when I first met your friend. I had this in a box of such things in my office, so as soon as I got home I dug it out to send to you. I'm sure you're familiar with it.

Try to stay out of trouble, Rev. Agnew. Your friend,

Bill

I could only stare at the note for a bit, thinking how he had written it without knowing about the divorce, losing my job, and everything else that had happened since we'd said farewell in Manaus. I felt my eyes watering, so I shook my head and turned my attention to the rolled canvas. I pushed the rubber band off and unrolled it as Amara looked on eagerly.

It was a 12x24-inch print of John Collier's *Lilith*. The nude succubus appeared as a beautiful red-haired woman standing in a jungle with a giant snake coiled around her from her ankles to her neck and she held the serpent's head in her right hand. Her breasts showed, with small pink nipples, but her pubic area was covered by the thick body of the snake.

"It looks like me," Amara said, laughing.

"It really does," I agreed. "I haven't seen this picture since college. I'd almost forgotten about it. I remember when I saw it I thought she was incredibly beautiful."

"Thank you," Amara said. She kissed my cheek and I laughed at her.

"You know, of course, that she is considered a demon?"

"Who?"

"Lilith," I said, nodding at the print. "Hebrew legends say—"

"That is not Lilith. Lilith is ugly. She is a vile creature," Amara said, her face becoming hard and angry as she spoke. "That is me, not Lilith."

"Whoa. Hold on there, Amara. It's not you or Lilith. It's a model John Collier used for his painting. He just named it *Lilith*. I don't know why."

"He should not have named it that," she said, her voice pouty.

"Well, if you say so. Too bad we're going to be living in a motel for a while. They won't let us hang pictures, I'm sure. It's just temporary, though, until we're back on our feet."

"You say you had not seen that painting since college," Amara said, her voice teasing. "But did you not ever think about finding that woman when you went into the jungle?"

I chuckled, a little embarrassed by her intuition. "Maybe," I admitted. "Maybe I'd thought once or twice about finding John Colliers' image in the dark jungle. I never expected it would happen, though. I figured there was a better chance of finding Tarzan."

"What if I told you that I was without shape until just before you saw me?" she asked, a playful light dancing in her eyes. "What if I pulled this image from your mind and shaped myself to become that?"

"I would either say that you are crazy, ornery, or just that we both have undergone huge changes since right before I saw you standing naked and alone in the rain forest. Then I would say that our cab is here." A car horn was blowing in the parking lot. We picked up the few bags and boxes going to the motel with us and hurried down the stairs, leaving behind yet another home we'd shared for a short time.

The ride to the motel was brief, but nonetheless expensive, teaching me why poor people rode the Metro Transit buses instead of hiring taxis. The motel was another reminder of our financial situation. One of several squatty hostelries located along South Shields Boulevard among dealers of portable outbuildings and trailer houses, it was made of bricks that had been painted a pale sea-green. The parking lot was covered in gravel and the owner or manager who checked us in was grossly overweight, unshaven and had a wet, unlit cigar hanging from his mouth as he threw a key on the counter and grunted, "Room Five." Then he scratched his groin, farted, and turned back to a small television on his desk. I took the key and led

Amara to our new home.

The inside of Room Five was no better than the outside. The outdated shag carpet was a mix of golds, browns and rusts, worn thin and ratty. The bed sagged, there was a dead cockroach two inches long in the bathtub and the sink groaned and spat before delivering any water.

"I miss your old house," Amara said.

"So do I. But, this is what God has provided for us right now."

"I thought you provided it."

"Only through the grace of God." The words didn't come easy as I looked over the stained ceiling and grimy framed prints of fruit. "We could be worse off than we are."

We soon were. Even if it looks like it should be condemned, torn down and the earth sewn with salt, living in a motel is not cheap. There was nowhere to store food, so we ended up spending money I hadn't accounted for eating fast food and riding the bus to get to the restaurants that sold it. Most of my next unemployment check went to pay another week's rent in the motel.

"I am going to have to call Karen," I announced one morning after determining our total finances amounted to just over three hundred dollars.

"Will you ask her to forgive you and take you back?" Amara asked.

Strangely, I hadn't even considered that. Would she take me back? I doubted it. But maybe she had calmed down by now. I looked at Amara and knew it was hopeless. Karen would never take me back when I'd continued to live with Amara— live as man and wife, no less. And could I really send Amara away to go back to Karen?

Amara sat in a wooden chair beside a small round table, one elbow propped on the table, her legs crossed. Despite the cold of the room, she wore a short dress and no shoes. Her pale legs were exquisite in shape and her dangling foot was perfect. I followed the leg up to her face and knew that, no matter how bleak our financial situation was, I could never give up Amara. "I think I have really, truly fallen in love with you, Amara,"

I said.

Her radiant face absolutely glowed like a star. She got up from the chair and came to me, pushing me down so that I sat on the bed. She straddled my lap and kissed me deeply, her tongue pushing into my mouth, hot and loving. She pulled her face away. "And I have come to love you, Milton Agnew," she said. Then she kissed me again, rocking her hips over my new erection. As she kissed me, she reached between us and pulled open the fly of my pants, freeing my penis so she could grip it firmly in her hand. Then she raised herself, slipped me under her dress and into her burning soft folds of womanhood. She rode me slowly, clinging to me as she pumped up and down on my lap until finally she threw back her head and gave a soul-wrenching moan. I came just as hard, burying my face against her neck and sucking on her beautiful flesh.

A moment later she relaxed and my lock on her neck was broken. I expected to see a deep red hickey where I'd been sucking, but there was nothing but my own saliva glistening in the overhead light.

"I do love you," she said, her eyes pulling mine to her face. "Will you call your wife now?"

"I have to," I said, the last feeling of orgasm now gone completely. "I can't pay her. I have to ask her—beg her—to let me miss a payment."

"But you will not go back to her?"

"I could never leave you now, Amara." I pulled her close and kissed her again, losing my hands deep in her hair until I felt her scalp and cupped it in my fingers. "Never," I said as I released her. She smiled and slid off my lap and I reached for the phone. It would cost extra to call long distance.

Karen answered on the third ring. "Hello," I said. "Karen?"

"Milton." Her voice was cold.

"How are you?"

"Fine."

"And Eric?"

"He's fine."

"I don't suppose you've heard anything about Lori?"

"No. Nothing. What do you want?"

"Karen, things are pretty tight for me right now. There's just no way I can go on paying you as much as I was. I—I'm sorry, but I can't pay you anything right now."

"Then I guess we'll be in court," she said.

"Karen, there's nothing you can do to humiliate me now. I'm living in a motel on Shields. My car was repossessed last month so I could pay you. I only have a few hundred dollars to my name. I can't find a job. I'm…I'm scared, Karen."

"I know about your jobs," Karen said, her voice softening just a little. "Milton, how could you lose a job over drugs? What has that woman done to you?"

"It isn't Amara's fault," I said.

"Fine. She's still with you, isn't she? If she hasn't run off yet, you must not be as destitute as you're playing."

"Where would she go?" I challenged. "She has less money than me. No friends here. Nothing."

"She can go be a hooker in Oklahoma City the same as she did in Brazil," Karen snapped back. "Make your payments, Milton, or we'll have you in court and up what you pay me."

I slammed the phone down and for the second time in my life I called my former wife a bitch.

"This will help," Amara said. I turned my head toward her and found that she was offering a lit marijuana cigarette. I felt weak, spiritually and physically, as I reached for it, but at that moment I just didn't care.

31

A couple of days later I saw an ad in The Daily Oklahoman newspaper that the local General Motors plant was going to hire thirty people for an assembly line job. I left Amara alone in the motel room, boarded a white and green bus and rode to the plant in Midwest City, a suburb on the east side of the Oklahoma City metro. When I arrived, there were close to two hundred people ahead of me. I was given an application and left to find a place in an empty warehouse to fill it out.

It was a long, grueling day. The plant did offer lunch of sandwiches and coffee and water to the people waiting for interviews. The turkey sandwich I got had mustard on it—I prefer Miracle Whip—but I ate it and was grateful for it, although my stomach continued to rumble afterward. The line of applicants moved slowly and, until noon, for every person called into the interview room two more job hopefuls entered the waiting area. After noon, the flow trickled to just a few new faces every hour. I finally got called in at about three o'clock. Hungry and nervous, I sat at a table facing two men and a woman in suits. They introduced themselves quickly and I promptly forgot their names.

Within the first two minutes I knew I'd wasted my day.

Before even asking about my background they inquired as to my physical strength and endurance. Could I lift forty pounds repetitively for at least eight hours a day, five or six days a week? I assumed I could and answered positively, but their faces showed their skepticism.

"You think I'm too old," I said during an awkward pause. "Fine. Maybe I am. But, do you have anything else? Do you need a plant chaplain?"

"I'm very sorry, Mr. Agnew," the oldest man, a rotund person with a shiny scalp and dark brown eyes, said. "We don't. Thank you for coming in today."

"What about a janitor?" I asked. "Anything. Please. I have to have a job." The frustration of waiting all day for nothing and the thought of going back to that nasty little motel room to tell Amara I'd failed again suddenly welled up in me, putting a lump in my throat.

"I'm afraid we don't have anything else open at this time, Mr. Agnew," the woman said. "Thank you for your interest in GM."

"Office work? I can do filing. Mailroom. Whatever. I'm not too proud to take anything."

"Mr. Agnew, please go now," the first man said. The three of them glared at me and I wondered how many other desperate people had sat where I was earlier that day. Reluctantly, slowly, I rose from the chair and slouched away.

I joined a couple of other applicants at the bus stop not far from the plant's entrance. The sky was overcast and the December wind blew hard from the north. I kept my long wool coat tight around me. One of the applicants, a young black man, was excited and said the interviewers had promised to call him for a second interview. The other was a dour woman who kept repeating that she had five kids to feed and no job, no health coverage and she was thinking of going back to Illinois where the state benefits were better. When the bus came, I sat as far away from them as I could, alone in the back, where nobody could see me weeping.

Amara greeted me at the door of the motel room, beaming with joy. She made a grand, sweeping gesture at the little round table of the room as she said, "For the master of the house." There on the table was a feast. T-bone steaks, baked potatoes, corn on the cob and fluffy white rolls with golden crowns steamed in the cool air of the room. In the center of the table, a bottle of dark wine chilled in a plastic ice bucket, flanked by smaller plates, each holding a slice of chocolate fudge cake.

"Where did this come from?" I asked.

"Please do not be mad, Milton. I took money from your wallet again. I called all morning until I found a restaurant that would deliver this. I just knew you would come home with good news today."

What could I say? I couldn't be mad at her. Her face showed she read the suddenly renewed slump of my shoulders to be bad news.

"You did not get the job?"

"No." I shook my head. "I'm too old and weak."

"That is silly," she said. "Then we will celebrate something else."

"Another week of no hope?"

"No, Milton. We will celebrate you saying you love me."

I smiled at her, but it was a sad smile. "That sounds good to me."

She helped me out of my coat and shooed me into a chair. My mouth watered so badly I was afraid I'd drool on my plate.

The aroma of cooked meat almost made me dizzy. Amara sat across from me and reached for the wine bottle.

"Wait," I said. "Let's say grace. We haven't in a long time. For this meal, we should."

"If you want," she answered.

I bowed my head. "Heavenly Father, we thank you for this food, for this feast in a time of famine. We do not know why we must struggle as we do, but we know that through faith in Christ Jesus we will prevail. In Jesus' name we pray. Amen."

"I hope you like the wine," Amara said, pulling the bottle from the bucket and jabbing a corkscrew into the top.

"I've never been a drinker," I said. Some of the light left her face, but came back when I added, "But there's no way I'll refuse your wine tonight."

Halfway into the meal I asked her how much it cost. "Seventy-four dollars and fourteen cents," she answered. "What? You're kidding me?" I dropped my fork and it clattered on the plate. "Seventy-four dollars?"

"The wine was thirty-two dollars and twenty-two cents," she added meekly, not meeting my gaze.

"Amara, how could you? How could you? That's more than half of all the money we had left. You took that much out of my wallet?"

"It looked like you had so much money in there," she said. "And I just knew you would be hired by the car factory. I wanted to give you a feast. I am sorry."

"Oh God, help me. Help us," I said, looking to the stained ceiling. Amara began to sob. I immediately jumped from my chair and turned her in her chair so I could hold her. "Don't cry," I said. "It's done. We have a wonderful meal. We'll enjoy it and figure out what to do later. On full stomachs."

"I am very sorry, Milton," she cried, her eyes streaming tears.

"It's okay. Really, Amara. It will be all right. Don't cry. Let's finish eating."

"Please say you forgive me and won't be mad at me," she begged.

"Of course I forgive you. You did a very sweet thing and I appreciate that you wanted to. Just, please, no more counting chickens until they hatch. Okay?"

"I do not understand."

"Don't spend money thinking I'll get a job. Obviously, it doesn't always work out."

She nodded. "You forgive me?"

"Yes, Amara. Let's finish our dinner. It's wonderful food."

Rent came due three days before my next unemployment check arrived. I didn't have the money to pay the rent for a week. Instead, I had to pay by the day, which was a higher rate. On the third morning, I turned over all the cash I had except for a quarter, a nickel and two pennies to pay for our previous night's stay. There was no food for breakfast. Or lunch. By midafternoon I was mad with hunger and boredom.

"I can hear your stomach growling," Amara said. It had been roaring for hours.

"I'm starving," I said.

"I have seen men holding signs that say they will work for

food. Can you do that?" she asked.

"Beg for food? I don't want to do that."

"You would rather be hungry?"

"Yes." My stomach rumbled long and loud. "Come on," I said, standing up and grabbing my coat. I helped Amara into hers and we left the motel room.

I led her on a walk I thought was aimless, though we walked directly north and soon came upon a KFC restaurant. It had always been one of my favorites; as a kid, my dad would usually stop at a KFC—still called Kentucky Fried Chicken then—after church on Sunday. We'd get a bucket of golden chicken and take it home for a feast, often reheating the thighs to eat during the late afternoon football games.

Now, I found myself standing apprehensively near the trash Dumpster at the back of the building, pretending to be studying a shopping store parking lot across the street from the Dumpster as cars moved in the KFC drive-through. The aromas of chicken and garbage were very strong.

"Are we going to look for food in the trash?" Amara asked. "I would rather do that than beg," I said.

"Why?"

"This way, you're getting what people didn't want and not asking them to give up something they do want just because we—I mean I—can't get a job."

The driver of a red Kia Sephia picked up his order from the window at the side of the building. There were no more cars in the drive-through. I pushed open the lid of the Dumpster and looked quickly at the contents. I spotted a white bag and could see a drumstick inside it. I grabbed the bag, let the Dumpster lid fall shut and pulled Amara out of the KFC drive-through area.

When we were far enough away to look like customers, I opened the bag and reached inside. There was the drumstick, with only one bite taken from it, half a serving of cole slaw and a few French fries. Dejected, I handed the bag to Amara. "There isn't much. You eat it. I'll find something else."

"No, Milton. You eat it," Amara said, pushing my outstretched hand back toward me. She smiled and turned away, walking briskly across the street to the grocery parking lot, heading toward the store.

I ate the food. Ravenously. The drumstick was down to the bare bone in a few bites. I scooped the cole slaw from the Styrofoam container with two fingers and then swallowed the cold fries. I did it all before Amara had found her first mark.

I was still twenty yards from her when she found a man coming out of the store and crossing to his car. She stepped beside him and walked with him. "I am very hungry," she said. "I have not eaten since yesterday morning. Could you help me by giving me enough money to get a meal there?" She pointed to the KFC. "My husband lost his job and hasn't been able to find another one." Now she pointed at me. The man she spoke with, a clean-cut man in his mid-thirties looked at me for a split second before turning his attention back to Amara. I hung my head in shame.

"Here's five bucks," he said, pulling out his wallet and handing her a bill. "That'll feed you. Your bum husband should find a job if he wants to eat." He slipped behind the wheel of his Ford Taurus and drove away. Amara came to where I was standing beside a light post.

"See, that was not so hard," she said. "Not for you."

"You can do it, too."

"I don't have the ability to entice people into giving me what I want the way you do, Amara. I'm just an out-of-work old man. Not a stunning young redhead."

"Did you not ask your congregation to give you money every week?"

"That was different. They were giving to the church, not to me."

"Then tell these people you are seeking money for your church."

"I don't have a church."

"They do not know that."

"I was never good at lying."

"Did your trash food fill your belly?"

I stared at her, surprised again by her bluntness. "No," I admitted. It had, in fact, only made me crave more.

"There is a woman coming out now. She looks very kind. Go and ask her to help you."

Like a child being sent to the principal, I moved toward a well-dressed woman of about my own age. She was following a store clerk who pushed her groceries. I caught up with them just as they entered an aisle of cars.

"Excuse me, ma'am," I said, approaching her, unable to hold her gaze. "My, umm, my—my wife and I are having some hard times and I was wond—" I'd gotten my hopes up when she reached into the pocket of her coat. The pepper spray was a complete surprise. It burned instantly. I screamed and fell to my knees, my gloved hands covering my streaming eyes. I heard her talking to the carry-out boy as they walked away.

"This city is just full of bums and perverts," she said. "I don't know if he wanted money or for me to go to bed with him and his wife, but either way I didn't want any part of it."

"No, ma'am," the boy answered smartly.

Amara pulled me to my feet and led me out of the way of traffic trying to move in the lane. I followed blindly, unable to see through the burning tears in my eyes. She sat me on a bench outside the front of the store and sat with me.

"I am sorry, Milton," she said. "I should not have made you do that."

"Not your fault," I said. My nose was running. I wiped it repeatedly with my sleeve. Slowly, my vision cleared.

"I am sorry, Milton."

"It's all right, Amara. I forgive you." Now that I could see, I felt very angry. "That woman had no Christian compassion," I said. "What kind of people shop here who would pepper-spray a man just trying to talk to them? I hadn't even asked her for money yet."

"She is a wicked one," Amara agreed. "Shall we go to the

restaurant and spend the money I earned?"

"No. Not yet." I wiped my eyes and nose one last time. "I'm going inside."

She followed me into the store. I went in with the sole intention of stealing something. I was hungry, angry over the treatment from the woman in the parking lot, angry at the world for my condition and craving more marijuana, which only made me madder. But, I almost lost my nerve. Finally, I snatched a bag of beef jerky from a rack, looked around quickly and stuck it under my coat and into my armpit. I made for the door, keeping my arm tight to my side.

Just as we were passing the check-outs before the door a voice behind me yelled, "Stop him! He's stealing!" All eyes turned to me. I didn't look back, I just ran.

The automatic door was open and I charged through it, Amara right with me, two young boys close on our heels. The bag of beef jerky slipped from my armpit and fell out of my coat, but I didn't stop to try to retrieve it. One of the boys did, leaving just one in full pursuit. We made it into the parking lot, Amara now a few steps ahead of me. She pulled a shopping cart from a return stall and shoved it at the boy following me. It hit him and sent him sprawling on the blacktop. She grabbed me by the arm and pulled me along.

I was puffing and struggling to breathe when she finally stopped running. I thought I was going to die. I bent over, my hands on my knees, coughing, and then suddenly the food from the Dumpster erupted from my mouth, splashing into the grass of somebody's front lawn.

"Come, Milton," Amara urged, pulling at my coat again. "We are close to home."

"Home," I repeated, thinking of the grungy motel room. I was breathing a little better when we stepped onto the gravel parking lot, but the aftertaste of regurgitated cole slaw was vile on my tongue. I stopped in at the motel office to ask for my mail. The fat man with his eternally wet stub of a cigar handed me a forwarded electric bill from the apartment, a few pieces of junk mail and a credit card bill. "That's all?" I asked.

"Yeah. That's all," he said around his cigar. He glared at me and I knew he was lying to me, that he'd taken my unemployment check. I would have to call the unemployment office the next day to verify it had been sent. I took what he'd given me and turned away.

"He is not telling you the truth," Amara said. I looked at her and shook my head slightly.

"What'd you say, honey?" the man asked, leaning over the counter, resting his upper body on a forearm the size of a ham. He looked sidelong at me, then back at Amara. "Is your pretty bitch here calling me a thief and a liar?"

"If you were a good Christian like Milton, you would not steal our money," she said.

"Amara, no," I said. "Don't do this."

"A good Christian does not steal, you said," she insisted.

Why is she doing this? She knows I just tried to steal from the grocery store. What is she trying to prove? *I had no answer.*

"Come around this counter here and I'll show you why I ain't never been called no good Christian," the man said.

"Let's go, Amara." I reached for her, but she moved away. "Tell him, Milton. Tell him like you would tell your church."

"Church?" the manager said, his voice filled with surprise and mirth. "You one of those street-corner preachers? I'd never a guessed that, what with the pot I smell coming outta your room all the time."

"Are you ashamed to be a Christian?" Amara asked me. "Will you not tell him?"

"I am not ashamed," I said quietly. "I just don't want to talk about it now and in this company. Let's go." I went to the door and opened it, waiting for Amara to pass through. Finally, she did. The manager was laughing as I let the door close.

"What was that about?" I demanded. "Haven't I been humiliated enough today?"

"Your religion humiliates you?"

"No, Amara, not my religion. You did. You humiliated me in front of that man. Probably he did steal my check, but I can't accuse him of it without some kind of evidence. I'll call the unemployment office tomorrow and ask if they sent the check. Then I'll go back and ask him about it."

"What if he still does not give it to you?"

I took a deep breath and blew it out slowly between pursed lips. It steamed on the cold night air and blew away. "I don't know," I admitted. "Let's go inside."

"You are angry with me," she said as I closed and locked the door.

"A little, yes."

"I apologize," she offered. "Fine."

"You forgive me?"

"Yes, Amara," I said, making it sound very dramatic. "I forgive you, Amara. Okay? I'm going to take a hot shower."

"I could join you. We could make love under the water."

"No. Not this time. I just need to be alone for a few minutes." I went into the bathroom and locked the door.

We didn't speak much the rest of that evening. Amara rolled our last joint, a puny thing, and we smoked it. It made my hunger even worse. At about 10 p.m. I shut off the television and we went to bed. I tossed and turned for a while, then fell into a deep sleep.

Belo was there. He reached out a hand and placed the palm on my forehead. Suddenly we were in another place and time— another ancient civilization. We hid behind some vegetation on a low hill; Belo pointed to the bottom of the hill. Amara was there, naked, sitting cross legged on the ground and all alone. As we watched, it began to rain lightly. Amara gathered dirt to her, fashioning something with her hands as the dirt grew wet. Soon, the dirt had taken the form of a great snake. Amara stood and walked away, leaving the snake to slither away.

"You are compelled to go to her," Belo said. "But it is not safe."

I was already pushing through the thick vegetation of the hill and hurrying after Amara's naked back. I ignored the snake until it bit me. I fell to the ground, paralyzed and in great agony as the serpent's venom burned through my body. Eyes bulging, I watched as the serpent lost its shape and returned to dust. It blew away and Amara was kneeling before me. When she spoke, I recognized the language as ancient Egyptian, something I could not have done while awake.

"I can cure you," she promised. "But first you must give me what I need."

Something shook me. I struggled to turn, expecting to find Belo behind me, trying to drag my stiff body away from Amara. As I struggled, I woke up and found myself back in the dark motel room.

"Milton, get up," Amara said. I rolled back and found her leaning over the bed. "Get up," she repeated. A dark shape loomed behind her, silhouetted by the neon lights shining behind the thin curtain over the motel window. I realized suddenly that it was a large man. I scrambled to a sitting position as the man moved closer.

He was a giant black man dressed in faded jeans, a gray T-shirt under an open flannel shirt. He wore a blue cloth as a headband. He looked down at me without interest.

"Tell your pimp to get his ass outta the bed," the man said.

"We need the bed, Milton," Amara said.

"What?"

"He is going to lay with me and pay us money."

"No. No, he's not," I said. "No. I won't have it."

"We have to have the money," she insisted.

"What the fuck's goin' on?" the man asked, beginning to sound angry. "This your pimp or your husband or what the fuck?"

"Amara, I won't let you become a prostitute."

"We must do something," she argued. "You cannot beg. You cannot steal and you cannot find work. Would you starve before you let another man lay with me?"

I'd gotten out of bed by this time. The room was cold.

"Where did he come from?" I asked.

"I went out when you had fallen asleep. He was not hard to find."

"Hey, my dick's tired of waiting," the black man said, throwing out his long, thick arms. "I done gave this bitch my money and I'm gonna fucking fuck somebody."

"You are not going to f—have sex with her," I said.

"Well I'm fucking somebody," he said, stepping forward and glaring down at me.

"Are you going to lay with him, Milton?" Amara asked. "What makes you think I wanna fuck this old white man?"

"That's perverse," I whispered, suddenly terrified. "No. Not that."

"You giving her to me?"

"No."

"Look at this, man. Look." He tore open his jeans and let them fall to the floor. In the dim light I could see his swollen penis, large and thick, pointing at me like a snake ready to strike. "This dick is saying it done paid for some pussy."

"I do not mind, Milton," Amara said. "I will do it for you."

Slowly, I shook my head. "No," I said. "I...I will do it. I can't bear the thought of anyone else touching you."

"That's sweet," the black man said. "But why the hell should I fuck you when this fine piece of pussy is offering it up? I paid for the pussy."

"I have never—I'm a—I have never known a man. That way," I said.

"Your asshole's a virgin?" I nodded.

"That don't sound so bad, after all."

My mind reeled and I thought for a moment I would fall. I closed my eyes and pictured this giant man rutting on Amara, his rough, dark flesh pinning her pristine pale body to the bed, humping, the bed squeaking, until he fully defiled her with his unclean lust.

"Do with me what you wish, but leave her alone," I whispered.

"Get them purty pajammies off," the man ordered, stroking his penis.

"You will do this to save me, Milton?"

"Yes, Amara. For you. God help me." I unsnapped the pajama pants and they fell to the floor. I pushed my underwear off and stood before them in only my pajama shirt. My own penis was tiny and shrunken and pathetic compared to the other man's.

"You want it on the floor or on the bed?" he asked. I shook my head to indicate it didn't matter. "Bend your ass over that bed, then."

I did as he commanded. Amara stood beside the bed, watching as the man positioned himself behind me. "It's only flesh," I said.

He grabbed my hips in his massive, calloused hands. I felt his penis poking at my doughy buttocks, finding the crack, searching. I closed my eyes and braced myself, but the moment of penetration was much, much worse than I could have anticipated. Without care at my inexperience, he rammed himself into me. I straightened my back, screeching, "Gaaaaa." It was unlike anything I'd ever felt, anything I could ever have imagined. My body went rigid with the agony as he continued to push himself deeper into me, tearing my flesh and, it seemed, shoving internal parts aside. I smelled excrement and blood. One of his hands released my hip, took my shoulder and pushed me back over the bed as he withdrew.

For one fleeting moment I thought he'd changed his mind and was going to pull out of me. Instead, he thrust forward even harder than the first time, moving more smoothly into me now that I was lubricated with blood and my own waste.

Tears flowed down my face. I braced myself on the bed with my hands, holding on just so he wouldn't knock me down with each merciless thrust. The agony of the initial penetration lessened only a tiny bit as he continued to work, pushing in, pulling out, each movement an excruciating testimony to my fall from prominence.

Then he pushed deep into me and stopped. His hands tightened painfully, pinching my buttocks as if he were crushing a grape. I cried out with the pain. He answered with a deep, throaty grunt and then I felt his penis throb and his hot seed burst into me. I cried openly, sobbing like a child, falling onto the bed, my eyes fixed on Amara as I wept bitterly.

Behind me, the man moved away toward the bathroom, then returned a moment later. He threw a stained, stinking white towel on the bed beside my face and then tossed a ten dollar bill on top of it.

"Since I was your first," he said. Then, to Amara, "You come find me again sometime and maybe I'll give you some of that." He left.

The towel was stained with my blood and excrement that he had wiped off his penis. I lacked the willpower to even turn my head away from it.

32

By morning, the pain had not left me, but lingered, leaving me feeling raw, stretched and as if internal organs had been displaced. And that was just the physical pain. Emotionally, I was a wreck. Over and over I pictured myself bent over the bed while the giant black man rutted behind me, Amara standing near, watching as if she were at a zoo and two animals were mating for her enlightenment.

When the man had left, Amara helped me clean myself and get into the bed. She snuggled close to me, covering my face and neck with kisses and thanking me for sacrificing myself for her. I couldn't speak to her; the pain then had been simply overwhelming. Eventually, I slept, though it was fitful and Belo came to me again.

It seemed he stood over me where I slept in my bed, his dark skin and ebony hair were shifting shadows in the dim motel room. He reached for me—into me—and jerked me into a dream world that was black, void and silent. "Will you see now what she has done to her own people?" Belo asked.

A female appeared before us. I could not place her, but I recognized her face, square, flat, with heavy features. As I watched, the woman put her hands on her legs and pulled out the femur bones from each. From them, she made a cigar holder. She then reached into her flesh and extracted tobacco, which she rolled into a cigar. Holding the cigar before her, she clutched a massive, firm breast in her free hand and squeezed it mightily so that a few drops of milk rose to the nipple and dripped onto the cigar. A burst of flame appeared before her face and the cigar was lit. As she blew out a stream of smoke, the air gathered and exploded in a clap of thunder and lightning. In the flash of light I felt her look at me. She puffed and exhaled again; another clap of thunder and now she stood before me.

And I knew her. It was Coadidop, the pagan goddess worshipped by the Amazonian villagers prior to the establishment of my mission.

"You are Thunder," she said. "I will call you Enu. I am your mother and grandmother. I have created you and will give you the power to create that which you need in the world. Make brothers for yourself," she commanded.

"I don't know how," I answered. She ignored me. I looked around, but Belo had abandoned me. "I want brothers," I called to the void. The darkness shimmered and became solid, taking the shape of three short jungle men. Delighted, I turned back to the goddess.

She also had created companions for herself. Two women, short and brown like my men, stood beside her. Coadidop tied a cord around her head, then removed it and dropped it at her feet. She took one of her breasts in her hand and again squeezed milk from it so that it fell on the circle of cord. The space within the cord began to fill, taking shape from her drops of milk until the cord held the very earth within it. The goddess addressed my creations and her females, "Go and live there and multiply." The people vanished.

"Come," a voice said. Belo had returned. He pulled me by the arm and we raced after the Indians, crashing into the jungle near the mission I'd helped to build. Yanmo, the chief of the village, was talking with Mike Page, a college professor of literature and an usher from the Prairie Valley Community Church. Tina Ford, Lori's friend, sat in a circle of children, reading from a Bible lesson book. Other people I recognized were all around. It was early morning and soon nearly everyone moved toward the gleaming white chapel for morning service. Outside, the air darkened as though night were returning, angry at the daylight that had driven it away. A feeling of gathering electric power filled the area around the village. The people who had not gone into the chapel looked at one another nervously. Someone cried out, "The goddess comes!"

They fled into the forest.

The air trembled, coalesced, and there in the center of the village stood Coadidop. She raised her thick brown arms and a flash of light exploded from her body in all directions, splintering the nearest buildings and setting everything afire. Even in the dream I was blinded for a time. When I could see again, the village was as I'd found it when I returned there after learning of the fire. I walked through the ruins just as I had that day that now seemed so long ago.

What is beautiful to you?

The voice wafted to me like the whisper of a breeze. For an instant as I stared into the ruins of the church the image of John Collier's *Lilith* snapped into my mind and was gone. I looked up and saw Coadidop watching me from the trees. As I looked, her shape melted and reformed and she was Amara.

"Now will you know the truth and guard your soul?" Belo asked. "Awake!"

"It's not true!" I yelled. I jumped toward Belo and found myself sitting up in the motel bed. The sudden movement and sitting position sent a sword of pain up my spine so I fell onto my back. Amara was not in the bed with me. I heard the shower running. Lying still, I tried to blot out memory of the night before. Then I heard Amara speaking. Carefully, I eased myself from the bed and went to the bathroom door to listen.

Her voice was too close, as if she was standing just on the other side of the thin door and not actually under the running shower. "He is not yet broken," she said. "No, I tell you he is not. He *can* grant it to me. He will. The time is near."

I knocked on the door. "Amara, who are you talking to?" Silence. "It is only me and my guardian angel," she said.

"Do you not say every person has a guardian angel?"

"Sounds like you're arguing with yours."

"That is silly, Milton," she said, and now her voice was farther away. The tone of the shower changed and I could imagine her putting her head under the streaming water. "I cannot hear you very well because of the water."

I moved away and sat carefully on the bed. Bored, I pulled open the nightstand drawer. A Bible placed by the Gideons lay at the bottom of the drawer. It looked as if it had never been opened. I shoved the drawer closed.

Amara emerged from the bathroom naked and wet, a dingy white towel wrapped around her head. She smiled at me and was still beautiful as ever.

"I had the strangest dream," I told her. "Please tell me."

"First, tell me, who are you? Who are you, really?"

"I have told you that," she answered, sitting beside me and taking my hands in hers.

"Yes, but I remember…this will sound really strange, but I remember thinking some of those things just before you said them."

"You believe you have the power of prophecy?" she asked.

"Nooo, not that." I wasn't at all sure how to say what I meant. "Do you have the power to read minds? Did you read what I expected you to say from my mind and then say it, knowing I would believe it?"

"That is silly, Milton," she said, laughing at me. "Tell me about the silly dream that would make you ask me that. Tell me about the dream as we eat breakfast."

"Breakfast?" The very word made my mouth water and stomach growl.

"We have money now, thanks to your act of sacrifice."

"Oh." The black man had paid Amara forty dollars when he thought he was going to have sex with her. With the ten he'd dropped on the bed after taking me, we had a total of fifty dollars. We splurged and rode the bus to an IHOP, where we both ordered large meals. The booth's bench was incredibly uncomfortable to my sore anus, but I was able to ignore that as I shoveled scrambled eggs, bacon and hash browns into my mouth.

"Tell me about your dream," Amara urged. I told her. She watched me, very seriously, as I told her all about it. When I'd finished, she only continued to stare at me, the small line of consternation creasing her forehead between her eyes. "You should not dream about that evil Belo. Did his own people not drive him away?"

"Something like that," I agreed. "It was a strange dream. Just…so vivid. Seeing the village again, just as it really was, was very weird."

"Are you ready to go?" she asked. I drained the last of my second glass of orange juice and we paid the bill, then went to the bus stop. "You should make that dirty man behind the desk give you the check he has stolen," she said.

And that was her topic all the way back to the stop nearest the motel. As we walked the short distance from the stop to the gravel parking lot, I agreed to confront the manager. He'd been waiting for me, I learned.

"There he is." The man beamed as we entered the office. His eyes blazed and his face was dark with stubble that had been left to grow now for several days. He reeked of cigar, coffee and stale beer. A large white onion sat on the counter; I put my hands on the counter, one on each side of the onion. "Ol' Duane told me he visited you last night. Said it wasn't at all what he'd wanted, but that it wasn't half bad. You're a new man today, preacher. Ain't ya?"

My voice faltered. I swallowed and tried again, though my mind was screaming: *How could he know?* "I want my check. I know it came in the mail and you have it. You'll be in trouble with the law if you try to cash it."

Suddenly he raised a black claw hammer from behind the desk. Startled, I staggered backward a step as the hammer came down on the onion, breaking it into numerous pieces and releasing the sharp, eye-watering scent.

"This onion's just as busted as yours," he growled. Then he brandished the hammer at me, the head wet with onion juice. You got ten minutes to pack your shit and get out, or I'll call the law myself and tell them how your whore over there's been buying dope and how you've been selling your ass to anybody with a ten dollar bill."

"You can't do that," I said. "It's my check. You have to give it to me."

"No. You got less than ten minutes now," he said. "You— bastard!" I lunged forward, completely mad with rage, and grabbed the hammer. I jerked it from his meaty hand and stepped back, unsure what to do next. He started to yell something at us again. I threw the hammer at him as hard as I could. He dodged, but it caught him on the side of the head. He dropped like a stinking sack of bricks.

"Oh no. Oh no. What did I do?" I looked at Amara. "Come, Milton. We must hurry." She pulled me out of the office. We hurried to our room. I grabbed the duffle bag I'd carried when we checked in, didn't pay any attention to what was in it, just shoved some clothes on top, and followed Amara back out to the parking lot; she carried only the small cheap purse I'd bought her in Manaus. We hurried back to the bus stop and boarded the next bus without looking to see where it would take us.

We rode the bus for two hours, until I realized it was bringing us back to the stop near the motel. Nervously, I looked out the window to see if I could see the flash of police lights in the direction of the motel. There was nothing. The bus stopped. No police boarded to look for the man who had attacked the manager. Had I killed him? Had he just been stunned or knocked out? I wasn't sure I wanted to know.

"Where will we go now, Milton?"

"I don't know, Amara."

"Is there no place in your city for people without homes?" I nodded. "There is."

"Should we not go there?" Reluctantly, I nodded again.

We left the bus at a stop on Reno Avenue, on the east side of downtown Oklahoma City. The air was cold, but the day was crisp and bright with not too much wind. I led Amara north from the bus stop, then alongside Interstate 40, which is an elevated highway running through the downtown area, carrying a huge volume of truck and passenger car traffic. The passage of vehicles was like thunder over our heads as we crossed under and then kept close to the bridge. Soon we came to an oblong box of a building with bars on the windows and "Jesus saves" painted on the cracked glass. Painted above the door in red letters were the words "Gospel Garden." The building was almost under one of the access ramps to the interstate, all alone in a cracked and broken area of blacktop. That was a Tuesday, December 12, 2000. I remember making a mental note of the date, the first night I would spend as a guest in a flophouse.

"What is this place?" Amara asked.

"A mission," I answered. "A place for homeless people. They provide meals and a place to sleep."

"You know the people here?"

I shook my head. "No, I only know of the place. I've never been here." I hesitated, then put a hand on the doorknob. "Are you ready?"

"Yes, Milton."

I opened the door and we stepped inside. The lighting was not good, but it was better than the smell. Several long portable tables stood lined end-to-end in a large room just inside the doorway. A half-dozen men sat at the table, some in pairs, playing cards. Others looked at newspaper parts. They all looked up at us as we entered and I heard a collective gasp as they took in Amara with her glowing face and flaming red hair. I put a protective arm around her and pulled her close to my side, staring back at the men.

"Hello? Can I help you?"

A man in his late fifties emerged from a hallway on the other side of the room. He approached us, a knowing but concerned look on his lean, worn face. His black hair had thinned greatly, but his dark eyes were friendly. He wore a water-spattered white apron over jeans and a red flannel shirt.

"I'm...we're...we could use some help," I said.

"Yes, I see," he said. "My name's Don Short. Most people just call me Pastor Don." He held out a hand made soft and wrinkly from dishwater.

I hesitated, then lied. "My name is Arthur and this is my wife Allison."

"Are you new in the city?"

"We've been here just a few months," I said. "I haven't been able to find work and now we're out of money. We don't have anywhere to go."

"Well, come back here to my office and let's talk about that." Pastor Don led us back to the hallway he'd emerged from, past a kitchen where he paused to tell two women he would rejoin them soon, and finally into a cramped office where we all sat around a small desk. "What kind of work do you do?" he asked.

"Oh, I'll do anything," I said.

"Yes, but what did you do? Before you lost your last job?"

I was at a loss for a bit, knowing I could never tell him I'd been a minister. Amara spoke up. "Arthur has never had one job very long," she said. "He likes to move around a lot and sample everything."

"Oh, I see." Pastor Don nodded. "You know, Arthur, not to point fingers, but I would think a man of your age would have settled into some job long enough to make a career of it. Is there anything you did longer than anything else? Something you enjoyed more?"

I shook my head. "No. Not really."

"Well, okay. I do learn of job leads sometimes, but they usually are things like mowing in the summer or cleaning graffiti off buildings. Hard jobs that not many people would want."

"I'll do anything," I said.

"That's the spirit. That's what we need to hear," Pastor Don said, smiling. "You'll be wanting to have lunch with us?"

"Yes. Please."

"Lunch is just soup with a piece of bread. Generally, we encourage our guests to get out during the day and search for work, even if it's only collecting cans."

"I understand," I said.

"We don't have too many rules," Pastor Don continued. "You're welcome to come in and eat with us. We serve breakfast, lunch and supper at eight, noon and five. We have a Christian service before breakfast and pray over each meal. No drugs or alcohol are allowed here. No weapons of any kind. If you spend the night, I'm afraid you'll have to be separated. We draw a partition through the main room, dividing men from women. It isn't a hotel." He looked from me to Amara. "Your wife is going to be a problem, Arthur. I'm sad to say that not every man who comes here has Christian values. Some will no doubt try to sway her with his affections."

"I can take care of myself," Amara said.

"We do have monitors—men and women volunteers—who stay at night to be sure no one is harmed," Pastor Don added. "But, some incidents have happened."

"I understand," I said again. "We'll be careful."

The Gospel Garden shelter became our base of operations. We would rise in the morning and eat breakfast; Amara never sang the hymns and never closed her eyes during the prayers. My own voice was dull and lifeless when I tried to sing the hymns and I gave up on it the first day, just mouthing the words. I couldn't pray; it seemed too much like God had turned his back on me. As those around us prayed, I held Amara's hand under the table.

We would slip away during the daylight hours, often walking aimlessly, trying to avoid the other people staying at the shelter. Most were older men, white, many with slight mental disorders, but there were others who came and went without staying long, and they were all races and ages.

I longed for an intimate moment with Amara, so one day we climbed a concrete embankment to a dark crevice right under the interstate. We could feel the earth vibrating as the trucks passed less than two feet above our heads. I took off my coat and spread it on the floor of the crevice. We lay on it, holding one another for only a moment before I pushed up the long skirt she wore and mounted her. The sounds of traffic faded as we enjoyed a brief but fierce moment of passion. When we finished, I slipped off and fastened my pants.

"Could I get some of that?"

One of the men from the shelter had followed us. He looked hungrily at Amara's groin; I pulled her skirt down to cover her. "No. This is my wife. You should leave," I said.

"But I want some of what you just got," he said. He was missing several teeth, had iron gray hair and faded blue eyes. A dirty hand fondled an erection through jeans made shiny with grime. "I can pay ya." With his other hand he pulled a wad of bills from a pocket. There were a few crumpled ones and a five.

"I said no," I repeated. "Now, go on back."

He tossed the money into Amara's lap and reached down to his pant leg. He lifted it and pulled a sharpened butter knife from his boot. "I just want some of your woman's pussy, Arthur. Don't make me get mean to get it. I always gotta go someplace else to live when I get mean with somebody."

"I won't let you have her," I said.

"My husband will let you lay with him," Amara said. "Amara!" I snapped at her.

"You did it for me once before," she said. "Will you not do it now?"

"Why'd you call her that? Amara?" the man asked. "Never mind," I said.

"You still tight?" he asked. "What?"

"Your asshole. Is it still tight?"

"He has only had intercourse with a man one other time," Amara said.

"Be quiet," I hissed at her.

"That sounds better'n pussy," the man said. "Get your pants back down and get on your knees. I like it doggy-style."

There's no use continuing to recreate the conversation. In the end, I complied and he rode me like an animal. It wasn't as bad as the first time, as this man was not nearly so endowed, nor did he last as long. Amara sat before me, cross-legged, caressing my face with one hand and clutching the offered money in the other as the homeless man did his business. The most climactic moment he left me with came after he had tucked himself back into his pants.

"You're gonna need to get yerself tested now," he said. "Clinic says I'm positive. That's why none of the guys down at the shelter will let me have a go with them."

"What?" The sinking feeling I had at that moment is with me to this day. My vision turned black around the edges and I could focus only on his guilt-ridden face. "Positive? For what?"

"HIV. AIDS," he said.

I lunged at him and grabbed him by the coat. I shook him, spitting profanities I'd never before uttered into his face. Finally, with all the force I had, I flung him from the concrete embankment. He sailed out over the sloping beige surface, then crashed into it. Blood spurted from his head and he rolled quickly to the bottom and into the street.

Once again, Amara pulled me away from a scene of my own violence. Had I killed the homeless man? I hoped so. Yes, at that moment I wanted to go down to the street and smash his face into the pavement until I knew he was dead. But Amara prevailed. She picked up my coat and pulled me away. We went back to the shelter and sat alone in a corner, not speaking. I sulked the rest of the day, fuming with anger, snapping at anyone who approached us.

In the middle of the afternoon two uniformed policemen entered the shelter and talked to the staff, showing them a photograph. They nodded and answered questions. The police walked around the shelter, showing a picture of the dead man to everyone. I looked at it briefly.

"Do you recognize him?" the officer asked.

"Yes. I've seen him here," I said. "I don't know his name."

"Have you seen him today?"

"I don't think so. He might have been here at breakfast. I didn't pay much attention."

"Have you left the shelter today?"

"Just for a little bit. My wife and I took a short walk a few blocks west and back." The place where we'd made love and I killed the man was east of the shelter.

"You didn't see him while you were out?"

"No."

"Thank you." The officer moved on, asking his questions, but not really caring. After all, it was just a homeless bum, not a tax-paying citizen.

Two days later, I very nervously went to Pastor Don's office and confessed that I'd had sex with a man for money. I expected quotes from Leviticus about the evils of homosexuality; that's what I would have offered. But Pastor Don only nodded sadly and wrote on a scrap of paper which he then handed to me.

"This is a free clinic where you can get tested," he said. "I know times are hard, Arthur. You want money. You want a job and to get on your feet, but there are better ways."

I nodded and left him. The clinic confirmed my worst fears. The test they did wasn't the most accurate available, but it was the least costly, the one they did first to see if further testing was warranted, a nurse told me. I returned the next day to learn the results. The test indicated I was HIV positive. In the lobby I broke down and sobbed like a child, clinging to Amara, my face buried in the shoulder of her coat. People stared, some whispered, but I couldn't think of them. *I have AIDS. I will die because of it. I'm going to die.*

Eventually Amara got me to my feet and we left the clinic. We paid for a day pass and rode the bus for a while, using the last of the money earned from my encounter with the dead man. As we passed a park on Northwest 36th I signaled for a stop and we got off. We walked around the park for a short while, then sat on a bench. We were alone in the park. There was equipment for children, but it was unused. Naked trees swayed under an overcast sky, their long, thin branches like accusing fingers.

"I'm going to die of this," I said aloud for the first time. "I killed him, but he killed me first. I just didn't know it for sure until now."

"All humans die, Milton," Amara said.

"I gave up everything to be with you. Now, you're all I have, but I can't even have you anymore."

"Why not?"

"Amara. I have AIDS. It's passed through sex. There's no cure."

"I am very sorry I offered your body to that man. I thought he was going to kill us and I knew you would die before you let him take me."

"You're right about that," I said. "I would have fought him. Maybe he would have just killed me with the knife then raped you and given you…this disease. That would have been awful."

"I am very sorry, Milton."

"It's not your fault," I said. "Please forgive me."

"Of course, Amara. Don't I always forgive you?"

"You do."

"We should go back."

We had to walk a ways to find a bus stop where the bus would take us near the Gospel Garden. We rode back quietly, hand in hand, and arrived in time for dinner. Afterward, Pastor Don called me to his office and asked about my visit to the clinic. I told him I had the dreaded virus.

"I am incredibly sorry, Arthur," he said. "You know we will continue to welcome you here, but please be careful now that you are infectious. Did they give you medication?"

"No. I have to go back and talk to a doctor about that."

"Please make sure you do that. I know there is no cure for AIDS, but there are drugs that can help you live and be happy longer."

"Happy?"

"I know life has not been kind to you, Arthur. But it's all in God's hands."

Without responding, I left him there and went to the main

room. Night had stolen in through the barred windows. I sat on my cot, staring out the window at the lights of downtown Oklahoma City. At long last I reached under the cot and pulled out my duffle bag. I unzipped it and dug through the dirty clothes to take out the Bible I'd treasured for so many years. It had gone untouched since we left the apartment. Idly, I thumbed through the pages. Finally I stopped and clutched the book tightly and bowed my head.

At first no words would come. And then three words did come. "You don't exist."

I left my cot. On my way out of the shelter I shoved the leather-bound Bible deep into a trashcan.

I roamed the night for hours, spending a good deal of that time at the memorial built to remember people who died when Timothy McVeigh blew up the Alfred P. Murrah Federal Building. Rows of stone chairs stood ranked before a shallow pool reflecting the night lights of the city. Across the pool a blasted tree stood silent sentinel. Two uniformed guards talked quietly under the Survivor Tree that had withstood the blast from the Ryder truck. I turned from the pool to face the chairs. "It's all so goddamn useless," I told them. "I'll join you soon enough, but there won't be any chair with my name carved on it."

I left the memorial and walked back toward the shelter. It was late morning; I knew I'd long since missed breakfast and was wishing lunch would be more substantial than bread and soup. As I approached the front door I heard Amara's voice coming from the west side of the building. Suspecting she was talking to herself again, I eased along the brick wall, hoping to catch her in the act.

I did catch her in an act, but she was not alone. She was tearing the clothes off a strong young man I'd noticed in the shelter earlier that day. He ripped the front of her dress open and grabbed her breasts. She pulled his jeans down and knelt to take his erection into her mouth. He rocked with pleasure as she bobbed her head. Then he pulled her to her feet and pushed her against the wall. She raised her skirt.

"Fuck me, Rick," she said. "Fuck me as hard as you can."

He began to do so. A moment later I somehow found his head in my hands. I slammed it against the brick wall and it bounced off like a large golf ball. Blood ran from a gash in his forehead and from his nose and lips. He shook his head and looked at me. "Oh shit," he said. He pulled up his pants and ran.

"Milton, please forgive me."

I turned on Amara. She was standing against the wall, her dress still open so that her firm white breasts gleamed in the moonlight. Overhead, trucks roared by on the interstate. Her eyes pled with me, her lips trembling. "You were all I had left," I said. "I had nothing. I gave up everything for you. And you betrayed me." I began to turn away, but she grabbed my arm and pulled me back to her.

"Please, Milton. Forgive me," she begged. "No. Not this time."

"Milton, what are you saying? You have to forgive me. This is not the final test."

"Test? What test? To hell with that. I don't even care. I don't forgive you, Amara. You *are* just a whore. Just like Karen said. Get away from me."

"Milton! No! Do not leave me." She came after me and grabbed my arm again.

I spun around and struck her hard across the face. She reeled away from me, one hand rising to the cheek I'd hit. Her eyes, her enormous green eyes, were filled with pain and disappointment.

"Then it is true," she said. "If the image of God cannot forgive me, God will never do so."

"God?" I spat. "God? There is no God. Do you think God would have allowed this to happen to me? Look at this. Look at this! Look at me. I've lost everything. My family. My home. My dignity. The faith I thought was so strong. And now I've even lost you."

"You have not lost me, Milton."

"Yes I have. Go away. Go sell your pussy to anyone who'll buy it."

She started toward me again and I raised my hand. She backed away and a new emotion flitted across her face. She was angry. Her eyes blazed and she stood erect. "I do not need your forgiveness," she said. "No more than I need his." With that, she turned and walked away from me and into the night of Oklahoma City.

33

I was alone. I'd never been really, truly alone in all my life. I left my parents' house for college, then lived with roommates until marrying Karen. Now, I had no one. Of course, I wasn't alone in the Gospel Garden, where I continued to flop at night, but I stayed to myself and didn't socialize. Most people there knew the beautiful woman I'd been with had left me. They knew I'd contracted HIV. Some, I believed, suspected me of killing the man who'd given me the disease. But that could have been my own paranoia.

Despite Pastor Don's decree, drugs were readily available at the Gospel Garden shelter. Generally, they weren't used inside the building, but outside, drug use was prevalent. I continued to smoke marijuana after Amara left. I took pills, usually painkillers, hoping to dull the sense of loss I felt over my plight. How I got the drugs varied. Sometimes trading a stale packaged dessert from lunch was enough for a joint. Sometimes it would mean a handjob in the bathroom. It no longer really mattered to me what I did.

During the days, I would either sit idly in the shelter, or roam the streets, watching people with jobs, homes and lives. My unemployment checks no longer came. I had called and asked that they be sent to me at the shelter, but I'd quit making my job searches and quit lying about it to the automated phone system. I didn't care. I had no need for money. I was just waiting to die, although I was not yet noticeably sick.

Then, one cold, blustery Friday before Christmas, as I walked through the small Kerr Park across the street from the Kerr-McGee office building, I saw a familiar face sitting on a stone bench by one of the water fountains that was turned off for the winter. I stared in disbelief, rubbed my eyes, then ran and threw my arms around my daughter.

"Lori!" I shouted, pulling her off the bench and hugging her so tightly she coughed. "Is it really you? What are you doing here? Where have you been?" I held her at arm's length and looked her in the face.

The face was Lori's, but different. She looked much older, with dark circles under eyes that seemed empty. She wore a great deal of makeup in an attempt to cover her listless features, but they could not hide the changes from the father who remembered when she glowed with life. Her hair was clean and blew in the wind and she wore a long coat of tan suede, but it was open and I could see that she wore a very short skirt and fishnet hose.

"Hi, Daddy," she said, her voice betraying very little emotion.

"Baby, aren't you glad to see me?"

"Sure."

"Where have you been?"

"I've been around. What happened to you? You kind of stink. And you look like hell."

How could I tell her? There was no soft way to put it. I couldn't look her in the eye, but I said, "Your mother left me.

She found me in bed with Amara and left me. Things pretty much fell apart after that. I live in a homeless shelter now and I have AIDS and Amara cheated on me and is gone."

"Whoa. And I was afraid you were going to start dropping the God-bomb on me when I saw you running over here," she said.

"That bomb is a dud. No God could let this much shit happen to me."

"Daddy. I can't believe you just said that. You *are* messed up. You said you have AIDS? Amara gave you that?"

"No, it wasn't her," I said. "Do we have to talk about this here? What are you doing here? Do you work in one of these buildings?"

"Sort of," she said. "A lot of the men like to relieve their stress during lunch."

"What does that mean? You give massages?"

"C'mon, Daddy. Don't you get it? Look at me." She stuck one of her legs out of her open coat. "They come out, give me money, and I go to their office, or car, or whatever and we have sex. I'm a prostitute."

"Oh Lori. No. Not that. Why?"

"You're a fine one to talk," she said.

I took a deep breath and let it out slowly. "You're right," I said. "I got AIDS because I let a man take me. He had a knife and was going to take Amara. But he wasn't the first. You don't have AIDS do you?"

"Oh no. We take care of ourselves."

"We?"

Lori pointed to two other young women positioned around the small park. "That's Daphne and that's Brenda. We share an apartment and kind of look out for each other."

"Oh." Suddenly it seemed there was nothing left to say. The silence was long and awkward. Lori broke it.

"Look, Daddy, I have money. I have plenty. Let me give you some."

"I don't want your money, Lori. I'm just so glad I found you." Suddenly I was crying, my body shaking with the sobs. "I didn't want to die without seeing you again."

"Oh Daddy." She took me into her arms and held me tightly as I wept on her shoulder. When I had quieted she said, "Listen, let's go to lunch. Let me buy you lunch." I nodded against her shoulder, then straightened up to face her.

"Thank you," I said. "I appreciate it."

Lori called out to one of her friends, pointed to me and nodded. The friend gave her a queer look, then shrugged and turned away to approach a young man in a suit. "Let's go," Lori said, taking me by the arm. She led me around a corner, past The Journal Record newspaper office and across the street to Leadership Square, another tower of glass with a strange red metal sculpture in the courtyard. She bought us overpriced sandwiches and coffee from a deli inside and we sat at round tables in the open first floor of the building. An indoor fountain seemed very loud as we tried to talk.

"Where is Amara?" Lori asked.

"I don't know. I don't really care. Why?"

She paused. "Do you remember that bite I had on my neck?" she asked. "Just before I got Dan to go to bed with me?"

"Bite?"

"You know, we thought it was a bug bite. A big one. Right here." She pulled down the collar of her coat to show me her neck. There were no marks on the flesh, but I did finally remember the bite.

"Oh, yeah. I kept telling you to put something on it and you wouldn't," I said.

"I have dreams that Amara bit me. In fact, I think I might have woke up while she was doing it and that's why I keep dreaming about it."

"She bit you?"

"And drank my blood, like a vampire. No, not like a vampire. More like, she bit me, sucked the wound like she was giving me a hickey, then was licking the blood off me."

"You knew that and you didn't tell me?"

"Like you would have believed me," she said and laughed. For the briefest of fleeting moments I saw my little girl again as Lori laughed. I smiled. She said, "You wouldn't have believed me. You wouldn't believe anything anybody said about Amara when you first brought her home. It was obvious you were in love with her. I saw it when I picked you up in the airport."

"Lori…" I looked away, watched people walking by looking back at me with turned up noses. "You're probably right. Still, you should have told me."

"It was too weird, anyway. I mean, like, why would she do that? That's what I thought then. And, you know, it was right after that I started feeling horny all the time. I felt constantly horny, like a nymphomaniac, all the time after that. Until about a week ago. One day, as I was going up the elevator with a john, I just didn't feel it anymore."

"What day was it?" I asked, a strange feeling tickling my gut.

"Last Thursday. That's what, like nine days ago?"

"I sent Amara away last Thursday. It was late morning," I said.

We stared at each other, wondering what it meant. "Lobishomen," I said quietly. "What's that?"

"Supposedly, a South American demon. It bites victims, drinks their blood and turns them into nymphomaniacs. The captain of the *River Lily* said Belo's wife had been bitten by one."

"That's kind of freaky, Dad," Lori said. "And who is Belo? Didn't he play Dracula?"

"No. That's Bela. Lugosi. Belo was a man on the boat. The son of a native shaman. He died while me and Amara were on the boat. He was very afraid of her."

"Too weird. You brought home a demon?"

"Lobishomen are supposed to be extremely hideous."

"Amara wasn't that," Lori said.

"No." We sat quietly for a time as I remembered the dream about Coadidop. *What is beautiful to you?* The dream voice played over and over in my mind until, suddenly, I had an idea. "So, if you don't feel that way anymore, why don't you stop? Stop...selling yourself?"

Lori shrugged and now it was her turn to look away. "I don't know," she said. "What else would I do now? I look in the mirror and see a whore that isn't very old but that's, you know, looking pretty used."

"Lori, a good night's sleep, some rest, and you'd look better. Stop doing this and you'll feel better about yourself. You *are* still young. You can do whatever you want. Please. Think about it. I know I'm in no position to be telling you what to do, so I'm asking—I'm begging you—think about it. For me?"

She nodded. "I'll think about it, Daddy. I really will. The money's easy, you know, doing what I do. But now that I don't feel like that, like I want it all the time, I do feel kinda dirty and cheap, even when they pay a lot."

Our sandwiches were gone and the dregs of coffee were cold.

She traced a long red fingernail around the lip of her cup. "What are you going to do now, Daddy?"

"Go back to the shelter, I guess."

"I'd ask you to come stay with us, but…Daphne and Brenda probably wouldn't like it."

"I understand. I wouldn't impose."

"The offices down here will shut down after today, you know. Christmas break. I'm going to Wichita with Brenda to see her parents. They think we're secretaries at Devon Energy. Otherwise, I'd say you'd have to come have Christmas dinner with us. I'm sorry. I could stay."

"No, Lori. You go with your friend. Have fun. But…could I see you again? After Christmas?"

"Of course, Daddy. I want to see you. I didn't want to leave home, you know. But I knew you and mom would just freak that I had that need. It was unreal. I just ached for sex all the time. Daphne said I was every man's dream become nightmare because nothing could ever satisfy me for very long." She paused, then blushed. "I'm sorry, Daddy. I guess you don't want to hear that."

I smiled sadly and shook my head. "No. I'm just glad it seems to be passing. Maybe you should apply for a real secretary job at Devon."

"Maybe. I did take a lot of math in high school. But I don't have my diploma."

"You could easily pass the equivalency test," I said.

"Yeah. I probably could. Daddy, I want to give you some money. I mean it." She reached into an inside pocket of her coat and pulled out a modest roll of bills. She peeled off three fifties and pushed them across the table at me. "Get some new clothes and eat a good Christmas dinner, okay? For me?"

"If you'll really seriously think about getting a new line of work," I said. She laughed again and I saw the old Lori one more time when she did.

"I promise," she said. I put the cash into my pants pocket. We stood and walked out of the building into the cold air as more people were coming back in after their lunch break. "I need to go back alone," Lori said. "I'm so glad you found me, Daddy." She threw her arms around me, hugged me and kissed my cheek.

"When will I see you again?" I asked, not letting her go. "We'll be back on Tuesday. When the offices reopen," she said, releasing me and sliding out of my arms. She reached into her pocket again and took out a wadded napkin and a pen. She wrote on the napkin and handed it to me. "That's my cell phone number. I gotta go, Daddy. I love you."

"I love you, too, Lori."

She started to turn away, then hesitated. "Daddy? Where is Mom?"

"Woodward."

"And Eric?"

"He went with her. He was…he was really mad at me." She nodded. "Bye, Daddy." She waved and hurried away, her heels a quick, delicate staccato on the stone courtyard.

34

Finding Lori was the first good thing to happen to me since Amara entered my life. As I walked back to the shelter that afternoon after we had lunch I vowed to give up all the drugs I'd been using. No more pot, no more pills and certainly no more disgusting acts to obtain the drugs.

It wasn't easy. I'd come to crave the marijuana desperately. When I was smoking, I could imagine myself back in the good days, when I was young and Karen had not become so distant, when Lori was a little girl sitting on my lap to watch "Sesame Street," or playing catch with Eric. Or the first weeks after I became Amara's lover.

I imagined pain where I had none. I'd begun taking the painkillers for emotional pain. Soon after vowing to stop using drugs, I began to have physical aches that made no sense. The next day was worse. I spent the weekend before Christmas either lying on my cot in the shelter, or sitting huddled in the doorway of a closed office building. I wouldn't tell anyone of my aches because I knew it was just withdrawal, but the urge to go to my supplier and offer to jerk him off for a couple of Valium was very strong. I resisted, though, and made it through the day and a mostly sleepless night.

Shortly after dawn, the Gospel Garden shelter began to fill with the aroma of baking turkey. Pastor Don and the other volunteers beamed at us, wishing us a merry Christmas, promising us a hot and delicious meal of turkey, dressing, mashed potatoes, hot rolls and the other usual trimmings. I sat on my cot, hunched over, my hands over my abdomen, rocking and wishing for a pill, a joint, anything to ease my mind. I didn't notice Pastor Don coming into the room until he began to speak.

"Ladies and gentlemen," he called. "We've had a bit of a

problem. Our oven quit working." There was a groan from the gathered homeless. I dully noted that there were more people in the shelter today than usual. There were many children and I supposed Pastor Don had promised them gifts.

"I came here for turkey," one large woman with a face that seemed frozen in a scowl shouted. A few others muttered in agreement.

"Now, not to worry," Pastor Don continued. "We have a bus coming to pick you up. We're going to take you, the presents and the half-cooked turkeys to the Myriad Convention Center and join the celebration going on there."

Most people cheered, others grumbled that the new plan was acceptable. I said nothing, just sat in my private hell and wondered if the food would stave off my other cravings for a while.

About an hour later a large bus from Pastor Don's Baptist church arrived. Everyone was shooed from the shelter and onto the bus. Well, I was shooed. Most went eagerly. The Myriad is not far from the Gospel Garden; we could have walked the distance in twenty minutes rather than waiting for the bus, but it was a very cold day despite the brilliant sunshine.

We arrived at the convention center and were greeted by more smiling volunteers doing their good deeds by giving up their holiday to help the outcasts of the city. These clean, smiling faces led us through hallways and into the main area of the center, a place that usually held rock concerts, monster truck events or popular speakers. I'd once gone there to hear Bill Cosby lecture. Now, the space was filled with long tables, hundreds of folding chairs, many of them already occupied by people who'd come for the free lunch.

Scores of conversations were going on, creating a loud din punctuated by dozens of rampaging children chasing one another around in various games. I hung around the edge of the crowd, toward the back, the collar of my coat turned up and my hands either in my pockets or my arms crossed over my chest.

The people were of various races and age groups, but nearly

all wore old clothes, some obviously hand-me-downs or thrift store fare. Their faces were animated, but it was plain to see the light within them was new for today, that their usual life was not filled with warm rooms and free turkey and gifts for their children.

In stark contrast were the volunteers in new clothes with smooth skin, manicured nails and styled hair. Their smiles were as bright as new holiday lights, but even when they weren't smiling their faces had an internal shine. Sullenly, I told myself the light was false. Or, not false, but that the faces had never known darkness and therefore took the light for granted.

I was just like that last year at this time.

The thought hit me hard. I *had* been just like them, helping people like those all around me without really giving them the thought they deserved. I looked again at the other poor people, wondering now why the woman with twin infants was here, how the man with the U.S. Marine Corps tattoo came to be dressed in tattered slacks and what did the children do when they were not running around the floor of the Myriad? What hope did they have of a future? Would they ever know a life that didn't involve receiving free Christmas dinners with other poverty-stricken people?

A line began to form at the serving table and I was herded into it by a cheery woman of about thirty-five who wore a hat with cloth reindeer horns sticking from the sides. It took several minutes to get to the table, where I was handed a tray and some plastic flatware. I shuffled along with the rest of the poor, accepting a helping of corn, of yams, beets, dressing and had my tray extended for turkey when I was addressed.

"Milton?"

I raised my eyes and found myself looking through gold-framed glasses into the widened brown eyes of David Ross. I dropped my gaze, my tray sagging in my suddenly weak arms.

"Milton? Is it really you?"

"Yes, David. It's me."

"What's happened to you, man?"

"Long story."

The line was backing up. Feet were shuffling and I felt eyes on me, trying to push me out of the way. David finally put a large piece of turkey breast on my tray. "Thank you," I whispered and moved on to a woman who was serving gravy. When I got to the end of the table, David was there waiting on me. "Shouldn't you be carving more turkey?" I asked, trying to move away, but he stayed with me, following me to the least occupied table in the room. I sat and he sat beside me.

"Tell me, Milton. What's happened to you?"

"Don't you know, David? Can't you guess?"

"I never could have guessed I would find you here. Like... like this."

I looked up from the tray of food I no longer wanted. "It's so much better than it looks, you know. Not only am I homeless, penniless, alone and aching for a joint or some pills, but I've gotten myself a good ol' case of AIDS by having sex with other men for money," I said.

"Oh my Lord, Milton. I had no idea." His dark, wrinkled face showed genuine compassion, and it infuriated me.

"No idea? You had no idea? What the hell did you think I would do when you fired me? Huh? Not a lot of jobs out there for preachers who get fired for committing adultery. Man, my life was falling apart already. Lori was gone. Karen was leaving me. My own son beat the hell out of me. And then you fired me. This may come as a shock to you, Mr. Accountant—Mr. Church Elder here to do your goddamn service to this shithole community—but I don't have any other skills besides telling people to follow the laws of some mythological character in an old book."

My voice had risen in volume the more I talked and I now realized that people all around us were looking at me, openly eavesdropping on the conversation. I glared back at them and when they didn't look away I became even madder. "Eat your damn turkey, you bunch of welfare grubbing leeches."

"Calm down, Milton," David urged. "I want to help you.

I can—"

"Help me? What? Are you going to give me second helpings of this turkey I couldn't afford to pay for? Ooo. Maybe another scoop of stuffing. I'd tell you to go to hell, but if there is a hell I don't want the company."

I shoved my tray across the table and stood up. I forced myself not to run, but I was practically doing so as I hurried out of the building and back into the cold afternoon. For a long time I walked, thinking I was moving aimlessly, believing my anger would dissipate, but it didn't. When I found myself on the campus of Oklahoma City University, a few miles northwest of the Myriad, I realized where I was subconsciously going. Now that the idea was in my thoughts, I decided I liked it.

The sun was sinking when I entered the Prairie Valley division in far northwest Oklahoma City. By the time I made it to my old church it was fully dark. I thought my legs should ache from the long walk, but they didn't. The desire for drugs was gone, drowned in adrenaline as I walked along one wing of the building, looking for something and finally finding a neat stack of branches trimmed from trees lining the fence of the playground behind the church. I picked out a nice thick one to use as a club and went back to the church sign near the street. The sign was one of those with a glass front, a black background with slots so you can arrange letters. For years, my name had been on the sign. Now, the message on the sign reminded readers that Jesus was the reason for the season. Somebody named Richard Robinson was named as minister. I swung the club and smashed the glass. It made a sharp cracking sound, followed by the tinkle of falling glass. I struck the sign several times, sending white letters flying like broken teeth. It felt good. The release of anger was better than smoking pot. I felt as if my veins burned with fire as I left the sign and approached the church.

The burglar alarm sounded with the first blow to a stained glass window. I laughed at it and smashed the window again. I raced all along the central hub of the building, breaking out the brightly colored stained glass of the sanctuary windows. They were all broken, like empty eye sockets where I could look into the darkness of a brainless skull, when I noticed the approaching police sirens. Something told me I should run, but instead I dropped my pants and began to urinate on the front door of the church.

Car doors slammed behind me. Red and blue light flashes were reflected on the surface of the door. "Put your hands where I can see them," a cop shouted. I finished urinating, shook myself, and lifted both hands. "Now turn around." I did.

There were two police cars. Four officers crouched behind open doors, guns drawn and pointed at me. For one euphoric moment I considered rushing them, letting them fire their guns at me, ending the misery that was my new life. But, I would have tripped over the pants wrapped around my ankles and simply fallen after the first step. Not a glorious end at all.

"Keep your hands on your head," one of the officers yelled. He moved slowly away from the door of his car and approached me. When he was standing about three feet from me he stopped. "Very slowly, pull up your pants," he ordered. I did as I was told. "Do you have any weapons on you?" he asked.

"No," I answered. I'd thrown my club through the last window I broke.

"Turn around and put your hands on the door. Higher," he ordered when I pressed my palms to the door at chest level. I moved them higher. He holstered his gun and frisked me quickly. Then he pulled my hands behind my back and put handcuffs on my wrists.

"Jail at last," I said. "I guess that's really all that was missing in my life."

The other officers had approached now and stood around me. Another car pulled in behind their patrol cars and a trim man in his mid-thirties jumped out and ran toward us.

"I'm Richard Robinson," the man said as an officer moved to stop him. "I'm the minister here." I laughed at him.

"Do you know this man?" one of the policemen asked him.

"I've never seen him before," the minister answered. The cop turned to me. "What's your name?"

"Milton Agnew," I said.

"Milton Agnew?" Richard Robinson echoed. "You know him?" a cop asked.

"He was my predecessor here."

"We're going to take him to the jail," a police officer said. "I assume you'll want to press charges?"

"Absolutely."

"A damn Christian act of you, Reverend Robinson," I said, still laughing. "Merry fucking Christmas to you, too."

"Are you under the influence of drugs or alcohol?" a cop asked.

"I'm just high on life," I answered. "It's a hell of a trip." They all gave me a dirty look and decided the time for conversation was over. I was pulled to a cruiser and pushed into the back seat. I don't remember what I was laughing about— probably just trying to keep from crying again—but I laughed all the way back downtown to the county jail. I laughed when they fingerprinted me, laughed when they took my mug shot and laughed when they put me in a tiny cell and closed the door—not the classical barred door, but a solid white steel door with a small square of reinforced glass at eye-level.

Alone in the cell, I sat on a steel tray mounted to the wall and covered with a thin mattress and continued to laugh until

I did begin to cry. Somebody yelled at me to shut the fuck up. I laid down and put my face in the pillow and continued to cry.

After a while, I slept.

35

"Agnew. Milton. Wake up."

I opened my eyes and looked toward the open door of my cell to see a tall, barrel-chested black man in a policeman's uniform. He was staring back at me as I rubbed my eyes and sat up, my body aching from the exertion of vandalizing the church. "Do I go to see the judge now?" I asked, all traces of last night's laughter gone from my voice.

"Nope. Charges been dropped. On coupla conditions."

"What's that?"

"They'll tell ya 'bout 'em out there." The cop pulled the door open and motioned for me to go down the corridor and through another open door. I was ushered into an office and the door was closed behind me. I was in the room with a bald white man in his late forties and David Ross.

"Milton Agnew?" the white man asked. "Yes."

"I'm Sergeant Nathan Singer. Have a seat." He waved to a wooden chair with a rounded back and reddish finish. It matched the one David sat in beside me. "You know this man?" the sergeant asked, motioning at David.

"Yes. He's David Ross."

"Mr. Ross is representing Prairie Valley Community Church this morning. He said he's willing to drop the charges against you if you'll agree to his conditions."

"What are those?" I asked.

"That you put yourself in the custody of Mr. Ross."

"What?" I couldn't believe what I'd heard.

"Milton, I want to help you," David spoke at last. "I want to help you get back on your feet."

"Why? To make yourself feel better for firing me?"

"I did what I had to do for the church. That has nothing to do with what I'm offering now. I'm not asking you as a church elder to a minister I hired. Or fired. I'm asking you as a friend who cares for you."

"Cares for me? You never cared for me. You rode my ass constantly."

"Milton…how do I say this? Since my wife died, I replaced her with the church. The business of the church. And I let the business overshadow what the church is really about. When I saw you yesterday, it hit me like a ton of bricks. I thought, 'My God, I let adherence to rules and public perception ruin this good man's life.' And I know you are a good man, Milton."

"Mr. Agnew," Sergeant Singer interrupted, "I think Mr. Ross here honestly wants to help you. I've talked with him for nearly an hour this morning and he's told me several times that seeing you was a wake-up call to him. I can release you to him, or you can go back to your cell. You'll be charged with destruction of private property, indecent exposure and we could probably throw in attempted burglary and a few other things if you want to make this difficult. This man wants to help you. I suggest you accept his offer."

"What do you want in return?" I asked David.

"I've talked with the people at Gospel Garden. I know you have a drug problem now. I want you to get over that. I'll help. Other than that…I want you to forgive me for my part in letting this happen to you."

"Nothing just happened to me, David. I made conscious decisions. They were just a long series of wrong ones."

"Please. Make the right one now." David's round, dark face was very earnest, drawn, his eyes filled with pain as he looked at me. I looked down at myself, my dirty, ragged clothes, filthy hands, and knew my face was now gaunt and wore several days' worth of stubble.

I nodded.

"Thank you, Milton," David said.

"You've done the right thing, Mr. Agnew," the police sergeant added. "I do want you to think about one thing for me." He made a dramatic pause and waited until I'd met his gaze before continuing. "If you betray this man's trust, if you break the law again while in his care, I promise you I will find every possible charge I can scrape up to bring against you and lock you away for as long as possible. You understand?"

I nodded again. "I understand."

"Good," Sergeant Singer said. "Now, you can go through that door, to your left and down the hall, turn right and you'll find the counter where you can pick up the belongings we took when you came in."

"Okay." I stood up; the officer and David stood, too. Sergeant Singer reached across the desk to shake my hand, then David's.

"Let's go, Milton," David urged.

I collected the few things I'd had with me when I was booked into the jail the night before. It was a sparse assortment—the napkin with Lori's cell phone number on it, the cash she'd given me, my wallet, which was empty except for a driver's license, a credit card I could no longer use, a bank debit card for an account with no money and pictures of Lori, Eric and Karen. And the canvas print of John Collier's *Lilith*, now folded into a square that fit into my coat pocket. The letter from Bill Barlow was folded into the canvas. I stuffed all these items back into my coat pockets after I put the garment on.

"Are you ready?" David asked. "I think so."

"Let's go."

Conversation came in spurts as we drove. David's Lincoln Town Car moved along smoothly, jazz music playing softly on the radio, the blue leather interior as spotless as the day he drove the car off the lot. I remembered my own Cadillac being towed away.

"How do you feel?" David asked.

I sighed. "I feel...empty. Tired, beaten down, hungry and...empty."

"I think I can help you on all accounts. We're going to my

house. You can take a long, hot shower, get yourself cleaned up, shaved, put on clean clothes while I make us some breakfast. Or lunch. Whichever you prefer. Then, if you want, you can sleep in the guest bed until you feel like getting up."

"What about the empty part? It's more than an empty stomach. Since...she left, I haven't had much purpose. At least, not until I found Lori."

"You found Lori? Where?"

"Downtown."

"What was she doing?"

"She...she's a secretary at Devon Energy. She's doing well."

"When you said you've felt empty since she left, who did you mean?"

"Yeah. All my women left me, didn't they? I meant Amara, of course. The last one to leave."

We drove in silence for a while, slipping up Classen Boulevard to the Northwest Expressway, then heading west.

"You told me you have AIDS," David prompted. "I'm very sorry. Are you getting treatment?"

"No. Not many homeless people have insurance."

"No, I suppose not." His glasses glinted in the late morning sun as he risked a quick glance my way. "I'll make sure you get treatment. I'll make the appointment today."

"Why? Why would you do that for me? Treatment for HIV is outrageously expensive. I probably will never be able to repay you for that."

"When you brought Amara back here, you said you wanted to continue the mission work with her. With that one person. Now, you're *my* mission, Milton."

I laughed softly. "There's every possibility I only brought her home because I subconsciously—or not so subconsciously—burned with lust for her the moment I saw her. Besides, my one-soul mission not only failed but destroyed my faith in some benevolent deity watching over us from a throne in the cosmos. It's all crap, David. Look at me, man. I am living proof that there is no God."

David looked at me and smiled. "And I'm living proof that there is a God and he still loves you."

I snorted, then laughed again. "If you say so. After all, Sergeant Singer basically said you're my daddy now."

As we left the Expressway and turned into the Prairie Valley subdivision, I had to fight down the urge to throw open the car door and jump out to run back to the jail. Familiar houses slid by as we drove. We passed the turn I'd made so many times to go to my own home I'd shared with an intact family. As we passed the church I stared at the gaping black holes of windows, at the door where I'd once greeted my congregation but last night had baptized in piss. People I recognized were cutting plywood to cover the broken windows.

"I always loved those stained glass windows," I said softly. "I shouldn't have broken them."

"It's just glass. It can be replaced."

"At great expense."

"There's more to life than money."

"Ah. That's so easy to say when you have it. But try living without it. Try wondering how you're going to pay for another week in a sleazy motel or buy a loaf of bread so you don't have to dig through the Dumpster behind a fast food joint. Money. That's the real god."

"In time, Milton, I hope you'll remember what you're saying now and wonder how such words came from you."

"It doesn't seem likely."

We pulled into David's driveway. The garage door was sliding up and he drove the Lincoln into the garage and lowered the door. His house was large, much too large for a man who lived alone. Every item—every book, every framed photograph, every record album, dish and piece of furniture—was in a place assigned for it. There was not a speck of dust, nor hint of cobweb. The furniture was heavy pieces, oak and tan leather mostly. He had shelves of books on tax codes, personal finance, investment strategies and numerous volumes of popular Christian writings. He showed me to the spare bedroom where several new shirts, two pairs of slacks, two pairs of sweatpants and a package of underwear and one of socks was laid out on the bed.

"I think I'm pretty good at guessing people's sizes," David said. "I think all these items will fit. You have a bathroom right off this bedroom. I'll leave you to get cleaned up. There's soap, shampoo, razor and shaving cream in there, as well as deodorant and a couple kinds of cologne."

Somehow, this moved me much more than his willingness to bail me out of jail. The barrier I'd put up between us when I found him in the sergeant's office crumbled a bit and I reached out and took his arm in my hand, then shook his hand. "Thank you, David," I said. "I've been an ass all the way up here, I know. It's been a life-changing few months. I can't believe you're taking me into your home and…" I gestured at the clothes. "And buying me clothes. Thank you."

"I'm glad to do it, Milton," he said, smiling so that his teeth gleamed as brightly as his eyes. I'm not sure I'd ever seen him look so happy. "Now, please, take that shower. I don't want to be rude to a guest in my home, but you smell horrible."

We laughed. He left the room and closed the door and I went to the shower. I made the water as hot as I could stand it, scrubbed myself furiously with a blue bar of Zest and a wash cloth, then stood under the spray for several minutes, trying to remember my last shower in a clean bathtub with plenty of hot water. At last I turned it off, dried myself, and shaved—no easy task considering how long I'd gone without doing it. Finally I applied deodorant, a few dabs of Old Spice and put on the gray sweat pants and a crimson University of Oklahoma sweatshirt. The smell of frying meat coming from the kitchen made me feel light-headed.

David had fried some thin steaks, eggs, hash browns and made toast. I had to swallow many times to keep my mouth from overflowing with drool as I waited for him to get the food on the table. It was delicious, the best meal I'd had since me and Amara had gone to IHOP after my first homosexual encounter, but now I was able to eat without that pain and fresh humiliation. David let me eat without trying to interrupt me with talk and I was thankful for that.

Finally, I shoveled in the last bite of eggs and swallowed some juice. I looked up from my plate to find David grinning at me. "You wouldn't have been so hungry if you'd eaten that turkey dinner yesterday."

"Maybe not," I agreed. "So…what's next?"

"That depends on what you're up to. We need to have a long talk, but if you want to sleep first, that's fine."

"What will we talk about?"

"First, I think we should talk about the HIV." I nodded and David asked, "What have you done so far?"

"After…after the incident, the guy told me he was infected," I said. "I told the minister at the shelter a few days later and he sent me to St. Anthony's Hospital to be tested. They did a preliminary test, something they said wasn't real accurate but could indicate if more expensive tests were needed."

"And you went back?"

"No," I said. "I never went back for the results, just assumed I had it. I mean, everything else was falling apart, so it just stood to reason I'd have it. Plus, I mean, that guy told me he was infected. He didn't use protection when…when he was with me. What chance was there I wouldn't have it?"

"I want you to go back to the clinic and have a more accurate test done. If you really are positive, you'll need to start taking medication. The state will provide that through the clinic at no cost."

"It will?"

"Yes," David said. "You forget, I haven't lived in Prairie Valley all my life. I grew up on the northeast side of town and I still have friends and family there. AIDS and poverty are problems there and I've helped several people get started on medication.

"Now, you know, you'll have to stop taking any other drugs

you're on. What have you been using?"

I dropped my eyes back to my empty plate before answering. "I can't even tell you the names. Mostly it's marijuana. But the pills...whatever people had that would dull my senses. Valium, mostly."

"When was the last time you took something?"

"A couple of days ago, I guess. I haven't taken anything since I saw Lori. That was the day before Christmas Eve."

"That phone number you have written on a napkin. Is that Lori's?"

"Yes. It's a cell phone."

"Do you want to call her?"

"No. Not now. I do want to call her later. More than anything, I want to stay in touch with her now that I found her again. But, she went to Wichita with...one of her friends at work. She'll be back Monday."

"We're going to get you cleaned up, Milton. No more illegal drugs. On AIDS medication, if that's needed. Then we're going to find you a job. You're welcome here as long as you need it, but I consider it my duty to get you on your feet and supporting yourself," David said.

"It's more than I have a right to ask," I said. "I really am sorry for the things I said to you there at the Myriad. You know, in years past I was one of the lucky ones, well off, well fed, making myself feel good by donating my time to scoop food onto the plates of nameless poor people. To have that reversed, and to be served by you...Well, it hurt. It really set me off. I'm sorry."

"Under the circumstances, it's understandable," David said.

"I have to say, Milton, I'm concerned for more than just your physical well-being. You mentioned earlier feeling empty. I've heard you use the Lord's name in vain and you just spoke now about doing charity work to make yourself feel good, making it sound like that was more important than the work. You're questioning your faith."

"No, David. I no longer have any faith. In anything. I thought my faith in the God I grew up worshipping was unshakable. I really did. But then, all this happened. It just kept getting worse and worse. I prayed, at least in the beginning, but it did no good. There was no help. No comfort, only more misery. Lori left. Karen and Eric left. My money ran out. My car was taken. All I had was Amara. And then she betrayed me."

"Did you ever think that maybe your faith was being tested?"

"Of course I did. But it went beyond a test. If God is out there, he's a sadist and I don't want any part of him."

"Hold on, Milton," David said, his voice becoming stern. "I want to bring you back to your faith. If you never want to do that, it's your own business. But I won't have you blaspheming in my house. I just can't allow that."

"I understand." I nodded. "I'm sorry. Just still bitter, I guess. I think I'll go take that nap now, if it's still all right with you."

"Of course."

We got up and I helped put the dishes into the dishwasher. I had turned away to go back to my room when David asked,

"Milton, you really don't know where she is? Amara?"

"No. I don't know. I caught her behind the shelter, having sex with another man. We argued and I sent her away, told her I never wanted to see her again. Called her names." I paused, seeing her again in my mind as she went after the young guy from the shelter.

"You know, it was the first time I didn't forgive her for something she'd done. She acted really strange about that. She said some things…she doesn't need my forgiveness, or his. Something like that."

"Whose? The other man she was with?"

"I have no idea. She used to talk to herself. I'd hear her in another room carrying on a conversation. She'd talk, pause, then answer as if somebody else had spoken."

David shook his head. "I'm glad that woman is out of your life, Milton. I only met her the one time, but she was trouble. Go on and rest now."

36

Yes, I dreamed of Belo again.

I sat at a table of hewn wood in a small hut. Belo sat across from me, bare-chested, his face painted with dark red and white swatches in the custom of jungle shamans. He watched me silently, his eyes large and white with deep pits in their burning centers.

"Why do you come to me in my dreams?" I asked.

"The shaman advises the chief in all things. Especially war," he replied.

"Am I at war?"

"You are."

"With whom?"

"It is because you do not know that I am here," he said. "Will you tell me?"

"You must learn the answer for yourself. But first you must find what you have lost."

"I have lost everything," I said. "You have everything to gain."

"You speak in riddles, Belo, son of a shaman."

"Come." He stood and beckoned to me. He led me to the door of the hut, which was covered with a heavy blanket of dark wool. With one hand he pulled aside the curtain and we looked out onto the blackness of space. "We must go." Belo took my arm and led me forward. We moved through the emptiness. Soon, the earth was visible. He continued to move, closer and closer, until I could make out oceans and continents. He dropped toward a point in southeast Europe. Our descent never stopped. The solid ground rushed to meet us. I closed my eyes and then we stopped.

I opened my eyes and found that we were in a cave. Light spilled into the cavern from an opening about fifty yards behind us along a steep incline. All around us were the bones of human skeletons. On a large flat rock lay a corpse, its wrists and ankles bound. The body was that of a woman, apparently in her early twenties. Her flesh was stretched tight over her frame, but her belly was distended. Thin coppery hair fell around her bony shoulders.

"She was left here to starve," I said.

"A sacrifice to the earth goddess," Belo agreed. "Returned to the womb at the time of planting to ensure fertility. Will you know the history of the goddess?" Belo gestured toward the altar. The eyelids of the corpse fluttered and opened. Dull eyes stared back at me. The mouth moved, opening and closing several times before words came.

"In the beginning there was the great earth goddess and she was worshipped in caves," the corpse said. "Men lived in peace and tended crops and there was only the great goddess. Then warriors came from the east, bringing weapons and bloodshed and male gods of battle. They divided the goddess into many names and made her submissive to the war gods, but she was still the goddess."

"What names?" I asked.

"Many names," the corpse responded, its voice becoming stronger as it spoke, its flesh growing healthier, pink with life and not so gaunt. "More men came, bringing more battle, more bloodshed, and they said there was no goddess, only a single father god who would tolerate no others. The people were forced to abandon the goddess."

The corpse was taking on a healthier shape by the minute, her cheeks filling out, her fingers and toes beginning to move, her eyes becoming less cloudy. "The goddess fled before the advancing armies, accepting the worship of those who still believed in her. She was driven to the edge of the sea, and then the armies came there. Battles raged, frontiers shifted, but the goddess was defeated. She fled over the sea in search of people who did not know the father god."

The woman's eyes, I now saw, were green. Her hair was red-orange. With a graceful movement she sat up on the stone altar, naked, looking at me with a face I recognized. "There she remained for centuries, but in time the warriors of the battle god came to her new lands and spread their religion. The goddess retreated to the jungle and again was at peace for centuries.

"And then you came, Milton Agnew," Amara said.

I reached for her…and fell out of the bed in David Ross' guestroom.

A familiar smell filled the air of the room. It was soft and feminine and made my heart ache with want and memories of betrayal. "Amara," I whispered as I pushed myself off the carpet. The smell faded and was gone.

My eyes found the clock on a bedside table. It was a quarter after nine in the morning. I'd slept nearly twenty hours. Fragments of my dream remained with me as I untangled myself from the blankets I'd pulled off the bed as I fell. My mouth was dry and felt gummy. Phantom aches made me wish for some pills. I stood up and left the room.

The house was quiet and I knew immediately I was alone. I went to the kitchen and found a note from David. The note said he had to meet with the other church elders then attend to a personal matter but would be back at about one in the afternoon. There was breakfast food and sandwich meat in the refrigerator; I could help myself to whatever I wanted to eat. The last paragraph made me press my lips together and glare at the note in anger.

I've taken all the medication I own out of the house to reduce any temptation you may feel. Also, I have set the security system to alert the police should any door or window be opened. I am sorry, Milton, but at this early stage I feel it is in your best interest that I take these precautions.

"I might as well be back in jail," I muttered as I wadded up the note and dropped it back on the table. I looked around the neat kitchen with its varnished cabinets, spotless countertops and refrigerator and cupboards filled with food I could choose from and knew my assessment wasn't at all accurate. I made myself a peanut butter sandwich and opened a bag of barbecue potato chips and a can of Diet Coke and sat at a coffee table in the living room to eat in front of the television.

I was about halfway through the sandwich when I smelled Amara again. Her fresh scent of sunshine on jungle leafs wafted across the room from a bookshelf. I stared at the shelving unit, a floor-to-ceiling piece, stained a deep mahogany finish. It was about half-filled with books. Each shelf was divided, one half filled with books and the other half occupied by items of African art or photographs of David's deceased wife. I went to the shelf and my hands instinctively went to a black vase trimmed in gold with figures outlined in white etching dancing around it.

I held the vase in my hands for a moment, then lifted the delicate lid off. Inside, I found one thousand dollars in cash and a Visa credit card, along with a copy of David's Social Security card, birth certificate and a photo of him and his wife as a young couple taken in front of a café.

"Emergency money and ID?" I mused aloud. That had to be it. I put the items back and replaced the vase, making sure it faced out exactly as it had. I went back to the television and my sandwich. The smell of Amara was gone.

David came home when he said he would. After that first morning he seldom left me alone. True to his word, he took me to St. Anthony's Hospital for a more accurate HIV test. A week later it was confirmed that I did indeed have the dreaded virus. A doctor at the hospital gave me pills, explaining that I would have to return weekly to get more. David promised we would. "Using any other medication or illegal drugs can have a serious effect while using this medication," the doctor, an old man with a thick nose, said. "It can be fatal."

"He's not using any drugs," David said. "I can promise he's not taken so much as an aspirin in the past eight days and that behavior will continue."

"Very good," the doctor said, then dismissed us.

David made sure I took my pills regularly. He made me eat when I didn't want to, talked me through spells when all I wanted to do was sit and weep or when the craving for some drug to dull my anguish threatened to overwhelm me. At night, though, he could not protect me from the dreams.

"I will open the door for another who will come to you," Belo said.

"Who?" I asked. "One who has fallen."

In this dream, I lay in my bed in David's house. Belo stood beside me as he spoke. He pointed toward the bedroom door. Between the bed and the door a fire without heat erupted from the floor, the silent orange flame reaching almost to the bedroom ceiling. The air around it vibrated. Then a figure stepped from the fire and faced me. Belo was gone, abandoning me to this newcomer.

The figure was male, very tall, his body lithe and elegant and perfect. Power emanated from him in forceful waves, making me want to fall out of the bed and bow at his bare feet. He was robed in white with flowing blond hair and deep blue eyes. His flesh was pale, almost translucent. His countenance, however, was sad as he beheld me.

"Greetings, Milton Agnew," the man said. "Who are you?" I asked.

"Azazyel, the Watcher."

"What do you watch?"

"The doings of Man. The rise of heroes, the fall of empires, the suffering of the many and the squandering of the few."

"You are not human."

"I have never been a Man, though I have worn flesh to my disgrace. Come with me." He reached a hand toward me and I took it. Without moving, I found myself in a lush green field, standing among dozens of tall male figures, all as perfectly beautiful as Azazyel. There must have been two hundred men in the field. They were all nude and all looking at me. One seemed familiar. Azazyel, his robes gone, addressed me. "Behold the Watchers," he said.

"You brought me here."

"I did," he said, his voice deep, rich and soothing. "Who are you?"

"Azazyel, the Watcher."

"You said that already."

"I am chief of the Grigori. We were charged with the watching of Man. But we did more." He raised his arms and night fell on the field. Women approached from all directions. The males around me chose partners and lay with them on the grass, coupling with the women. For their part, the women, every one, seemed transported with ecstasy as the perfect men made love to them. One by one, the couples finished, rose and the women went their ways. The one with the familiar face hovered near as Azazyel dismissed his concubine and returned to my side.

"They will bear our children," Azazyel said. "Only the females can reproduce, so we must take the shape of males."

"You aren't really men?"

"We are spirit. Without gender, but with the ability to incarnate as we choose." As I watched, his perfect manly face and figure dissolved, shifted and reshaped itself as the perfect woman. Its chest swelled and expanded into two shapely breasts. The penis shrunk and vanished into the torso, replaced by the female genitalia. All around me, the other male figures also changed, becoming female. When Azazyel spoke again, his voice was now feminine and sweet, like the tinkling of bells. "Our children will be called heroes and monsters and will be wiped from this earth in a great flood," she said. "We will be punished for polluting ourselves with pleasures reserved for those created to be flesh. We will be bound to this earth, unable to ascend back into the heavens. We will become gods of men."

"There is no Heaven," I argued.

"You are wrong," a new voice said. It was the figure who had seemed familiar as a man. Now it was Amara, standing before me naked as when I'd first seen her. "Eons ago we revealed ourselves to another and he petitioned for our return, but it was denied."

"Asaradel, whom you know as Amara, believed she had found the secret to returning," Azazyel interrupted.

"You were talking to him," I said. "Or her. All those times I heard you talking alone, you were talking to…others like you. Other…"

"You would call us angels," Amara said. "Angels of the second fall."

"Not those who followed Lucifer. You told me that," I said. "What was the secret?"

"While you are faithless, it does not matter," Azazyel said. "Asaradel's plan has failed."

"Tell me, Amara. Tell me there was purpose to everything you did."

She stepped closer and lifted a hand to touch my face. "Of course there was purpose. Go. Awaken. You will find a gift."

"Asaradel, you must not," Azazyel said, her voice firm and commanding.

"Wake up, Milton!" Amara yelled.

I snapped up in the bed, my eyes wide and staring at the closed bedroom door. There was no fire burning between me and the door, no burned patch on the carpet to indicate there had been a fire. But I smelled Amara in the room. It was the scent of her hair, always fresh, always overwhelming and intoxicating. Of course she was not in the room.

Slowly I let myself sink back onto the pillows. I looked toward the clock, but something was blocking my view of the red digital numbers. The room was still dark. I guessed it to be a couple of hours before dawn. I closed my eyes.

Belo's voice whispered in my mind. "Enoch walks with God."

"Enoch?" I said the name aloud, opening my eyes again.

The smell of Amara's hair and flesh vanished from the room as if sucked into the central air vents in the ceiling. I shook my head to clear my senses. I looked at the clock again and was angry that I couldn't see it. I reached out to move the obstruction. It was a book. I lifted it and it felt familiar. My heart beating like thunder in my chest, I sat up and flicked on the bedside lamp.

In my hands was the Bible I'd shoved deep into the trashcan

of the Gospel Garden shelter soon after catching Amara cheating on me. The scuffed brown leather cover and blue ribbon marker sewn into the spine were all familiar to me. I opened the cover and saw the inscription written by my father when he gave me the book.

The hair stood up along my neck then. I slid out of the bed, settling onto my knees on the floor. I hunched over, clutching the Bible to my chest and prayed for the first time in months. "Dear God, I have been a fool. You gave me an opportunity to do something great in your name and I failed. Worse, I turned away from you. I come back to you now, humbled but enlightened and prepared to do your work. Forgive my transgressions. In Jesus' name I pray. Amen."

I remained curled around the Bible for hours, thinking of all that had happened since that first time I'd found Amara in the jungle, through all the things she did to me, from that first time she watched me urinate when I'd asked her to give me privacy to ruining my family to betraying me with another man. It all made sense to me now.

When the smells of David cooking breakfast came wafting through the house, I went to the kitchen and sat down, putting my recovered Bible on the table beside my plate. David looked at the book, then at me, a question bringing more wrinkles to his brow.

"I hadn't seen that here," he said. "It wasn't with the things you collected at the police station."

"You're right," I said, laughing. "And you wouldn't believe me if I told you where I found it."

"Perhaps you can tell me later," he said. "I have to leave for a while this morning. We're having a pancake breakfast at the church. I should be home around noon."

"Take your time," I said.

David left. I ate the waffles and bacon he'd prepared, then stood to take my dishes to the dishwasher. That's when I noticed a gap in the pages of my Bible. I opened it to that place and found my passport lodged between two pages.

"Yes, Lord, I understand," I said. "But I have to do one thing first."

I called Lori right after I put my dishes away. The conversation was short. As much as I wanted to talk to her, I was too excited to remain on the line very long. Lori expressed her amazement that I was living with David and that he was taking care of me. She was having trouble with her roommates. She'd told them she wanted to stop hooking, that she no longer felt the need for sex. They argued with her, saying she'd never make such easy money and she should get all she could while she was young enough to be desirable to young men with big salaries.

"I haven't given it up completely, Daddy," she said. "I have to pay my share of the rent and I can't afford that on what most of the jobs I've applied for will pay."

"Keep looking, Lori," I urged. "You'll find something. I know you will."

"I'll keep trying. Daddy, you sound so much better than you did when we talked before Christmas. Are you happier?"

"Yes, Lori, I am," I said. "I found something that was lost. Listen, sweetie, I have to go. There's something I have to do this morning. It might be a while before I talk to you again. I have to tell you I love you and I believe in you and I know you'll pull yourself through this problem and get back on the right track. I have faith you can do that. Okay?"

"What is it you have to do, Daddy? Now you sound serious. Almost scary. What are you doing?"

"I can't tell you now. Just remember I love you and do what you know is right, okay?"

"I will, Daddy. I love you, too."

I hung up, went to David's black vase and took out the credit card and cash. I found a phone book and called United Airlines. "My name is David Ross," I said. "I need to book the next available flight from Oklahoma City to Manaus, Brazil. The tickets will be in the name of Milton Agnew, an employee working for me."

My flight left in less than two hours. I called a taxi and went to the airport. Trusting me at last, David hadn't bothered setting his home alarm to sound when I opened the front door. On his kitchen table I'd left a note apologizing for using his credit card, taking his money and his hospitality. I wished him well and said I hoped to see him again someday.

My plane landed in Houston and I was transferred to a bigger jet. As it flew over Mexico, I slept for a short while and dreamed of Belo for the final time. We stood in the jungle. He held a spear in both hands across his chest, blocking me from the path I meant to take.

"She will destroy you," he said.

I laughed at him. "She can't hurt me," I said. "I know what she wants now."

37

Once again I found myself puttering up the Gualones River in an American-made johnboat. I'd rented the boat from a crippled fisherman in Manaus and paid for passage up the Amazon on a barge, all with cash I'd taken from David Ross. The heat was oppressive, so much different than the winter I'd left behind in Oklahoma. All around me, tropical birds and monkeys called out in greeting, warning, fear or lust for one another—I didn't know what they said and it didn't matter. I knew what I had to do.

After a long trip, I came around a bend and found the village where my mission had been. Much to my surprise, I saw new huts were built and dark-skinned villagers moved about between the buildings. As I drew near, the activity stopped and every eye watched me approach. My boat bumped against the bank and I tied it to a shrub growing near the river. As I stepped ashore, two men came running toward me, yelling in their native tongue for me to get back into my boat and leave. "Greetings to you, Yuma," I said, raising a hand. Yuma had been one of the most ardent protesters to the Christian mission. After the dream I'd had in which I saw some villagers flee the arrival of Coadidop, I was not so surprised to see that Yuma was alive, though I hadn't expected anyone to return to the site of the old village. "You have re-established your home here?"

"You angered the goddess," Yuma shouted. "You drove her to destroy our families and animals and homes. You are not welcome here."

The other man gestured toward my boat with a spear he held in his hands. I looked from the bone tip of the spear to the man's angry face and back to Yuma.

"I have come to make peace with your goddess," I said. "You lie. You follow your own god. You say there is no other. You are

309

wrong and you lie."

"I have learned a great deal since we last met, Yuma. I speak the truth. I will go into the jungle and make my peace with the goddess, then I will leave and never return. Let me pass."

Yuma hesitated for a long time before he spoke again. "You will go into the jungle," he said. "I shall come with you so you do not profane the goddess again."

"Very well," I said.

The other man lowered his spear. Yuma commanded the man to follow, then motioned for me to follow him. We went through the village, a couple dozen people parting to let us pass, and entered the deep shade of the Amazonian forest, following the path Amara had once led me along to the old totem pole. After a short time we found the pole; Yuma and the other man stopped and bowed to the hideous image of Coadidop.

I looked around and did not feel right. "This is not the right place," I said. "I don't feel her here." I thought for a moment, wondering where I was supposed to meet Amara. Then enlightenment came. "The pool," I said. "Take me to the pool where the goddess bathes."

"It is sacred. Forbidden," Yuma said. "You cannot go there."

"I will go there," I said. "I know the way from the village." I turned and started back. Yuma and his guard spoke quietly for a moment, then joined me.

"The goddess will strike you dead if you enter her pool," Yuma said. "Just as she destroyed our village."

"It would be for the best," the other man said. I laughed at him.

We skirted the edge of the village and re-entered the jungle. From memory, I made my way along the unmarked path Amara had shown me on the day we buried the missionaries and villagers. After a few moments, we came into a silent clearing and faced the pool. I could smell the perfume of Amara's hair and flesh on the air. The two natives also sensed her presence; I could feel them tensing for flight.

"Amara, I am here," I called. "Where are you?" No answer.

"Asaradel, I summon you," I called.

The heat was suddenly sucked out of the clearing as if it all had been quickly inhaled by a giant unseen being. The cool air shimmered and the ground shook. Yuma's guard dropped his spear and fled; Yuma stayed a moment longer, then also broke and ran from the clearing.

"Come to me, Amara," I whispered.

The air filled with swirling colors, bringing to mind the day I had cut Amara with a paring knife—the strange phenomenon I thought I'd seen then, of colors like a rainbow caught in a tornado, was what I was now seeing on a larger scale. As I watched, the shimmering, colored air moved to a central location over the pool of water, took on a human shape and hung there. I felt miniscule things racing past me; I looked around but could not see what they were. But they were moving toward the shape over the water and as they reached her they covered the colorful form, becoming flesh and hair and…Amara.

A clap of mighty thunder shook the forest, knocking me off my feet. I put out my hands to keep from slamming my face onto the solid earth. When I looked up I found Amara standing before me, naked as when I'd first seen her, her hair like the waving lava of a volcano, her eyes the color of fresh spring foliage. Her hands were clasped behind her back.

"Do you worship me, Milton Agnew?" she asked, her voice like tinkling bells, stirring my emotions and bringing tears to my eyes.

"Amara," I said, sitting back in a kneeling position. "Worship you? No, you know I do not. Adore you? Yes. I've missed you."

"You come to me to ask me to return with you to your life of poverty?"

"No, Amara. You know why I've come."

"I see images of myself in your mind, Milton Agnew. I see Azazyel and I see the guises I have worn for other men in other times. What do you want of me?"

311

"I want to forgive you," I said. "Forgive me?"

"Yes. For everything."

"Do you even know all that I have done?"

"It doesn't matter," I said.

"How can you forgive if you do not know my sins? I stirred the lust in your daughter so that she would lie down for any man who desired her. I visited your wife in her dreams and set her mind against you. I told your son I would have you and that you would abandon him. When you attempted to steal from the grocer I put the image of your crime in the mind of people in the store. I chose the men who would take you, even the one who gave you the disease you now carry."

I hesitated. This was more than I expected. She had deliberately attracted the man who had given me HIV? She had used her supernatural powers to invade Karen's mind, to poison her and Eric against me.

"Do you still offer your forgiveness, Milton Agnew?"

That was in the past. There was nothing to be done for it. "I do," I said.

"It was I who killed your people in the village," she said. "Your people and those they came to lead away from worshipping me. I killed them and burned them so that you could not tell one from another."

"I know," I said. "I forgive you."

Her eyes softened and the line that showed she was thinking appeared on her brow. "You have indeed changed, Milton," she said. "When I first showed myself to you and committed little sins, you forgave me easily, without thinking. The words held little meaning to you. But now, you know what it is you say."

I stood up finally and dared to put my hands on her angelic arms. "I have changed," I said. "You are so right. I did forgive you without meaning before. It was my Christian duty to forgive and I did it because I had been taught to do so. But now, because you have stripped me of everything I held dear, including my faith in God, I have had to discover truths that before I had only known from books or from the words of other men. "For every crime you have committed against me, I forgive you, Amara," I said.

"Even now, you hold hope of returning home," she said. "You would go home to your daughter who is no longer under my spell. You would make a life with her. You have found your faith in God, but you also have found hope. I do not need your hope."

She raised a hand and stroked my cheek, then she kissed me on the mouth, a soft, loving kiss without the passion of lust. "I must steal your hope, Milton."

She raised her other hand and for a moment I saw that it held a long knife. Her hand on my cheek became a vice on my neck, holding me in place as she sank the knife's blade into my chest. The pain was sharp, immediate and agonizing. I screamed, a sound that bounced among the massive trees and died a tortured death in the darkness of the rainforest. I felt the hot blood running from the wound, coating my shirt in coppery stickiness. My eyes fixed on Amara's, I sank to my knees. She knelt with me, one hand holding the hilt of the knife, the other still on my neck.

"You will die here, Milton Agnew. The villagers will not touch your body. You will have no burial. You will not go home. You will not see your daughter. You will die here. Now. With me. Do you forgive me for this?"

I nodded. "Yes, Amara. I forgive you."

Her hand on my neck released its grip and slid back to my cheek. She stroked me gently, her face softening again, her eyes brimming with tears. "Eons ago, when the world was young, we went to a man named Enoch and asked him to petition God on our behalf. We only wanted to go home. Enoch did this for us, but God refused our request. We dispersed and did what we felt was best. Some sought revenge, spreading disease among men. Some simply did nothing. And others, like myself, convinced humans to worship us instead of God. I thought that if I showed God that I was good he would have to let me return. But always my followers were killed or converted. I fled. Always I fled, until I came here. I listened to the message of you and your people and learned that

God had done that which we wanted to do."

She paused, one hand still on the handle of the knife. She looked at the blood, then back to my face. She smiled sadly. "We did lie with human women out of lust, you see. Not sexual lust. We wanted to experience the mystery of flesh. We had intercourse with women thinking we could put ourselves in mortal wombs and be reborn into this world with flesh of our own. But it did not work. God had foreseen our thoughts and created us in a way that would not allow such a sin. Instead, we released monsters on the world.

"But you and your followers said that God had become flesh and lived on this world and that his flesh was slain so that all men could be forgiven of sins. Forgiven, Milton. Surely, if all men are forgiven by this gift, surely I, too, can be forgiven." I had no answer. I had read the apocryphal Book of Enoch, written centuries before the birth and crucifixion of Christ. I knew that in the book Enoch petitioned God to forgive the fallen angels and that God had refused, saying they would be bound on earth forever.

"Yes, bound on earth forever," Amara said. "But that was before he made his own sacrifice. Maybe now is different. But, after so long, how would I ask him to forgive me? I did not know, Milton. I did not know. But an idea came to me. Man is created in the image of God. If a single man can forgive me for every crime I commit against him, surely God will forgive me." I nodded. The loss of blood was making me feel weak. "I will die soon, Amara," I said. "My vision is getting dark. I forgive you. I will die looking at your face."

She smiled at me one more time. "You will accompany me," she said. "Or, rather, I will accompany you into the presence of God and you will beseech him to hear my plea. Shall we go?"

Now it was my turn to smile. I nodded, the slight motion bringing waves of blackness to my vision. Amara released her hold on the knife handle. As I slumped to the side, my face brushed her hand and then her touch was gone. She stood and extended her arms out at her sides. Just as the particles of dust and ash had accumulated to create the layer of flesh she wore, they now dissolved and flew away. In a moment she stood before me in her full angelic glory. The light emanating from her pierced the blackness of my fading vision. She was even more beautiful than before, a thing of pure spirit, created by God before Man ever walked in Eden.

"Come, Milton Agnew," she called. "Forgive me one final time for taking your life, give up the ghost and join me in Heaven."

"He will not go," another voice, male, booming and authoritative filled the glen. "Go if you will, Asaradel. But this man has suffered enough at your hand."

"I forgive you, Amara," I said, my voice hoarse. "Go and sin no more."

There was another clap of thunder. The air was electric with ozone. The burning figure of Amara shot into the sky, breaking through the branches of the towering trees so that they fell back into the clearing, burning, hissing as they fell into the pool of the goddess. Then the light was gone and it was only the diffused green daylight of the forest, a little brighter than usual because of the hole Amara had burned through the canopy.

And then all was black.

Epilogue

Well, I didn't die from the stab wound. So, if you thought you were reading the narrative of a ghost, I guess you're disappointed.

Whose voice did I hear in the glen? Who was it that told Amara, or Asaradel if you prefer, that she would not take me with her? Was it Azazyel, chief of the Watchers banished from Heaven for mating with mortal women? Was it God himself? I do not know.

It was neither of my rescuers, though. Of that much I'm sure.

I awoke to find myself in a hut made of mud and logs with a roof of grass. Daylight spilled through the open doorway and there sitting beside me was Bill Barlow, my archeologist friend. "Have I died and gone to Texas to pay for my sins?" I asked.

For a man with a slight figure, Bill has a rich, hearty laugh. He laughed for several minutes, long enough for me to know not all the laughter was at my joke, but mostly the simple fact I was alive and speaking.

"You haven't parked your Sooner Schooner at the pearly gates just yet, Milton," he said at last. "Though I don't mind telling you that you were damn close. Damn close."

"What are you doing here, Bill?" I asked. "For that matter, where am I?"

"We're still in your village deep in the Amazonian rainforest."

"How did you get here?"

"Through the air and over the river, same as you."

"Okay, okay. *Why* are you here?"

"I was sitting in my office last week, minding my own business, when the phone rings," he said. "It was some guy named David Ross, calling from Oklahoma City. Said you'd just stolen a wad of cash and a credit card and headed for South America. He asked if I knew how to find the village where your mission had been."

"David called you? How did he know—"

"I found a letter he sent you when he sent a print of Amara," David said. I turned my head and found him standing in the door of the hut. He came in, smiling broadly. "I'm glad to see you're finally awake. You owe us both a lot of cookies and juice."

"Cookies and juice?"

"That's what I usually get when I donate blood," David said.

They both laughed at my confused expression. Of course they'd both given me blood transfusions while I was unconscious. It was a trick Bill had learned on one of his artifact expeditions.

"Lucky for you we all have compatible blood types," Bill said.

"Luck is a word for heathens and Texans, not that there's much difference," I told him. "No, I doubt it was luck. I don't really believe in luck anymore."

David had discovered my theft sooner than I'd anticipated. He'd arrived at the church for his pancake breakfast and realized he'd forgotten some papers he needed and came home for them. He found my note, searched my belongings I'd left in the nightstand drawer in his guest bedroom and immediately called Bill. They'd met in Houston and flown to Manaus, where they'd rented a faster boat than the barge I'd hitched a ride on or the little johnboat I'd brought up the tributary. We estimated they'd arrived in the village just about two hours after I did.

"We found you bleeding to death in that little glen by the spring," Bill said. "The villagers would only point the direction. They were terrified. They said the goddess was tearing you to pieces for defiling her bath."

"Is that all you saw?" I asked.

Bill and David looked at each other, then David spoke. "We saw a light. We have argued over what it was while you lay here near death. Bill says it was an underground eruption of gas that shot into the air from the pool. Light reflected in the water from the explosion, making it look...like something else."

"Do you believe that?" I asked.

"No," Bill said after a moment. "To be honest, I don't. I didn't believe it then, but I believed it even less when we found this sticking out of your chest." He reached under the cot on which I lay and pulled out the knife Amara had used to stab me. "Have you ever seen one like this?"

I shook my head.

"I've never seen one in this condition. Hell, I've only seen one in my life and it was locked in a glass case in Iraq. It's Sumerian. Older than the Egyptian pyramids, though it looks like it was made yesterday. I'm almost sure it's not a reproduction. To find a knife like this, most often used for sacrifice, in the Brazilian rainforest is unthinkable."

"Then you admit we saw something not of this world there in the clearing?" David asked.

Grinning sheepishly, Bill nodded. "Light shaped like a human, shooting out of the clearing like a rocket, setting the trees on fire as it went. Yes, I saw it."

That knife now hangs on the wall in the small house I share with Lori. We live in Bethany, a little town that has been swallowed by Oklahoma City. We're not far from Lake Overholser. I like to walk along the lake's shore in the evenings. Lori often walks with me and we talk of many things both important and trivial.

Lori earned her high school equivalency diploma and is enrolled in a community college. She'll go on to a university soon. She says it will be a local one so she can remain near me. She is everything a man could ever hope for in a daughter. Despite carrying a full class load and working part-time in the college's library, her looks have returned to her. Nearly all traces of her life as a prostitute are gone from her sweet face. She is happy. She smiles and laughs and has high hope for a future in which she will teach theology. I am very proud.

Karen and Eric still live in Woodward. There has been no reconciliation, though our relationship has improved to that of wary friends now that Amara is gone. I have apologized to both of them for my betrayal. I tried to tell them the truth about Amara and how she had influenced them, but they attributed my ravings to a side effect of the HIV medication. We may never reconcile completely, but I hope in time we will become close again.

Oh yes, I'm still HIV positive. No Heaven-sent cure for that from the mysterious voice in the forest. The medication keeps most of the symptoms at bay, though I can feel differences in my body. I know there is not a lot of time left to me. Perhaps years. Perhaps only months. Whatever there is, I will treasure every moment of it.

I no longer dig through trash bins for my food nor rely on handouts from the Gospel Garden. David Ross, who is a truly remarkable man, organized three churches and opened a new shelter not far from where I live with Lori. He said the shelters downtown were too crowded. With help from the Prairie Valley Community Church and two Bethany churches, the shelter was opened and David made sure I was hired as director, offering me the position as my new missionary work. The hours are long; I am seldom thanked for the assistance I provide, but it is very rewarding to feed someone who would not have had a meal at all if they had not entered my mission.

I've kept only one secret from those closest to me. I have not been able to tell Lori or David how I killed the homeless man who infected me with HIV. In my heart, I've forgiven the poor soul and I know I will answer to God for killing the man, but I can't answer to the police. Perhaps I'm a coward, but I cannot bear the thought of giving up my remaining time with Lori to spend the end of my life in a prison cell. When she reads this, I think Lori will understand. The other man, the motel manager I hit with the hammer, did not die as a result of my act.

As to Amara, I know nothing more of her. Was she accepted back into Heaven? Did God forgive her? Or, is she back in the forest of Brazil, or maybe the deep African jungle, once again playing the role of goddess? I suppose it's something I won't know until I slough off this mortal coil and go on to the next world myself.

What I do know, what I learned from my experience with the fallen angel, is that there truly is a spark of the divine within every human heart. A quote I found in my recent reading sums it up best. In *The Note Book*, Elbert Hubbard said, "The ineffable joy of forgiving and being forgiven forms an ecstasy that might well arouse the envy of the gods."

Yes, the envy of the gods. We can do good deeds. We can help little old ladies across streets, we can hold doors open for people with their hands full of boxes and bags. We can even provide food for those who cannot buy it for themselves. But, finally, the closest we come to being divine is when we forgive our fellow man for his transgressions against us.

The sun is sinking. It will be a glorious summer sunset where the sky will blaze orange before fading to purple and slowly revealing its twinkling stars. Lori has finished her homework and is waiting for me to join her for our walk around the lake.

Life is good.

Author's Afterword

Amara's Prayer was born of hate. Hate and questions and soul searching.

I was raised in a Pentecostal Christian church and I knew early on that the tongue-speaking, glory-shouting fundamentalist beliefs of that branch of faith was not for me. But what was? What did I believe?

Many of my friends have "found Jesus" over the years. They'd go on and on for a while about how strong their faith was. They never really did anything with it, though, and after a while the fervor would fade. It led me to ask if faith was real if it was never put to any kind of test.

In 1999 friends and people I trusted betrayed me in a way that changed my life. Added to the above questions was: How much can a person forgive?

Amara's Prayer is the culmination of those questions, at least as of 2004, when I finished the book as my thesis project for a master's degree at the University of Oklahoma. During the research and writing of the novel, Dr. Laura Gibbs directed my reading into channels I might never have found on my own, and that research and study has continued to this day, and likely will for the rest of my life.

You are invited to join my quest for gnosis at a site created for open discussion of spiritual matters, www.whoisamara.com.

Thanks for reading,
Steven E. Wedel
December 29, 2015

ABOUT THE AUTHOR

Steven E. Wedel lives in central Oklahoma with his wife and most of his kids…the ones who haven't grown up enough to leave the den yet, anyway. He began writing in the mid-1980s and has kept at it despite numerous disappointments and setbacks. Steve has a bachelor's degree in journalism from the University of Central Oklahoma and a master's degree in liberal studies from the University of Oklahoma. He has worked as a machinist, bookseller, stock clerk, journalist, public relations specialist, and is now a high school English teacher most of the year.

Visit him online at www.stevenewedel.com.